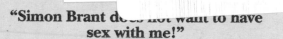

3 12

D0378145

"Simon Brant does not want to have sex with me!"

"Are you sure about that?" The words were spoken in a deep, masculine voice from behind her.

Her heart plummeting to her toes, she spun around with the cell phone stuck to the side of her head like a hi-tech earmuff. Simon lounged in the guest room doorway; the formerly closed door swung carelessly against the wall.

She opened her mouth, but the only thing that came out was air. Jill was saying something, but Amanda couldn't make any sense of it. She was too busy hyperventilating from embarrassment.

"Simon," she choked out.

"Yes, Simon. You're obviously interested in the man." Jill's impatient voice in her ear had a dreamlike quality to it.

Reality was six feet, two inches of masculine perfection and a sardonic gleam in gunmetal gray eyes.

"*Jill*," she said, breaking into her friend's familiar tirade on Amanda's lack of a love life.

"What?"

"Simon's here. I think he wants to talk to me."

Jillian's gasp was audible. "Simon's there?"

"Yes."

"How much did he hear?" Her friend's whisper was too little, way too late.

"Enough."

BOOK YOUR PLACE ON OUR WEBSITE AND MAKE THE READING CONNECTION!

We've created a customized website just for our very special readers, where you can get the inside scoop on everything that's going on with Zebra, Pinnacle and Kensington books.

When you come online, you'll have the exciting opportunity to:

- View covers of upcoming books
- Read sample chapters
- Learn about our future publishing schedule (listed by publication month *and author*)
- Find out when your favorite authors will be visiting a city near you
- Search for and order backlist books from our online catalog
- Check out author bios and background information
- Send e-mail to your favorite authors
- Meet the Kensington staff online
- Join us in weekly chats with authors, readers and other guests
- Get writing guidelines
- AND MUCH MORE!

Visit our website at
http://www.kensingtonbooks.com

The
Real
Deal

Lucy Monroe

KENSINGTON BOOKS
KENSINGTON PUBLISHING CORP.
http://www.kensingtonbooks.com

KENSINGTON BOOKS are published by

Kensington Publishing Corp.
850 Third Avenue
New York, NY 10022

Copyright © 2004 by Lucy Monroe

All rights reserved. No part of this book may be reproduced in any form or by any means without the prior written consent of the Publisher, excepting brief quotes used in reviews.

If you purchased this book without a cover you should be aware that this book is stolen property. It was reported as "unsold and destroyed" to the Publisher and neither the Author nor the Publisher has received any payment for this "stripped book."

All Kensington titles, imprints and distributed lines are available at special quantity discounts for bulk purchases for sales promotion, premiums, fund-raising, educational or institutional use.

Special book excerpts or customized printings can also be created to fit specific needs. For details, write or phone the office of the Kensington Special Sales Manager: Kensington Publishing Corp., 850 Third Avenue, New York, NY 10022. Attn. Special Sales Department. Phone: 1-800-221-2647.

Kensington and the K logo Reg. U.S. Pat. & TM Off.

First Trade Paperback Printing: September 2004
First Mass Market Paperback Printing: June 2005
10 9 8 7 6 5 4 3 2 1

Printed in the United States of America

*To Lori Foster for her generosity and friendship,
which are an indescribable blessing to me
and to her Book Junkies, authors and readers
that have enriched my life
by letting me hang out with them online.
Thanks, guys! Major hugs.*

Prologue

Thunk.

Pain jarred through Amanda's shoulder as the baseball bat connected with the treadmill, but the darn thing didn't even shift. The black metal monster taunted her just as it had for the past two years. Her nemesis.

The symbol of her husband's dissatisfaction with her body.

Of her failure as a woman.

Swinging the bat in a high arc above her head, she then brought it down with all the force of the anger and despair warring inside her.

Thunk.

This time the pain was so great her fingers flexed open in an involuntary spasm and she dropped the bat.

"No. You aren't going to win!"

For one horrifying second, she saw herself as someone else might see her—a madwoman in a Jackie-O dress and heels, attacking a piece of exercise equipment with a baseball bat and screaming at it as if it were animate.

She didn't care. She hated that pile of molded metal as much as she hated what she'd allowed herself to become. She bent over, her shoulder and arm throbbing, and grabbed the bat again. Melodious chimes, discordant with her mood, halted her mid-swing.

She spun on her heel and stomped through the perfect Southern California showplace that had never felt like a home. Sun glinted off the polished tile floor of the foyer, causing a white glare that hurt eyes gritty from crying.

She didn't want to deal with a visitor. Didn't even know if she *could.* It was probably someone for Lance. Today was Saturday, golf day. Her husband usually spent it with his tanned and toned business associates on one of the many prestigious private courses found along the Southern California coast. Only, today, Lance was otherwise occupied.

Which was something she had every intention of telling whoever was on the other side of that door, right before telling them to go away.

It would serve the lying swine right if she told his visitor just what was occupying her faithless wretch of a husband.

Red hair sticking up in a wild tangle showed through the glass semicircle insert in the door. *Jillian. Thank you, God.* Amanda could deal with Jillian. Jill would understand. Heck, she'd probably ask for her own bat.

Amanda yanked the door open. More sunlight glared and little black spots wavered before her eyes, obscuring the flamboyantly dressed woman in front of her. "Hey, Jill."

"Amanda! What happened?" Jillian swept inside with her usual dramatic flair, her Day-Glo™ orange dress competing with the sunlight for brightness. "I came by to talk you into some serious mall-walking, but you look like you're competing with Tammy Fay what's-her-name for the Miss Raccoon title."

Amanda scrubbed at the hot wetness on her

face with one hand. "I'm thinking more along the lines of Lorena Bobbit."

"What did that SOB do this time?"

Amanda almost laughed. Almost, but she couldn't quite make it. Jillian was the only person in her life who considered Lance less than an ideal husband.

"You're implying that he makes a habit of screwing me over." Which couldn't be further from the truth.

Jillian's brightly painted lips twisted in a grimace. "He's a condescending jerk who wouldn't know a truly sexy woman if she fell on her knees in front of him and offered him a blow job."

Humiliation mixed with anger as Amanda recalled doing almost exactly that—and getting turned down. A sob tore from her already raw throat and she felt her knees buckle. Wiry but strong arms wrapped around her, stopping her descent to the floor. A string of curses that would do any movie director in Hollywood proud stung Amanda's eardrums.

"Come on, honey." The familiar fragrance of Jillian's perfume wrapped around her, as soothing as her friend's voice. "Let's go in the kitchen and get you something to drink. You look a little shocky."

Shock didn't begin to describe how Amanda was feeling. "He was in his office. He was naked, Jill. It's been so long since I saw him that way, I almost didn't recognize him." Her pathetic joke fell flat as another keening wail snaked up from her battered soul. She gulped and breathed before trying to talk again. "He wasn't alone."

"I kinda figured that, you being so upset and all. I didn't think him jacking-off to a copy of *Playboy* would have left you white-faced and shaking."

That did make her laugh, just one small, choked giggle, but it was better than the crying that had been making her throat raw for the past two hours.

"So, who was it? The new paralegal?"

Three little words. *Who was it?* And it all came rushing back. Walking into the anteroom of his plush law office. The sounds coming from the other side of his door in an otherwise silent building. The mesmeric pull of those sounds. The long walk across deeply piled carpet, making no sound herself except for shallow breathing that seemed to grow thinner with each step. The feel of the cold doorknob under her hand. The excruciating slowness as she turned it. The door swinging inward on silent hinges and the tableau that burned like acid against her mind's eye.

"No. Not his assistant." Amanda stopped abruptly, pulling Jillian to a standstill beside her. She leaned back against the white wall, needing the support, the connection with something solid and real. "He was with . . ."

She took a deep breath and Jillian waited for Amanda to continue, for once totally silent.

She closed her eyes, trying to block the picture swimming before them, but the image only grew more prominent against the inside of her eyelids. "He was standing there. Naked." She'd already said that. "He wasn't alone."

Jillian didn't remind her she'd already said that too and Amanda was grateful.

"He had his arms around a woman. She was up against the wall. H-he was inside her. Standing up. I don't know who she is." Amanda didn't know if she could finish it. "A m-man was standing behind him, only he wasn't just standing. Lance was . . . he was . . ." She couldn't say it. Couldn't repeat the exact nature of the threesome's lewd activity, couldn't tell her best friend who the man copulating with her husband had been.

She didn't even want to think it. The double betrayal was ripping her guts out.

"Both of them? He was screwing both of them?"

Amanda's eyes flew open at Jillian's shriek and she stared into green eyes dilated by the same shock that had her trapped.

"Yes. Well, Lance was doing it to the woman and the other man was doing it to him." Even saying it made her sick and she felt bile rise in her throat.

Jillian followed her mad dash to the bathroom, handed her a glass of water afterward and kept up a steady stream of cursing the whole time. "What did you do?" This time her friend's voice came out in a whisper.

"They were really into what they were doing. They didn't notice me. So, I snuck out."

"He doesn't know you saw him?"

Amanda shook her head, her formerly neat French twist rubbing against the wall. She could feel hanks of her long hair coming loose and settling against her shoulders.

"What's the bat for?"

Her mouth twisted. "I was trying to beat up the treadmill, but it didn't work. The damn thing is indestructible."

Jillian made one of the expressive sounds she was so good at. "Honey, you said the d-word. Next thing I know, you really will be sharpening the knives."

Amanda grimaced. "I'd rather destroy the treadmill. I can't go to prison for that one."

Jillian nodded, her red hair waving like some mad monkey on top of her head. "You've got a point."

The next thing Amanda knew Jillian had grabbed her wrist and she was being dragged toward the garage. "Come on, I bet even Lance has a cordless screwdriver. All men have them. Even men who don't know the difference between a flathead and a Phillips. They're status symbols or something."

"And do you know what to do with one?"

"Sure. I've been living on my own since I was seventeen. I even know how to use a snake on a backed-up toilet."

Amanda chose not to comment on that dubious accomplishment.

Ten minutes later, she and Jillian were both armed with cordless screwdrivers. Her husband, who Jillian had guessed rightly wouldn't know how to use one, had not merely one, but three screwdrivers. All different models.

It didn't take long for Amanda to get the hang of using the tool under the competent instruction of her friend. Soon, the whirring of the battery-powered motors mixed with metal scraping against metal. Before long, the treadmill lay around them in pieces. They moved onto the StairMaster and even managed to dismantle the pneumatic weight bench.

Amanda squeezed the trigger on her screwdriver, making it whir noisily. "This is really therapeutic. I wish my aerobics tapes could be dealt with the same way."

Jill grinned. "Hey, the baseball bat oughtta work on those."

It did, but Amanda still felt dissatisfied. She needed more. She'd spent two years married to the food and exercise gestapo and she wanted revenge. She let the bat fall to her side and wiped the sweat from her forehead. "It's not enough."

Jillian's eyes twinkled with a look that had been scaring those who knew her since before she could talk. "Come on."

Amanda followed her into the entertainment room and her gaze fell on the giant screen TV that filled up half of an entire wall, Lance's newest and most prized toy. She swiveled her head and met Jillian's eyes. Their green depths reflected the same sense of purpose beating a rhythm in Amanda's breast. It took a lot longer than the treadmill and they both had to jump out of the way when the heavy screen crashed to the floor, splintering into pieces, but when they were done, she felt better than she had in months.

They both stood, staring at the remains of the exorbitantly expensive piece of equipment, and then Jillian looked up. "Anything else?"

Amanda thought about it. She could think of several things it would bother her husband to lose, but her blind desire for destruction seemed to be satisfied.

"No. I just want to pack my stuff and get out of here."

A curious sense of relief was beginning to pervade her being as she realized she never again had to suffer the critical comments and sexual rejection that typified her marriage to Lance. She was tired of feeling like a failure.

Maybe her womanly attributes were overblown in comparison to the boyishly thin chick her husband had been boinking. Maybe she was too pale for Southern California beauty, too short, too chesty, too hippy, too pretty much everything, but who said a woman was defined by her sex appeal?

She was on the inside fast track at Extant Corporation. Investing her time, energy and emotion in her career made more sense than giving those precious resources to her jerk of a husband, or any other man for that matter.

One thing was certain—she was never going to make the mistake of giving a man the power to hurt her again.

Chapter 1

With an accuracy born of years of practice, Simon brought the *katana* down in a precise arc that left the silk scarf hanging in two even sections from the hooks in the ceiling. Moving into the next position, he swung the Korean sword in a horizontal path that sent two scraps of red silk fluttering to the floor.

Pushing his muscles to the burning point, he worked through his form three times and completed an entire set of stretching exercises before taking care of his *katana* and hanging it back on the wall of his private gym. A few swipes with a small towel took care of the wet sheen of sweat on his chest and arms.

He crossed the room and turned out the lights, leaving as the only source of light the moon's rays filtering in through the windows that made up one wall of his gym. Returning to the center of the room, he sank to a cross-legged position on the floor mat. The dark waters of the Puget Sound glimmered, their cold depths calling to the chill in his soul as they always did.

He'd built his home on an island, less than an hour's ferry journey from the mainland and only two hours from Seattle. The perfect location for a man who liked his privacy, it was also easy access to the technology resources he needed for his research.

The entire computer industry was racing to see who could develop a usable prototype of a fiber-optic processor, and he was determined to be the first. It was that need that had sent him in here looking for clarity of mind and an easing of the physical tension that always accompanied his deep immersion in a project.

He hadn't found it. His mind, usually so clear after a workout, spun from one thought to another.

For some reason, instead of focusing on the results of his most recent experiments, old memories demanded his attention tonight. Memories he would have been happy to bury into oblivion, five-year-old memories that had no place in his life today.

He could see Elaine's face, the beautiful features taut with stress, her eyes glistening with tears as she said good-bye. "You've got to understand, Simon. You live in the shadows. I want to live in the light. Eric likes being around people. You're always looking for excuses to avoid them. You want to spend all your time in that stupid lab of yours. A woman can't live like that."

He remembered each word verbatim.

A woman can't live like that.

At the time, he had wanted to believe she was wrong, that she'd been making excuses for her own choices. But five years on, he had to concede she was probably right.

After Elaine, he hadn't had a relationship that lasted long enough for him to even start considering marriage. His infrequent girlfriends invariably bailed after the novelty of the sex wore off. He was too intense. Insensitive to their needs. Too wrapped up in his designs and experiments. Too cold. Too uncommunicative.

Some had even decided after having sex, that he was just too big. He wasn't a monster, but damn it, he couldn't help the fact he was not average.

He wanted marriage. A family. A life like the one he had known so long ago before his mother's death, one that had warmth and companionship. Hell if he knew how to go about procuring one, though. He didn't know how to turn down the intensity. He could no more give up his computer experiments than he could will his sex to stay at half-mast during intercourse.

His current project fascinated and challenged him in a way that nothing, particularly no woman, had since he was six years old and programmed his first robot. So, why was he letting old memories taunt him?

But he knew. Eric's ecstatic voice over the phone. Elaine was pregnant with their second child. He was hoping for a girl this time. Simon wasn't jealous of his cousin's relationship with Elaine. He had accepted a long time ago that they made a more natural couple than he and Elaine had ever done.

The fact that their relationship had never progressed to the bedroom should have clued him in long before Elaine's big good-bye scene. But part of his problem, he freely admitted, was a certain amount of cluelessness where women were concerned.

Simon counted Elaine as both family and friend now, just the same as Eric. He made himself a frequent visitor to their home so he could spend time with them and their little boy. The kid called him Uncle Simon and he liked it. It made him feel like he belonged to someone.

But none of that changed the velocity of the lonely winds that howled through his soul as he contemplated a bleak future.

He picked up one of the pieces of red silk that had landed near where he sat. It was soft against his skin, but so light it weighed almost nothing. If he closed his eyes, it would be like it wasn't even there.

Just like him.

Sometimes he thought if he closed his eyes long enough, he would cease to exist, fading into the cold mists that often surrounded his home.

Amanda mentally went over the game plan for her upcoming meeting with the president of Brant Computers as the elevator made its ascent.

She could barely believe her luck. When she had put the proposal for a friendly merger before the Executive Management Team at Extant Corporation, she hadn't been sure they'd go for it. She'd been almost positive if they did pursue her plan, they would choose someone higher in the management hierarchy to negotiate terms.

That hadn't happened. She'd been chosen over several colleagues to make the initial approach to Eric Brant. He had been receptive and the Executive Management Team had appointed her point man for negotiations.

Her boss had wanted her to take a team with her, but she had convinced him the rapport she had established with Eric could be undermined if other negotiators were introduced at this juncture. Daniel had acceded to her arguments, allowing her to make the trip to Port Mulqueen, Washington, to talk to the president of Brant Computers alone.

Her relief had been enormous since a representative from the company's law firm had been one of the suggested team members. It was inevitable that she have business dealings with her ex-husband given that his firm handled all of Extant's legal issues, but the last thing she wanted was for her first really big break with her company to depend on Lance Rogers's cooperation.

So far, negotiations had gone very well indeed.

She watched the buttons light up as the elevator went past one floor after another without stopping to pick up further passengers. She willed each little circle to lighten and darken without the elevator stopping. She didn't want any delays in her meeting with Eric Brant today, not even small ones.

She wasn't nervous, not exactly. Just impatient. It was a honey of a deal. She couldn't imagine Brant's board of directors not going for it. Not once she'd gotten buy-in from the company president and that's what she was here for. After his encouraging reaction to her first proposal, she wasn't expecting a lot of resistance.

When the deal closed, she'd be one step closer to that position on the Executive Management Team she coveted. At twenty-six, she was the youngest female junior executive in the firm. Her goal was to be the youngest executive, male or female, and she was two years into a five-year plan to make that happen. Her plan would get a major boost when she successfully negotiated the merger with Brant Computers.

A smile of professional satisfaction hovered on her lips as the elevator doors slid open. She adjusted the strap of her purse over the shoulder of her ultraprofessional, favorite red blazer and tightened her grip on her briefcase before stepping out of the elevator. Taking a cleansing breath, she walked toward the semicircular desk in the center of the large reception area. Her two-inch heels made whisper soft noises on the carpet that seemed to fit with the soft music playing in the background and the almost silent clicking of the receptionist's keyboard as she worked at her computer.

Amanda stopped in front of the desk and a blonde of indeterminate age turned to greet her. "Ms. Zachary?"

"Yes." Amanda smiled.

"I'll just call Mr. Brant's executive assistant and let her know you're here."

The receptionist picked up the phone, dialed a number and spoke into the mouthpiece attached to her headset. As she listened to what was being said, her gaze flitted to Amanda and then back to her computer screen. "All right. I'll tell her."

She hung up the phone. "Mr. Brant's earlier meeting has run over. If you would like to take a seat, his executive assistant will come for you when he's finished."

Amanda acquiesced with carefully concealed impatience, seating herself in an armchair on the wall opposite the elevator. She ignored the magazines laid out in an attractively arranged pile, in order to spend her time waiting in thought.

What was going on?

It could be that a meeting had legitimately gone overtime. The man was president of a major company after all. He could also be exercising psychological strategy in making her wait. But to what purpose? Her previous meetings with Eric had led her to believe he was as excited about the possible merger as she was.

Several minutes passed before an older woman in a dove-gray suit cut in classic lines approached Amanda. "Ms. Zachary?"

Amanda stood. "You must be Fran." She had

spoken to the executive assistant several times on the phone, but this was their first opportunity to meet.

The older woman's mouth tilted slightly in what might be considered a smile. "Yes, won't you come this way?"

Amanda got up and followed the other woman. They stopped in front of double doors, one of which was cracked open a few inches.

"What the hell is the matter with you, Eric?" The deeply masculine voice came out in even tones, but was laced with unmistakable anger. "This is a family held company. Merging with Extant would destroy everything our grandfather and fathers built here."

"Nonsense." Eric's voice sounded conciliatory, but louder than the other man's. "Look, Simon, you promised to give her a fair hearing and I'm holding you to your word."

"I would have promised anything to get Elaine to turn off the waterworks, including listening to some snake-oil salesman's pitch."

"Our arguing upset my wife, and Amanda Zachary is no snake-oil salesman."

Before the other man could respond, the executive assistant had knocked on the already opened door.

The voices ceased abruptly.

Fran pushed the door open. "Eric, Ms. Zachary is here."

There were two men in the room. One stood in front of the windows so his face and expression were cast in shadow, but she could tell he was big, easily six-foot-two.

The other man wasn't quite so massive. His sandy brown hair and engaging smile gave him a look of boyish charm, but his blue eyes glinted with unmistakable intelligence. "Thank you, Fran. We'll take it from here."

The other woman turned and left. For one completely insane moment, Amanda wanted to call her back. The brooding presence of the man by the window unnerved her.

Then Eric caught her attention by coming forward to take her hand. "It's a pleasure to finally meet you, Amanda."

She shook his hand, being sure to grasp it firmly. "The pleasure is mine. I'm looking forward to our discussion."

Or rather, she had been before this other man had entered the equation.

Eric released her hand and turned slightly. "Amanda, this is my cousin, Simon Brant. He's in charge of research and development for Brant Computers. Simon, this is Amanda Zachary, the representative from Extant Corporation."

Simon stepped away from the window and she got her first clear view of the man. She knew her negotiator's smile had slipped a little, but she couldn't help it. Simon Brant was a force of nature. Dark exotic looks mixed with a smoldering presence in a Molotov cocktail that set something on fire inside her, something she had been absolutely sure no longer even existed.

Desire. Hot. Molten. Unstoppable. And it washed through her body as if her receptors had forgotten, or never even known, that she wasn't a very sexual person. She felt betrayed by her body. Now was not the time for it to rediscover long-dormant feminine hormones.

Everything important to her was on the line with this deal.

"M-Mr. Brant." Great. She'd stuttered. She never tripped over her words, not since going through an endless series of speech therapy sessions as a child. However, she'd also never met a man who looked like a cross between a Scottish warlord and Apache chief.

She put out her hand and wished to Heaven she'd ignored the urge for politeness when his big, warm fingers enclosed hers.

For the space of seconds, she didn't speak. Couldn't speak. Something elemental and downright terrifying passed from his hand to hers as he completed the shake.

"Ms. Zachary."

"Call me Amanda." The words slipped out, unbidden. She wouldn't have taken them back if she could. It would be awkward to have his cousin calling her by her first name while Simon stuck with the more formal address.

He dropped her hand, his gray eyes roaming over her with tactile intensity. "Simon."

That was it. Just his name, but she knew what he meant.

"Now that the introductions are over, why don't we all sit down?" Eric's voice sounded far away and Amanda had to force herself to decipher the words before nodding her agreement.

Despite the fact it was Eric's office, Simon led the way. He waited for her to sit in an armchair across the room from Eric's large executive desk. Eric and Simon sat at either end of the matching black leather sofa, with Simon taking the end furthest from her. She should have felt relief that his choice had given her a reprieve from his proximity, but the angle at which they sat gave him a clear view of her and vice versa.

It was an effort to turn her attention to Eric. "I didn't realize your cousin would be joining us for the meeting."

"It's a family held company, Amanda." Simon gave special inflection to her name. "I'm family and I happen to own a sizable chunk of the business."

"I see." She smiled tentatively. "But I had the impression from Eric that none of the other family played a principal role in management of the company."

"That's true." Eric gave Simon a hard look. "I'm the president of the company and my cousin rarely shows interest in my day-to-day decision making."

"I don't call proposing a merger with one of our chief competitors your average day-to-day decision. Wouldn't you agree, Amanda?"

He'd put her on the spot and, in all honesty, she couldn't gainsay him. "It is a big decision, but certainly not one Eric has entertained lightly. We've been discussing the possibilities and ramifications of a merger for several weeks now."

"It's a pity I wasn't brought in before this then, because you've wasted your time talking to my cousin. I'll never approve what you propose."

"You don't own controlling interest in the company, damn it." Eric glared at Simon.

"Neither do you," Simon pointed out with a silky menace that sent shivers down the back of Amanda's legs.

"What do you plan to do, make this a family war?"

Simon's shoulders tensed infinitesimally and Amanda had the distinct impression that war was the last thing he wanted.

"Perhaps if you would allow me to present Extant's proposal, there won't be any need for bloodshed." It was a weak joke, but Eric smiled.

"Great idea."

Simon settled against the sofa cushions and kicked his denim clad, long legs out in front of him.

He crossed them at the ankles, one booted foot resting on top the other. His arm stretched along the back of the couch, pulling the knit of his dark crewneck shirt taut over the well-defined muscles of his torso. He was the epitome of "relaxed."

So, why did she get the feeling he was a tiger waiting to pounce on her unwary person?

One black brow rose. "I'm ready for you to begin, Amanda."

She'd put up with all the patronizing from men she was going to tolerate in her lifetime during her marriage. She didn't care how sexy this guy was, no one knew their job as well as she knew hers. It was after all, her life. And she was no snake-oil salesman as he would soon see. She gave him a smile meant to convey her confidence in what she had to say, and then launched into the initial proposal she'd given to Eric.

The smile would have knocked him on his ass if he hadn't already been sitting down.

Man, this woman was hot. Beautiful. Built to stop a strong man's heart, even if she did hide it behind a boxy jacket and long skirt that only hinted at the legs underneath. And she was the damn enemy.

Simon's jaw set and he listened while a husky voice that could have played a starring role in his favorite wet dream told him why he should let his cousin go through with his plans to destroy their family held company.

All right, so she didn't see it as destruction. Why should she? It wasn't her grandfather's dreams at stake here.

She was going on about the increased market share the two companies would enjoy once they were merged.

"Where did you come up with those figures?" he asked, interrupting her mid-flow.

He had to give it to her. She didn't so much as frown at his rudeness, nor did she hesitate before explaining the marketing statistics she'd used to develop her proposal.

"What about the employees? I'm still unclear as to the effect this will have on overlapping human resources."

He wasn't unclear at all. It meant letting people go. Loyal employees that had a right to expect some loyalty back from the company they worked for. But he wanted to hear her say it. He wanted to see his cousin's face when she said it. Didn't Eric care?

She sat forward on the edge of her chair, her expression earnest. "Not unexpectedly, there will be a certain amount of employee attrition, but nothing on the scale of a major layoff."

"What do you consider a major layoff, Ms. Zachary?"

"Less than five percent of the total workforce for both Brant and Extant will be affected." She said it like she was expecting accolades for keeping the numbers down.

Eric sat there looking as if he thought laying off five percent of their workforce was no big deal.

Simon uncrossed his legs and leaned forward. "Do you realize how many jobs we're talking about here? I'd be willing to bet that for the guy who loses his job, just one person let go seems pretty major."

It interested him that she scooted back in her chair even though he was several feet away from her. "The computer industry is dynamic. Employees who have chosen their career in it understand that."

"How would you feel if it was your job on the line, Amanda? Would you still be in favor of the merger?"

She blanched, actually flinching at the question. Her job clearly meant a lot to her.

He waited to see how honestly she would answer the question, but Eric intervened. "That's not a fair question, Simon. This is about what is best for the company, not individual employees."

Simon stood up, his patience disintegrating with his mood. "Maybe I think the company's welfare is tied up with that of the employees."

Eric ran his fingers through his hair, disturbing the usually immaculate style. "Calm down, Simon."

"I'm not upset."

Eric's expression said he wasn't fooled. Simon wasn't shouting, but his cousin knew he was pissed. Big-time.

"Mr. Brant . . . Simon . . . you agreed to hear me out, I thought. I'm barely through the first point in my presentation."

She had guts, and eyes the color of Hershey's dark chocolate syrup that a man could happily drown in.

Nothing about this merger appealed to him, but the woman did. He'd listen, if for no other reason than to spend more time in her company, learn more about what made her tick. He sat back down.

"I'm here." He turned to Eric. "But don't you ever use your wife to manipulate me again."

Eric's relieved smile froze on his face. "It wasn't like that."

Suddenly, Simon knew it had been exactly like that. He'd been spouting off, but Eric had known Simon couldn't withstand Elaine's tears. He'd also known his pregnant wife was bound to be upset by their argument. "You son of a bitch, you brought it up in front of her on purpose."

Eric had the grace to blush. "We'll talk about this later."

"Why? Don't you want Amanda privy to family business? You seem pretty free with the idea of handing over the family company to her."

Eric's eyes narrowed and the muscles of his jaw tightened. "I'm not handing the company over to her. I'm not handing it over to Extant for that matter. We're talking about a merger, a friendly merger."

"Eric is right. Brant Computers isn't going to cease to exist, it's going to be bigger than it has ever been." She was leaning forward again and her blazer parted to reveal the thin white silk of her blouse.

Did she know he could see the shadow of the top swell of her breasts when she did that?

Somehow he doubted it. She seemed completely focused on business. It wouldn't hurt him to do the same thing. He hadn't had as much trouble with his libido since he was a fifteen-year-old wiz kid attending college with fully developed, sexually active women who had turned teasing into a national league sport.

"There may be a company left. Hell, you might even agree to keep the Brant name, but the company my grandfather founded and my father spent his life building will cease to exist, and all the soft-soap in the world isn't going to make that any less of a reality."

"I don't think you're looking at the big picture."

"Maybe that's because the picture of Brant employees standing in the unemployment line keeps getting in the way."

She frowned at that. "Over the long term the

employees will be better off because stability will be increased for both the companies." She grabbed her briefcase and started pulling papers out. "If you just look at these long-term sales forecasts, you'll see that the initial five percent of employee attrition will not only be made up, but there will be steady growth in the number of positions available within the merged companies."

Simon looked at the papers, but all he saw were two exquisitely feminine hands with neatly manicured nails. He'd give his most recently acquired antique *katana* to have those delicate fingers on his body. He'd give the whole collection to have met this woman in other circumstances.

"Eric, trade places with Amanda. Presumably, you've already seen these numbers."

Her head came up and he read startled uncertainty in those gorgeous brown eyes before she masked her reaction.

Eric was already standing and the poor little darling had no choice but to do what Simon had suggested. Her initial reaction told him that the idea of being in close proximity to him made her nervous. Was that because he was on the opposite side of this issue from her and she saw him as the enemy?

Or was it because she felt this gut-wrenching physical attraction too?

"Here, let me see that." He let his hand brush against hers as he pulled the paper from off the top of the pile.

Her fingers trembled.

An immediate and unexpected reaction took place just south of his belt buckle. He started a mental recitation of the laws and formulas related to thermal dynamics.

"As you can see, future employment projections are quite good."

He didn't comment. The recitation of the formulas sparked an idea related to his latest fiber-optic experiment. He needed a notebook. Dropping the paper in his hand, he stood up and crossed the room to Eric's desk. It took rifling through three drawers, but he found a legal pad. He started taking notes as rapidly as possible.

He had to test this.

The pad in one hand, he started from the room. "Simon!"

He stopped at the door and turned his head to the sound of his cousin's demanding voice. He didn't see Eric though, his mind's eye was too focused on his project.

"What about Amanda's presentation?"

"If I've said something to offend you . . ." The soft, husky voice trailed off and succeeded in claiming a corner of his attention.

Amanda.

He wanted to see her again.

"Bring your proposal to my house."

Her eyes widened and he heard Eric groan.

"My cousin can give you directions." Then he turned and left, his thoughts consumed with his upcoming experiment.

Chapter 2

Amanda watched the maddening man walk out of the office, feeling like Dorothy before she'd found the yellow brick road. What had just happened?

"He wants me to go to his *house*?"

Eric's expression was one of rueful resignation. He nodded. "Don't take this personally. Simon's brilliant and his mind doesn't work like everyone else's. When he gets an idea, it holds his complete attention."

"But . . ." One second he'd been reading her figures and the next he'd gotten up and was rummaging through Eric's desk.

"One Christmas, when he was about nine, I think, he got up in the middle of opening his presents and disappeared into his lab until New Years Day."

"When he was *nine*?" Eric had to be exaggerating.

"Simon was a child prodigy. He graduated from high school when he was eleven. He had a double bachelor's degree in physics and computer design engineering by the time he was fifteen. Four years later he had a Ph.D. in physics."

She knew what Eric was telling her. Simon was a genius. A cold, sinking sensation settled somewhere around her stomach because that genius didn't want his company merged with Extant. She could see all her carefully laid plans crashing and burning.

"Why does he want me to go to his house?"

A wrinkle appeared between Eric's brows. "I'm not sure. I think he wants you to finish your presentation."

"But why at his house?" A straightforward business deal had taken a distinctly unbusinesslike turn.

Eric's expression turned thoughtful. "I really don't know. He's a total privacy nut. Him inviting you to his house is out of character, but then so is his showing such a strong interest in the business side of Brant Computers."

"I'd feel better about finishing the presentation here in your office." She'd feel more comfortable not having to be in the disturbing man's presence at all, but going to his house seemed way too intimate.

Eric shook his head. "If he's on a new project, it could be days, weeks even, before he comes back to the mainland."

"Comes back to the mainland?" Her voice came out faint as she considered how disastrous that would be for the timetable on the merger.

"He lives on one of the islands. The Puget Sound is full of them. At least he opted for a home on one that has regular ferry service. You should be able to go and come back in one day."

Was that supposed to make her feel better? "But couldn't you call him and ask him to meet me here?"

Eric shook his head again, his mouth twisted grimly. "No. Simon is stubborn and like I said, his mind doesn't work like the rest of us. If we want him to hear your presentation, you'll have to go to him."

"Won't you be participating in the meeting?"

"Like Simon said, I've seen all the numbers." Eric stood up. "I can't really take the time from my schedule for a duplication of effort. You convinced me. I'm sure you can convince Simon and until you do, further meetings on the subject between the two of us would be ineffective."

She wasn't sure of any such thing, but she had no choice other than to try. She couldn't let Simon Brant unravel her plans and jeopardize her goals. If that meant visiting him at his island home, that's what she would do.

Which was how she found herself breathing in the smell of burning diesel fuel on a ferry bound for a small island in the Puget Sound the next day.

She'd tried calling Simon to ask him to meet her again in Seattle. According to the crotchety old man that identified himself as Simon's housekeeper, Simon wasn't available for phone calls. When she identified herself, she'd been told Simon was expecting her.

Since he hadn't so much as given her a time or day for their meeting, she didn't see how that could be, but apparently Eric was right. Simon didn't think like other people.

His housekeeper had told her she was expected for lunch today.

William Tell's *Overture* started chirping away in her purse and she grabbed for her cell phone. Flipping it open, she put it to her ear. "Hello?"

"Hey, chicky-poo, how's it hangin'?"

"Jillian. Why aren't you on the set?"

"We finished taping early. They wanted to do this sunrise scene. I've been up since two-thirty this morning."

"Uh . . . Jill, we live on the West Coast. Sunsets over the ocean are beautiful, sunrises hidden behind LA's smog and skyline aren't exactly awe-inspiring."

"We did a desert taping, smarty-pants."

"Oh."

"Anyway, I called to say you've gotta watch today's episode. I've got amazing dialogue and I emoted with all the energy of Bette Midler."

Shoot. "Honey, I've got an afternoon appointment and the VCR in my hotel room doesn't have a timed taping function." She thought fast. "But my Ti-Vo is saving it for me at my condo. I'll watch it the minute I get home, I promise."

"Amanda . . ." Jillian drew her name out for at least six syllables. "I really wanted you to watch this. It's just the first half of the show. Can't you sneak away to the bathroom or something and find a television?"

What would Simon think of taking a thirty-minute break in the middle of their meeting to watch Jillian's soap opera?

"Jill—"

"Please, Amanda. I haven't been this excited about my work since I got the job."

That was saying a lot. Jillian had had her bit part on the soap for the past six years, longer than Amanda's marriage had lasted. She was a regular, if not a star.

"Okay, I'll try." She couldn't believe she was saying this. "But I can't promise anything."

"Thanks, hon! You're the best friend a girl could have. Have I told you that lately?"

"Not in the last week, no," Amanda said, laughing. Jillian had always been there for her. Through a disastrous two-year marriage and an ugly divorce that took a year to finalize, she'd been a rock in Amanda's life. "But listen, if I can't watch it, can you Fed-Ex me the tape?"

"The way I feel today, I'd fly the tape up to you to watch myself if I didn't have to work tomorrow and Friday."

Jillian was right. Amanda hadn't heard this much enthusiasm in her friend's voice concerning her work in years. "Hey, maybe you can fly up for the weekend anyway."

Silence met that. "Are you okay, Amanda?"

Darn. Why were best friends so discerning? "I just asked if you wanted to come up for the weekend. We could do the Seattle thing. Why does something have to be wrong?"

"Because when it comes to work, you are worse than anal retentive. You're so focused, you could give a Zen Buddhist monk lessons."

She sure didn't feel like a monk, or rather, a nun, not when every time she thought about Simon Brant her hormones started hopping around like rabbits hyped up on sugar. "There's a glitch in the deal I'm trying to work out," she admitted.

"What kind of a glitch?"

"A big one." About six feet, two inches, of glitch.

"Bummer, hon. I'm sorry."

"Me too, but I'm not about to give up."

"Of course not. The only thing you've ever given up on is men. Everything else gets your try-till-you-die mentality."

Driving down the same road for the third time in twenty minutes, she was having difficulty applying the try-till-you-die approach. Where the heck was the turnoff? She'd missed it twice and was now driving slower than she could be walking in the attempt not to miss it a third time. Wait. Was that an opening in the trees? It was. Carefully camouflaged, the opening to Simon's drive could have easily been taken for a natural break in the flora and fauna alongside the road.

Eric had said Simon was a privacy nut, but this was ridiculous. One of them could have mentioned that the entrance to his property was as well hidden as your average state secret. Not that Simon had mentioned anything. He'd told Eric to give her directions and then dismissed the whole situation by leaving.

It was a good thing he was just a business associate and not her boyfriend. That kind of behavior would be really hard to take in a lover.

Fortunately, she reached the gate before her wayward thoughts had a chance to go any farther afield.

She stopped the rented Taurus and pressed its automatic window button. It whirred softly as the glass disappeared between her and the small black box she was supposed to talk into. She reached through the window, inhaling a big breath of fresh, forest-scented air, and pressed the red button below the box.

"Yeah?" There was no mistaking that crotchety voice. She'd only heard it once, but Simon's housekeeper was unforgettable.

"It's Amanda Zachary."

"Expected you here a good twenty minutes ago, missy. It don't pay to be late if you expect to catch the boss out of his lab."

She glared at the box and reminded herself that this was business. For business, she could put up with a cranky old man.

"I'm sorry. I missed the turn."

"Guess you missed it more than once if it took you an extra twenty minutes."

What was this guy, the timeliness cop? "Perhaps, since I am already late, you would be kind enough to buzz the gates open so that I won't keep your employer waiting any longer."

"He ain't come out of the lab yet."

She ignored that bit of additional provocation and simply said, "The gate?"

"Can't."

"You can't open the gate?" She stared stupidly at the black box, at a complete loss.

"Right."

"Is it broken?"

"Nope."

Anger overcame confusion and good sense. *"Then what exactly is stopping you from opening the darn thing?"*

"You got to get out of the car. I need to make a visual I.D. before I can open the gate."

"Since you've never seen me before, what exactly are you trying to identify?"

"No need to get snippy. I done my job. I got a picture of you. No use you asking how. I don't share my trade secrets with just anybody."

For Heaven's sake.

She got out of the car and stood so her head and shoulders were clearly visible above the car door.

"You'll have to step around the door, if you don't mind."

Now he decided to be polite, while asking her to do something totally ludicrous.

"What difference does it make?" She glared with unconcealed belligerence at the camera at the top of the gate.

"You got something to hide, missy?"

"Not if you discount a body that isn't femme fatale material," she muttered to herself as she stepped around the silver car's door.

Thoroughly out of sorts, she threw her arms wide. "Look, no automatic weapons, no hidden cameras, no nerve gas. Are you satisfied?"

"I think I could be."

No! No. No. Darn it. No. This had not been the housekeeper's voice, but another, unforgettable one—that of Simon Brant. In a reflex move, she crossed her arms over her chest as she felt heat crawl from the back of her ankles right up her body and into her cheeks. She was going to kill that housekeeper when she got her hands on him.

She was going to pick him up by his toes and hang him above a tar pit. And then she was going to let go.

"Hello, Mr. Brant. I've been informed that I'm late."

He didn't answer, but the gate swung inward.

If Simon tried to talk, he was going to laugh and that would just encourage Jacob in his irascible ways. So, he pressed the button for the gate release without answering Amanda. He watched as she climbed back into her car, her dark hair all twisted on the back of her head in a tidy knot. The severity of her hairstyle and the suit she was wearing could not erase the image he had of her with her arms flung wide, her generous breasts pressing against the fabric of her blouse and her eyes glittering with pure temper.

"She's a tad feisty, sir."

Simon didn't know why the old man called him

sir. He'd never been in doubt who was in charge between the two of them, and it wasn't Simon Brant. "I have no doubt she has cause."

Jacob just shrugged his thin shoulders. "Might have upset her a bit, I suppose. I got poor company manners, sir."

Considering the fact the man had at one time been on the presidential detail of the Secret Service, Simon took that comment with the credence it deserved. "What you have is an unfulfilled wish to go undercover and it comes out in the different roles you like to assume here."

Jacob's gray head cocked to one side. "Could be. Or could be I'm just a crabby old geezer who's lucky to have an eccentric millionaire for a boss."

Simon didn't have a chance to answer as the first few bars of Beethoven's Fifth played over the house-wide sound system. He did not like doorbells.

"I'll get it. I think Amanda could do without another dose of your company manners." And he wanted to be alone when he greeted her. He didn't want any distractions when he discovered if his reaction to her in Eric's office had been an anomaly.

Amanda's hand clenched and unclenched on the handle of her briefcase while she waited for the door to open.

Okay, the guy was a genius and so sexy he made her heart imitate a Morse code operator, but that did not mean he would succeed in scotching the deal. If he was so smart then he would definitely see the benefits of merging with Extant.

She had a briefcase full of reports and graphs that he'd have to be a fool to ignore.

So, stop worrying, already.

He was just a man with some preconceived notions she needed to help him reprogram.

The door swung open.

Simon Brant stood with his strong, masculine hand curved around the edge of the door. "Amanda. Welcome to my home."

How did he do that? Five words, none of them remotely sexual, and her insides were turning into warm honey.

Just a man.

Uh huh.

Right.

Her professional, let's-talk-the-deal smile fought with her rebellious lips' urge to pucker up and beg for the gorgeous man's kisses. Oh, man, she was losing it.

"Mr. Brant."

Firm lips curved in a smile, revealing perfectly even, white teeth. "I thought it was Simon."

"Simon," she conceded. "Thank you for inviting me."

He inclined his head and stepped back, indicating she should come inside.

She stepped over the threshold of the door and for one disconcerting second felt as if she'd made an irrevocable decision that would change the rest of her life. Shaking the feeling off as highly fanciful, she extended her hand toward him. "I look forward to showing you the many benefits of the proposed merger between Brant Computers and Extant Corporation."

Simon took her hand, but he didn't shake it. He squeezed her fingers and bent forward. For one incredulous moment, she thought he was going to kiss her hand, but he didn't. He simply dropped his head forward in a cross between an Oriental bow and an Old World gesture.

He straightened and dropped her hand. "Jacob's prepared lunch. It's waiting for us in the great room."

Was that a veiled hint about her slight tardiness?

He turned and led the way down a hallway, his feet making no sound on the hardwood floor while her shoes tapped out a firm tattoo with each step.

The hall took a sharp right and she stopped in awe at the entrance to the room. It gave the term *great room* new meaning. It was huge, at least twenty by forty feet, but it wasn't the size that had her so captivated. The entire forty-foot wall opposite the entrance was glass with a view of the Sound and Mt. Rainier off in the distance.

Simon stopped and turned to her. "Like it?"

"It's fantastic." No wonder the guy preferred to work out of his home, with a home like this.

"Other than the necessary structural bracing, this entire side of the house is made up of reinforced glass and windows."

"How many floors are there?"

"Three. The pool and gym are on the floor below us. Jacob's living quarters, the kitchen, guest room, and this room are on this level, and my living quarters and lab are upstairs."

Her gaze slid around the room they were in. Its simplistic design and furnishings had Oriental overtones, but nothing glossy and lacquered. It was all fruitwood, simple lines and natural hues for the upholstery. "This really is magnificent. You must enjoy living here quite a bit."

The house was much bigger than the home she had shared with Lance and in many ways more grand, yet it still felt like a home. It reflected its owner's complex, but deceptively simple-appearing approach to life.

"Thank you." He took her arm and led her to the dining table in front of one of the massive twin stone fireplaces at either end of the room. "Let's have lunch and you can tell me a little about yourself."

She allowed him to seat her, feeling strange about a business associate observing the courtesy. In LA, she was used to being treated the same way as her male counterparts in the corporate world.

Flicking her cloth napkin open and then laying it across her lap, she said, "I'm not all that interesting, but I don't think you'll find the same true of Extant's proposal."

His smile flashed along with a determined glint in his gray eyes that gave her pause. "I prefer to know a person before I discuss business with them. It probably comes from working for a family held company."

"I see."

"Good."

She looked down at the pasta in pesto sauce attractively presented in a flat china bowl. "This looks wonderful."

"Jacob's rather proud of his culinary talents."

"He's a unique individual." She meant to be diplomatic.

He laughed, the sound affecting her already off-balance equilibrium. "That's one way to describe him. Cantankerous is another."

She didn't bother asking why Simon kept such a rude man working for him as she took her first bite of the delicious pasta. She thought it was probably just as hard for a recluse genius to find household help as for a cranky old man who cooked like an angel to find a job.

"So, tell me about yourself, Amanda." It was a line tossed out as easily as a common greeting, and yet his intent stare and deep, controlled voice made her feel like he was asking for more than a rundown on the highlights of her résumé.

She fought against giving in to the compulsion to share on a personal level with him. "I've been working for Extant Corporation since graduating from college with a degree in business. This is my second year in the corporate planning division."

"Are you married?"

Her fork paused midway to her mouth. "I don't see how that relates to the merger."

One black brow rose. "I thought I explained I like to know the people I do business with."

"I believed you meant my business background."

He poured wine into her glass and then his own. "Did you?"

No she hadn't. Not really, but it was so ludicrous to think he wanted to know about her. She wasn't the type of woman to inspire personal interest from a man like Simon, from any man for that matter. Or so her ex-husband had taken pains to point out. "I assure you the most interesting aspects of my life relate to my career."

"I'm *interested in* your marital status."

"Why?"

He shrugged. "It seems relevant to who you are. I'm single and I've never been married. I rarely date and I spend long hours in my lab ignoring the rest of the world."

"Oh . . ." What was she supposed to say to that? She couldn't begin to understand why he was telling her this stuff. He must be very serious about wanting to personally know the people he did business with. She supposed that made sense considering most of his current business associates were family or employees for his family's company.

"I'm not married." She didn't add that she was

divorced. "I don't have time to date." Something flickered in his eyes at that. She supposed he was noticing, as she was, that they had quite a bit in common. "And I'm focused almost exclusively on my work." In fact, her only friend outside work was Jillian.

Which reminded her. "Do you have a television?" She couldn't believe she was asking him this. It was totally unprofessional, but then the man insisted on having a business meeting in his home and grilling her about her marital status. He couldn't be *that* concerned about professional behavior.

His black brows rose. "No."

She couldn't quite stifle a sound of regret. Jillian was going to be so disappointed.

"I believe Jacob has one, however."

"Jacob?" Asking Simon to allow a thirty-minute break in their meeting so she could keep her promise to Jillian was not nearly as intimidating a prospect as asking Jacob for the loan of his television.

"Yes. He likes British comedies."

That would mean he had cable. He'd definitely get Jillian's soap opera. "My best friend is a regular in a daytime drama. She wants me to watch her show today. She's really proud of her scenes."

It had been worth asking, to see the bemusement on Simon's features. He'd been knocking her off-balance since they met and she found herself relishing this small opportunity to get her own back again.

"You want to watch a soap opera?"

"Yes. My friend said it was only the first thirty minutes I needed to see. I hate to ask for a break like that and realize it isn't quite professional, but I promised." Waiting for Simon's answer, she realized she would never have made the same request of his cousin, Eric Brant.

"What time is the show on?"

"At one o'clock."

Simon twisted his wrist so he could see the face of his ultra-sleek hi-tech watch. "That's in less than an hour."

"I suppose you want to conclude the meeting as soon as possible so you can get back to your project." She'd just have to have Jillian Fed-Ex the tape of the program.

Simon shook his head. "It's important to keep promises to friends. I don't mind taking a little break. I've never seen a soap opera, excuse me, daytime drama before."

That didn't surprise her, his intended desire to watch Jillian's show with her did. "You don't have to watch it with me," she assured him.

"I wouldn't miss it."

"Thank you." It seemed to be the thing to say. "Would you like me to start going over some of the figures for the merger?"

"I prefer not to discuss business while I'm eating. Tell me more about you. Your best friend is an actress?"

"Actor." She smiled. "Actress is considered a sexist term and she'd tear a strip off you if she heard you using it."

"It's fortunate she isn't here to have heard my *faux pas* then, isn't it?" Silver flecks of humor twinkled in his gunmetal gray eyes.

"She's a little militant," Amanda admitted.

"What about your family?"

"What about them?"

"I presume they aren't all actors."

Actually they all had a fair amount of acting ability. "My parents own a real estate agency in Carlsbad. My brother is a lawyer." And the most accomplished actor of them all.

"No sisters?"

"No. What about you?"

"No."

"No sisters?"

"No brothers either."

She knew his father had died in a plane crash with Eric's father several years ago. "What about your mom?"

Simon's face went blank. "She died of ovarian cancer when I was ten."

She sensed the loss still affected him deeply and that touched her. If her mother died, would her father and brother even bother telling her about it? Yes, for appearance's sake, probably. Not because anyone in her family felt that connected to her. She was the cuckoo, unwanted and unloved by her parents, dismissed by her brother.

"I'm sorry," she said to Simon and meant it.

"Thank you."

"Eric told me you got your Ph.D. when you were nineteen. That's very impressive."

He shrugged. "Intelligence is something you are born with. My mother and father encouraged me not to squander mine."

"But to have accomplished so much by such a young age."

Instead of answering, he reached toward her and she watched in mesmerized fascination as his darkly masculine hand came closer and closer to her chest. She couldn't seem to open her mouth to protest, nor could she move.

He stopped, his fingers a centimeter from her body. "You've got a noodle here." Then he pulled the offending piece of pasta off the lapel of her jacket without so much as brushing her chest with the backs of his fingers.

Chapter 3

_____

It hadn't been a fluke.

Simon's reaction to Amanda was as devastating today as it had been in his cousin's office.

And Amanda was just as affected.

She'd thought he was going to touch her. He could see it in the dilation of the black centers in her eyes, in the way her breath had caught and held, pushing her beautiful curves into prominence. Yet she hadn't protested, hadn't moved.

She wanted him.

Perhaps as much as he wanted her.

But he couldn't let it happen. Not yet, probably not ever.

In the current situation with his family's company, she was the enemy. He wouldn't risk the possibility she might try to use sex to manipulate him into agreeing to the merger. He was almost positive she wouldn't stoop to such tactics. His instincts told him that though she tried to be all business, she wasn't barracuda material.

In fact, she seemed like a really sweet, beautiful woman almost absurdly unaware of her feminine appeal. He wanted time to see if that was true. He wanted to observe her and get to know her. She intrigued him. He wanted to understand what made her tick, what put shadows in her eyes when she said she wasn't married. He wanted to know why her voice had changed tenor when she mentioned her family.

For the first time in five years, Simon was interested in a woman's friendship. His body craved hers with feral intensity, but he wasn't going to risk her deciding he was too big or too intense, and putting up her guard against him.

His gaze flicked over her heart-shaped face. "So, do you usually watch your friend's show?"

"Every day, faithfully."

"You keep a television in your office?"

She looked appalled at the idea. "That would hardly be professional. I record it on my Ti-Vo and watch it when I go to bed to relax me."

"You like to watch television in bed?" He went to bed to sleep, or to make love, period.

She fiddled with her fork, her gaze not quite meeting his. "Yes." For some reason his question had made her blush.

Maybe it had been his mentioning the word bed. He knew simply thinking the word in her proximity brought all sorts of interesting, but impossible, scenarios to his own mind.

"What part does your friend play in the show?" he asked in order to get his focus off those scenarios.

"She started off playing the long lost teenage daughter of one of the love interests on the show. They kept her on. It's a small role, but she gets to do what she has always wanted to do, act."

"And are you doing something you love?"

"My career is very important to me."

"But do you love it?"

"Of course. I'm well on my way to meeting all my goals."

No doubt the intended merger with Brant Computers was a big part of that. It was unfortunate, but she would have to find some other way to pursue her ambitions. Brant Computers was going to stay a family held company as long as Simon had anything to say about it. Considering the fact he had no intention of ever selling his share of the company, that would be for his lifetime.

He searched his mind for a way to steer the direction away from her work. "A friend of mine from my university days is an actor in New York."

They spent the remainder of lunch discussing her girlfriend's soap opera and the difference between stage acting and television.

Following Simon into Jacob's quarters, Amanda couldn't believe she had gotten so sidetracked.

She'd spent forty-five minutes talking to Simon and after her initial sally, she had not once brought up her proposal. The only other person in her life that kept her so enthralled in conversation was Jillian. Because she was so outrageous. Simon was eccentric, not outrageous, but he was interested in everything and his mind was like a mainframe computer stored to capacity with data.

"You got an addiction to soap operas, have you?" Jacob asked as she took a seat on the sofa opposite a big screen television.

The old man's sneering got her back up. "My best friend is one of the actors in a highly acclaimed daytime drama."

"Ho, is she now? What's her name then?"

"Jillian Sinclair."

Jacob sat in the recliner, leaving the only seat for Simon on the couch with her. "Point her out when she comes on screen." His tone implied he questioned her story.

She consciously refused to grit her teeth. "I will."

Simon sat beside her rather than taking a position by the other arm of the sofa. "This should be interesting."

She turned her head to look at him and couldn't help smiling. His expression was dubious. For a man who didn't even own a television, daytime drama probably had very doubtful appeal. She wasn't sure why he'd decided to watch it with her. Perhaps that genius brain of his, so interested in everything, wanted to taste a new experience, even a questionable one.

The show's theme music started and she forced her attention back to the television. Opening credits rolled. Jillian wasn't in the first scene, so Amanda allowed herself another peek at Simon, but he wasn't watching the television.

His gunmetal gaze was settled on her. "You don't like the woman on the screen."

He was right. Amanda didn't particularly like the grand dame of the show, but how could he tell? "It's not my favorite story line."

"If you two are going to talk, sir, there's no sense you staying in here to watch the show, is there?" Jacob's irascible voice interrupted them.

Simon chuckled. "We'll be quiet. It is, after all, your television."

Silence between them did not diminish her awareness of Simon Brant. On the contrary, it heightened it. She had to be imagining that she could feel the heat of his body from six inches away, but the impression would not leave her. The side of her closest to him flushed with warmth.

It got worse when Jillian's initial scene came on screen. "That's Jillian, the redhead," she said, pointing her friend out for Simon and Jacob.

She could have said the half-naked woman draped like a blanket over the blond hunk. *Jillian had a love interest.* No wonder she was excited. That increased her caché with the show big-time. It was, however, not a scene Amanda would have preferred to watch sitting next to the first man in years to spark sexual feelings in her.

She licked her lips as Jillian and the blond hunk kissed. It wasn't a get-to-know-you kiss, but one of supposed overwhelming passion and both actors portrayed the emotion in an amazingly realistic way.

Amanda's breathing hitched and she tried to mask her reaction with a cough, which earned her a glare from Jacob.

Simon caught her eye and winked.

She felt heat crawl up her face. He couldn't possibly know she was thinking about his lips on hers while Jillian and her lover kissed. Could he?

At the next commercial break, Simon turned to her. "Your friend is quite talented. You'd never guess watching her with that guy that they aren't really madly in lust with each other. Or are they?"

She shook her head and laughed a little. "No way. He's married with four kids and the sweetest wife. He dotes on her and she adores him, not at all your average Hollywood marriage." Or any marriage as far as she could tell.

Simon's expression turned thoughtful. "Is Jillian married?"

Why was he asking? She knew her friend was gorgeous. Did Simon want an introduction? "No, but she's got a boyfriend."

More like six of them. Where Amanda lived like

a nun, Jillian was out to enjoy male companionship to its fullest.

Gray eyes narrowed, Simon studied her, making Amanda feel like he was looking into her soul. "I don't know. I think I'd go ballistic if my girlfriend kissed a guy like that."

He couldn't be thinking of her when he said that, no matter what his expression indicated. She didn't engender those sorts of thoughts in men, especially gorgeous, sexy men like Simon. "It's not real."

"How can a kiss not be real?"

Amanda wasn't very clear on that herself. Jillian had tried to explain it to her, but for Amanda it always came down to lips against lips, bodies touching bodies. Intimacy.

She shrugged. "She says acting is putting yourself in that person's perspective, so it's not really you doing the kissing."

"And when his penis gets hard and presses against her belly, is that just the character reacting or the man?" He sounded as if he was asking a wholly clinical question.

She didn't feel in the least scientific, or qualified to answer the question in any case. Erect male flesh wasn't something she had a lot of experience with. "He probably doesn't get th-that way."

She'd stuttered. Again. With the exception of the other day, when she'd first met Simon, she hadn't stuttered since spelling militant in her sixth grade spelling bee. She'd dropped out because she'd said too many m's.

"Come on." Incredulity laced his voice. "He's got a beautiful body pressed against his, their tongues are doing the mating dance and did you see where she had her hand?"

Something twinged in her heart when he called

Jillian beautiful. She and Amanda were complete opposites physically. "Jill says that with the lights, the people all around, and the pressure to get it right for the first take, she doesn't have any inclination to get excited."

How had they gotten into this conversation?

Simon looked at her with an expression she couldn't begin to decipher, but which left her feeling ridiculously vulnerable and short of breath. "It wouldn't matter."

Did he mean it wouldn't matter if he had Jillian pressed up against him?

Thankfully, the show came back on and she was saved from having to pursue the conversation further.

They had to sit through another scene without Jillian and a second commercial break, during which Jacob grilled her about Jillian's start in show business.

Then Jillian's subsequent scene came on.

It was in the bedroom and all Amanda could think was how it would feel to be in a similar situation with Simon. Which was highly unprofessional as well as dangerous to her personal well being. She'd never before had a physical reaction to watching a love scene on Jillian's show and goodness knew she'd seen enough of them. But this time, her body was reacting as if she was the one in the bed.

She could feel arrows of sensation shooting down her thighs from their apex and her nipples were pressing against her bra like when she was freezing cold. Only she wasn't cold. She was hot. So hot, she wished she could take off her blazer, but she couldn't. Not with the nipple problem.

She'd die if Simon saw the evidence of her desire, not to mention Jacob. He'd probably say something nasty about it and Jillian's show. As if the show had anything to do with it.

Her wretched imagination was to blame. And the man beside her. Eccentric geniuses had no business being sexy and ultramasculine. He should wear wire-rimmed glasses and dress in polyester pants with checked, cotton button-up shirts, not form fitting shirts and jeans that accentuated his incredible body.

Simon's nostrils flared in primal recognition of the subtle scent coming off Amanda.

Her friend might not be affected by doing the love scene on-screen, but Amanda was affected by watching it. Her breath was coming in shallow little pants and he'd bet his newest computer that if she took off her jacket, her blouse would be inadequate for the task of hiding twin mounds topped by turgid peaks. Imagining the way they would feel against his palm was driving him crazy.

Were they pink or brown? Did she have big aureoles? Were her nipples big or little? Damn. He wanted to touch her. He wanted to see her. Neither was a wise or even possible course of action, so he sat there stewing in his desire.

And getting hard, which could be a problem if Amanda noticed, not to mention uncomfortable.

Stretching his legs out in front of him to relax the constriction around his crotch, he laid his arm along the back of the sofa. He didn't touch her, but she went as stiff as his sex was getting.

He turned his head slightly to see her face better and wanted to explode at the way she was biting her lip.

The sound of the phone ringing came as welcome relief. He jumped up before Jacob could. "I'll get it."

Jacob eyed him speculatively while Amanda kept her gaze set on the television.

"Amanda, go ahead and finish watching the program."

Her head came up then, her features schooled into a blank mask. "All right. Thanks. Jill said she had one last scene in the second half-hour, but it wasn't as big. I'd like to see it."

He nodded, already headed toward the nearest telephone.

Amanda went back to the great room after Jillian's soap opera ended, expecting to find Simon waiting for her because he'd never come back to Jacob's quarters.

The room was empty.

Should she go looking for him?

Maybe he was still on the phone. She didn't want to interrupt and surely he knew the show was over by now.

Her gaze moved to the huge wall of windows. The water of the sound was different than the ocean in Southern California. Even in the bright sunlight of late June it looked like smoked glass rather than the shimmering blue she was used to. Simon had a dock that extended over fifty feet out into the water and a sailing yacht moored at the end.

It didn't look like a modern vessel, which surprised her. She was familiar with the sleek lines of the latest boating designs since her condo was located on the bay above an exclusive marina. Simon's yacht looked like something from a 1940s movie.

Even from the distance, its dark wood exterior shone with the gloss of a meticulous finish.

As her gaze skimmed the glass wall, she noticed deck furniture to her right. A pitcher of what looked like ice tea and two glasses sat on the cedar table. Presumably, they were going to continue their meeting out on the deck that extended the length of the house. She picked her briefcase up from where she'd left it earlier and looked for a way outside.

Just like everything about Simon Brant, the exit was cleverly concealed. It took her several minutes before she found the small lever that, once pressed, sent a door-size piece of glass sliding to the right. She carried her briefcase to the table and set it on one of the empty chairs. Since Simon was not yet there, she didn't sit down but went to lean against the rail, breathing in the warm, salty air.

A small breeze blew across her face, and she closed her eyes, reveling in both the warmth of the sun on her skin and the smell of air free of Southern California smog. She couldn't remember the last time she'd allowed herself the luxury of stopping and just *being*.

Her conscience reminded her that she could be at the table setting up her facts and figures to present to Simon, but for once, she ignored the inner prompting.

This felt too good.

The quiet was broken only by the distant chatter of seagulls.

A strange inertia settled over her body as if the overwhelming pace she'd been keeping for the past two years had caught up with her all at once. She'd lived for her job since walking out on Lance. Why that sparked a sense of discontent at this particular moment, she could not understand.

Taking a deep breath, she opened her eyes and forced herself to turn back toward the table. She flicked a look at her watch and was shocked to see she'd stood at the deck rail for half an hour.

Where was Simon?

She scanned the great room, but it was empty.

No doubt Jacob knew where to find his boss. She'd have to locate the cranky housekeeper and ask him what was going on.

Luckily she found him in the kitchen. She hadn't really wanted to wander around the huge house trying to find one of the two men who lived there.

"Jacob, do you know where Simon is? I've been waiting on the deck for him since Jillian's show ended."

Jacob turned from where he was doing something at the sink. "The boss went back to his lab."

"But there's a pitcher of ice tea with two glasses on the deck." They were supposed to talk about the merger.

Jacob nodded. "Told me to put it there."

"But he didn't come out."

"Never does. Not once he gets that look in his eyes and goes off to his lab. Be lucky to see him again today. Probably won't."

"Do you mean he won't be coming out of the lab again this afternoon?" It was the experience at Eric's office all over again. He'd just walked away.

She had an urge to pound on the door to his lab and insist on him coming out and listening to her, but if she got militant, how receptive would he be to what she had to say?

"Not likely."

"You don't think he'll come out again today?" she asked, just to clarify.

"That's what I said, ain't it?"

"Couldn't you knock and remind him I'm here?"

"Wouldn't do no good. He don't hear when he's thinking."

She had some ideas on how to get Simon's attention, but since it had never been her goal in life to get arrested, she put them in the back of her mind.

"When do you expect him to come out of his lab? Surely he has to eat sometime."

"Has a kitchen up there, but he comes out to exercise."

Remembering Simon's well-developed muscle tone, she had no problem believing that even if he didn't put his work aside to eat regular meals, he did in order to work out. No one got muscles like those by default. "When does he exercise?"

"Depends."

"On what?"

"On when he wants to."

"I see." What she saw was that Jacob wasn't going to cooperate with her and her patience was a second away from disappearing altogether. "Will you please give your employer a message from me?"

"That's my job."

"Oh, really? Somehow I thought your job was to drive Simon's visitors crazy enough so that they wouldn't come back. Then he can live as a total recluse." The sarcastic words just tripped off her tongue and she wasn't even slightly apologetic.

Jacob had the gall to look offended. "My company manners may not be what they once were, but I don't try to chase off Simon's friends."

"Merely irritating business associates he has no desire to talk to in the first place. Does he pay you a bonus for your efforts, or do you consider it one of the perks of the job?"

"The boss didn't tell me to try to run you off."

She wasn't buying it. And she wasn't sticking

around for more of Jacob's annoying half-answers. Eric Brant wanted this merger too. He could convince his cousin to meet her. She spun on her heel and marched out of the kitchen.

After retrieving her briefcase from the deck, she had her hand on the front door handle when Jacob came into the entry hall. "There's no need for you to leave all in a huff, Ms. Zachary."

"I'm not in a huff. I'm cutting my losses."

"You wanted to leave the boss a message."

"There really isn't any point, is there? He'll just ignore it as effectively as he's managed to ignore me."

Only he hadn't ignored her over lunch, or during Jillian's show. He'd focused his considerable concentration on her and their discussion, which made his subsequent snub feel personal. She was used to male rejection. It wasn't something she would probably ever take in stride, but she had learned not to set herself up for more of the same.

She turned the doorknob. "Good-bye, Jacob."

"Wait."

The command shocked her into stopping. Not only in the fact that the irascible man was actually encouraging her to stay, but also by the authoritative tone of his voice. "What?"

"He doesn't mean anything by it. He's a genius."

"So I'd heard." She found it very difficult to believe Jacob was defending Simon's actions to her, as if her opinion mattered.

"He's not ignoring you so much as he's so focused on the complexities going through his mind, he's not even peripherally aware of what is happening around him."

"What happened to your bad grammar?"

Jacob's skin took on an interesting burnt hue. "I talk the way I want to."

She let that go. Jacob, she was discovering, was an entity unto himself. "You don't think it was on purpose?" she asked, referring to Simon's second abandonment.

"No, Ms. Zachary. The boss doesn't mean to do it. It's just the way he is."

"No wonder he doesn't have a lot of friends." She was making an assumption based on Simon's lifestyle, but Jacob sighed.

"He's spent his whole life out of step with his peer group one way or another. The boy is more comfortable experimenting in his lab than making friends. I think he finds his computers easier companions than people."

The boss had become the boy and she realized the relationship between Simon and Jacob was more multifaceted than it appeared on the surface.

"If I leave him a message to call, do you think he will?" The prospect of talking to Simon on the phone and seeing him again, even after his habit of disappearing without a word, was much too appealing.

"Yes."

She gave Jacob her cell phone number as well as the name of her hotel and room number. He wrote them down and she left.

The ferry ride back to the mainland passed quickly as she tried to strategize a foolproof plan for presenting the proposal to Simon. Unfortunately, by the time she reached her hotel over an hour later, she was no closer to a solution.

Both Jacob and Eric had made a point of telling her how wrapped up in a new project Simon could become. He was evidently in full new-project-mode now and she couldn't help thinking that any hope of presenting the merger to him in its entirety was doomed from the outset.

* * *

When she got back to her hotel room, there was a message from her manager requesting she call him. She wasn't surprised. She'd had to tell him about the glitch with Simon Brant when her last meeting with Brant Computer's president did not end in a concrete step toward the merger.

"How did Simon Brant respond to the proposal?"

"He didn't."

"What do you mean, he didn't? Is he a deep player, keeping his thoughts close to his chest?"

"He's deep all right, but he didn't express any reaction because I didn't get a chance to present the benefits of the merger to him."

"I thought you were meeting with him this afternoon."

"So did I. He didn't want to discuss business over lunch and afterward he disappeared into his lab."

"Don't tell me you couldn't steer the direction around to the merger over lunch. It was a business meeting."

"Simon doesn't see business in the same light most people do. He wanted to get to know me over lunch. He's not comfortable doing business with someone he doesn't know."

Her boss snorted. "And you went along with that? This is no time to decide to let your ice queen persona melt and start pursuing a personal agenda on company time."

"I am pursuing Extant Corporation's agenda to the best of my ability." The ice queen crack hurt, particularly because it wasn't true. She wasn't an ice sculpture, just a flawed one. "I'm not sure trying to convince Simon to support the merger is a practical direction to take right now."

"I talked to Eric Brant and according to him, we

need his cousin's cooperation, or the deal is dead in the water. Or at least close enough to justify calling in the coroner." The fact that her boss and Eric had been talking took her aback. She'd been under the impression she was on her own during the preliminary negotiations. Her stomach knotted at the idea that she might be judged and found wanting as a negotiator.

She explained about Simon's preoccupation with his current project. "Even his housekeeper warned me that trying to pin Simon down in one place long enough to hear the presentation is going to be difficult."

"I don't care if you have to camp out on his doorstep until you get him to listen to you. We need that man's cooperation for this deal to go through. If you don't think you can get it, maybe I'll have to come up there and take over the negotiations."

The knots in her stomach drew tighter until she felt in desperate need for an antacid tablet. "I can handle it, Daniel."

"Prove it."

The words echoed through her mind that night, making it hard to go to sleep.

In one way or another, she'd been trying to prove herself her entire life and somehow she'd always ended up falling short of the mark.

She was determined that this time would be different.

Chapter 4

She bolted upright in bed, her heart beating erratically. She'd had the dream again, the one where she got fired and where, driving home to her condo, she started shrinking until she wasn't even tall enough to touch the gas pedal. She usually didn't wake up until the car started veering wildly toward the edge of the coastal highway, coming awake just as the car started going over the cliff.

Ring.

She turned toward the sound, still disoriented by her dream and the brutal return to reality.

Ring.

It was the phone.

It had woken her, stopping the nightmare right after she started getting smaller.

She fumbled for the receiver in the darkness of her room.

"Hello?"

"Good morning, Amanda."

"Simon?" Was it morning? She blearily tried to focus on the clock beside her bed. Twelve minutes after five A.M. "Do you have any idea what time it is?"

"It's still dark, so not yet six."

"I was asleep."

"I'm sorry I woke you." He paused. "Would you like me to call back later?"

Remembering how easily he lost track of his surroundings and her, she jumped in with a very hasty, "No."

"Jacob said you wanted me to call."

"That's right. You didn't listen to my presentation. You said you would," she reminded him. "I believe it was something you promised your sister-in-law?"

"I promised Eric because Elaine was getting teary eyed. Pregnant women are emotional."

"I wouldn't know."

Lance hadn't wanted children right away and neither had she. She didn't regret that, not since it would have meant putting any child they'd had through the upheaval of divorce. Still, sometimes when she saw mothers with little babies, she felt like she was missing something pretty important in her life.

"Jacob also said I upset you when I disappeared into my lab." He sounded almost apologetic.

"You forgot about me."

"I didn't mean to."

"Don't worry about it. I'm used to it." Why had she said that? She was still too rummy from sleep to control her tongue.

The tendency that first her family, and then her ex-husband, had had to dismiss her as of little importance, was not something she wanted to share with Simon.

"You're used to being forgotten?"

"Never mind." She scooted into a sitting position, dragging the covers with her to maintain their cocoon of warmth. "I'm not quite awake. I don't know what I'm saying. Are you calling to reschedule our meeting?"

Another pause, longer this time. "Yes."

"Can we meet today?" The sooner she got this situation handled, the faster she could put Simon Brant and her strange reaction to him out of her mind and life.

"Yes."

That was promising. "When?"

"I'll be between timed experiments late this afternoon."

She took a second to go back over what she remembered of the ferry schedule. "I can be on the three o'clock ferry."

"I'll see you about four then."

"Right."

"Okay, then."

"Simon . . ." What did she want to say? She had an inexplicable urge to keep him on the phone with meaningless chatter. "Thank you for calling."

"I woke you up."

"I don't mind, really."

"I'm going to bed. If you call me in about fifteen minutes you can repay me in kind."

"You haven't been to bed yet?" He must be exhausted.

"No."

"I'm not into revenge."

"I'm glad. I can use some sleep."

"Sweet dreams."

"I believe they will be. Until later."

She was foolish to think the words had special meaning, particularly directed at her. She was dynamite in the boardroom, but more like a wet sparkler in the bedroom. No fizzle at all. She stifled a sigh. "Bye." She listened for the click on his end before she hung up.

She wished her dreams were sweet, but too often she had the Amanda-shrinks-to-nothing nightmare or one where she relived walking into Lance's office while he had sex with two people. Only in her dream, they realized she was there and they all laughed at her.

She snuggled down into the covers and thought about Simon. She liked his voice. It was deep and masculine, but smooth too, like well-aged scotch. He had very sexy lips. She recalled how they moved when he talked and wondered how they would feel moving on her own.

She was still chastising herself for her totally inappropriate, not to mention incredibly unlikely, thoughts when she slipped back into sleep.

This time when she arrived at Simon's, she didn't give Jacob a chance to harass her. She stopped her car, got out and pushed the button to call him. She barely refrained from a few choice expletives when he informed her that now they had met, a visual I.D. through the car window was sufficient.

Jacob answered the door when she rang the bell and she was immediately concerned that Simon hadn't come out of his lab after all.

"Has he surfaced, Jacob?"

"The boss is not a submarine, Ms. Zachary."

That was a matter of opinion. He certainly disappeared as easily as if he were one, and a stealthy one at that. "Is he available?"

"Not strictly speaking, no."

"I knew it!" She dropped her briefcase and glared in disgust at Jacob. "He woke me up before dawn this morning and then he didn't even bother to come out of his lab when he promised he would." She dug through her purse looking for headache medicine. She came across an antacid tablet and popped it for good measure. "No wonder the man isn't married. If he had a wife, she would have killed him by now."

"I did not say that my employer was still in his laboratory."

She stopped trying to get the stupid cap off the small white bottle of pain reliever she'd found and looked up at Jacob. He was looking down his nose at her in the best tradition of a snobbish English butler.

"You play more parts than Jillian!"

Jacob in his superior butler mode didn't deign to answer.

"If Simon's not tied up with his experiments, where is he?" She managed to get the cap off and tossed back two small caplets without water.

"Mr. Brant is on the level below."

Hadn't Simon said something about having his gym down there? "Is he exercising?"

"As I cannot see him at this moment in time, I cannot answer that question with any degree of accuracy."

"Jacob, I bet there's a spear somewhere in Africa with your name on it."

The left corner of his mouth tilted up before he schooled his expression into somber regard. The old faker. "I will escort you below stairs if you would like."

She waved her hand in front of her. "By all means."

All humorous irritation with Jacob faded when Amanda found herself standing inside the open doorway to Simon's gym. Everything faded except the sight of him, as his foot repeatedly connected with the kicking bag hanging from a ceiling beam.

He was fast, faster even than her Tae Bo instructor. His ponytail flipped from side to side like a short black whip.

And graceful. He moved with the lithe agility of a human panther.

He was also almost naked.

Wearing a pair of black karate pants and nothing else, sweat glistened on the smooth, tan skin of his body. His chest had a neat triangle-shape patch of black hair centered between his male nipples. The dark copper circles drew her eyes as did the rippling muscles below them.

He had a six-pack of abs that most weight lifters would die for. The shoulders of his six-foot-two-inch frame were broad and well-developed, as were the bulging biceps of his arms.

He was devastating.

And she was standing there, ogling him like a star-struck teenager on her first visit to Universal Studios.

"It appears he is exercising, Ms. Zachary."

"As shocking as you may find this to believe, I'd figured that out for myself." She couldn't make herself stop looking at Simon while she spoke to Jacob, which she had no doubt the old man noticed and found highly amusing.

She might find her behavior amusing too, in someone else, but in herself, she found it both unexplainable and embarrassing. Nevertheless, she could not look away.

Without warning, Simon whirled on his bare feet to face her. "Amanda. You came."

Had he doubted she would? "Hello, Simon. I can wait for you upstairs while you finish your workout." Even as she said the words, she regretted them. What if he disappeared while she was waiting for him again?

"There's no need. You can talk while I exercise."

"You must have better concentration than me. I can't even tell someone my name in my Tae Bo class, or I lose count of where I'm at."

"You practice Tae Bo?"

She laughed self-consciously. "Not exactly. I'm taking a class in it, strictly for the exercise. My form is terrible."

"I can help you with that." He eyed her as if already determining how best to work with her.

Just the thought of being in her Lycra leggings and sports bra in the same room with Simon in his loose fitting karate pants was enough to send her temperature spiking. "Well, uh, thanks for the offer, but I doubt I'll have the opportunity to take you up on it."

One black brow rose. "What's wrong with right now?"

She gave him an incredulous look. "I'm not dressed for it." Her smart ice-yellow suit had not been designed with strenuous exercise in mind.

"Take off your shoes."

What? "No."

"Come on. You can be my dummy. Watch my form and later you can work on emulating it."

"I don't need to watch your form." Watching him stand there doing nothing was bad enough on her equilibrium. "I've got an instructor back home."

"He can't be very good if your form is still choppy. You're too supple not to excel at it."

He was a she, as was the entire class, but Simon didn't need to know that.

"You're mistaken." She'd fought the blasted treadmill for supremacy, how in the world could Simon believe she was supple?

"She moves with innate limberness, doesn't she, Jacob?"

She'd forgotten the eccentric housekeeper.

"Yes, sir. She does."

"Oh, please. This is ridiculous. You're not going to talk me into being your Tae Kwon Do dummy by complimenting me on the way I move."

"You said you wanted to talk to me. I'm offering you the opportunity to do so while I exercise." His gaze shifted to the left of her shoulder. "I'll take care of Ms. Zachary, Jacob."

The other man must have left because Simon's gray gaze returned to her. "Take off your shoes," he repeated.

She stared down at her sensible pumps. She couldn't exactly wear them on Simon's exercise mats, even if she didn't act as his dummy.

She slipped the shoes from her feet and lined them up neatly beside the doorway.

"I think you'd better lose the jacket too."

Simon had several panels of glass open in the wall of windows and there was a nice early summer breeze. "I'm sure it won't be necessary. I'm not going to work up a sweat talking to you."

"That's true, but you'll have more mobility without it." Then he stepped forward and started to help her out of her short-waisted blazer.

It was halfway down her arms before she got enough wits to voice a protest. "I don't need mobility to talk."

"But it *will* make playing my dummy easier."

She was about to tell him what he could do with the idea of her playing his dummy, when the conversation she'd had with her manager the day before came back to her. This was for her job. She could and would do a lot to clinch this deal.

Playing dummy for Simon's Tae Kwon Do workout was neither immoral, nor demeaning. No matter how stressful she found it personally, she couldn't justify saying "no" simply because she was attracted to him.

She had to drop her briefcase before she could let him pull the jacket the rest of the way off.

Goose bumps broke out on her bare arms. From the breeze, she told herself, not because his fingers had brushed against her skin while pulling off the ice-yellow blazer.

He folded her jacket and laid it on top of her shoes, placing her briefcase neatly beside the pile.

Then he looked at her feet. "Those nylons will make you slide on the mats. You could fall."

"They're not nylons," she said before thinking.

"You wear stockings?" For some reason his voice sounded quite strange when he asked that.

Her gaze flew to his face, but his expression gave nothing away.

"I wear thigh-highs. They're more comfortable than either nylons or a garter and stockings." *Shut up.* Stop blabbering on. He doesn't want to know about the comfort level of your stay-up stockings.

"Thigh-highs?" There went that quizzical brow again.

"They stay up with a lacy elastic band around your thigh."

"Not my thigh." His deep rich chuckle and flashing white teeth made her insides curl.

"You know what I meant."

He smiled. "Yes."

"Why are we talking about my thigh-highs anyway?"

"You need to take them off."

If he'd looked even the least intrigued by the idea, she would have refused, but he spoke completely dispassionately. It was as if the thought of her taking off her semi-intimate apparel was no more interesting to him than the latest stock figures. In fact, those might have excited him. She'd seen that the market was up just a bit today.

She'd look a fool playing the outraged Victorian maiden when he so clearly saw her as the perfect sparring dummy, not as a woman.

There was nothing new about that.

The knowledge should not have the power to hurt her anymore, but it did.

While not surprising, it was still lowering to admit that the first man she'd been attracted to in years saw her as nothing more than a nuisance he had to spend time with in order to keep his promise to his cousin.

She turned away from him and reaching up under her skirt, she removed first one stocking and then the other. Air brushed her naked legs like a touch and she shivered again.

Schooling her expression into impassivity, she turned back to Simon.

He wasn't even looking at her. He was drinking out of a water bottle she hadn't noticed earlier.

"I'm ready."

He took another pull off the bottle and then put it down. "Okay. Come stand over here."

He maneuvered her into position with his hands on her shoulders. He was so close, she could smell his body's unique fragrance enhanced by sweat from his workout. Would he smell like that after making love?

She would never know, and with that acknowledgment, she slammed the lid on that particular line of thought.

"You stand like this." He grabbed the wrist and

elbow of her right hand and put it in a blocking position. "Switch arms when I switch sides of attack. Can you do that?"

"Sure." *Just stop touching me before I do something we'll both regret.*

He looked at her strangely. "Are you okay? I'm not going to hit you. I just want a target to aim for. The sparring routine will be completely noncontact."

She nodded. "You can start."

He did and true to his word, though he came within a breath of touching her with each blow, he never made contact. They'd been working out for about five minutes when he reminded her she was supposed to be talking.

"Right. First, I think you need to consider the merger in terms of future growth rather than the minimal cost to the current pool of employees."

Simon didn't respond, he just let her talk. Not by the flicker of an eyelash did he indicate if he was even listening.

Every once in a while, he would change her position to facilitate his workout. He did it silently, but regardless, each time she lost her train of thought and had to search her mind for the point she'd been making.

"You need to change your blocking arm faster."

She stopped in mid-spate of telling him about the projected increase in market share the combined companies would have. "What?"

"I need you to be faster in changing your blocking arm."

So, she increased her speed and found herself moving into basic Tae Bo blocking positions. Pretty soon she was panting between words and sweat was trickling down her back, making the silk of her white tank top stick to her.

"Okay, now let's work on your form."

Without knowing how it happened, she was surrounded completely by Simon with her back brushing against his chest. He took hold of each of her arms and put her into position. "Relax, Amanda. Let your body move with mine."

She was really glad her back was to him and they were facing the windows with a view of the water, not the mirrored wall that would have reflected their tableau with entirely too much realism. Because the thought of her body moving with his had her nipples puckering painfully. Both layers of her silk top and bra were not adequate to hide the evidence and she prayed he would stay behind her.

She tried to concentrate on doing as he'd said and following his movements with the same fluidity his limbs enjoyed.

"This isn't necessary, you know."

He didn't answer, but one big hand landed on her thigh, the fingers exerting pressure for her leg to move into position.

She'd wanted fluidity of movement, but she was in danger of losing control over her muscles as her bones literally turned to water. Her body wanted to melt into a puddle of sexual need on the floor mat below her feet. Only sheer force of will kept her knees from buckling as his fingers moved against her thigh.

Oh, mother! She'd never been this excited, not even in the act of copulation with Lance. And Simon wasn't even trying to turn her on. He was teaching her form, for Heaven's sake.

She stumbled on her stance and Simon's hand slid toward her inner thigh. Only the fact she was wearing a straight skirt that had been stretched taut by her current position stopped his fingers from going between her legs. Nevertheless, his fingertips brushed the very top of her mound and three layers of fabric did not dull the impact on her senses.

She yelped and twisted out of his arms, almost running in her desire to put some distance between them.

"What's the matter? Do you have a cramp?"

Crossing her arms over the telling evidence prominent on her overgenerous breasts, she shook her head. He didn't even know what was bothering her. That knowledge, more than any other had her crossing the room and yanking her jacket on.

"You're done with your workout, right?"

He nodded. "But we still need to work on your form."

She slid into her shoes without putting on her stockings. "I'd rather finish giving you my presentation on the merger."

"All right, but I had planned to take a short swim. Would you like to join me?"

Not in this lifetime. How did he expect her to swim? Naked? As her body exhibited further evidence of increasing arousal, she chastised herself. *Bad thought, Amanda, bad, bad, thought.* "No, but I wouldn't mind taking a shower." She wished she had some clean clothes with her. She could feel her perspiration not yet dry on her body.

Simon walked to a small speaking unit on the wall and pressed a button. "Jacob?"

"Yes, sir," came the disembodied voice of Simon's housekeeper.

"Amanda got a little sweaty playing my dummy and she wants to take a shower. I think you two might be similar in size. Could you dig up some clean clothes for her to put on when she's done?"

If Simon had asked, she would have refused the

offer of clothing, but he hadn't asked. Hearing that he considered her five-foot-four-inch curvy frame on par in size with his housekeeper's masculine, but wiry five-foot-nine, did nothing for her sense of self-confidence.

She could almost feel the sting of one of Lance's *love pats* on her thigh and hear the words that invariably accompanied it. "Did you get your exercise in this morning, hon?" He'd always managed to make it seem like he doubted the possibility.

When she'd called him on it, he'd told her she was reading things into his words and gone into psychobabble about how damaging that was to the communication of free ideas in a marriage. He'd had the gall to tell her that her reactions made him feel intimidated about being open with her.

She allowed herself a small smirk, remembering she'd told him the same thing about his reaction after she destroyed the big screen television.

"Amanda?"

She looked up and realized that Simon had been saying something to her that she hadn't caught. "I'm sorry. I missed that."

He looked at her quizzically, but she blanked her expression.

"Jacob will show you to the guest room shower and bring you some clothes to wear. I'll see you upstairs in the great room after I've had my swim and shower."

"You won't disappear into your lab again, will you?"

Color burnished his taut cheekbones, but he didn't make any promises. "I don't think so."

She glared at him. "Simon, you're a grown man. Are you, or are you not going to meet me in the great room after your swim? If you aren't, I'd rather go home and shower."

"I have every intention of joining you for dinner after taking my swim."

She picked up her briefcase and shoved her thigh-highs into it. "Okay."

Jacob had materialized at the door and she turned to follow him. "I'll see you shortly, Simon."

He didn't answer and she refused to let that worry her.

His interpersonal communication skills weren't that great, but she'd gotten through at least a third of her presentation already. She could easily outline the last two-thirds over dinner.

If he made it to dinner.

Chapter 5

She wasn't going to wear a pair of bulky men's sweatpants.

This might not be Southern California, but it was early summer and the weather was warm. She had no intention of sweating it out in the thick fabric. If a niggling sense of feminine pride refused to be seen dressed like someone's dotty old uncle that was all right, too.

Tossing the pants aside, she picked up the charcoal gray cotton T-shirt Jacob had lent her and pulled it on. The dark color prevented her lack of a bra from being indecent. She didn't like putting on the same pair of underwear after a shower, but she consoled herself with the knowledge that it had been the top half of her body perspiring during the workout.

She tugged her skirt up over her hips and zipped it, before turning to look in the full-length mirror.

The T-shirt didn't look too bad with the skirt, but tucked in, it outlined her breasts a little too smartly. She pulled it out and the hem fell loosely around her hips. She bit her lip. That was better, but her hair was a bedraggled mess. She'd used a shower cap to keep it somewhat dry. However, that had only aided in ruining the style.

Its customary sleek French twist was coming apart and several hanks of hair hung down her neck. She pulled out the pins she used to secure the bun and then gave it a vigorous brushing with the brush Jacob had left for her.

She didn't have any hairspray to smooth the style back into place, so she used a hair tie from her purse to secure it into a high ponytail on the back of her head. The ends of her hair brushed between her shoulder blades, but the tie kept it off her neck.

Foregoing her shoes, she left them in a neat pile with the rest of her things in the bathroom. She could get them later.

She could not imagine attending a business meeting with anyone but Simon Brant barefoot and in borrowed clothes. She could not imagine playing sparring dummy for a Tae Kwon Do session for anyone else either. Life around him was as full of eccentricities as he was.

She liked it.

She made her way to the great room, her feet drawing her to the wall of windows of their own accord. It was an irresistible view, the ocean looking both infinite and ever changing.

She pressed her hand against the glass, not worried about leaving prints because of her recent shower. It was warm from the sun, its hard, smooth surface a tactile pleasure for her. How long would Simon's swim take?

Movement to her right caught her attention and she watched as Jacob set the table outside for dinner. He crossed the deck and disappeared into the house to her left.

She was still standing at the window when Simon came in.

"You should see the view when there's a storm."

Muscles tensed and her lungs seemed to contract. All this because the man had walked into the room? She needed to get out more. Thinking back over the dearth of dates in the last two years, she amended that to she needed to get out, period.

She forced herself to respond to what he'd said instead of her reaction to him. "I would probably be nervous. Having the only thing between me and the elements, a thin wall of glass."

"It's not thin."

That's right. He'd told her it was reinforced. "It's still glass."

"I suppose you'd be more comfortable if there were drapes to draw across the windows so you could block out what is beyond them." He didn't sound condescending, just thoughtful.

And he was right. She shrugged. "It's not my house, so it hardly matters." She turned to face him.

His black hair was still wet and though it was slicked back from his face, he hadn't confined the shoulder-length strands into a ponytail. He was wearing a pair of jeans and nothing else. Didn't the man ever wear a shirt? With his dark skin tone, he looked like a tribal warrior.

"Did you enjoy your swim?"

It was his turn to shrug and the naked skin on his chest rippled with his muscle's movement. "I don't swim for pleasure. Doing the laps is the most efficient way to end my workout."

"You're not going to convince me you don't enjoy your martial arts sessions. You're way too proficient just to do them for exercise. What color belt are you anyway?"

She'd be surprised if he wasn't a black belt.

"Does it matter?" He was looking at her like she

was a bug on a pin, all scientific curiosity and something else that could have been mistaken for male interest if she didn't know better.

"Not really. I'm just making conversation." His social skills were not on par with his other abilities. For some reason, she found that rather endearing. "It would be polite for you to answer the question, unless you have some reason for not wanting to do so."

Two thin streaks of red burnished his high cheekbones, indicating he was aware he'd blundered in the politeness arena and was actually bothered by the fact. "I am a Grand Master Black Belt."

"That's pretty impressive."

"Is it?" He seemed genuinely interested in her answer, the storm-cloud gray of his eyes reflecting curiosity.

"Yes. I'm impressed anyway. It takes a lot of self-discipline and work to make it that far."

He appeared to contemplate that. "There wasn't anything else to do."

"What do you mean?"

"I started studying Tae Kwon Do with my mother's uncle when I was four years old. I was already in school by then with children that were older and bigger than me. I didn't have playmates, so studying with my great-uncle gave me something to do."

It was hard to imagine a time when he'd been smaller than his peers. He was such a big man now. "Eric said you were a child prodigy."

"Yes."

"Was it hard always being younger than everyone around you?"

An expression that hinted at deep loneliness and pain crossed his masculine features before he nodded briefly.

"Jacob has put dinner on the table."

The abrupt change in topic jolted her.

He stepped around her and pushed the button that slid the glass panel open. "After you." He brought his right hand out with an Old World flourish.

She smiled and walked by him, shocked when she felt a tug on her ponytail.

"I like this. It's not so stuffy." He let go immediately, so she didn't take umbrage.

She looked down at her attire and lack of shoes. "I'd say we're both as far from stuffy as it's possible to get right now." But something twinged inside her at his description of her usual mode of dress. He made it sound like she dressed like an old lady, but though her clothes were conservative in style, she'd always tried to maintain a certain level of chic.

Admittedly, she did not wear anything even remotely sexy or excessively feminine.

"That gray looks good on you. You've got such pale skin for your hair color. It's a fascinating contrast."

She let him seat her before answering. "I take after my great-grandmother and fascinating isn't how most Southern Californians view my pasty white skin tone."

"You make it sound as if you look ill and you don't."

"I don't tan. I burn. To most Southern Californians, *that is an illness.*" She laughed lightly, making a joke of it, but she could still remember the sessions in the tanning beds trying to cultivate the right look in her teens.

"People who sunbathe frequently are at higher risk for skin cancer. Their skin ages prematurely as well."

She gave a speaking look to his naked torso. "I

appreciate that now, as an adult. As a teenager, I didn't really care. I wanted to look like everyone else." Even if she'd tanned, she still would have had more curves than most of the other girls.

He looked down at himself and then back at her. "I like the feel of the sun on my skin after spending so much time inside my lab, but I don't lay around in the sun for hours on end cultivating a tan."

She looked at his olive skin tone. "You don't need to."

"Neither do you."

That was nice of him to say and maybe he did find pasty white a fascinating skin tone. "It doesn't matter. I gave up trying to tan years ago."

"Good."

She smiled.

"I know what it feels like not to fit in, but trying to be like everyone around you doesn't work."

"Your looks weren't your problem." He was too gorgeous.

He didn't preen under the compliment like so many of the plastic men from her Southern California world would have. "It was my age," he said, repeating what he'd said earlier.

"Did it ever get any easier?"

"I thought it did, for a while when I was a teenager."

"What happened?" Would he slap her down for prying into things that were none of her business, that were, moreover, totally unrelated to why she was there? She couldn't help the interest that burned inside her to know him better.

"I tried doing what the adults around me did."

"That's pretty typical for a teenager."

"Yeah, well, most teens try to act like adults with each other. I was surrounded by people several years older than me and light years ahead of me in life experience."

"You got hurt."

"You could say that. I learned some important truths in the process though."

She didn't push for more, but maybe one day he would tell her. Then she chided herself. What was she thinking? Once this merger went through, she'd never see him again.

"Is that why you live on an island now and work at home, so you don't have to worry about fitting in?"

"Maybe. I've never thought about it, but what I do could not be done in a nine-to-five environment."

"No, I don't suppose it could. Did you always want to be an inventor?"

Jacob materialized, putting a bowl of chilled mango soup in front of each of them. Then he left.

Simon tasted the soup, smiled and took another spoonful before answering. "I've always hungered to discover new things, new ways to accomplish the same tasks, and more efficient use of the resources at hand."

"That sounds a lot broader than new computer design."

"Computers have always played a central role. It's only natural considering who my father was, but I experiment in other areas as well."

"What are you working on right now?" She tasted the soup. It was ambrosia. Creamy and smooth, it had a hint of coconut flavor as well as peach mixed with the mango.

"One of my current projects is wind powered fuel cells as an alternate form of energy."

Of course he wouldn't work on one thing at a time.

"Any success?"

"Mild."

"What's a fuel cell?" She knew what a windmill was. There were hundreds of them in the California desert. However, she'd never heard of a fuel cell.

"It's like a super-efficient battery run on hydrogen and air. When you need the energy, you run the gases through the layers of the cell, with one of the by-products being electricity."

"What are the other by-products?" She remembered that nuclear power had been touted as a clean source of energy, and look at the problems the waste by-products had made for the power plants.

"If hydrogen and air are used for the fuel, the secondary by-product is pure drinking water. Hydrogen is the most abundant chemical in the universe and preliminary tests have shown the fuel cell to be at least twice as efficient as other energy sources. And there are no moving parts to wear out."

He was so enthusiastic, he was positively chatty.

"It sounds too good to be true."

"There are still a lot of variables that need to be dealt with before it will be a viable alternative for mass energy use."

"And you're working on those variables right now in your lab?"

"Me and probably a hundred other alternative energy source enthusiasts."

She laid down her spoon and stretched her bare toes toward the warm sun. Simon had led her to a seat on the side of the table shaded by an umbrella. "When do you find time to develop prototypes for Brant Computers?"

"I'm not responsible for all prototype development."

"But I thought you were the top design engineer at Brant." She was sure that was how Eric had explained Simon's role in the company.

"I think my title is something like Design Engineer Fellow."

She smiled. "You don't know?"

Gray eyes bore into hers. "It doesn't matter. I do what I do because it is what I like to do."

"But you do design for Brant Computers?"

"I bring new technology to proof-of-concept phase. Sometimes that means creating a working prototype, sometimes not. Once I turn it over to the design team, I'm pretty much out of it unless they get stuck."

"I hear your design team is one of the top in the industry."

"We like to think so."

"Extant Corporation has some of the most innovative design engineers in the country as well. Can you imagine what the two could do if their resources were pooled?" Surely that was one of the benefits to the merger that would appeal to him.

He frowned. "Forcing the two teams to work together could just as easily destroy the effectiveness of both."

"Why should it do that?"

"New product design is a creative process."

He'd finished his soup before she realized he wasn't going to add anything else. She waited until Jacob had taken away the bowls and laid down plates with their main course before speaking again. "So why does it being a creative process mean it would be bad to bring the two teams together?"

"I don't know that it would be bad. It's a possibility."

"But why is it a possibility? I would think the more brain power the better."

"Haven't you ever heard the old saying, *too many cooks spoil the broth?*"

"Simon, we're not talking about cooking here."

"But we are talking about the possibility of adding too much of a good thing to the mix."

"What exactly are you saying?"

"One of the reasons I work here is that I have complete creative freedom. That makes it possible for me to try things I wouldn't or couldn't in a corporate environment. Other people don't always spark creativity, sometimes they stifle it. Maybe they've tried something similar before and it didn't work."

"But that could happen in the groups now."

"That's true."

He did it again. Went silent.

"Is that all you're going to say?"

"For now."

Jacob came out bearing a tray with two crystal dishes filled with fresh strawberries topped by heavy cream and a mint garnish.

She gave the old man a dazzling smile just to confound him. "Dinner was fantastic, Jacob. Thank you. And dessert looks sinfully delicious."

"Nothing sinful in fresh berries, missy." He refilled their wineglasses before leaving, the dishes from dinner now on the tray in his hands.

The strawberries were so juicy, they slipped across her tongue with a burst of sweet sensation. "Mmmm," she hummed with pleasure as she took another bite.

She looked up to find Simon watching her, a curious expression on his face. "They're locally grown."

"They're yummy." She scooped another berry out with her spoon, making sure it was coated with the heavy cream. As she went to put it in her mouth, she realized Simon was watching her with disconcerting intensity.

Were his eyes really trained on her lips, or was that her imagination running away with her good sense? She was so attracted to him, she wanted to believe the attraction was reciprocal, but he'd done nothing so far to indicate it was.

More likely he was wondering why a woman with her figure hadn't foregone dessert. If she'd been with her parents or her ex-husband she would have.

"Aren't you going to eat?" she asked, waving her now empty spoon toward his crystal bowl of fruit.

"I'll eat it later." He looked at the hi-tech watch on his wrist and grimaced. "I need to check on my timed experiment."

"But we're not done discussing . . ." She didn't finish the sentence, seeing as how she was already talking to his back.

"Simon Brant, someone needs to teach you some manners."

He stopped at the door and turned. His expression registered a vague sort of chagrin. "I'm sorry, but three days of experiments will be wasted if I don't go to my lab right now."

At least he'd stopped to explain. She nodded, but didn't bother to ask if he'd be back down. He wouldn't.

She allowed herself the luxury of finishing her dessert in peaceful silence, the summer evening air cooling around her and bringing out goose bumps on her skin.

"The last ferry sails in thirty minutes." Jacob's voice came from behind her.

She turned to face him. "I guess I'd better be on it."

"Unless you want to spend the night."

"I can't see myself borrowing your pajamas."

The older man shrugged. "Suit yourself, but if you're wanting to talk to the boss, you'd do better to move in here than try to catch him like you've been doing."

She laughed. Right. Move into Simon's house, just so she could be there to talk to him when he surfaced from his lab.

Three days later, she wasn't laughing. She'd called Jacob each day, leaving a message for Simon to call. According to the housekeeper, Simon hadn't been out of his lab in all that time.

He certainly hadn't called her.

When the phone rang, she couldn't help hoping it was him.

"Hello."

"How's it going, doll?"

"Jillian! Your new story line is to die for."

Jillian's husky laughter echoed across the phone lines. "Yeah, ain't it just? Even the Grand Dame complimented me on yesterday's takes." The words fairly gurgled with happiness.

"I'm so glad, sweetie. I wish my job was going so well."

"The resident geek still giving you trouble?"

"Simon's not a geek." He was way too sexy to fit that label. "He's a genius. He's also a Grand Master black belt in Tae Kwon Do."

"You're kidding me. The computer nerd is a Chuck Norris wannabe?"

"Simon isn't a wannabe anything. He's completely his own man."

Silence crackled for several seconds.

"You sound really impressed by this guy."

"I am. I'm also totally frustrated."

"Are we talking work frustration here, or something more exciting and totally alien to your lifestyle for the last three years?"

If she said both, Jillian would be on the next flight out of LAX for Seattle. "I still haven't given him the complete presentation, much less convinced him of the advisability of merging with Extant and I've met with the man three times."

"That does not sound like your usually super-efficient self. Are you sure there's nothing else going on here I should know about?"

"Positive." She didn't want Jillian deciding Simon was the answer to Amanda's lack of a social life. "It's just that he's so wrapped up in his work, it's hard to get more than five minutes of his time. I had to play his Tae Kwon Do sparring dummy to get him to listen to the marketing estimates."

"You played a sparring dummy?" Shock laced Jillian's voice. "I don't believe it."

"In my skirt and blouse no less."

"No way!"

"Yes. You know how important this is to me, Jill. I'd do anything to get this merger tied up."

"And what kind of anything does Simon want you to do?" The suggestive tone of Jillian's voice made Amanda laugh.

"With an eccentric inventor, your guess is as good as mine. I was totally disbelieving when he wanted me to play the dummy. He even insisted on working on my Tae Bo form."

"He did, huh? I gotta tell ya, Amanda, things are sounding pretty interesting around there."

"That's one word for it."

"Have you considered camping on his doorstep until you get his attention?"

Amanda didn't laugh like she knew Jill expected

her to. "I'm thinking about moving into his house for the duration."

Jillian sucked in a shocked breath. "Tell me you're kidding."

"It was his housekeeper's idea and I think it has merit. How else am I going to get this deal closed?"

"You mean Simon won't mind you just moving in?"

"I don't know, but at this point, I'm willing to risk it. Daniel has been calling nonstop wanting a report on my progress. He's threatened to come up here. If I don't do something, I'm going to get taken off the negotiations."

Telling Jillian she was moving in with Simon and doing it were very different animals, Amanda discovered the next day as she nerved herself to press the red button on Simon's gate call box.

"Hello, Ms. Zachary."

"Hello, Jacob. Could you release the gate, please?"

"You got an appointment?" He was back to playing belligerent-butler again.

"No."

"Mr. Brant invite you?"

"No."

"You got a reason for coming?"

"Yes, Jacob. Now, are you going to open the gate?"

"Maybe."

She was on to his tricks and she wasn't going to lose her cool this time. "Open the gate, Jacob."

Then before he could reply, she pressed the up button for her window and just waited. He kept her waiting for a full minute before the black iron gate slid open.

She rang the doorbell a minute later, her laptop, briefcase, suitcase and toiletries bag stacked beside her on the porch.

The door opened to reveal not Jacob, but Simon and he looked terrible. His eyes were bloodshot, he had several days of stubble on his face and his skin had the pallor of a sick man.

"Amanda." He shook his head. "Was I expecting you?"

She stepped inside and laid her hand on his arm before thinking. "Simon, are you all right? You look ill."

"I'm not sick. Just tired."

"Hasn't slept more than a few minutes at a time since you was here last." Jacob's irascible voice reached her from further down the hall.

"That's terrible. Simon, you need to be in bed."

He wasn't listening. His focus was on something behind her. "You brought a suitcase."

She sucked in air and courage with the same breath. "Jacob invited me to stay awhile. I'm taking him up on it."

Simon craned his neck around to look at Jacob. "You invited Amanda to stay?" He sounded so confused, she felt sorry for him. He was too tired to understand what was going on, but he wasn't too tired to toss her out on her ear if Jacob gave lie to her bold claim.

"I may have said something to that effect."

She let out the small breath she'd been holding.

Simon stepped back. "Come in then. Jacob, will you see that Ms. Zachary's things are put in the guest room?"

Jacob's wizened gaze caught hers as she passed him and he winked.

It surprised her so much that she stumbled and crashed into Simon. Even tired, he had the reflexes of a trained warrior. He caught her and set her back on her feet without taking so much as an extra breath. "You okay?"

"Yes. Thanks. I'm clumsy today."

Simon covered his mouth and yawned.

"You need to go to bed, Simon."

"I'm hungry. I think Jacob's going to make me something to eat. I don't remember." He was so rummy, his words were slurring.

"I made some beef stew. It's simmering on the stove. Ms. Zachary, you could see the boss gets some while I'm busy with your things."

"No problem. Come on, Simon." She led him to the kitchen where she could smell the savory aroma of simmering stew and recently baked bread.

Simon sat down at the small kitchen table and she served him in a bowl Jacob had left sitting on the counter. She also sliced and buttered some of the bread.

Simon ate in silence while she watched over him like a broody hen. He really did look awful. There was no way they were going to have any sort of intelligent conversation before the man had gotten a good night's rest.

He finished and laid down the spoon. "Can I get you anything, a glass of wine maybe?" he asked her politely, just as if he wasn't practically dead on his feet.

"No, thank you. Go to bed, Simon."

He nodded and stood, swaying slightly on his feet.

She rushed forward and put one arm around his waist. He draped his arm over her shoulder, but didn't put his whole weight against her. For which she was grateful. He let her lead him out of the kitchen.

"Which way is your bedroom?"

He waved his arm to the left. It didn't take her

long to find the stairway. They managed to get up it without mishap, but when they reached Simon's bedroom he seemed to lose steam all at once. He went tumbling toward the oversize king bed and took her with him. They landed in a tangle of arms and legs with Simon's body half over hers.

He didn't move.

"Simon."

Nothing.

She fought her head clear of his heavy arm and looked up at his face. His eyes were closed. He was asleep.

No problem. She only had to slide out from under him and he'd never even know she'd been there.

She levered her arm out from where he had it pinned beneath his chest and pushed against him, trying to scoot backwards at the same time. His eyes opened and she fought between relief and embarrassment.

"Uh, Simon . . ."

He smiled, the beatific smile of a very happy child, said her name and then closed his eyes again.

Without moving.

She pressed firmly against his chest. He said something indecipherable and moved, dragging her into his body like the lover she wasn't. When he was still again, she was wrapped firmly in his arms, his face buried in the curve of her neck and his heavy thigh trapping both her legs.

Chapter 6

———

She should absolutely get up.

Right this minute.

But she didn't want to move. Simon's breath warmed her throat while the feel of his muscular body wrapped around her gave a sense of warmth and belonging she'd longed for all of her life. It was that sense that had her trying to peel out of Simon's arms. It was way too dangerous.

She wasn't any good at the man-woman thing and if she let herself fall for Simon, she was going to end up hurt.

Badly.

When it came to relationships, she always lost.

Remember the job.

She was here for the sake of her career, not to put her damaged heart at risk again.

Unfortunately, even in sleep, Simon was strong. Too strong for her to get away from.

She tried shaking his shoulder to wake him. "Simon. Wake up. You've got to let go."

His face nuzzled more firmly into her neck and his hand shifted until it was cupping her right breast.

Her brain short-circuited while her body started pulsing with unfamiliar desire.

"Simon!"

His hand squeezed and her nipple went rock-hard. She gasped. He squeezed again and darned if it wasn't with just the right amount of pressure.

Okay. She wasn't going to try to wake him up again. At the rate they were going, he'd be inside of her before she ever got him out of his comatose state. And she'd be loving it.

Which made her wicked and pathetic. For surely only a wicked woman would consider taking advantage of a man's actions while he was sleeping and only a pathetic one would need to.

Maybe if she lay there until he went into a really deep sleep, his muscles would relax enough for her to extricate herself from his arms.

The hand on her breast was heavy and she was tempted to pretend for a little bit. To pretend he meant it to be there. To pretend a gorgeous, sexy man like Simon found her desirable. It should be too much of a stretch for even her imagination. It wasn't. Not with his arms around her and his hard, masculine body pressed all along her side.

Fantasizing was risky.

She might start believing her own delusions.

She had to get her mind off the way it felt to be in Simon's unconscious arms.

She stared up at the ceiling. Not a lot of inspiration there. Simon had a ceiling fan. She wondered if he liked to lay naked on his bed and let the gentle air brush over him like she did. She preferred the fan to running the air conditioner, except on the hottest days.

As things started happening in her body, things like swelling and moistening, she realized that wondering about Simon's naked sleeping habits was a bad idea.

She let her gaze roam around the room, at least

as much as she was able to without turning more than her head. The stark simplicity of Oriental design was in here too, but so was Simon's love of hi-tech. The bed and matching bedroom suite had been designed in molded metal with a flat finish. It didn't look like office furniture gone bad, but rather sleek and almost soothingly simple.

The headboard and footboard on the bed were slatted with horizontal bars. She'd never seen a bed like it.

An image of her lying on the bed, naked but for a silk nothing of a nightgown, with her hands tied to the headboard, popped into her mind. Simon leaned above her, his hands teasing her body while he whispered shocking things in her ear.

She groaned. Simon's leg insinuated itself between hers, his thigh pressing against the apex of her thighs and the image in her head exploded in favor of tormenting reality.

She had to get out of this bed. She made her body go completely motionless and concentrated on breathing as quietly as possible. Anything not to jar Simon into further movement.

She snuggled into the delicious warmth of her bed, fighting consciousness and trying to cling to the sweetness of her dream. It had been so real, she could still smell the masculine scent of her lover, still feel the strength of his arms around her, the erotic pleasure of his legs twined with hers in the aftermath of loving.

She shifted one leg and fancied she could feel denim rub against the smooth sheerness of her stockings.

Stockings?

She wasn't wearing stockings in her dream. She

was naked—Oh, my gosh! Her eyes flew open to a patch of dark blue.

It was a shirt and the shirt covered a male chest. Simon.

Her head snapped back.

He was still asleep.

That was the only good news she could discern as she came fully alert with a mental bump of huge magnitude. Her legs were indeed twisted together with his, right up to their thighs. This was possible because her skirt was twisted up to her hips, exposing the tops of her stay-ups.

Somehow several buttons had come undone on her once crisp white blouse and Simon's hand was inside, resting against her silk-clad breast. Her hand was underneath his untucked T-shirt, pressing against his well-defined abs.

If he woke up right now, she would have a heart attack and die of humiliation.

With all the caution of a thief leaving the scene of a crime, she gently withdrew her hand from under his shirt. His body shuddered in sleep as her fingertips brushed along his skin and she was terrified he'd waken. He didn't.

He was sleeping too deeply.

Thank you, God.

She'd been right that his muscles would relax in sleep. Moving slow centimeter by centimeter, she withdrew from his embrace until her body was no longer touching his at any point. Heaving a sigh of relief, she rolled onto her back and only registered her nearness to the edge of the bed a second before landing on the floor with a solid thump.

"Not a real graceful way to get out of bed, if you don't mind my saying so, Ms. Zachary."

Jacob? Jacob was here? How much had he seen?

She scooted to her feet in a flurry of movement,

yanking her crumpled skirt down over her exposed legs.

"Thought you were going to use the guest room."

She could feel heat scorching into her cheeks. "I am. This was a mistake. He . . . I . . ." How did she explain the events that had led up to her sleeping in Simon's arms?

"I don't pry into the boss's private affairs."

"For goodness sake, we are not having an affair. I was trying to help him to bed. He fell asleep with me under him. I mean. He fell. We fell. I couldn't get away. I guess I fell asleep waiting for him to relax."

A lot of falling had gone on.

"Whatever you say, Ms. Zachary. I came to see if you wanted dinner."

"Um, that would be great." She surreptitiously did up several buttons on her blouse, keeping her body angled away from Jacob's too knowing gaze. "I'll just go change my clothes."

She was a wrinkled mess and maybe a return to her usual put-together appearance would harbinger a return to sanity as well.

One could only hope.

Eric Brant called after dinner. As soon as Amanda heard his voice, her stomach cramped with worry over his reaction to her coming to stay with his cousin.

"He let you move in? Just like that?" Eric sounded stunned.

"It was Jacob's idea," she defended herself.

"But Simon hardly ever has company and now he's letting a complete stranger live in his house. I have to tell you, Amanda, this is the strangest business deal I've ever been involved in."

"Simon doesn't do things like normal people," she said, throwing his own words from before back at Eric.

"But he doesn't do stuff like this either."

"It was the only way I could think of to catch him often enough to convince him of the merits of the merger."

Eric's laughter jangled against her already stretched nerves. "Well, I've got to hand it you, Amanda. You've got real dedication to getting the job done. I only wish my junior executives were half as ambitious and creative."

She warmed under the praise. "Thank you." She only hoped her boss, Daniel, agreed with Eric.

Amanda popped the green stem out of the strawberry and tossed it in the waste bin to her left on the deck. She dropped the berry in the ceramic bowl and picked up another one. She'd eaten breakfast an hour ago, but the juicy berries were still tempting. The only thing that stopped her popping one in her mouth was the certainty that Jacob would walk out on the deck at that exact moment and catch her.

She wouldn't put it past him to be watching her from the kitchen just so he could do that very thing.

She hadn't seen Simon since practically running from his room the previous afternoon. She didn't even know if he'd woken up from his restorative sleep yet and she didn't have the nerve to ask Jacob. Not after what he had witnessed in Simon's bedroom.

"That doesn't look like the normal occupation for a dedicated career woman."

She looked up at the sound of Simon's deep

voice and smiled, albeit a bit nervously. She didn't know how much he would remember from her so-journ in his bed. Not that it hadn't been pretty tame as sojourns go, but since she hadn't been in any man's bed in over two years and hadn't done anything worth mentioning in a bed in more than three, she was still uncomfortable about facing Simon.

"Hi. Get enough sleep?"

"I did."

He certainly looked it. His eyes were clear and he'd taken the time to shave. He was shirtless again, this time wearing a pair of cutoff denim shorts. Her gaze slid to his muscular legs with their light covering of black hair and stayed there for way longer than was politic. She forced herself to meet his eyes again.

They glinted with something she couldn't inter-pret and a funny half-smile had formed on his lips. "I need some exercise. I came out to see if you wanted to work out with me again."

"You mean play your sparring dummy?"

"I thought we could go through a couple of TKD routines."

It actually sounded like a great idea. Her body was craving a workout and she hadn't quite nerved herself to ask Jacob if he thought Simon would mind if she used the pool.

"I'm almost done with these and then I'd love to."

"How did Jacob talk you into doing that?"

"It wasn't hard. I wanted an excuse to sit outside and he gave me one."

"Is he making jam?"

"That's what he said. I've never seen anyone make homemade jam before. He told me I could watch later."

"Your mom didn't do any canning?"

"Are you kidding? My mother's idea of domesticity is having the local maid's service number memorized."

He laughed. "My mom wasn't much better. She was too involved with her painting to want to do much around the house, but she still managed to make it feel like a home."

Then she'd been a world ahead of Amanda's mother who had always managed to make her daughter feel like an intruder in the perfectly decorated and maintained California mansion she'd grown up in.

"What was she like?" she asked him.

"Warm. Alive. Fun. She smiled a lot. She could make me and Dad laugh until our sides ached."

"It must have hurt so much to lose her."

"It did. Everything changed."

"Your dad probably took it really hard."

"He found comfort in his work."

"What about you?"

Shrugging those incredible shoulders, he frowned. "I followed my dad's example, I guess."

"You were only ten years old, you said." She couldn't fathom a child getting lost in his work.

"And close to graduating high school. Between my experiments and my studies, I got by."

And learned how to shut out the rest of the world in the process.

She finished hulling the last berry and wiped her hands on the wet tea towel Jacob had left with her. "I'll just go throw on something I can do kicks in."

Simon slipped out of his shorts and pulled on a pair of *dobok* pants. The loose-fitting bottoms designed for martial arts would be better at concealing his reaction to Amanda when they worked out. He was still reeling from the vivid dreams he'd had of her while sleeping off his three-day-long work binge. They'd been so damned real, he could have sworn her scent clung to his pillow when he woke up.

A cold shower had helped calm his raging hormones, but seeing Amanda dressed in a tank top and jeans had sent his libido into orbit all over again. No wonder the woman hid herself in those boxy looking suits. If she dressed in anything formfitting at work, none of her male colleagues would get any work done. Not with those curves.

Funny, but he could swear he knew the weight of her breasts in his hands. Wishful thinking, no doubt.

He ran into Jacob as he headed down to the gym.

"Dinner at six."

"Okay, but we haven't even had lunch yet."

"Warning you in advance."

"You mean it's not stew tonight." Jacob occasionally warned Simon when he planned to make a meal that would spoil waiting for Simon to come out of his lab.

"Right. Thought I'd make something special for our guest."

Simon was still having a difficult time believing Jacob had invited her. "Did you really ask her to stay?"

"Told her staying would be the only way to catch you long enough to talk."

Simon didn't want to discuss the merger, but he didn't mind spending more time with the intriguing woman. She was such a mixture of confidence and reticence. She was completely confident in her guise of career woman, but when it came to simply being a woman, he sensed that she was not nearly so sanguine.

"I assume you entertained her while I slept the afternoon and night away."

"You did a fair job of that yourself, from what I saw."

Simon stopped walking and turned to Jacob. "What do you mean?"

"Came upstairs to check on you. To make sure you made it to the bed all right."

Simon had been known to collapse on the floor in sleep after a work fest like the one he'd just finished. "And?"

"And you were wrapped around a living, breathing teddy bear."

"*What?*"

"She said you fell on her when you got up to your room."

Simon didn't remember anything past the vague recollection of Amanda helping him up the stairs. "I fell on her?"

"Yeah. You were snug as bugs and both sleeping when I came to check the first time."

He couldn't believe it. He'd slept with her, collapsed on top of her in fact. No wonder she'd seemed a little nervous out on the deck. He wondered why she hadn't said anything.

"I assume you checked again."

Jacob's smile was smug. "I thought she might have wanted some dinner."

"I'm sure she appreciated your concern. Was she still asleep?" He wasn't sure he understood how she'd fallen asleep in the first place. It seemed very out of character for a woman with her professional demeanor.

Evidently he'd dragged her down to the bed when

he fell asleep practically standing up, but why hadn't she gotten up immediately?

"She was trying to get out of bed without waking you up."

"Obviously, she succeeded." He hadn't even known she'd been in his bed.

"Some might say you succeeded too."

The cryptic comments were getting irritating. "In what way?"

"Had your hand inside her blouse. *Her unbuttoned blouse.* I don't think she minded though. She had her hand up under your shirt."

The scene Jacob was describing had Simon almost bent over double with desire. He'd had his hand on her breast and had been too unconscious to appreciate it.

"Could have been worse, sir."

"How is that, Jacob?"

"You've been known to strip completely naked when you fall asleep in your clothes like that."

Simon positioned Amanda in the correct position for the *poomse's* third step. "Snap your arm like this." He moved her through the correct motion.

"Okay. I think I've got it."

They went through the entire form together and he cursed the clever mind that had come up with this idea. Watching her body move through the *poomse's* steps after what Jacob had told him was driving Simon right to the edge of his control.

His hand had been on her breast.

One of the two fleshy mounds that moved so enticingly under the oversize T-shirt she'd put on to exercise in. She probably thought the thigh-length shirt masked her body's attributes adequately. She was wrong.

The Lycra shorts came down about two inches below the hem, leaving the rest of her perfectly formed legs bare. She had such beautiful curves, totally unlike the emaciated look popular among so many women.

He wanted to ask her why she'd stayed in bed with him, but had a sneaking suspicion it could have been his fault. If he'd fallen on her, he could have held her pinned to the bed with his unconscious body. It was just as likely that the tableau Jacob had described finding them in had been Simon's fault as well. His dreams had been vivid.

They finished the form.

Amanda swiped the moisture from her temple with the back of her hand. "That was fun."

"I'll show you some one-step sparring."

Her Hershey-brown eyes lit up. "Like what you were doing the other day when I played your dummy?"

"A little less advanced."

"Let's do it."

His phallus reacted immediately to her words, disregarding the fact she was talking about martial arts form, not bodies melting into bodies in wild abandon.

He willed his libido to take a vacation.

Sex was completely out of the question right now, maybe ever. He wasn't going to make another mistake with a woman. And sex muddled a man's ability to reason. Amanda wanted a merger between their two companies, something he was determined to prevent. He couldn't afford to let his hormones put doing what he knew to be right at risk.

His body might disagree with his decision, but

he'd learned to control his sexual urges after his disastrous years in college and the lessons they'd taught him about women and making love.

She caught on to the one-step sparring very quickly. "You're good at this, Amanda."

"Thanks. You're a lot more patient than my Tae Bo instructor. She thinks I'm a dead loss."

"Your Tae Bo instructor is a woman?"

"Sure." She worked through the series of one-step sparring techniques he'd shown her without a single mistake. "Simon?"

"Yes?"

"Can we try some sparring? I'm tired of doing everything in order."

"You don't know any kicks yet."

"Sure I do. I haven't been going to Tae Bo classes for a solid year for nothing."

"All right." He was careful to temper his abilities to hers, but what she lacked in skill, she made up for in enthusiasm.

Soon they were both sweating.

She made a reckless move with her leg that was probably supposed to be an axe kick. He pivoted, avoiding contact completely. She lost her balance and pitched forward, her center of gravity thrown off by the kick.

He caught her, instinctively pulling her into his body.

Her palms landed against the sweat-slicked skin of his chest with a loud smack. "Ungh!" she grunted.

"You okay?"

She nodded, her gaze locked with his. "Thanks for catching me."

"No problem." He had to let her go, but his fingers weren't listening to the message his brain was sending. They were too busy enjoying the feel of her silky smooth skin, hot from exercise.

Her lips looked hot too, all red and swollen. The small pink tip of her tongue darted out and wet the fullness of her bottom lip.

Physical sensation coursed through him with an ache that could only be assuaged one way.

He started to lower his head.

Her lips parted on a soft puff of air. He could smell her sweat. It was different from his. Female. Sweet. His body twitched in primordial response to the olfactory message his receptors were getting.

She came up on her tiptoes, her head tilted, her mouth reaching for his. "*Simon.*"

His name on her lips was like an aphrodisiac. He could already taste the ambrosia of her lips, could imagine how good it would feel to rub their two sweat-slicked bodies together. He could picture them writhing on the floor mats in exercise totally unrelated to martial arts.

Sexual energy vibrated between them until his body was tight with it.

Her eyelids slid shut, making her look both vulnerable and ready for his kisses. His mouth was centimeters from hers when the last thread holding him to sanity asked him what he thought he was doing?

He said a silent four-letter word that perfectly described what he wanted to do to her and stepped back.

"I think you could stand some work on your axe kicks."

Her eyes flew open and she landed back on her heels from her tiptoes with a double-thud. "Axe kicks?"

"Yes. You don't want to fall flat on your face when you miss your opponent. You need to work on your center of gravity." He dropped one of her arms and used his hold on the other to pull her over to the kicking bag. He let her go and demonstrated an axe kick. It wasn't his best, but he was still hampered by aching stiffness below his waist. "Try a few of those."

It took Amanda several seconds to accept what had just happened. She'd been prepared for the kiss to end all kisses and he'd been thinking about her center of gravity.

Humiliation crawled along her skin, burning and prickling like overexposure to the sun while rejection pulsed through her with the impact of an invading army. She'd wanted him to kiss her and he'd wanted to improve her kicking form.

It hurt. She felt like his foot had connected with her breastbone instead of the sandbag.

Her chest muscles tightened until pulling in air was an Olympic event. How could she have been so stupid? Hadn't she had her undesirability indelibly stamped on her consciousness by her exhusband? Did she really need a refresher course in that particular lesson?

The questions spun through her mind, along with a far more humiliating one. Did Simon realize she had wanted him to kiss her? Was he aware she had wanted it so much she'd gone up on her tiptoes to meet him halfway? She'd learned to avoid the degradation of rejection by not initiating sex somewhere in the second year of her marriage. So the fact that she had been so close to initiating the kiss both shocked and horrified her.

She forced herself to search his face for pity.

He wasn't looking at her. He was looking at the kicking bag. He executed another perfect axe kick. *Thwap.* The sound could have been her heart slapping against her chest in mortification. The bag moved.

"Are you going to try it?" He turned toward her, but his gaze was fixed somewhere over her shoulder.

Oh, he knew all right. And was embarrassed by it.

She desperately wanted to run away, to find someplace safe to hide and lick her wounds, but she had to brazen it out. If not for the sake of her own pride, for the sake of him.

It wasn't his fault a pathetic, sexually starved creature like her had fixated on him as fantasy fulfilling material.

She kicked the bag. "Like that?"

She knew it had been a pathetic attempt, but he didn't criticize her.

"Try it again."

She did. She forced herself to perform several more kicks. She even asked him to demonstrate a snap kick and copied him before telling him she thought she'd had enough and was ready for a shower.

She managed to hold it together until she got under the spray of hot water. Then she let the tears fall.

Chapter 7

Simon forced himself not to watch Amanda leave the gym, but focused his energy on a series of dragon kicks. They did nothing to relieve the physical frustration of his body. He wanted her, damn it. But she was off limits for too many reasons to count.

So, he'd backed off from kissing her and she'd followed his lead, pretending like nothing had happened.

She was probably relieved.

The more he got to know of her, the more convinced he was that she wouldn't intentionally use sex to try to convince him of the merger. She simply didn't seem like the type of woman to make a practice of sleeping with her business associates.

She wouldn't have thanked him for taking their relationship to an intimate level. It would probably make her feel like she'd let herself down professionally. He knew the type. Brant Computers had its own share of serious career women.

The computer industry was changing, but there was still a certain amount of prejudice against women making a career in the hi-tech field. Female employees often fought harder for respect in their industry and were less apt to risk their professional standing by engaging in a meaningless sexual fling.

Are you sure it would be meaningless?

He ignored the taunting words in his head. Amanda clearly had her life mapped out and it didn't include making room for a man who spent more time in his lab than he did talking to other people. She'd never give up her job to come live on his island and he couldn't see himself living the fast-paced lifestyle of Southern California.

He was still interested in her friendship. She fascinated him even more now, but he had no clue how to make room in his life for a long-term relationship with a woman; had nothing of value to offer a wife.

Hadn't Elaine made that clear five years ago?

Amanda came out of her room after her shower to discover that Simon had disappeared into his lab again. No matter how much she needed to talk to him about the merger, she couldn't help feeling thankful for the respite from his presence.

The only thing that could make her situation worse would be for Jacob to tell Simon about finding her in bed with him. He would surely think it had been the act of a woman desperate to seduce him.

"He'll be out for dinner, though."

"How can you be so sure?" she asked Jacob after that pronouncement. "From what I can tell, food is no bigger a draw when he's working than people are."

"The boss invited Mr. Eric Brant and his wife to dinner."

"Eric's coming?" Relief swept through her. Maybe Simon's cousin could help her convince the stubborn man about the merger. Then she could get herself back to California before she made an absolute fool of herself doing something stupid like climbing naked into Simon's bed and completing her humiliation.

At least she had a positive prospect to report to Daniel when she returned the call he'd made while she'd been busy in the gym with Simon.

"You spent the morning working out with him instead of going over the proposal?" Daniel's scathing tones lacerated already taut nerves.

"I told you. He wasn't about to discuss anything until he got his exercise in. He's almost as dedicated to his martial arts as he is to his work."

"I thought you were dedicated to Extant Corporation."

This was not going well. "I am."

"Yet he went back to his lab without you discussing one word on the merger with him."

Guilty as charged. "Yes."

"What's he working on?"

"A fuel cell alternate energy source."

"What? That's got nothing to do with the next generation of computers."

"Simon is an inventor. He works on more than one project at a time. Evidently only some of them are for Brant Computers."

"So, what's he working on for Brant right now?"

"I have no idea." Did Daniel really think Simon was going to share that kind of information with the competition? And until the merger went through, Brant Computers and Extant Corporation were direct competitors.

"You don't seem to know a whole lot about anything of value right now." Daniel's sarcasm hurt.

She was good at her job. It wasn't her fault that Simon was being so recalcitrant about discussing the merger. And the idea she should know what he was working on for Brant was ludicrous. "I didn't get sent up here to be a corporate spy, Daniel. Frankly, if Simon did drop proprietary information, I wouldn't pass it on. It wouldn't be ethical."

"I suppose not." But he didn't sound convinced and that worried her. "You said Eric Brant is coming to dinner tonight."

"Yes. He and his wife."

"Well, let's hope he can accomplish what you haven't and get Simon to listen to the merger proposal."

She fumbled in her purse for an antacid, but couldn't find one. She started digging through her briefcase, her cell phone pressed to her ear. "I'm trying my best."

She found a tablet and popped it in her mouth.

"Your best isn't cutting it."

The words sliced through her like a well-sharpened blade. She'd spent so much of her life being judged and found wanting that her reputation as a professional was incredibly important to her. The only place she had ever excelled had been first as a student and then as a career woman.

She couldn't screw that up.

It was the one thing she had left that stopped her from shrinking away to nothing like she did in the nightmare that plagued her.

"Have I ever let you down before, Daniel?"

"No." It was begrudging.

"Then trust me now."

"Don't make me sorry I did."

She was shaking as she hung up the phone. Two weeks ago she'd been on the fast track to success at

Extant Corporation and now she felt like her job was hanging by a thread.

Eric and Elaine arrived for dinner before Simon came out of his lab.

"Are you having any success discussing the merger with him?" Eric asked her over drinks in the great room.

Jacob had served them and then said something about fetching Simon.

"I've gotten to tell him the marketing estimates for the merged companies and we discussed the combination of design engineering power." She didn't elaborate on that, as the discussion hadn't been a rousing success.

"Simon can be very stubborn." The blond Elaine relaxed elegantly against the sofa's cushions. She had delicate features and was boyishly slender, even with her obvious pregnancy. Her chic mint-green silk sheath made Amanda feel oversized and dowdy in her black pleated skirt and lightweight houndstooth sweater set. "And when he's not being stubborn, he's simply ignoring the rest of the world in favor of his experiments."

She smiled at Amanda. "I don't envy you the task of trying to hold his attention long enough to convince him about the merger."

"I have to admit his antipathy toward the merger surprised me." Eric took a sip of his scotch. "Half the time I think he doesn't even realize Brant Computers exists."

"His biggest concern seems to stem from the jobs that will be lost."

"I can see that being the case. Simon has a tender heart," Eric said musingly.

"You should see him with our little boy," Elaine added, "he's a total pushover for Joey."

Amanda could picture Simon teaching a little boy basic Tae Kwon Do moves and she smiled. He'd be an interesting father, but a good one. "He should have children of his own."

She had no idea why she said it. She didn't know the Brants well enough to make comments like that.

Elaine's eyes widened. "I can't see him noticing a woman long enough to marry her, much less manage to father a child."

"I can't complain about Simon's absentminded approach to relationships. If he'd been more attentive, you might have married him instead of me." Eric's warm regard for his wife left Amanda in no doubt how he felt about the slim woman.

"You silly thing. I loved you almost from the moment I met you. Even if Simon and I had been engaged, I would have ended up with you." She smiled wryly. "That makes me sound awful, but love has its own rules."

"You and Simon dated?" Amanda asked.

"Yes, but dating a genius inventor isn't all it's cracked up to be, let me tell you."

Amanda could not imagine dumping Simon for Eric Brant. It wasn't that Eric wasn't an attractive and powerful man, but Simon was ultra-attractive and ultra-powerful in his masculinity. He was simply ultra-everything.

"So you rightly decided to cut your losses and let my cousin convince you to take a chance on him." Simon's voice sent Amanda's heart skittering.

She schooled her features and turned to him. "Hi, Simon."

He nodded at her.

Elaine got up and went to Simon for a hug. "Hello, stranger. You need to come and see Joey. He's wondering where his Uncle Simon has gone to."

Simon wrapped his arms around her and kissed her cheek. "Tell him I'll be by to see him next week sometime."

Seeing Simon in an embrace with his former girl-friend caused a jealous reaction in Amanda that she had no reason and even less right to feel.

Elaine stepped back. "All right, but a three-year-old's concept of time isn't that precise. He's going to badger me until you come." There was humor in her voice when she said it, so Amanda assumed Elaine didn't really mind.

Simon and Eric shook hands. "How are the experiments coming along?"

Simon shrugged. "I'll let you know when I have something concrete."

"So, what do you think of Amanda's proposal?"

Simon had been waiting for the question since coming downstairs to discover Elaine telling Amanda why he was a bad relationship risk.

"She hasn't finished presenting it."

Eric laughed. "Well, my money is on Amanda. Any woman who would brave moving in with an old curmudgeon like Jacob and a total eccentric like you has got the moxy necessary to get the job done."

The warm pleasure reflected in Amanda's eyes at Eric's compliment irritated Simon. "I said I'd listen to what she had to say, not that I would agree with her."

"But, Simon, it makes sense." Elaine smiled appealingly. "Extant and Brant together can compete with the bigger companies for market share in a way Brant could never do on its own."

"Market share isn't the only consideration worth looking at." There was so much more to the company than how big a chunk of the market they commanded.

"But it is a big consideration." This was from Amanda.

Simon turned his attention to her. The way the thin fabric of her sweater stretched across her breasts had been distracting him all evening. "That depends on how you look at it."

"Why don't you tell us how you're looking at it," Eric said, throwing the ball firmly back into Simon's court.

"Extant Corporation is our competitor, not to mention a publicly held company. The only way we could merge would be to go public ourselves. That's not a consideration I dismiss lightly."

"I haven't dismissed it either, but times change, Simon. If we want to stay competitive, Brant Computers has to change with them."

Simon shook his head. "You're not talking about gaining a competitive edge. You're talking about changing the face and direction of our company. No offense, Amanda, but it's a lousy idea."

She looked at him and her expression revealed almost anguished disappointment, but she didn't say anything.

Eric wasn't so reticent. "It's a natural progression for Brant Computers. Your job won't change. You can still do your research and development at home, in your preferred isolation."

"You're assuming I will continue to work for Brant."

He watched as the shock from his words changed his cousin's expression from exasperation to chagrin.

Elaine gasped. "Of course you'll still work for Brant. You're family. You couldn't even consider selling your designs to another company."

He turned to the woman he'd once considered marrying. "Why not?"

"Because it would be betraying your family!"

He leaned back in his chair and crossed his arms over his chest, taking in the others at the table with his gaze. "Not if Brant Computers is no longer a family held company."

Eric said something succinct and ugly. He ran his fingers through his sandy hair, leaving it disheveled. "I didn't expect you to look at it that way."

"Obviously."

"Look, why don't you let Amanda finish giving you her presentation and then we can talk more later?"

"Listening to more statistics on sales and growth estimates isn't going to change my mind." He and his older cousin rarely argued, mostly because they usually agreed, but also because they were both stubborn. Eric being four years older had never mattered to Simon.

"What will it hurt? I think you owe it to me to at least hear her out."

"How do you figure that?"

"I've been managing the company with very little input from you for five years. If you ask me, you've chosen a darned inconvenient time to start showing an interest in the way Brant Computers is run."

"You were just as happy with the division of labor between us after the crash as I was."

Eric ran his hand over his face and then dropped it to the table. "I was. I am. I don't think you and I could have worked together the way Dad and Uncle John did before they died. They made a great team because they saw things from the same angle. I'm not sure there's a person on the face of the earth that looks at life quite like you do, Simon."

Simon didn't take offense. He knew Eric didn't mean anything derogatory by the remark, but it landed with dead center accuracy in that empty, cold place inside him. The place swirling with the chilling fog of loneliness that had opened when his mom died and never gone away.

"I'm not going to kick Amanda out and send her back to Seattle with a flea in her ear."

"And you will listen to what she has to say?"

"I'll listen."

Eric nodded, looking satisfied.

"Thank you." Amanda's voice pulled his attention back to her. The dark brown eyes were filled with a determination he could not help admiring, no matter how misplaced it was.

Eric and Elaine left for the ferry and Amanda once again found herself alone with Simon.

He poured two glasses of brandy and handed her one before sitting on the opposite end of the sofa from her. "Okay, fire away."

"You dated Elaine before she married Eric?" Oh, my gosh. What was she thinking? That was not what she'd meant to say.

Simon looked as startled by her left-field question as she felt. What had prompted her to ask that? She knew he meant to talk about the merger with her. Maybe it had been the three glasses of wine she'd consumed over the course of the evening. They'd loosened her tongue to the point of revealing a personal interest that was better left completely under wraps. If so, she was never going to drink again.

She set the balloon glass of brandy down on the coffee table with an audible thud.

"I wanted to marry her."

If her question had surprised him, his answer shocked her speechless. She stared at him. He'd wanted to *marry* Elaine?

Simon grimaced in acknowledgment of Amanda's reaction. "Yeah. It was completely impractical. She's much happier with Eric than she could have been with me."

"Did you love her?"

He shrugged. "I wanted her warmth. When she was around the shadows receded."

That sounded like an eccentric inventor's definition of love to her. "How did she meet Eric?"

"I introduced them. He's my closest friend, my family. It seemed like the thing to do."

"And they fell for each other."

"Yes."

"You all seem like friends now."

"We are. I didn't hold her choosing him over me against either of them, if that's what you're thinking."

"It was," she admitted.

"What would be the use? Neither of them hurt me on purpose."

But he had been hurt. She could see it in the depths of his somber gray eyes.

"I'm not that understanding, I guess." Lance's betrayal still rankled and she would never trust the man she'd found him with again.

"You know that for a fact?" he asked probingly.

"I do." Maybe she would have understood better

if she hadn't been married to Lance, though, if her discovery had come before they'd gotten engaged.

"What happened?"

"My husband had an affair."

"You told me you aren't married."

"I divorced him." And her parents still hadn't forgiven her. Neither had her older brother. According to them, she was the one who hadn't lived up to her wedding vows.

"And you haven't forgiven him."

She thought about all the pain still roiling around inside her from marriage to a man who had rejected her femininity so completely. "It's not that simple. If you mean I'm not in a place where I can be his friend like you are with Eric and Elaine, you're right. But I don't wish him ill. So, in that sense I've forgiven him."

"Does he want your friendship?"

"Of course. It's all about appearances in his and my family's circle of acquaintances. He wants everything to look amicable even though it wasn't."

"Did he marry the woman he had an affair with?"

It was her turn to grimace. "No." To this day, she didn't know who the woman she'd seen with Lance and the other man, was.

"Did he want the divorce?"

"No."

"But you weren't willing to forgive him his lapse and stay married."

She had grown steadily tenser as the conversation progressed. She felt like a pane of fragile glass on the verge of shattering. "No, I wasn't." Then she looked Simon straight in the eye. "Would you have?"

"No."

Some of the tension drained out of her. At least

he understood. That was more than her family had been able to do. "We've gotten very profound in our conversation."

His smile dispelled another layer of tension. "Yes."

Maybe asking about Elaine hadn't been such a huge faux pas after all. She picked up her brandy and took a small sip.

"Jacob told me he found us asleep together in my bed."

The strong spirits went down the wrong pipe and she coughed until tears streamed from her eyes. Simon had jumped up when she started coughing and now he handed her a glass of water. She took it gratefully, taking a big gulp immediately.

He extended a box of tissues to her. She pulled one out and used it to wipe the wetness from her face.

"Better?" Simon asked.

She nodded.

"Jacob said you told him I fell on you."

Had he also told Simon about the compromising position she'd woken up in? She could only hope *not*.

"You fell asleep standing up and on the way to the bed, you somehow took me with you."

"You fell asleep too?"

This was less easy to explain. She averted her head, not wanting to look at him when she tried to make him understand.

"You wouldn't let go. I couldn't wake you up and I couldn't move you. I decided the only thing to do was to wait until you'd gone into a deep enough sleep to relax your muscles." That sounded much better than she had thought it would. "I fell asleep waiting. I'm sorry that I did so. I realize it was a completely unprofessional thing to do."

She peeked at Simon out of the corner of her eye to see how he was taking her explanation.

His expression was unreadable. "I think we can agree it was an irregular situation."

She nodded. That had been easier than she could have imagined. She barely stifled a sigh of relief.

"Why didn't you call for help from Jacob?"

No way was she going to tell him it was because she hadn't wanted to be caught with Simon's hand on her breast. Her reticence had been for nothing as that was exactly what had happened, but at the time she'd been trying to protect her professional reputation. "I didn't know if he would hear me, or not. He spends most of his time at the other end of the house and on a different floor."

Even though the explanation made sense, Simon could tell she was holding something back. He wanted to know what. Had she done it on purpose?

He would have sworn not, but the way she was avoiding looking at him was suspect. She could simply be embarrassed.

On the other hand, if what she said was true, she had no reason to be. She hadn't done anything to be embarrassed about.

"Eric seems very impressed by your business acumen."

That brought her attention around. "I'm glad." She looked it, her eyes glittering with happiness.

For no reason he could think of, that annoyed the hell out of him. "Maybe he'll offer you a job if your superiors are too disappointed when the merger doesn't go through."

She blanched, her head snapping back and her

skin going pale. "You said you'd listen to the proposal before making up your mind."

"I did not. I said I would listen to the presentation, period."

He watched with interest as her brown eyes went almost black with irritation. "But if you've already made up your mind and nothing I can say will change it, why listen at all?"

"Because I promised Eric that I would."

"But you will *listen*, right?"

"Yes, I'll listen," he said for the second time that night.

That impressive determination burned in her expression again. "And I'll do my best to convince you that your mind should not be made up."

He stood up. "But not tonight. I've got several experiments to catalog before going to bed."

Surprisingly, she didn't complain. She simply nodded and actually smiled. "I'll look forward to seeing you tomorrow then."

By five o'clock the following afternoon, Simon hadn't made an appearance and Amanda's spirits were pretty much in the toilet.

He had as good as said his mind was already made up. His affirmation that he would listen to her arguments had less ability to buoy her up today than it had the night before when she had been mellowed by his company and three glasses of wine. However, even if she thought it would be a complete waste of time, she had to present her ideas to him.

What other choice did she have?

The deal was as dead as her love life without his cooperation.

His threat to start selling his ideas to the highest

bidder instead of using them for the good of the company was an impressive one. She'd spent the morning clarifying some things with Eric. One of them had been Simon's agreement with the company for his computer designs. He didn't have one.

There was no way Brant Computers could force Simon to give them even first right of refusal on his future technical discoveries. She could not see Eric Brant dismissing such an eventuality as of no consequence. Even if he did, she was sure the rest of the family who held stock in Brant Computers wouldn't.

Though Simon and Eric owned the biggest blocks of stock, with thirty-five percent each, there were five other cousins who did not work with or for Brant Computers that held the remaining thirty percent of stock between them. In other circumstances, she would have considered going to the other stockholders to solicit support of the proposed merger.

But Simon's threat put paid to that idea.

It wasn't one she'd relished anyway. The company was family held and such a move by her would cause untold damage in the relationships among them. No. If this merger was going to go through, she needed the cooperation of one eccentric genius.

And each progressive hour without him coming out of his lab saw her grow further and further depressed.

She was going over her e-mail from work with desultory interest when her mobile phone rang.

She flipped open the palm size unit and said, "Amanda Zachary."

"Amanda, Daniel here."

Already dragging spirits plummeted.

"Hello, Daniel. I'm just putting together that report on the Garvey deal you asked for in this morning's e-mail." Okay, she'd been thinking about it rather than doing it, but she'd send it off soon regardless.

"Great, but I wasn't calling about that. I wanted to know how dinner with Eric and Simon Brant went last night."

Of course he did.

"And don't tell me you didn't discuss business again." Daniel's voice was laced with a fair amount of sarcasm and warning at the same time.

At least she could refute that. "We discussed the merger."

"Good."

Her next words were a lot harder to say. "Simon is still very much against it."

"What the hell . . ." Daniel's growl left no doubt as to his reaction to Simon's continued reserve regarding the merger.

"He's worried about the employees." Among other things.

"How commendable of him." The tone of Daniel's voice made it clear that employees were the last consideration he would have when looking at a lucrative deal like the one Amanda had proposed. "But that's not as serious as we first anticipated, is it? I read over your latest report and with the cooperation of the other stockholders, Simon Brant's vote can be overruled at the board meeting."

Chapter 8

She could feel the beginnings of a tension headache throbbing behind her eyes. She rubbed her forehead. "Neither Eric, nor Simon, want a family war over this."

"But Eric Brant wants the merger," Daniel's voice came out as smooth as a viper striking.

"They're friends and cousins. It's a tight relationship." She pointed out what should be obvious, even to a Southern California businessman. "I don't think Eric wants the merger at the expense of Simon's goodwill."

"Then, I guess it's your job to make him want it, isn't it?"

Bile rose in her throat and she swallowed it down. Daniel could not possibly comprehend what he was suggesting. "You're not talking about a disagreement between faceless stockholders here, Daniel. You're talking about me instigating a war between two men who are not only friends, but are also family."

She hoped reiterating the facts would make them sink in to Daniel's mind.

Pain pounded in her temples. "I think the original plan of trying to gain Simon Brant's cooperation is still the best one."

Eric had two sisters living in Arizona and a mother who split her time between the states her children resided in. He also had a wife and a child, with another one on the way.

Simon had no one but Eric.

She could not come between the two men.

"Then I suggest you use the opportunity of staying in his house to better advantage."

"I'm talking to him every chance I get."

"Perhaps you should consider more than verbal persuasion." Simon had once called her a snake-oil salesman. Daniel sounded like one now.

She stood in stunned silence for several seconds. "What exactly are you proposing?"

"Men are more vulnerable to certain types of persuasion than others. If the lure of getting rich through the merger isn't enough to sway Simon Brant, you might want to consider taking your negotiation tactics to a more personal level."

She would have laughed at the ridiculousness of the suggestion if it wasn't such an offensive one. "Are you implying I should try to convince Simon with sex, Daniel?" She really couldn't believe that was what her boss was saying.

"Don't be so crude, Amanda. You're obviously personally involved on some level or you wouldn't be living in the guy's house."

He believed she and Simon were already having an affair.

"I'm staying here so I can talk to Simon, not because we're sleeping together!"

"Right. Look, all I'm saying is that you should use every weapon at your disposal to ensure the success of this deal. You've got a lot riding on it. Some might even say your whole career path is at stake here. This is a big deal, Amanda, and I showed a lot of faith in your professionalism when I sent you up there to handle the preliminary negotiations alone."

Anger and fear warred inside her, leaving a metallic taste in her mouth and pushing her tension headache into the realm of a migraine. "We must be thinking about two different kinds of professionalism here, because the one you're talking about is illegal in this state."

"Don't be so damn naïve."

Lance had said the same thing when she had insisted on getting a divorce after seeing him engaged in that lewd *ménage à trois*. She hadn't told him what she'd seen, simply that she knew he'd been having affairs.

He hadn't even denied it. He'd told her not to be so naïve, that all men had affairs. He'd then laid the blame squarely back on her for not being a sexually satisfying partner. She was willing to accede that she'd failed in the sex stakes, but it wasn't all her fault. How could one woman possibly fulfill the sexual function of both a man's female *and* male lovers?

"Amanda? Are you there?"

"Yes, I'm here."

"Good. I thought the call had been dropped."

"No. Port Mulqueen has excellent cell phone coverage, being so close to Seattle's transfer towers." Why was she going on about cell phone service when her boss had just suggested she engage in a sophisticated and modern version of the oldest profession in the world?

"Whatever. I've got a meeting in another five minutes, so I've got to go. If you don't think you can get Simon's cooperation, cut your losses and start working on Eric Brant. One way or another, this deal is going to go through."

"Simon threatened to start selling his computer

designs to the highest bidder if Brant Computers goes public with its stock in order to accomplish the merger." That ought to spike Daniel's guns. "I don't think you'll get anyone in his family to agree to the merger if it means losing his brilliance to one of the bigger companies."

Even merged, Extant and Brant would find it difficult to compete with the biggest companies in the industry if Simon submitted his designs to an industry-wide bidding war.

The word that came out of Daniel's mouth was only four letters long and very unpleasant. "He'd be cutting his own throat."

"That's not how he sees it."

"He'll still own his share of the merged company, damn it!"

"Yes, and he can still draw income from it, but he'll personally make more money selling his designs to the highest bidder."

"Not if it means Brant and Extant going under."

"Why should it? Simon's just one man, Daniel. He may be brilliant, but the design teams for both companies are some of the brightest in the industry." She wasn't arguing because she wanted to dismiss Simon's threat, but because Daniel seemed oblivious to reality.

"Simon Brant *is* Brant Computers."

"Eric wouldn't agree with that sentiment, I'm sure."

"Eric is management. Simon's working on things that could change the face of the entire industry. We want him part of the merger. He has to be part of the merger."

We who? Extant's executive team? They hadn't even mentioned Simon Brant to her when she'd made her proposal for the merger.

"I can't believe Eric hasn't had him sign an intellectual property rights agreement." Daniel sounded aggrieved.

"Simon owns a big chunk of the company. I doubt Eric ever thought there would be a need. Besides, there's no saying Simon would ever have agreed to such a thing." The man was pretty independent and he definitely saw his work as his own.

"All the more reason for you to use your influence to get Simon Brant to agree to the merger."

Anger overcame her fear for her career. She was not a prostitute, glorified or otherwise. "You know, I don't think you could possibly mean what I think you mean, because if you did, you'd be making Extant and yourself vulnerable to a huge sexual harassment lawsuit."

When she hung up, Daniel was still spluttering.

Amanda slammed her taped fist into the sandbag. It made a satisfying thud. She did it again. And again. And again.

She was sweaty. Her knuckles hurt. Her muscles ached. And still, the anger burned inside of her. How could Daniel have suggested something so repugnant? She'd worked for Extant for five years and she'd never been asked to do anything remotely unethical.

Now this.

She'd never been so high up on a project before either. Is this the way Extant did business at the executive level? She couldn't believe it was, but Daniel *had* hinted that she should use her sexual prowess to convince Simon of the merger. There was no getting around, under, or over it.

Her boss expected her to use her body as a bargaining chip.

She laughed out loud as she stepped back and

connected with the sandbag with several round-house kicks, one right after the other. Daniel knew she was no sex kitten. She could no more convince Simon of her point of view using her nonexistent sensuality than she could teach Chinese as a second language.

But Daniel was convinced she was already sleeping with Simon and that was why he thought she could use her body for the cause. Which didn't alter her disgusted reaction to his suggestion. If she were involved personally with Simon, she would never use emotional or sexual blackmail to try to get his agreement on a business proposition.

With that thought, she switched legs and continued the roundhouse kicks with her other leg.

A disquieting thought nagged at her as she sought physically to alleviate the rage bubbling through her like hot lava. Was she most angry because her boss had suggested something so completely unethical, or because she knew there was no chance she could ever follow through on it?

She shook her head at the unpalatable idea and went through the entire repertoire of one-step sparring techniques Simon had taught her, using the bag as a dummy.

Her emotions began to separate themselves as the roiling mass of sensations inside her ebbed slightly. Okay, the anger was definitely at being told to do something so underhanded; but the accompanying pain had nothing to do with tender knuckles or aching muscles. It was the result of knowing she was as attractive to Simon as a carp to a salmon fisherman.

She didn't want to use her body to seduce Simon, but knowing she couldn't was really bad for her feminine ego. Almost as bad as night after night of no sex with Lance had been. And why

Simon, who was nothing more than a business associate when all was said and done, should have that kind of power over her feelings was a mystery she didn't want to solve.

"He wanted you to do what?" Jill's shriek was every bit as indignant as Amanda could have wished.

If there was one thing she could count on in her life, it was Jillian Sinclair's loyalty.

"He suggested I use sex as some kind of weapon in convincing Simon to go along with the merger. He thinks Simon and I are already sleeping together."

"The son of a bitch. I can't believe it. That kind of stuff is only supposed to happen on daytime drama."

Amanda found herself laughing when she was sure she couldn't. "Right. It's the sort of scenario one of your script writers could have come up with."

"Not our script writers. They've got better taste than that."

"Right. I mean that story line where the show's major male lead's current love interest turned out to be his long lost sister from an affair his father had with his gardener's daughter, was more tasteful than Daniel's smarmy suggestion. And more believable too," she admitted ruefully. "I'm not Mata Hari material."

"Mata Hari was a spy, not a corporate negotiator. Of course you would be a poor casting for that role, but if you're trying to imply you couldn't seduce Simon Brant, you're way off." Jillian made an indignant huffing noise. "The male of our species are not all like Lance Rogers."

Remembering the almost-kiss that had been all

on her side, Amanda laughed with black humor. "I couldn't heat Simon up with a blowtorch, much less use my imaginary sex appeal to manipulate him."

"Just because you don't have an emaciated body like half the women in Southern California, doesn't mean you have no sex appeal." This from the woman who made Twiggy look like an overeater. "If you'd let me fix you up with somebody decent, you'd find that out in a hurry."

"Jill, we've been down this conversational byway."

"And we'll keep going down it until you give in. Though from the sound of things, you don't need fixing up so much as loosening up with the man you're living with."

"I am not living with Simon Brant." Why did everyone seem so confused on that point? "I'm living in his house. It's not the same thing at all." She did her own huff of indignation. "Besides, if you had seen the woman he once considered marrying, you would realize he could never possibly find me attractive. I'd make two of her and she's pregnant, for Heaven's sake."

"Well, he didn't marry her, so that means he couldn't have been that taken with her."

Amanda wished she could convince herself of Jillian's perspective, but she couldn't. "She married his cousin instead."

"That definitely puts her out of the picture," Jillian said with unhidden satisfaction. "There's nothing to stop you from pursuing something fun, if not meaningful, with this guy."

"*Simon Brant does not want to have sex with me!*" she yelled, totally exasperated and over the edge of her control.

"Are you sure about that?" The words were spoken in a deep, masculine voice from behind her.

Her heart plummeting to her toes, she spun around with the cell phone stuck to the side of her head like a hi-tech earmuff. Simon lounged in the guest room doorway; the formerly closed door swung carelessly against the wall.

She opened her mouth, but the only thing that came out was air. Jill was saying something, but Amanda couldn't make any sense of it. She was too busy hyperventilating from embarrassment.

"Simon," she choked out.

"Yes, Simon. You're obviously interested in the man." Jill's impatient voice in her ear had a dream-like quality to it.

Reality was six feet, two inches of masculine perfection and a sardonic gleam in gunmetal gray eyes.

"Jill." she said, breaking into her friend's familiar tirade on Amanda's lack of a love life.

"What?"

"Simon's here. I think he wants to talk to me."

Jillian's gasp was audible. "Simon's there?"

"Yes."

"How much did he hear?" Her friend's whisper was too little, way too late.

"Enough."

Simon's black brow rose in question.

Jill said "Oh."

"Exactly. Look, Jillian, I've got to go."

"Sure. Call me later."

"Maybe tomorrow." If she hadn't died of mortification by then. Could one die from that sort of thing?

She snapped the cell phone shut. "I didn't hear you knock."

"I think your concentration was elsewhere."

It had been. Oh yes, it had been. "You're right."

"You, however, are wrong."

She was wrong about her concentration? Her usually efficient brain was not functioning at anything near normal capacity at the moment. "About what?"

"I do want to have sex with you."

Her knees gave way. Luckily the bed was right behind her and she landed precariously on the edge. "W-what?"

"I think you heard me."

She shook her head, but the buzzing his words produced did not abate. He hadn't moved a centimeter. His entire posture where he leaned in the doorway, filling it, was one of relaxation. He couldn't possibly be discussing sex with her and maintaining such insouciance. It wasn't possible.

"You did, but I'll say it again. I do want to have sex with you."

She lost her hold on the bed. The carpet muffled the thump as she landed on her bottom on the floor with her back against the mattress and box spring. "You didn't just say that."

. He moved. Finally. It was to come across the room and offer his hand to her. She took it and he pulled her to her feet. Her bum was sore.

"I did, but that's not what I came in here to talk about."

"It's not?" A modicum of sanity reasserted itself in her beleaguered brain. "Of course it's not."

"I'm truly sorry, but I'm in the middle of an experiment I can't leave right now."

"But you're here." Okay, so her thinking processes weren't completely restored.

"For just a minute. I came down to tell you and Jacob I wouldn't be joining you for dinner. I don't know when I'll be able to break away from the experiment again tonight."

Why was he telling her this?

"We'll have to put off the rest of your presentation until later."

Two things struck her at once. The first was that Simon was capable of divorcing himself from whatever small desire he felt for her pretty darn easily. The second was that he was explaining himself in a way he hadn't so far in their brief acquaintance. She liked it.

"Thank you for telling me."

He nodded. "You're welcome."

His hands dropped from her shoulders. "I've got to go."

"Right."

"We'll talk later."

"Later," she parroted.

Then he left, taking his sinfully sexy body with him. She collapsed back on the bed and wondered if the Peace Corps had any use for a slightly damaged corporate negotiator in a country like Zimbabwe or something.

Simon picked up the calibrator, made note of what it read and wrote a number down on the pad beside his right hand. It was just about what he had expected, but the slight discrepancy bothered him. He would have to find the reason for it before he could go forward with the fuel cell energy project. He started mentally ticking through the list of possible reasons, writing down ideas on isolating root cause as he went.

He stalled at the second likely test while his thoughts went winging back to his brief discussion with Amanda earlier. He could still see the look of shock on her face when she realized he had overheard her telling her friend, vehemently no less, that he did not want to have sex with her.

Was she blind?

Just because he wasn't acting on his desires didn't mean they had suddenly disappeared. She'd been there in the gym when he'd almost kissed her and she'd known what he'd been about to do. He might be clueless about women sometimes, but he knew when one was gearing up for a liplock with him.

He'd been so irritated with her feigned ignorance that he'd told her she was wrong. Not the brightest thing he'd done since first discovering sex. He shouldn't have admitted it out loud. It was a weapon she could use against him.

He wasn't about to give her the chance. He would listen to her proposal and then she could go back to her hotel in Port Mulqueen. With the temptation of her body gone, maybe he would get some actual work done.

He'd never experienced this kind of distraction before. His concentration was usually absolute, but since meeting Amanda he had found himself thinking about her when he should be analyzing a problem. Even the multiple projects he had going right now were not enough to keep his mind off the tantalizing woman. One of the reasons for his three-day work fest had been a test he was forced to restart when he'd messed it up daydreaming about Amanda instead of keeping track of the energy levels.

He could not afford to be distracted right now. Not if he wanted to be the first designer to get proof of concept on a fiber-optic computer processor. His fuel cell project was an interesting diversion, something to keep his mind from getting locked into a single mode of thinking. He'd learned long ago that working on more than one project at a time, projects that were vastly different, kept his thought processes fresh.

Amanda was interfering with that. No doubt about it. Images of her in his bed plagued him far too often. He'd never been so obsessed with the idea of having a woman, so consumed with the desire to know what she looked like out of her clothes, how she felt, how she tasted. Not even his precocious adolescence had elicited this kind of absorption in him.

It was an absorption he could not afford if he wanted to prevent his cousin from merging Brant Computers with Extant Corporation. Amanda's ideas were good, but she and Eric were considering too many of the wrong things in their enthusiasm for the merger. Simon refused to let them forget the company's beginnings, the commitment Brant Computers had always had toward its employees.

The temptation of Amanda's body could very well undermine his efforts in that direction. She had to go.

Out of his house and preferably back to California with a "No," from Eric ringing in her ears.

Warm, salty wind caressed Amanda's face as she sat on the bobbing dock, her feet dangling in the chilly water of the Puget Sound. There were a lot of things she didn't miss about home. She didn't miss the smog, or the stalled traffic on the freeway. She didn't pine for the fast pace or the crowded malls, but she did miss a warm ocean.

Her feet were going numb from the cold. Was that a bad thing? You couldn't get frostbite from water, could you? It probably wasn't worth the risk.

Sighing, she pulled her feet from the water and drew her knees to her chest. She watched with much more attention than it deserved as a puddle of water formed around her feet on the sun washed gray wood.

Simon had said he wanted to have sex with her and her mind had gone as numb as her feet were now. Her thought process was still sluggish as she attempted to deal with the ramifications of his statement.

He wanted her.

So, why had he pulled away from kissing her in the gym? Or had he? She still couldn't be entirely certain he had meant to kiss her at all. When it came to men's passion and their desire to act on it, she was a total novice despite having been married.

She'd been tempted to call Jillian back and tell her everything, but in the end, Amanda had decided against making the call. Because she already knew what her friend would say.

Jill would say, "Go for it."

No hesitation. No other considerations. She would expect Amanda to ignore her own less than successful attempt at sexual intimacy in the past, to ignore the fact that Daniel wanted her to use sex as a weapon against Simon and to forget her sense of propriety when it came to business relationships.

The truly terrifying reality was that Amanda was considering doing just that. Without Jillian's cajoling.

Amanda wanted Simon.

More than she had ever wanted another man. More than she had believed possible. She had long ago come to the conclusion that all the hype about making love was just that, hype. Or at least an aspect of reality she was not destined to experience.

She'd read somewhere that there was no such thing as a frigid woman, just an inept lover. She didn't believe it. Or hadn't . . . until Simon.

Her desire for him put paid to her certainty that she was not a very sexual being. She certainly felt sexual around him. In fact, it was hard to focus on any other aspect of her humanity when he was around. She wanted to touch him. To be touched by him.

Just thinking about it had all sorts of interesting things happening to her body. Her nipples were tightening, puckering, getting hard. The rigid buds pressed against her legs that were drawn close to her chest. Her nipples had never before manifested any sort of sexual excitement until manipulated physically.

She could never remember feeling this throbbing ache between her thighs either, or the fluttery sensation in her stomach. Her breathing didn't usually go ragged and uneven, not even in the act of intercourse.

But all of those things were happening right now and they were all for Simon. And not even Simon in the flesh, but the simple thought of him.

Her body wanted his possession. Okay, it wasn't PC and she'd never say it out loud, but that was what she wanted. She wanted to feel him *inside her, surrounding her, owning her* for that brief time when their bodies meshed and sought the ultimate pleasure. An experience she'd never actually had.

She was too repressed to pursue it on her own. The mere thought of using mechanical devices made her blush. She'd definitely never known such a thing with Lance. She thought maybe she'd come close once or twice, but now she realized that what she'd mistaken for passion had been at best lukewarm physical pleasure.

"Some people have better things to do than to track down wayward guests and give them messages."

Her head snapped up as a shadow fell over her and Jacob's irascible voice jarred her from her thoughts. "Hello, Jacob. Am I the wayward guest?"

"Don't see nobody else staying in Simon's house, missy."

She was getting used to his bouts of surliness. "I don't either, so that must mean the message is for me," she said with a sunny smile.

Was that approval she could see in his eyes? Maybe the old man was starting to like her.

"The boss said to tell you he would come down about nine o'clock."

"Tomorrow morning?" She had to stifle her disappointment at having missed Simon when he'd surfaced from his lab.

"Tonight. Said to tell you he'd come to your room." Jacob managed to lace the words with disapproval and a fair dose of innuendo all at once.

"At nine o'clock?" Her voice squeaked on the word nine. "In my room?"

"That's what he said. I retire before that unless the boss instructs me otherwise."

So, she and Simon would effectively be alone. In her room. She felt like sticking her head in the frigid water of the sound. Anything to clear the morass of thoughts chasing themselves through her mind.

Was he planning to pursue his desire to have sex with her? She couldn't believe he would have sent the message through Jacob, but then Simon didn't do things the normal way. And she hadn't been around when he'd come out of his lab, presumably to tell her himself.

"Simon wants to meet me at nine o'clock in my

room?" she asked to verify the improbable message.

Jacob's snort of impatience barely impinged on her consciousness. "That's what I said. Do you need it in writing?"

She shook her head, as much to clear it as to negate his statement. "No. I've got it."

Simon wanted to meet her in her room at nine o'clock that night. After Jacob had retired to his own quarters. Not exactly at bedtime, but too late to be considered strictly appropriate for a casual visit.

Oh, she had it all right.

The only problem was—what was she going to do with it?

Chapter 9

Simon laid down the calibrator and stretched. Flicking a glance at the digital atomic clock above his main workbench he winced. Nine-thirty. He'd told Jacob to tell Amanda he would be down at nine.

He hoped she wasn't too irritated.

The thought annoyed him. He'd pretty much dismissed the frustration others had with his work habits since he was ten years old. Why were the worries coming to surface now, with a woman who was nothing more than a business contact and an unwelcome one at that?

Even if she was mad, he knew she'd still be up. She wanted a chance to convince him of that damn merger.

She was too dedicated to her job to go to bed in a huff of offended feminine pride at being forgotten. And he hadn't forgotten her. If it had been anyone else, he would probably still be at his workbench. Not doing a quick finger-combing of his hair as he rapidly descended the stairs to the second floor.

* * *

The sweet fragrance of the peaches and cream candle she'd lit an hour ago filled Amanda's room, but instead of soothing her, it mocked her attempt to create a mood of romance. *He wasn't coming.* It was after nine-thirty. He'd definitely decided against acting on the mutual attraction between them.

She should be feeling relieved.

After all, she'd only decided at eight-thirty to take the advice she knew Jillian would have offered and go for it. Until then, she'd vacillated between the sane thoughts of her business-conscious brain and the insane urges of her heretofore unknown feminine desires.

She should be glad that his decision to stay away had saved her from herself. Maybe if it didn't feel so much like a rejection, she would be. Certainly it made sense that he would have realized the inappropriateness of pursuing any kind of intimate relationship in their current situation. But why in Hades hadn't he figured that out before sending that stupid message through Jacob?

And why hadn't he had at least the courtesy to come down and tell her himself?

The thought that he'd gotten caught up in his lab experiments and forgotten her was no consolation.

That smacked of unpleasantly familiar rejection as well.

A sharp tattoo sounded on her door and all the air in her body seemed to expel.

He was here. Heavens. What should she do now?

The knock sounded again. "Amanda?"

Open the door. That's what she had to do. She walked across the room on bare feet, the shimmering burgundy of her painted toenails flashing in the periphery of her vision with every step.

The color went nicely with the Bordeaux satin tap pants and camisole she was wearing. She'd spent a full fifteen minutes applying the nail polish, letting it dry while she brushed her long hair into a dark brown curtain that gleamed like silk in the flickering light of the candle.

She reached for the door handle with a trembling hand and then pulled it open.

Simon's fist was raised to knock again. He let it drop while shock registered on his face. "I know I'm a little late, but I didn't think you'd be going to bed so early."

Why was he looking so surprised?

"It's only nine-thirty," he added.

She looked over her right shoulder at the red glow of her digital alarm clock. "Nine-forty-two actually."

"Look, I know it probably irritated you that I forgot the time, but I didn't forget you completely." Far from looking like a man bent on seduction, Simon looked tired and cranky. "I'm here, aren't I?"

"Yes." Was she acting annoyed? She didn't think she was.

"I can't believe you're going to dismiss the chance to talk about the merger just because I'm a half an hour later than I said I'd be." Outrage laced his voice. "Hell, you moved into my house so you could catch me between experiments. Going to bed right now is hardly the behavior of a professional career woman intent on pursuing her objective."

On that he had her complete agreement, but the rest of his words weren't making any sense.

"You think I'm angry with you?" she asked, while trying to understand what was going on here. The sensual fog she'd been in since deciding to "go for it" was clouding her ability to reason.

He tipped his head and rubbed the bridge of

his nose with his thumb and forefinger. Gunmetal eyes reflecting weariness pinned her with unconcealed annoyance. "Don't play this *I'm not mad, just tired* routine. It's such a female thing to do and not at all what I would expect of a woman dedicated to getting the job done."

As the desire that had overridden her usual caution began to wane under Simon's anger, the inconsistencies in the situation infiltrated her consciousness. Inconsistencies she would have noticed immediately if she hadn't been so overwhelmed by the prospect of going to bed with him.

He was not acting like an amorous lover. In fact, nothing he'd said so far indicated any sort of desire on his part whatsoever. As her now nimble brain went back over what he'd said so far, the sick feeling of embarrassment started to crawl along her nerve endings.

He hadn't meant making love at all.

Simon had wanted to meet her to discuss the merger.

How stupid could one woman possibly be? "Why did you insist on meeting in my bedroom?" Her voice was too high, but there was nothing she could do about that.

He frowned. "I didn't insist. I told Jacob I'd look for you in your room so I wouldn't spend a half an hour searching the house for you when I came downstairs. What does where I asked to meet you have to do with your childish display of temper?"

He thought she was being childish? Everything finally made sense. Simon had wanted to discuss the merger. He believed that because he was late, she'd gotten ready for bed in some kind of juvenile act of rebellion. While not exactly flattering, it beat the truly mortifying truth that she'd thought he'd wanted her.

She stepped back into the room, flipping on the overhead light as she went. "I'll just get on some jeans and a sweater, all right? It gets cold in the evenings here. Really chilly, to tell you the truth." She blew out the candle on her way by. "I'm not used to these kinds of temperatures."

She was babbling, but she didn't care. Maybe if she kept talking it would prevent him from clueing into what she'd really thought. Shame so familiar, it was almost a friend, surrounded her like the hot oppressive air of the Mojave Desert.

"It won't take a sec," she continued her babbling litany as she yanked on a pair of jeans right over her tap pants. "I'm sorry if you thought I was being childish. I thought you'd forgotten completely. That's all," she lied.

She grabbed a red turtleneck from the top drawer of the dresser she'd been using. She tugged it on over her head, pulling her hair in the process. She ignored the pain as she ripped it loose of the constricting neck on the top.

"Let me just clip back my hair." She hadn't looked at him once since realizing her mistake and she didn't do so now either. She spoke to the wall in front of her as she headed for the en-suite.

"Don't pull it back on my account. It looks beautiful down like that."

She wanted to spin around and start screaming invective at him. *Beautiful?* She wasn't beautiful. She knew it and he knew it. He didn't want her. Not really. She didn't know what he'd meant by telling her he wanted sex with her earlier. It had probably been some kind of joke. An amusing bit of sarcasm she should have recognized as such.

How could a woman with an IQ in the top two percent of the populace continue to be so dim about some things?

She didn't bother responding to him as she walked into the bathroom, shutting the door behind her. She needed a minute to collect herself. *She needed a lifetime, but she could take a minute.*

She searched for the light she hadn't bothered to turn on before coming into the small room, found it and flipped the switch up.

The sudden brightness illuminated a picture in the mirror she could have gone forever without seeing again. Brown eyes dark with hurt and humiliation were opened wide to prevent the moisture gathering in the corners from spilling over. Her face was crimson with embarrassment, her mouth a tight line of pain.

It was a familiar sight. How many nights in the first year of her marriage had she tried to interest Lance in making love only to have him reject her for one reason or another? How many times had she stood in front of the mirror just as she was doing now and tried to see what was wrong with her?

The sad-eyed woman in the mirror was someone she knew intimately, someone she had vowed never to see again.

She'd promised herself, damn it. She was never going to let another man close enough to hurt her this way again. But she had and she was paying the price. The mire of humiliation was closing over her head, suffocating her with its terrifying inevitability.

She hated feeling like this. Hated it!

Suddenly the slide of satin against her skin was as painful as a hair shirt and just as effective a reminder of things she would rather forget. She ripped off her outer clothes, then tore the camisole and tap pants from her body and threw them with all her might into the garbage can beside the sink vanity.

She'd only started wearing pretty feminine undergarments in the last year, having cut every negligee she owned into shreds and disposed of them the second year of her marriage after a particularly brutal rejection from her husband. He'd told her that fat women shouldn't expose so much of themselves to view.

Fat!

She had been five pounds under her ideal weight, but that hadn't been good enough for her husband.

Why had she stayed married to the man so long?

She didn't have an answer now, any more than she'd had the one hundred and ten other times she'd asked herself that question.

The closest she could come was to acknowledge that she'd grown up with the feeling that she had no right to be happy. She'd been unlovable to her family. It was only natural her husband had decided he didn't love her too.

The pounding on the door brought her gaze away from the mirror.

"Amanda, are you all right?"

She must have been longer than she thought. "I'm fine. I'll be right out," she called in a credibly even voice.

The only way she could think of to mitigate the pain of Simon's unwitting rejection was to prevent him from knowing how much he had hurt her. At least her humiliation wasn't public, not like it had been with Lance.

She threw her clothes back on, not worrying about a lack of underthings. Simon wouldn't know. It took her longer than usual to clip back her hair because her hands were shaking so badly. She had to get herself under control before she went out there. Closing her eyes, she inhaled deeply, concentrating on breathing in peace and breathing out her stress.

It was a psychological trick one of her friends from high school had taught her. Most of the time, it worked.

Amanda finished zipping up the leopard print suitcase. She'd been up since five that morning after sleeping very little the night before.

Simon had listened to the initial proposal in its entirety, had not interrupted when she outlined her thoughts on the best strategy for joining the two businesses. He had even allowed her to present the rest of her arguments in favor of the merger, all of it with very little comment from him. He hadn't argued a single point, thus not giving her the opportunity to press her own ideas forward.

And she hadn't cared.

She'd been relieved that he didn't want to get into a major discussion because all she had wanted to do was finish the presentation and get away from him. She'd been back in her bedroom by eleven and had started packing five minutes after that.

She *should* stick around and try to bolster the arguments she'd offered the night before, but she couldn't. While her job was the most important thing in her life, she could not stand the crawling sense of humiliation her mistake the night before had left her with. Not even for a major bump up in her five-year career plan.

She'd done all she could do.

If Simon wasn't convinced, maybe Daniel *should* consider sending another negotiator to Port Mulqueen. Her stomach cramped at the thought, but she was leaving. Today. This morning. She had every intention of being on the first ferry off Simon's island.

Fifteen minutes later, she went looking for Jacob to tell him she would be going. She found him in the kitchen.

He looked up when she entered, his wizened gaze taking in her perfectly pressed suit. "I'll have blue corn cakes ready in a few minutes. Did you want bacon or sausage with them?"

"Neither, thank you."

"It's not a good idea to start the day without putting a bit of protein in you."

"I'll stop for breakfast when I get back to Port Mulqueen." It was a lie. She knew she wouldn't be eating any time soon, but the small deception didn't hurt anyone and it would keep Jacob from haranguing her.

"You going to the mainland today?"

"Yes."

"Will you be back in time for dinner?"

"I won't be back at all. I came in to say thank you for your hospitality and let you know I was leaving."

"Wasn't my hospitality, missy. The bed you slept in belongs to the boss. He bought the food you ate."

"Then please pass my gratitude on to him."

"Why don't you do it yourself? He'll probably be down for breakfast before too long."

Just the prospect of seeing Simon again made her sensitive stomach twist with nausea. "I don't want to miss the ferry." Good. Her voice was steady, professionally void of emotion. She even forced what she hoped was a credible smile to her lips. "Let's be honest, Jacob, there's no guarantee Simon will come down for breakfast at all."

"Thought you were supposed to convince him about that merger Mr. Eric Brant wants."

"Simon listened to the proposal last night." And if Eric wanted the merger so darn bad, he could convince his cousin of its merits. Brant Computers stood to gain by the merger just as much as Extant Corporation did.

"And he agreed to it?" The incredulity in Jacob's voice left her in no doubt how unlikely he found such a scenario.

"No."

"Then shouldn't you be staying to try to talk him into it?"

She didn't know why Jacob cared about her business, but she wished he didn't. "I've done what I could. I can't force Simon to my point of view."

"Seems like a pretty sloppy way to do business to me."

Her tolerance and patience dried up at the same time. "This may come as a debilitating shock to you, but what you think of the way I conduct my business is of no concern to me whatsoever."

Jacob's eyes narrowed. "No need to get snippy with me, missy."

She closed her eyes and counted to ten. It worked in all the books she read. Real life was less disciplined. "You're right, Jacob. I'm leaving now," she said through gritted teeth, and then turned on her heel and did just that.

Simon walked into the kitchen, irritated by the anticipation he felt at the prospect of seeing Amanda.

"Good morning, Jacob."

"Morning, sir."

There was a pile of shiny fabric on the counter next to where Jacob stood putting blue corn cakes and bacon on a plate for Simon. The material was the same color as Amanda's pajamas. The pajamas responsible for a night filled with restless sleep interspersed with highly erotic dreams.

"Is Amanda up yet?"

"Up and gone."

"Gone?" Was she walking along the water again? She seemed to really enjoy doing that.

Jacob laid Simon's plate of breakfast on the table. "Took the first ferry to the mainland."

She'd probably gone to have a war council with Eric now that Simon had listened to her arguments. He wondered what her next step in her campaign to convince him would be. He should tell her now that he had listened to her proposal, there was no reason for her to stay on the island.

But what he should do and what he wanted to do were poles apart, especially after seeing her in that wet dream–producing nightwear.

"What time do we expect her back?"

"We don't."

Simon paused with a loaded fork halfway to his mouth. "What?"

"She's not coming back, sir. Said to tell you she appreciated the hospitality."

"The hell you say."

Jacob just shrugged. "Thought she'd stay to do a little more convincing on that merger business. Told her so, but she pretty much told me to mind my own business."

Amanda had left? Without saying goodbye? There was something about this situation that didn't feel right. Like Jacob said, it made no sense for her to leave without making at least one more effort to convince him about the merger.

"Was there some reason she had to go back to the mainland so early this morning?"

"Don't know, sir. She didn't say anything. Just that she didn't want to miss the ferry."

Simon's gaze slid to the clock on the kitchen wall. The ferry had left the dock twenty minutes ago.

Amanda was gone. Telling himself that was exactly what he wanted did nothing to alleviate the hollow sensation inside him.

Why the hell hadn't she even bothered to say goodbye?

Jacob held up the pile of rich burgundy satin. "She left this behind."

So it *was* her pajamas. "We'll have to get it back to her." His spirits lifted at the thought of having an excuse to see her again.

"Don't know if she wants it. Found it in the garbage in the bathroom, sir."

"You found Amanda's pajamas in the garbage?" That didn't make any sense. "Were they damaged in some way?" Maybe her woman's thing had started last night and she'd been surprised by it, ruining the silk bottoms to the nightwear.

"Not a thing wrong with them, sir."

"Then they must have fallen into the garbage by accident."

"Could be. Don't see how, but it could have happened."

"Well, what do you think happened?"

"Think she threw them away, sir. She was meticulous in cleaning her other things from the room. Don't see how she could have overlooked these."

Simon measured Jacob with his eyes. The older man had a studiously blank expression on his face. Why had he brought the pajamas to his attention, if he believed Amanda had tossed them on purpose? More worryingly, why had she thrown them away?

* * *

The ferry announcement had ended several minutes ago, but the words were still echoing in Amanda's head. Ferry service had been suspended until further notice. There had been an accident on one of the major routes and the single ferry that serviced Simon's sparsely populated island had been re-routed to the busier one. Ferries didn't have accidents, did they?

They were big. They traveled the same stretch of water over and over again. So, how had this happened?

More importantly, what was she going to do? The only public facility she knew of on the island was a small general store and deli—deli being a euphemism for a two-foot-long glass case with lunchmeats and potato salad on display. There was a single table with two chairs for customers to sit on. It was not somewhere she would be comfortable staying for several hours while waiting for ferry service to resume.

She could just stay where she was.

She grimaced. She'd been sitting in this poky little waiting room for two hours already. There wasn't even a vending machine where she could buy a bottle of water. According to the ferry officials, it could be hours before service resumed. Considering how much she wanted to get off the blasted island, it would be just her luck that the ferry wouldn't be available until the next morning.

Surely not. She tried to console herself with the thought that they had to have at least one trip to the mainland that day. She wasn't the only one who wanted to get off the island. Okay, maybe she'd been one of three cars that had been in line for the morning ferry and the other two had left after the first announcement of delay. Looking around the now empty waiting room, she had to accede it was possible she was the only passenger *desperate* to leave the small island.

"You might as well go back to wherever you've been visiting, ma'am. It's going to be a while before we get a ferry off the dock."

She turned her head at the sound of the man's voice. He was wearing the bright orange vest that indicated ferry personnel.

"How did you know I was visiting?" she asked, apropos of nothing.

"It's a small island. Working the ferry, you get to know all the residents after a while, even the weekenders."

"Oh." What an intelligent response, Amanda. But she felt fresh out of intelligence at the moment.

"Who are you visiting?"

She thought about refusing to answer, but it wasn't a state secret after all. "Simon Brant."

The sandy haired man's blue eyes widened. "He doesn't have a lot of visitors, *especially overnight ones*."

She made a noncommittal sound, not liking the implication of his emphasis on "overnight visitors."

"The security at his place is pretty tight," the ferry official remarked, obviously fishing for more information on the elusive islander.

Remembering Jacob's insistence on making a visual identification the first time she visited, she had to agree. "I suppose he sees the need for it, being both an inventor and computer designer."

It struck her that Simon had shown a lot of trust allowing her to stay in his home like he had. What if she had been a corporate spy for Extant, more interested in his designs than the merger? The thought brought forth a niggling memory. Daniel had commented on Simon's current project like he knew what it was. How could that be true?

Jacob was as loyal to Simon as any person could be. She would stake her life on that. So, how had Daniel found out anything about Simon's work? Or had he? Perhaps she had misunderstood what her boss had said. She'd been pretty hot about his suggestion she use her body for the cause.

"They say he's a genius."

She nodded.

"And eccentric."

Her lips tilted in a wry smile. "You could certainly describe him that way. You said, *they say*. Don't you know? Haven't you met him?"

The young man shook his head. "He keeps to himself. Him and that old man who lives there with him."

"Jacob is the housekeeper."

"A security expert too, according to gossip."

She looked more closely at the sandy-haired man. He looked young, but his eyes were filled with the avid curiosity of an inveterate gossip. "For not knowing him, you certainly know a lot about Simon."

"Not as much as you do, I bet." His smile once again implied an intimacy between her and Simon.

She wouldn't let this one slide. "It's strictly a business relationship." Still smarting from her humiliating mistake in the other direction the night before, she was sharper than she intended to be.

The ferry official's smile didn't dim. If anything, he contrived to look smug. "He doesn't bring business acquaintances to the island."

"I suppose gossip said that too," she said in scathing tones that once again went right over his head.

He shrugged. "Yep."

"Well, he brought me and I can assure you there is nothing except business between Simon Brant and myself."

"You'd say that wouldn't you? Not wanting gossip and all." His knowing look indicated that gossip about Simon's houseguest would be rife on the island, regardless of what she might want.

She stood up, a sense of righteous indignation coursing through her. "Your implication is out of line, not to mention archaic in its perception of the relationship between men and women." Taking a step toward the ferry official, she grimly enjoyed watching him back up. "This is the twenty-first century. Women are a fact of reality in the business arena. I suppose you think we should all stay home and pop out babies until menopause takes us over."

He was starting to look seriously worried. "I don't think that at all, ma'am. Lots of women work for the ferry service."

"But you don't think we have the education or the intelligence to compete in the technology industry. You just assume that a woman could not possibly have business dealings with Simon Brant because he's a genius in a male dominated field. I resent that implication very much."

"I didn't mean that, ma'am."

She ignored his lukewarm self-defense, now in the full stride of her ire. "I will have you know that I have a very successful career at Extant Corporation, a company on the forefront of design in the hi-tech industry. Furthermore, there are several women at the executive level with my company. It's attitudes like yours that kept women in strictly supportive roles for so many years."

"He's not old enough to have fought the vote, missy."

She swung around, her finger still pointed accusingly in front of her. "Jacob! What are you doing here?"

Chapter 10

"Ferry's not running."

His laconic answer did nothing to clarify the situation. "I know that, but how did you?"

"News travels fast on an island."

That sent her spinning back toward the hapless ferry employee. She glared at him. "I suppose gossip accounts for this sort of thing too."

The young man appealed to Jacob over her shoulder. "I didn't mean to offend her. Really. We were just talking."

"Have I suddenly disappeared now that another man is in the room?" she demanded with bite.

"Leave the poor boy alone." Jacob came to stand beside her. "You've got him scared to death."

"Scared of a woman?" she asked derisively, somewhere at the back of her mind realizing she was overreacting, but unable to stop the words from flowing out of her mouth. "Imagine that."

"I'm not a chauvinist," the ferry official asserted, his courage apparently bolstered by Jacob's presence.

"Then how do you explain your inappropriate comments earlier? The result of a bad breakfast?" Her stomach growled, reminding her she hadn't eaten anything yet that day, bad or otherwise.

"He made inappropriate comments to you?" Suddenly Jacob's voice had gone arctic, his homey accent dropped for precise diction.

"He implied that rather than business associates, Simon and I shared some kind of *personal* and *intimate* relationship."

"My employer does not appreciate speculation regarding his private life."

The ferry official blanched.

Amanda didn't blame him. The deadly tone even sent a shiver up *her* spine.

"I didn't mean anything by it. Honest."

"The implication that a man and woman must have more than a business relationship is never a welcome one," she said before Jacob could reply.

"It was just the shock of you staying overnight. That's all. Mr. Brant hasn't had an overnight visitor since his cousin missed the last evening ferry a couple of months back."

"The Secret Service has nothing on Washington State ferry personnel, does it?" She was amazed the man knew so much about Simon's life. She didn't even know that much about the neighbors she'd been living next door to since leaving Lance two years ago.

Apparently realizing that everything he said made the situation worse, the orange clad official started backing away toward the office. "I've uh . . . got a lot of paperwork to catch up on. I'm sorry about the inconvenience the cancelled ferry has caused you, ma'am."

"You intimidated him."

She stared at Jacob, disbelief warring with offense inside her. "I intimidated him? You were the one that turned into The Enforcer. You were so cold, I'm surprised the guy didn't get chillblains standing next to you."

Undeniable satisfaction reflected in Jacob's expression. "It's a role I play rather well."

"I'd say you play all your parts with the professionalism of a trained thespian."

"For that sort of flattery, I'll make you a Napoleon for dinner."

Just thinking of the flaky crust and sweet custard filling of the decadent dessert had her mouth watering, but she had no intention of going back to Simon's. "I'll just wait here until the ferry resumes service."

"Not a good idea. Could be tomorrow morning before you can get back to the mainland."

"I find that difficult to believe. They can't just leave passengers stranded without a means to get off the island."

"The island's population is so low it has the least priority of all the ferry routes. Besides, most residents have their own boats to use if they're in desperate need of getting to the mainland."

She remembered the yacht moored on Simon's private dock. "But I have a car. I can't just hire someone to take me across." Though the thought was a tempting one.

"Couldn't hire someone anyway. Jim Fletcher's the only resident that takes paying passengers and he's off-island right now."

"So, I'll wait here."

Jacob looked around the sparsely furnished, miniscule room. "Be more comfortable at the boss's house."

That's what he thought. She'd be more comfortable in a thicket of blackberry bushes than she would be at Simon's. "I'll be fine here. If I get tired, I can take a nap in the car."

"What about food?"

She didn't feel like eating, even with her stomach growling, but she was thirsty. "I'll go to the general store for supplies."

"You're being stubborn."

"Think what you like, Jacob. I just don't want to inconvenience Simon anymore. I'll stay here, if it's all the same to you."

"The boss ain't going to like it."

"He won't even notice. By the time you get back he'll have forgotten why he sent you out to begin with."

"The boss ain't senile."

"No, but he is preoccupied with his work. Thank you for your concern, but I'm fine where I'm at."

Jacob left, muttering about intransigent women who might be better off if they never had got the vote.

She couldn't help smiling. Jacob was an irascible old codger, but he'd gotten defensive on her behalf before she mentioned the nature of the ferry official's inappropriate comments. The old faker liked her, even if he would never admit it.

Amanda grabbed the six-pack of bottled water and headed toward the antique looking cash register. The clerk, a middle aged woman in an oversize T-shirt bearing a picture of cats on the front, was talking animatedly with an elderly woman in white slacks and a sweatshirt.

Neither one of them noticed Amanda waiting to be rung up.

She didn't say anything. Why interrupt their discussion when she only planned to take the water and go back to the ferry terminal? She had thought about taking a drive around the island, but what if the ferry came while she was gone? She was fairly certain there would only be one sailing today. She was determined to be on it.

The bell above the entrance jingled. Both she and the chatting women turned to look at the new-comer.

It was Simon.

"Morning, Mr. Brant," the clerk called.

He nodded politely to the two women and then turned to walk toward Amanda. He stopped less than a foot away. "Jacob said you didn't want to come back to the house."

The accusation in his voice was unexpected.

"I didn't want to put you out any more than I had already," she said, giving him the same excuse she'd made up for Jacob.

He flicked a glance to the water in her hand, his expression enigmatic. "I don't mind."

"Thank you, but I wouldn't feel right imposing." He looked like he was about to argue, so she went on. "You allowed me the opportunity to present the merger proposal to you. Our business is concluded and there's no reason for you to feel responsible for my comfort. It's not as if I was a guest in your home."

His mouth quirked. "So you told the man at the ferry. Jacob said you were pretty adamant about it."

She bristled with remembered indignation. "It's the truth. That man had no right to imply otherwise."

"Living on a small island is like living in a *very* small town." Simon's gaze went temporarily to the two women who pretended to be talking, but were clearly more interested in his conversation with Amanda than their own. "Everyone knows every-one else's business, or thinks they do."

"Well, it's not right. That sort of gossip is intolerable." She didn't realize her voice had risen until the woman talking to the store clerk gave up all pretense of not listening and stared at her with blatant curiosity. *Great. More gossip.*

She smiled and nodded, hoping they would go back to their previously absorbing conversation, then turned back to Simon. "There's really no reason for you to wait around here. I've got refreshments." She lifted the six-pack of water. "I'll be fine until the ferry gets here."

"But you'll be better at my house. Jacob's set on spoiling you." Simon's voice had taken on a seductive quality that her body did not identify with food. "He's working on the pasty crust for a napoleon even as we speak."

Her face felt tight. The last thing she needed after Simon's unknowing rejection was the high-calorie dessert. "I'm sure you will enjoy it then."

"He's making it for you." Simon slid his hands into his jeans pockets, outlining a certain male part of his anatomy she was better off *not* noticing.

She forced her gaze to his face and kept it there. "I'm sorry I won't be there to eat it," she said, adding another lie to the ones she'd already told that morning.

"Why won't you be there?" He frowned at her, his sensual lips forming into a thin line. "There's no reason for you to wait around in that dinky room when you can relax in comfort at the house. We could even get some sparring in."

He said it like that should be some sort of incentive, but she flinched at the thought.

No way was she going through another tortuous session of touchy-feely martial arts training with Simon. "I don't mind. Really. I'm sure you've got experiments or something." She waved vaguely toward the door. "I won't keep you."

She started to turn away, hoping he'd finally get

a clue and leave. She wasn't going back to his house. Period. If he thought she was being neurotically polite, so be it. Better that, than the chance he would discover the desire that seemed to grow with each lungful of air she took in his radius.

The in-drawn hiss of his breath was all the warning she got. He grabbed the water from her hands, dropped it right there in the aisle and then swept her up into his arms like she was some damsel in distress. Only, the real distress started the moment he touched her because her senses went haywire.

"Well, I'm damn well going to keep you. You're being too stubborn for your own good."

"Simon! Put me down. You're causing a scene. It's going to be all over the island by the time we reach my car." And judging from the twin expressions of avid interest on the other two women's faces, Amanda didn't think she was exaggerating.

Simon ignored her and carried her outside. He stopped behind her car. "Push the unlock button."

She didn't even think of arguing with him. If she didn't get out of his arms soon, she was going to do something drastic. Like kiss him. Or bury her fingers in the black, silky hair he'd left loose to hang around his shoulders today.

The snick of unlocking doors sounded and Simon went around to open the passenger door. He bent down and put her inside.

"What are you doing?" She was shrieking. She never shrieked, but then she'd never been kidnapped by an eccentric genius before either. "This is my car."

"I'm driving." And his tone suggested she not argue about it.

She'd never been all that great at taking suggestions. *"But the rental agreement doesn't have you on it."*

He just looked at her.

"Well, it doesn't." She turned to face the front, her mouth in a mutinous line.

He shut the door. Firmly. Seconds later he was sliding into the driver's seat. "Keys?" He put his hand out.

She glared at him in mute defiance. No way was she giving him her keys.

With the incredibly swift reflexes he had exhibited during their Tae Kwon Do sessions, he snatched the keys from her.

She yelped.

He didn't respond to the sound of outrage, but put the key in the ignition and started the car. "Fasten your seat belt."

She glared at him. "Make me." Where had that come from?

He didn't hesitate. While the car idled, he reached across her, his chest pressing against her breasts and he grabbed the belt. Every rational thought in her head went on vacation and it was all she could do to limit her reaction to breathing in little pants and a heart rate that could be measured on the Richter scale.

He pulled the seat belt across her and clicked it into the lock. "You're hyperventilating. Calm down. I'm not going to hurt you."

He thought she was frightened? She was, scared silly, but not of him. Of herself.

He put the car into reverse and pulled out of the small store's two-car parking lot. "I need a ride back to the house. I had Jacob drop me off when we spotted your car."

"If you needed a lift. All you had to do was ask." At least her voice worked and she hadn't warbled on a single word. "There was no reason for the he-man kidnapping or for you to appropriate my keys and my car."

His smile was devastating. "Wasn't there?"

She crossed her arms over her still heaving chest. "No."

"You weren't going to come back to my place without an order from the Senate."

"That's ridiculous."

"No, what's ridiculous is your stubborn insistence on waiting out the ferry at the terminal! What would you have done if ferry service didn't resume? Slept in your car?"

Since that was exactly what she had planned, she didn't feel the need to answer him.

"This may be a small island, but that doesn't mean it's safe for a beautiful woman to sleep alone in her car all night."

Beautiful woman? Right. She made a rather rude noise in response to his blatant attempt to win her acquiescence with a falsehood.

"And I'd like to know what you were going to eat. All I saw was bottled water. Jacob said you didn't have breakfast. Did you plan to starve yourself?"

She went cold at the question. She didn't starve herself. Not anymore. *She wasn't anorexic.* It was just that rejection had a negative impact on her ability to eat. "I wasn't hungry."

It was his turn to make a rude noise of disbelief.

"What I eat, or don't eat, has nothing to do with you, Mr. Brant."

"Why not? I thought we were friends."

"We're business associates."

"We can't be friends too?"

Not when she wanted him more than she wanted to breathe, more than she wanted to guard herself against rejection. She'd allowed that want to dictate her actions last night and look what had resulted. She'd been humiliated, even if he didn't know it.

"I doubt I'll even see you again after today."

"You will if you continue to pursue the merger."

They'd reached his gate, which Jacob had left open for Simon. No cat and mouse games from the old codger for the boss.

Simon stopped the car in front of the house and got out. She opened her door and was climbing out when she realized he had popped open the trunk and was pulling out her suitcase.

"What are you doing?"

"Getting your things."

"There's no need." She tried to grab her suitcase and put it back in the trunk, but he placed it on the other side of his body. An impossible barrier in her current state. "I'll be on the ferry in a couple of hours."

He shook his head while reaching in to pull out her laptop. "I don't think so. More likely the first ferry out will be tomorrow morning, but even if it is, you won't be on it."

"What do you mean I won't be on it?" she asked with a fair amount of panic.

"We aren't done discussing this merger business, which I would have told you if you'd bothered to stick around long enough this morning to say goodbye." He sounded really miffed by the fact she hadn't.

But why would he care if she said goodbye, or not?

She ignored the part of her brain that insisted he was right that they weren't done discussing the merger and said, "I've told you all the facts."

"What if I have a question?" He pulled her briefcase from the trunk and turned to look at her with nothing less than accusation. "Or want to *discuss* some aspect of the proposal?"

"You don't want the darned thing!" This was stupid. Simon wanted that merger about as much as she wanted a cozy friendship with her ex-husband. "Why would you ask me any questions?" she demanded. "You didn't bother to last night."

He picked up her laptop and swung the case strap over his shoulder, then picked up her suitcase. "I was busy listening."

More like ignoring her. "*Right.*"

His eyes narrowed. "I can prove it." Then he started spouting facts at her like bullets out of an automatic pistol. Every one of them accurate, every one of them something she had told him the night before. When he was done, he looked smug. "Maybe I don't want the merger, but I thought you were going to try to change my mind."

This was too much. He could quote her words back to her verbatim, but that didn't mean he believed a single one of them. "You can't turn a stone into water."

"Are you saying I'm dense like a rock?" Amusement twitched at the corners of his mouth and her temper exploded.

"No, stubborn as a mountain of rock!"

He threw back his head and laughed.

Heat surged into her face as her temper continued to escalate. She wasn't embarrassed; she was angry. "It's not funny. This is my career we're talking about. You won't even consider the merger regardless of whether or not it's the best thing for both of the companies."

Suddenly the laughter stopped and his gray eyes fixed on her with serious intent. "And your job is all that matters to you, isn't it?"

"A career doesn't let you down like people do."

"And if this merger doesn't go through are you saying you'll get what you want out of your career anyway?"

Remembering the silken threat in Daniel's voice, she grit her teeth against an honest answer. "What difference does it make to you?"

"Maybe I care." He slammed the trunk shut with an excess of force and grimly finished picking up her things. "Maybe I don't want to see you hurt by this, but I don't have any choice about it because what you want *isn't* best for Brant Computers. You just think it is."

She didn't know what to say. He made it sound like what happened to her really mattered to him and she knew that wasn't possible. She was nothing to him but an irritant. A blip on the radar of his life and just as temporary.

Without another word, he turned and headed for the house, leaving her to follow or not. She followed.

He went directly to her former bedroom and deposited her things on the end of her bed, then turned to face her. "I can't promise to change my mind, but I can promise that if you leave I won't have a chance to."

There was no compromise in his expression. If she stayed, there was a slight chance of success. If she left, the merger was dead. It was blackmail. Plain and simple. Effective too. He'd chosen to hold the lure of the one thing she valued in her life besides her friendship with Jillian. Her career.

She didn't have a clue why Simon wanted her to stay. She couldn't believe it was because he really wanted to consider her arguments in favor of Extant's proposal. But what if she was wrong? Even if she wasn't, the longer she held Daniel off from going after the other cousins' support, the better. She refused to be responsible for igniting a family war.

The arguments chased themselves in her head until she was dizzy. She felt torn between the familiar hell of staying with Simon and wanting him when he didn't want her, and the unfamiliar hell of knowing she had let herself and her company down professionally.

What real choice did she have? She'd survived marriage to Lance. She could withstand a few more days in Simon's home.

"I'll stay."

Simon watched Amanda meander along the shoreline from the lab room window. She'd changed from her starchy suit to a cotton shorty top and matching Capri pants. She'd even pulled her magnificent hair back into a ponytail, letting it loose from that neat bun she constantly wore. She looked incredible, not at all like the buttoned-up woman he'd come to know so well in such a short time.

A timer went off, reminding him he was supposed to be working, but then so was she. She'd told him she had a couple of hours of online work to do before lunch after once again refusing any sort of breakfast. That bothered him, but he'd won a major concession and had sensed he wouldn't win another one.

He'd come up to his lab to try to gain some perspective. He had several puzzles that needed solving in his two major projects and that should have been enough to take his mind into a realm populated by circuit wires and computer code instead of people. It hadn't been.

For the first time in his memory, he could not dredge up enough interest in his projects to focus on them. He was too busy thinking about Amanda. Forcing her to stay had to be one of the least logical things he'd ever done. There were several very good reasons for letting her leave and never seeing her again. Reasons he had been convinced were paramount until that morning when he walked into the kitchen and she hadn't been there.

None of those sound arguments stacked up against the reality of her being gone. He'd expected to see her eating at the table and when he hadn't, the light had gone out of his morning. When Jacob told him that Amanda had left without saying goodbye, cold winds had blown across Simon's soul—winds that had been silent since her arrival at his home.

He hated that cold and the shadows that accompanied it. She filled the empty places and pushed the shadows away.

That's why he had kidnapped her from the island's one small grocery store, why he had blackmailed her into staying. It didn't have anything to do with the merger, no matter what he had told her to get her to stay. He wasn't being fair to her. He knew it. He had no intention of changing his mind about the merger. It was the wrong move for a family run company and given enough time, Eric was bound to see that as well, but Simon had still used the carrot of his possible change of heart to lure Amanda into staying.

Because as of this morning when he'd faced a day without Amanda in it, and the prospect of endless more to follow, he had become as determined to keep her as he was to reject the merger.

"I thought you needed to take care of some e-mail."

Simon watched with fascination as Amanda jumped and whirled at the sound of his voice. She acted like a jackrabbit startled by a fox.

She stepped backward, away from him. "I didn't hear you come up."

"You must have been thinking pretty hard."

The twist of her lips could be called a smile, but there was something not quite right about it. She said, "Or you walk as quiet as a panther."

He shrugged at that. "I walk the way I walk."

She chewed on her bottom lip, which looked like it had already had a fair amount of that treatment. It was red and slightly swollen, all of the lipstick eaten off of it. Finally, she sighed. "You're so sure of who you are."

"Are you trying to tell me you're not?" She was easily as focused on her career as he was on his projects.

She looked away toward the water, her expression pensive. "I suppose I am when it comes to my job."

"But not when it comes to being a woman," he guessed, remembering his initial impression of her.

Her laugh was almost brittle. "No, not when it comes to being a woman, but then I'm much better at being a junior executive than I am at being female." The last words came out in such a low voice he had to strain to hear them.

"You don't think you're any good at being female?" he asked for confirmation because he found the idea so laughable. If she were any better at it, he'd need a straitjacket to keep his hands off her.

She whirled to face him, her dark brown eyes shooting sparks like a metal cup in the microwave. "Stop it. I know what I am. And while we're at it, you can quit making those stupid comments about my supposed beauty. I know what I look like, all right? I don't need you patronizing me with false flattery or your sarcastic little jokes about wanting to have sex with me." She sucked in air, drawing his attention to the charms she was so certain she did not have.

"We've got a business relationship. That's all. I don't need you to pretend like you notice me as a woman when you don't. Heaven knows I'm used to it."

"Used to what?" The conversation was not falling into any sort of logical pattern he could recognize.

"Used to being seen as my job rather than myself." She closed her eyes and seemed to battle for control before opening them again. "It's not important. I don't need you to see me as a woman. I'm here to do a job, nothing else."

He had never said otherwise. He might have thought it, but he hadn't said it. "Are you trying to convince me, or yourself?"

Unexpectedly, her eyes filled with tears, their brown depths awash with pain as well as wetness and he felt like a total bastard for having hurt her. He hadn't meant to. All he wanted was to understand what was going on inside her mind right now. He wanted to know why she had left without a word to him, why she had been so adamant about not coming back.

"I need to go." She turned back toward the house.

He could no more let her dismiss him right now than he had been able to leave her in the grocery store and his hand shot out to grab her shoulder. "Wait. I don't understand, baby. I didn't mean to hurt you with that question."

"Don't call me baby," she said in a choked voice without turning to face him.

He hadn't realized he had. It fit her though. So tiny. So vulnerable in ways others probably wouldn't notice. "It suits you."

She shook her head, her long hair swinging against her petite back.

Taking her other shoulder in his free hand, he

started pulling her back toward him. He didn't know what he planned. To comfort her, maybe, but as soon as her body was flush with his the idea of comfort took on a very intimate connotation.

He wrapped his arms around her front, locking them right under her breasts and nuzzled her shell-pink ear. He couldn't seem to help himself. Touching her seemed both natural and right.

She was in pain and he wanted to make it better. "I don't want you to hurt, Amanda. Tell me what I can do to make it go away."

She'd gone completely still in his arms. He wasn't sure she was even breathing.

"Amanda?"

"You don't want me any more than he did." The words were filled with so much pain, he winced.

He ignored her ludicrous assertion that he didn't want her. If she couldn't feel the erection growing against her back, he wasn't going to point it out to her and scare her half to death.

But the other part of what she said intrigued him. "Who didn't want you?"

"Lance."

"Your ex-husband?" he guessed.

She nodded, causing her ear to brush against his lips, making them tingle. She gave a convulsive shudder.

"Are you crying?" He didn't know what to do with a crying woman, but somehow he couldn't just leave Amanda to her misery, whatever the cause.

"No." The broken syllable gave lie to her word, but he didn't tax her with it.

"Tell me about Lance," he said instead.

"I told you." She sounded belligerent. "He didn't want me."

Zebra Contemporary

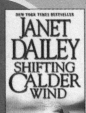

Whatever your taste in contemporary romance – Romantic Suspense … Character-Driven … Light and Whimsical … Heartwarming … Humorous – we have it at Zebra!

And now Zebra has created a Book Club for readers like yourself who enjoy fine Contemporary Romance written by today's best-selling authors.

Authors like Fern Michaels…Lori Foster… Janet Dailey…Lisa Jackson…Janelle Taylor… Kasey Michaels… Shannon Drake… Kat Martin… to name but a few!

These are the finest contemporary romances available anywhere today!

But don't take our word for it! Accept our gift of FREE Zebra Contemporary Romances – and see for yourself. You only pay $1.99 for shipping and handling.

Once you've read them, we're sure you'll want to continue receiving the newest Zebra Contemporaries as soon as they're published each month! And you can by becoming a member of the Zebra Contemporary Romance Book Club!

As a member of Zebra Contemporary Romance Book Club,

- You'll receive four books every month. Each book will be by one of Zebra's best-selling authors.

- You'll have variety – you'll never receive two of the same kind of story in one month.

- You'll get your books hot off the press, usually before they appear in bookstores.

- You'll ALWAYS save up to 30% off the cover price.

SEND FOR YOUR FREE BOOKS TODAY!

To start your membership, simply complete and return the Free Book Certificate. You'll receive your Introductory Shipment of FREE Zebra Contemporary Romances, you only pay $1.99 for shipping and handling. Then, each month you will receive the 4 newest Zebra Contemporary Romances. Each shipment will be yours to examine FREE for 10 days. If you decide to keep the books, you'll pay the preferred subscriber price (a savings of up to 30% off the cover price), plus shipping and handling. If you want us to stop sending books, just say the word… it's that simple.

FREE BOOK CERTIFICATE

Yes! Please send me FREE Zebra Contemporary romance novels. I only pay $1.99 for shipping and handling. I understand that each month thereafter I will be able to preview 4 brand-new Contemporary Romances FREE for 10 days. Then, if I should decide to keep them, I will pay the money-saving preferred subscriber's price (that's a savings of up to 30% off the retail price), plus shipping and handling. I understand I am under no obligation to purchase any books, as explained on this card.

Name _____

Address _____ Apt. _____

City _____ State _____ Zip _____

Telephone (___) _____

Signature _____

(If under 18, parent or guardian must sign)

Thank You!

Offer limited to one per household and not to current subscribers. Terms, offer and prices subject to change. Orders subject to acceptance by Zebra Contemporary Book Club. Offer Valid in the U.S. only.

CN065A

THE BENEFITS OF BOOK CLUB MEMBERSHIP

- You'll get your books hot off the press, usually before they appear in bookstores.
- You'll ALWAYS save up to 30% off the cover price.
- You'll get our FREE monthly newsletter filled with author interviews, book previews, special offers and MORE!
- There's no obligation — you can cancel at any time and you have no minimum number of books to buy.
- And—if you decide you don't like the books you receive, you can return them. (You always have ten days to decide.)

llₐₗₐ.llllₐₐ.llₗlₗₗₗ.ₗlₐ.ₐlₐ.ₗₐ.ll.ₐl.ₐₗₐ.llₐ.ₗlll.ₗll.ₐl

Zebra Contemporary Romance Book Club

Zebra Home Subscription Service, Inc.

P.O. Box 5214

Clifton , NJ 07015-5214

PLACE
STAMP
HERE

Chapter 11

"But he was your husband."

"Yes."

For some reason hearing her affirm it made his gut tighten uncomfortably. He hated the thought of any other man having claim to this woman.

She exhaled on a broken sigh. "And he did everything in his power to mold me into someone he could desire. It didn't work."

What kind of eunuch idiot would want to change her? She was sexy, beautiful and perfect just as she was. "What? Was he gay?"

Her laugh was so far from humorous, it hurt to hear it. "No. He just couldn't force himself to make love with such an inadequate woman."

"You believed that bullshit? That you were inadequate as a woman?" He knew he sounded angry.

He was. Furious, in fact. If Lance were within kicking distance, he'd be bruised and bloody right now. While the image gave him some satisfaction, he knew it wouldn't do anything to help the misery he sensed in Amanda right now. He didn't know what would.

She tore out of his arms and whirled on him, her expression feral. "Yes, I believed him! Why shouldn't I? You don't want me either! You made that obvious."

"When have I made that obvious?" He'd told her he wanted to have sex with her. Did she think he made a habit of lying?

"Oh, please! Like you don't know."

Her sarcastic words were the last straw and he stormed forward. She backed up, but he caught her with no real effort. They'd have to work on her fighting technique when an adversary had her cornered.

He grabbed her wrist, careful not to bruise her pale flesh, but with a grip she wouldn't be able to get out of easily, and pulled her forward. In a crude act that shocked him even while he was doing it, he placed her small hand against the much larger, irrefutable proof that she was wrong.

"Feel that? I don't walk around with a lead pipe in my jeans, so what do you think that tells you about how much I want you?" He let go of her wrist prepared to take a slap in the face for what he'd done. Or worse.

She didn't slap him, or kick him, or even scream at him. She didn't jerk her hand away either. Instead she pressed her open palm against his erection and stroked its length. His knees almost buckled.

Her tear drenched gaze lifted to his, her expression filled with wonder. "You meant it."

He couldn't make his voice work, not with her hand still pressed against his sex. So, he nodded, but still could not comprehend why she acted so shocked by his arousal.

Her fingers convulsed, squeezing him and his eyes slid shut at the pleasure of it. "If you don't stop, I'm going to take you right here, in front of God, Jacob, and the seagulls."

* * *

It wasn't the mention of God or the seagulls that did it, but when he said Jacob's name, Amanda forced her hand away from the physical evidence of Simon's arousal.

She felt exultant, like she'd just landed the deal of her career. Simon wanted her and he meant it. There could be no mistaking it this time. A man could not fake an erection, or get one on command. Lance had made sure she knew that. To get hard, a man had to be aroused and Simon was. Very aroused.

She wanted to shout hosannas.

He pulled her against him, letting her feel the hard length of his erection against her stomach. It was an incredible heady sensation and one she had never had before, this standing fully clothed against a man in a state of obvious sexual excitement.

His arms wrapped tightly around her. "You're so sexy. It's all I've been able to do not to lay you down in my bed and keep you there for three days straight."

Bliss shivered through her at the thought. "So, why haven't you?" she asked into his chest with no thought of being coy or playing hard to get entering her mind.

He rubbed himself against her, his hands pressing into the small of her back to increase the friction between them. "I didn't want to cloud our relationship."

"You mean because of the merger?" Remembering Daniel's crude advice for how to get Simon to agree to the proposal, she had to admit Simon had a point if that had been his concern.

"That, and the fact your life is in Southern California and mine is here."

This evidence that casual sex did not interest him warmed her, but depressed her too. Because nothing could change the fact that their lives were lived in entirely different spheres.

"There's still the merger," she said aloud. "We're business associates, not lovers." Melancholy settled over her as she said the words. Simon might want her, but not enough to overcome the issues holding them apart.

His chin dropped against the top of her head and rested there. "Yes."

Her heart lost its tenuous hold on a possible positive outcome and plummeted. "I guess that means making love would be a bad thing?" she couldn't help asking, even though she knew his answer before he gave it.

His heart sped up at her words, thumping loudly against his chest. With her face pressed against his sternum, she could feel it as well as hear it.

"Depends on how you define bad." One big hand slid down to cup her bottom. "My definition of the word is changing with the speed of a sonic jet."

He had such a sexy voice. She bet he could talk her to an orgasm if he put his mind to it. Just the thought had her growing damp and hot between her legs. "It is?" she asked in an embarrassing croak.

The hand on her bottom squeezed. "Oh, yeah."

She heard his words, but her attention had been caught by his scent. She found herself nuzzling the denim work shirt stretched across his impressive chest muscles. Lance had never smelled like this. No other man in the world had Simon's scent. It was unique and it was intoxicating.

Her fingers lifted of their own volition and started undoing buttons. She wanted skin.

His arms tightened around her. "Keep that up and *bad idea* is going to lose all meaning for me."

She undid two more buttons for good measure and then kissed the bronzed chest she had just exposed. "Really?" She wanted to taste him. Almost insanely and with a complete lack of her normal sexual reticence, she flicked her tongue out and licked delicately. Salty. Warm. She licked again. Sort of spicy.

His big body shuddered.

For the second time that day she found herself being swept up into his arms.

"*Simon!* What are you doing?"

Had she pushed him too far? Would he make good on his threat to make love to her outside? The thought intrigued her far more than it worried her. To have the ability to push her lover beyond his normal bounds of control was something she had never experienced.

She'd read about it though, and it sounded like a lot of fun, if incredibly far-fetched.

His laughter sent sensual shivers arcing through her. "I'm carrying you off to my lair to have my wicked way with you." Suiting action to words, he started making ground-eating strides across the lawn toward the house. "To the victor go the spoils, or some such thing and I did capture you this morning."

"You kidnapped me!"

He shrugged and she clung to his neck, not wanting to fall.

"Same thing," he said.

"Are you saying you see yourself as some kind of conquering warrior?"

He smiled down at her, his eyes full of sensual heat. "You make an incredibly sexy and beautiful captive."

A warrior? She had no problem seeing Simon in the role. He'd struck her as innately dangerous since the moment they'd met. It was only now she was coming to appreciate the true nature of the danger involved. He had the power to stir her emotions in a way no other man ever had, not her few boyfriends and not even her ex-husband.

But her, sexy and beautiful? Now that was a lot harder for her to wrap her imagination around.

Not so *captive.* Ooh . . . she liked that word. After the sexual debacle of her marriage, she was ready to indulge in a decadent fantasy. It might be the only chance she'd ever have. If she disappointed Simon in bed like she had Lance, he wasn't going to play conquering warrior for her again.

She shoved the depressing thought away. No matter what happened in the aftermath, for right now, Simon wanted her. So much, he was *carrying* her off to bed.

"I'm too heavy to cart all the way to the house and up two flights of stairs." It was a half-hearted protest because she found the experience so delightful, but she felt it had to be made.

"Be quiet, captive." His voice came out in a disconcerting predatory growl. "None of your arguments will gain you freedom." His hold on her tightened. "You're mine now."

It was just a game, but it seemed like there was an element of real warning in Simon's voice. She dismissed the thought as fanciful. *She was really getting into her role of captive.*

"Fighting would be a waste of effort," she agreed, burying her face against him. She inhaled more of his scent, absorbing his essence skin to skin.

If she was dreaming, she'd kill the sleep police if they woke her up before Simon made love to her.

Simon's heart was trying to pound out of his chest as he laid Amanda down on his oversize bed. She looked so incredibly small laying there, her beautiful skin flushed with arousal, her eyes dark pools of sensual promise.

He started reefing off his clothes, stopping when all he had on was a pair of unbuttoned jeans. He didn't take them off. Not yet. He wanted her a lot more excited before he bared himself to her. He would expire from unsatisfied desire if she bolted after seeing his full erection. And it was *fully erect*, so hard it ached and pulsed with a need only this tiny woman could satisfy.

She hadn't taken anything off.

"If you don't undress, I'll rip your clothes off your body," he said in his conquering warrior persona, but only half-joking. He wanted her so much that if he tried undressing her, that cute little cotton top would probably end up without any buttons left.

Those startled doe eyes looked at him, doubt lurking in their depths. "You want me to take off my clothes?" She sounded just like a nervous virgin.

Another shot of desire surged through him. He didn't know how much longer he could keep up the game. He'd started it on a whim, sensing a need to put their lovemaking on a less intense level for Amanda, but far from lessening the tension, the role-playing was increasing it. At least for him.

He mock-glared at her and started toward the bed. "Yes."

Something shifted in her expression and she scrambled to her knees, her hands on the buttons of her blouse. Her eyes questioned him.

"Take it off." Was that guttural voice his? He sounded like a primal male intent on subduing his mate.

Her fingers trembled, but she undid the top button.

He didn't want to scare her. Stopping at the

edge of the bed, he reached out and covered her hands with his. "The game doesn't matter, sweetheart. I just want you."

She swallowed. "I, um . . ."

He slipped his fingers under hers and undid the next button, exposing the top of her generous cleavage. He couldn't help himself. "What?"

She cleared her throat. "Simon?"

"I'm right here, baby." He liked calling her that, he decided.

"Could we, um . . ."

He put his knee down on the bed and loomed over her, slipping the third button out of its hole and giving himself a view of creamy white mounds. She wasn't wearing a bra and for some reason that knowledge upped his excitement ten more notches. He had every intention of seeing her fully naked before long, but there was something about knowing that thin cotton was all that stood between him and her magnificent breasts.

She took a deep breath, pressing soft flesh against the back of his fingers. "Oh!" She blinked her big, brown eyes at him.

He smiled and lowered his head until their lips were a centimeter away from meeting. "Could we what, sweetheart?"

"I want to play."

"I want to play too." And he wanted to play for a very long time. He kissed her, nibbling at that delicious bottom lip that had tantalized him with its fullness earlier.

She tasted so good, better than he'd fantasized. Her mouth was sweet and warm and he explored all of it, starting with her lips and then moving with gentle forays into the interior. Her tongue was shy, but when she let it slide along his, fireworks exploded in his head.

They stayed like that for endless minutes, her shirt half undone, his hands buried in her hair and their mouths molded together like two halves of a work of art by one of the great masters.

Finally, he pulled back. He wanted to finish the job of undressing the treasure in his arms. "Is that the way you wanted to play?" he teased as he undid the final three buttons in quick succession.

Her hands grabbed his wrists before he could peel the fabric back and expose her flesh to his hungry gaze. "I mean I *want* to play conquering warrior and captive." She said it all in a rush and then blushed crimson.

He'd never seen a woman do that before, but Amanda's cheeks were as red as a ripe apple.

He let the pads of his thumbs caress the inner curves of her breasts. "You want to keep pretending to be my captive?"

Did she have any idea what the scenario was doing to him?

Amanda nodded, terrified of how he'd respond to her request. What if he didn't want to keep up the pretense? She might annoy him with her silliness, but she'd thought that if she could get him to play the game, he would be in charge. He wouldn't expect her to *do* anything. After all, a captive wasn't required to seduce her captor.

Simon might even mistake her sexual ineptness as an attempt to play inexperienced virgin. It would be his job to seduce her and then maybe she wouldn't mess everything up.

His hands slid inside the opened edges of her top and cupped both her breasts, sending her heart into her throat. "You make a very alluring captive, Amanda."

"I do?" she choked out.

"Oh, yes." His hands squeezed and she felt her

pebble-hard nipples brush against the hard skin of his palms.

She moaned.

"You may be a virgin, but you cannot pretend you do not want me." Heavens, he really sounded like the conquering warrior now.

Her hands were still on his wrists, but she wasn't trying to stop him from caressing her intimate flesh. She wanted it so much. "Yes, I want you," she said, giving him the words.

Then he kissed her, not gently and tentatively like he'd done before, but with all the passion she'd dreamed of sparking in her lover. His mouth claimed hers with a marauder's skill and she went under without a count.

Her sensory universe shrank to include only this man. His taste. His smell. The way it felt to have his mouth sucking at hers, his tongue invading her mouth. She let her hands slide along his arms and up to his chest, touching him like she had craved doing that first Tae Kwon Do sparring session when he had teased her with his naked torso.

His skin was smooth over rock-hard muscles and she brushed the fan of silken black hair on his chest with her fingertips. She was glad he wasn't hairy all over. She much preferred the velvety expanse of his skin, so warm, so vibrant.

Suddenly the hold on her breasts changed. He took each swollen bud between a thumb and forefinger and began to roll them. She screamed into his mouth, the feeling so electric her fingers dug into his pecs.

His mouth broke away from hers. "I've got to taste you, baby." Then he was tearing her top off and his hot mouth closed around one nipple.

He sucked.

She screamed again, the sound unmuffled and shocking to her.

He sucked harder and it became a pleasure this side of pain, but she would die if he stopped. *She knew she would die.* He started to play with her other breast again, using his fingers to torment the peak to a level of sensitivity she had never known.

She couldn't talk. She couldn't even beg. All she could do was make incoherent noises with her mouth while the pleasurable tension inside her coiled tighter and tighter. She felt like a spring, ready to snap, but there was no letup of the pressure. She couldn't stand it. It was too much!

She tried to pull away, but only succeeded in falling backward on the bed, Simon still in possession of her sensitized flesh. He used his knee to push her legs apart and then settled between them, his big body pressed against the heart of her.

She could no more help arching her pelvis toward him than she could stop the feelings shooting straight from her nipples to the core of her femininity.

She reached her hands above her head, needing something to hold onto as the maelstrom of sensations threatened to overwhelm her. Her fingers encountered the bars of the bed. She grabbed them, her whole body tensing as Simon ground the hard muscles of his stomach against the throbbing flesh between her legs.

He released her nipple with a pop and air rushed against the wet, engorged tip. His head came up and his gunmetal gaze raked over her, his eyes narrowing when he saw where her hands were.

He seemed mesmerized by the sight of her fingers clinging to his headboard. "Good idea."

"What do you mean?" Her voice came out in a husky whisper, which was all she could manage at that point.

"A captive should be restrained, don't you think? So she can't run away."

Simon almost laughed at the look that crossed Amanda's face at his suggestion, but he wasn't capable of laughter right then. He was barely capable of speech. He wanted to bury himself between her legs, to feel the liquid heat of her swollen lips and blood-engorged tissues surrounding him.

"You want to tie me to the bed?" she asked, her voice squeaking like Minnie Mouse.

He cupped her tip-tilted, luxuriant breasts and squeezed them together, then buried his mouth against the nipples he'd pressed so near one another. "Yes."

She was silent for so long, he thought she was going to say *no*. He laved the sweet reddened berries with his tongue, totally willing to let the game go if that was what she wanted. He needed her, her body, her generous and giving passion. Her. Nothing more. Nothing less.

"All right."

His head shot up and he looked into doe-brown eyes glazed with desire.

"You can tie my hands to the bed."

He felt a spurt of pre-ejaculate come. Not at the thought of tying his lover up, but at the knowledge she trusted him enough with her body to let him do it.

He came up on his knees and straddled her right over the apex of her thighs. Her breath heaved in and out, making her flushed and excited flesh quiver.

If he didn't need to be inside her so bad, he could watch her just breathe all night. He traced the smooth skin of her abdomen with one fingertip. "Baby, you are beautiful."

"I'm not."

Anger equal to his passion coursed through

him. "You are, and you can damn well stop accusing me of lying. You're the prettiest, sexiest, most incredible woman I have ever known and if you try to deny it again, I'll gag you."

She laughed, the sound almost as beautiful as she was. "You can't gag me because then we couldn't kiss."

She had a point. "Then I'll just have to kiss you silent."

Her mouth curved in a Mona Lisa smile. "Is that supposed to encourage me to be good . . . or bad?"

He groaned. "Minx."

Leaning over her, he reached for the nightstand drawer and slid it open. The box of condoms Jacob had presented Simon with the day after catching Amanda sleeping in his arms winked up at him, but it was the antistatic straps he had stashed there at some point that interested him at the moment. Their soft composition and Velcro fastening made them ideal for what he had in mind.

Pulling two out, he sat back up, grunting as the movement caused his iron-hard flesh to brush against her mound in a way guaranteed to drive him crazy. He wanted to get her pants off and see that place reserved just for him.

She stared at the EST straps in his hands, then looked up at him and smiled such a sweet smile he had to lean down and kiss her.

Amanda reveled under the onslaught of Simon's kiss. She was so close to orgasm that one more movement down there and she was going to go off like a model rocket on a short fuse. He had no idea how tantalizing she found the prospect of having her hands bound. If she couldn't touch him, she couldn't mess up touching him. It was a win-win scenario for her.

And he was so good at this touching thing. He

ground himself against her and she felt herself right on the verge of ecstasy, but she needed more, just a little more.

She pressed against him with herself, spreading her legs wider to increase the friction between their bodies. Rotating her hips in a circle, she fought frantically for that final touch that would make the explosion nuclear.

But, cruelly, he pulled away, moving his body so that no matter how she arched and twisted, she couldn't get the contact she needed.

She tore her lips from his. "Simon! Please, I need you to make me come. I'm so close," she whimpered.

His hands cupped her face. "Baby, I want to taste you. I want to touch you. I want some part of my body, and I don't care if it's my tongue, my finger or my sex, inside you when you come for me for the first time. Please."

She stared up at him, frustration warring with the undeniable need thickening his voice. His need and hers . . . to be desired that strongly . . . won. "All right."

He smiled and kissed her with obvious approval. Then she felt his fingers at work at each wrist and she found herself bound loosely to the bed. If she yanked or worked the bindings, she could get loose, but she didn't want to.

Then he climbed down her body until he could reach the button and zipper on her cotton Capri pants. He undid them and began to pull them off, taking her panties with them as they went. When he reached her feet, her tennies and socks came off too, leaving her completely naked and open to his gaze by the time he stood erect at the end of the bed.

She looked so vulnerable lying there, like she

expected him to find her lacking. Her expression of nervous worry was impossible to misinterpret.

He shook his head. "You are gorgeous." Dark brown curls hid the secrets of her femininity and he climbed back onto the bed so he could brush his fingers through the silky fluff.

Her eyes slid shut and she moaned as he pressed one fingertip between the plump lips. He sought out her clitoris and touched it. Just lightly. He didn't want her going off yet. She'd come so close earlier and he hadn't been lying when he said he intended to be inside her when it happened.

He wanted to taste her, to get her so mindless with pleasure that when he went to join their flesh, she wouldn't have enough wherewithal to get nervous about his size. He would never hurt her, but she wouldn't know that until after they'd made love, would she?

He told himself to stop worrying. She'd trusted him enough to play sexy games with him. She wasn't going to freak out when she saw his straining erection.

She arched off the bed, her body flushed with passion. "If you don't do something soon, I'm going to scream."

"You're going to scream all right, but it will be *because I'm doing something.*"

She gave a choked laugh that cut off when he pressed her silky thighs apart and buried his mouth against her wet and swollen flesh. She was slick and sweet and hot, so damn hot. He'd done this for other women, but he could never remember being as turned on by it as he was right now.

Every ripple of pleasure in her flesh echoed in his own.

Every sexy little moan brought a responsive groan from deep inside him.

And she tasted like every erotic fantasy he had ever had.

Her body writhed against him. "Simon, oh . . . ! That feels so good. I've never . . . Oh . . ."

He slipped his tongue inside and used his thumb to draw circles around her hardened clitoris. She went ballistic, screaming his name while pressing herself against his mouth with so much force he was afraid she'd hurt herself on his teeth.

"More!" she shouted.

And he gave her more. And more. And more. Until she was sobbing with pleasure. Until she was begging him to stop, her body convulsing and jerking with every slide of his tongue, every glide of his finger. *And more.* Until with a groan of utter abandonment, she went limp beneath him.

He kissed her labia softly, then the sweet spot he'd pleasured so unmercifully and then finally paid homage to it all with a gentle kiss on the very top of her mound.

She expelled a shuddering sigh.

He stood up and shucked out of his jeans and black knit boxers, the relief of letting his sex free an overwhelming pleasure in itself. He walked around the bed and dug a condom out of the drawer in the nightstand. It took two tries to rip open the foil packet because his hands were shaking. He finally got it on and turned to look at Amanda, ready to gauge her reaction to his size, but her eyes weren't even open. Her face wore the most blissful and sweet expression he'd ever seen, but tears ran unchecked down her temples.

Chapter 12

Oh, man. Was she okay?

Amanda felt a tentative fingertip trace the path of her tears and smiled.

"I didn't hurt you, did I?" He sounded so worried.

She didn't want him to worry, not when she was as close to Heaven as a woman could get and still be living. "No. It just feels so *good*." She forced heavy eyelids up and turned her head toward the sound of his voice.

He was beside her and leaning above her, propped up on one arm. "You're crying because it feels good?" His tone was one of disbelief.

"Yes." She looked deeply into his storm-gray eyes. "Thank you. That's the most beautiful experience I've ever had."

The worry cleared from his expression to be replaced by masculine arrogance. "There's more."

"Not possible."

That made him laugh. Low and husky, sending a skirl of pleasure through her when she thought all pleasure had been wrung from her body.

"Do you want me to release your arms?"

She thought about it. Everything had gone so well so far. He didn't seem disappointed and she'd experienced the most amazing sensations of her life. There was an old saying, "If it isn't broken, don't fix it." It definitely wasn't broken.

"No." Then she peeked at him to see if her answer had disappointed him, but he was already moving over her, pressing her legs apart with his muscular thighs.

He hooked her knees with his forearms, pulling them up, exposing her to him in a way she could not have stood with anyone else. "You wanted more, Amanda, and I'm going to give it to you."

She remembered screaming that at some point during him making love to her with his mouth. Unbelievably, renewed desire sparked to life inside her. She thought she'd been beyond arousal, so satiated her senses could not take in any more pleasure.

She'd been wrong.

At the first tender probe of the blunt tip of his erection, her thighs quivered and the engorged tissues of her feminine core sat up and took notice. He pressed himself inside her opening, stretching her and she felt her eyes widen. "Simon?"

The tentative way she said his name made something protective expand inside him. "What, sweetheart?"

"Are you awfully big?"

"I won't hurt you."

Her smile warmed him. "I know."

"Trust me." He pressed forward a little more and she sucked in air. "I'll be careful. We're going to fit just fine. We just need to take this part slow."

"I do trust you, Simon, but I don't know how slow I can stand for you to take it."

She still wanted him.

Relief had only a second to make itself felt, as sexual excitement vied for his attention and won. "I want to bury myself so deeply inside you that our pelvic bones touch."

Her inner flesh contracted at his words. "Oh, yes."

He rocked forward, gaining another full inch and making her moan. "You feel so good, so perfect for me."

She arched toward him, her fingers gripped around the bars of the headboard with white-knuckle intensity. "Stop playing, Simon. You said you wanted to go deep. I want all of you!"

He would have laughed at her demanding tone if he'd had enough breath. He moved again, gaining more, but she was so tight, he couldn't go farther. "Relax for me, baby. Please."

"How?" She sounded both bewildered and as on edge sexually as he felt.

How? He didn't know how. It was her body.

Some of his frustration must have shown on his face because her brows puckered and her lips trembled. "I'm sorry. I—"

He cut off her apology with his mouth. He didn't like hearing her apologizing when she was giving him so much pleasure. When she was once again straining beneath him, he lifted his head. "Can you tighten your inner muscles?"

"I think so." The flesh around him squeezed and he groaned. Okay, she could definitely tighten them.

"Now, try reversing that."

Her face took on the most endearing expression of concentration. He didn't think another woman had ever been so concerned about getting it right for him. And she did get it right, all at once the pressure around him relaxed and she spread her thighs wider. He'd been afraid to press her legs that far apart, but she was incredibly limber.

Hell, she was plain incredible. He rocked into her, finishing the penetration easily now. And then he was where he had most wanted to be, sheathed by her wet, swollen tissues, his sex throbbing from the pleasure her body gave him.

Her entire body went stiff and her gorgeous brown eyes flew wide with shock. "Simon?!"

Had he gone in too far? He'd promised not to hurt her.

Her inner muscles contracted around him again and she shuddered. "So good," she panted, and he relaxed.

Oh yeah, it felt good all right. It felt better than anything he'd ever known and he stayed perfectly still savoring the completeness of their joining. He'd been right. She fit him like her body had been made to accommodate his.

As he strained the limits of his self-control by remaining immobile, he could feel sweat soaking his back and muscle burn like he'd been doing a major workout.

"Move, Simon!" She squirmed under him, but she couldn't do much with her knees hooked over his forearms and her hands tied. She glared up at him. "Don't tease me."

"I'm not teasing you, baby. I'm enjoying you."

"Please move. Please, oh please, oh please . . ."

The begging did it.

He moved. Pulling out until only the head of his sex remained in her warmth, he then surged deep with one thrust . . . two . . . three . . . and suddenly her hot, wet flesh was pulsating around him in release. She screamed, she cried, she writhed and then she demanded more again. He let go of her legs to reach between their bodies and massage her sweet spot with his thumb.

She convulsed again, her body going so taut, she lifted them both up off the bed. He went over the brink, his raw shout joining with her uncontrolled whimpers of surrender and ecstasy. They strained together for endless moments of shared rapture before she collapsed back on the bed.

He went with her, his body feeling boneless. With the last bit of strength he had, he reached above them and undid the restraints on her wrists.

"I don't think I can move them."

His head came up at her ruefully uttered words. She didn't look upset, so he didn't think she meant he'd hurt her.

Her eyes slid shut. "I want to hold you," she whispered on a yawn, "but I can't seem to make my arms work."

He discovered that with the right incentive, he had reserves of energy he had not known he possessed. Reaching up, he grasped her wrists and pulled her arms gently down. When he placed them on his shoulders, she linked her hands behind his neck and hugged him to her.

It felt good.

She kissed his collarbone. "I like this."

He sighed with pleasure. "Me too."

He was still erect inside her, his orgasm having exhausted him, but going nowhere toward slaking the desire she engendered in his flesh.

"Thank you, Simon."

He pulled back so he could see the sweet contours of her heart-shaped face. "*Thank you.* I've never had it so good," he admitted truthfully.

Hershey brown eyes widened, glistening with suspicious moisture. "Really?"

He kissed her. "Really."

"Me neither."

For some reason that admission made him feel ten feet tall. "You liked making love with a conquering warrior, huh?"

"I adored making love with *you*." Her fingers

speared through his hair and she nuzzled his chest. "I've never climaxed before."

The words were muffled and whispered sort of low, so at first he doubted he'd heard her correctly. "Did you just say you'd never come before?"

"Yes." She wouldn't look at him.

He tilted her chin up with his free hand. "Say that again."

She shook her head. "You heard me."

"But you're so responsive!"

She attempted a shrug, but it didn't work very well with his bulk on top of her. "I never have been before."

He liked hearing that. He didn't care if it was a totally non-PC attitude to have, but he felt like a true conqueror at her halting admission. Definitely non-PC. "You mean you've never had an orgasm with a man," he said for clarification.

"Did I say that?" she asked, turning her face from his scrutiny.

"No." But the alternative was unthinkable. She was twenty-seven years old, or so Jacob had informed him after the initial security check. She was divorced. She couldn't be that innocent. He felt like he'd just made love to a virgin. "But, baby, there are things . . ."

She glared up at him. "I didn't feel comfortable trying *things*, alright? If it bothers you, I'm sorry. I just thought you might like to know."

Hell. He had offended her. "Shh." He kissed her until all the tension that had been seeping into her limbs eased away. "It doesn't bother me. It surprised me. That's all. You are the most sensual woman I have ever been with, but I'd have to be a fool not to like knowing you had your first climax with me."

Her smile was a little watery. "I guess that means you won't mind trying it again sometime."

They were still intimately connected, he could feel her soft wetness clinging to him and she was talking about *sometime* as if what they were sharing right now was over. He stared down at her. Did she think this had been some casual sexual encounter, like sharing a really decadent dessert that they both might want to taste again, but nothing serious?

The hell with that.

But all he said was, "Sure." If his tone was a little surly, she'd have to forgive him. "Sometime" could mean anything from the next time she was in Washington to the next five minutes. He knew exactly which *sometime* he intended to make happen and it wasn't some nebulous date in the future.

But first there was something he had to do.

He carefully withdrew from her body and rolled away from her. He stood up and turned away from her in pretty much the same motion, still a little leery about her seeing him in all his aroused glory. It was getting more *glorious* by the second as he contemplated how best to seduce the pocket Venus in his bed all over again.

Amanda watched Simon walk into the bathroom in a state of confusion. He'd sounded angry. Had her question made him mad? Maybe she was clinging. For all she knew, this was a one-off deal for Simon. They hadn't said anything about the future. He might want to go back to business as usual.

Maybe once had been enough for him.

He'd said she was the most sensual woman he'd ever been with, but she knew that wasn't true. Couldn't be true. She was about as sensual as a Raggedy Ann doll, but she *had* satisfied him. She knew she had. His release had been every bit as loud and wild as her own.

So, why had he vacated the bed so quickly?

Maybe she had *disappointed* him in some way.

Was she supposed to get dressed and leave while he was in the bathroom? She didn't know the protocol for this sort of thing. She felt lethargic from the surfeit of pleasure he'd given her, but she didn't think he'd appreciate coming back to find she had crawled beneath the sheets and gone to sleep in his bed. She wasn't even sure he'd want to come out and find her in the room at all.

Cold seeped into her where the heat of passion had burned so brightly just minutes ago.

She heard the sound of water running, but it wasn't followed by the distinctive patter of a shower.

What was he doing?

She sat up and scanned the room, looking for her clothes. She could see one tennis shoe over by the door, a sock on the chair by the bed and what looked like her pants in a heap of cotton on the bottom corner of the huge mattress. She got up on her knees and crawled across the bed to retrieve her pants.

When she reached them, she spied her top on the floor about a foot from the bed. She leaned over and reached for it.

"Nice view."

Realizing exactly what he was seeing, her naked backside up in the air, she screeched and scrambled back onto the bed. She turned on her knees to face him. He looked amused, darn him.

Just once she'd like the naked view of her body to inspire uncontrollable desire. Not contempt. Not humor. Passion. Right. That was going to happen in this lifetime, not.

Her top was still on the floor, so she grabbed up her pants and held them in front of her in an attempt at modesty. They'd made love on top of the covers, leaving her nothing to hide behind. The thought of Simon looking at her naked body and noticing her deficiencies made her cringe.

"I thought you were going to take a shower."

But he hadn't. He'd come back wearing nothing but a towel slung low on his hips.

"You look very good sitting in my bed, Amanda." He walked over to the bed. "But you will look even better in my bath."

He reached out and tugged at her pants. "You don't need these right now."

"I . . ."

He managed to prise the meager cotton barrier to her nudity from her tight grip. He tossed the Capris on the floor where they landed almost on top of her shirt.

"They're going to get wrinkled all wadded up like that."

"Jacob can iron them for you." With that, he scooped her up in his strong arms.

"This is becoming a habit with you," she said breathlessly as naked skin met hot, naked skin.

His answering smile was that of a buccaneer who had appropriated a cargo hold full of bounty. "You're such a tiny thing, all my primitive instincts come out. Do you mind?"

"No." Actually, she kind of liked it.

But *tiny*? She supposed compared to his six feet, two inches, her five-foot-four seemed small, but still . . . tiny?

"I wear a thirty-four D cup bra," she said, stating the obvious, "and I bet I wear the same size all the time that your cousin's wife," *the woman he'd cared enough about to want to marry*, "wears pregnant."

"Yeah. You're perfect, but so small it scares me a little. I'm really lucky your passion makes up for your size."

Were they talking about the same body? Had he heard a word she had said? Her mother had been after her to go for a breast reduction since she'd finished developing. Lance had joined her mother's urgings, but she had refused. She'd never had surgery and frankly the idea of having such an operation had scared her.

"You really think I'm perfect?" she couldn't help asking.

He stared at her like she'd lost her mind. "You have a luscious body, sweetheart. But I'm not telling you anything you don't already know. Other men must have told you the same thing, ad nauseum."

If she admitted they hadn't, would that lessen her in Simon's eyes? She shrugged noncommittally, not saying anything else until they arrived at Simon's bathtub. It looked more like a small Jacuzzi to her. There was definitely room for two and it occurred to her that Simon meant to take advantage of that fact.

"We're taking a bath together?" Was that squeaky voice hers?

His answer was to step with her into the swirling water.

Simon had come into the bathroom to take care of the condom when the sight of his oversize, jetted tub had given him an idea for his "captive's" next seduction. He'd never bathed with a woman. He'd taken showers with lovers, but never a bath.

She'd had her first orgasm with him. He decided he would take his first coed bath with her.

She made no move to slide off his lap once their bodies were immersed in the hot, scented water. He'd tossed in some aromatherapy bath salts one of his cousins in Arizona had sent him for Christmas. It smelled pretty nice. He hoped Amanda thought so too. Besides it had an oil base, turning the water into an all-over body lubricant.

He cupped one of her D-cup breasts, smiling at how she had admitted to her bra size like it was a crime. Was she really that ignorant of a man's desires that she didn't realize his reaction to her generous curves would be *anything but* revulsion?

She circled one of his masculine nipples with a forefinger, making his sex bob in the water beside her hip.

"This is kind of fun, isn't it?" she asked.

Cupping his hand, he scooped up some water and let it trickle over swollen peaks the color of ripe raspberries. "Fun is a pretty tame word for what I feel right now, Amanda."

She laughed, the sound exultant. "Oh, Simon."

He palmed her cheek, angling her head for his kiss. Her lips were pliant and warm. As he played with the ripened flesh of her breasts, she opened her mouth with a purring sound and he took instant advantage of the chance to taste her again. *So sweet.* He could never get enough of her mouth.

She sucked on his tongue while kneading the muscles of his chest like a cat and he felt like exploding right then. He put up with the torment of her mouth for as long as he could before he knew that, one more second, and he would come without even having her touch his arousal.

Tearing his mouth from hers, he broke the kiss to suckle the rapid pulse at the base of her throat.

"That feels so good," she groaned, letting her head fall back. "Simon, everything you do to me feels good." She sounded really surprised by that fact.

Maybe she was. She'd been married, but never had a climax. Her husband had to have been a lousy lover because she was amazingly responsive.

She wiggled her bottom against him, but didn't make a move to bring her body into contact with his hardened flesh. He couldn't stand that kind of teasing. Not this time. Maybe never. This woman affected him in ways he would earlier have denied were possible.

He reached down and grabbed her hips, turning her toward him and letting her float in the water just long enough to separate her legs. When he pulled her back onto his lap he made sure she was straddling him.

Her head came up and she stared at him, her eyes glazed with passion. "Simon?"

"I want to feel your sweetness against me, baby."

"Oh, yes." But she didn't move.

Too impatient to wait, he pressed against her tailbone and her bath oil slickened thighs slid along his until their bodies met. He shuddered. So did she.

He adjusted her until her swollen outer labia were lined up with his erection, then he reached around and gently separated the lips. He arched up so his sex pressed against her most sensitive flesh. "Pleasure us, sweetheart."

She made a broken sound. "How?"

Grabbing her bottom with both hands, he slid her up the length of his erection, pressing in when her hardened clitoris was aligned with the mass of nerve endings near the tip. Then he slid her down again until her labia met his sacs.

Her mouth formed a surprised little *O* that he just had to kiss. "Ride me."

"But you aren't inside me."

Never having taken a bath with a woman before, he didn't know how well a condom worked in that environment. He also didn't have the patience to find out. "This will be good, trust me."

She must have because she started moving against

him, doing a little circular motion every time her sweet spot met the ridge at the broad tip of his arousal.

"This is so amazing. I can feel bubbles in my . . ."

"Do you like it?" he asked as he moved his hand around so his fingers could play where the bubbles had found their way.

"Oh . . . Oh . . . Yesss . . . . I like it."

Her movements were voluptuous and he was glad they'd already made love. He wanted this to last. And it did.

She rode him for a long time while wave after wave of pleasure washed over him with the oil-slick water. Eventually, her movements grew more frantic until she stiffened against him, crying out his name as her body convulsed in what felt like a never ending orgasm.

He came then, too. Shooting into the water. The sensual feel of the bubbling wetness all around him increased the intensity and his orgasm lasted longer than any he had ever had. When it was over, his head fell back against the rest and he closed his eyes. Amanda sank against his chest like a wilted flower and he hugged her to him.

She kissed his chest and he felt that tender salute to the bottom of his soul.

Amanda woke up to the disorienting sensation of being surrounded by living heat. Then she remembered. She was in Simon's bed, in his arms. His quite naked arms. It was almost identical to the time she'd fallen asleep waiting for him to relax his hold on her. His hand was on her breast, hers was against his chest, and their legs were entwined.

Only this time, she knew she belonged.

He'd pulled her into his bed after their bath

without giving her the option of returning to her own room.

She hadn't minded.

Given her druthers, she'd never leave Simon's bed again.

She allowed herself a small smile at that bit of fantasy. She could just see Jacob bringing them the necessary provisions while they pursued a life of debauchery, never leaving the haven of Simon's bedroom.

It didn't feel like debauchery when their bodies were joined, though. It felt spiritual. Did Simon experience the same thing? She had no way of knowing. She'd been a virgin with little heavy petting experience when she'd married Lance and she'd never had sex with another man. Until now.

It felt funny, knowing they weren't married.

She supposed in that way too, she was anachronistic. Even feeling odd about it though, she wasn't going to walk away from her first experience with real passion. Because something had hit her about halfway through their decadent bath. It wasn't just a matter of passion, but of love.

She was in love with Simon Brant. Really in love. It was only as the overwhelming emotions coursed through her that she accepted that the lukewarm feelings she had had for Lance had been as much to do with seeking her family's approval, as they had to do with any sort of attraction she'd had for the smooth manipulator.

What she felt for Simon was so elemental, it was scary. The thought of him with another woman made her sick and she could not imagine ever letting another man touch her the way Simon had touched her. She wasn't naïve enough to think Simon was considering a long-term commitment to her, but that didn't alter the way she felt.

He'd told her one of his objections to getting involved was the fact their lives did not mesh. Which said to her that he wasn't looking for ways to make them mesh.

Because of her past, she wasn't sure that even if he did want a permanent future with her, she could pursue it. The thought of being married again terrified her. Men changed after marriage. Lance had been complimentary and charming, right up until the honeymoon.

The little digs had started on their wedding night.

Rationally, she knew Simon wasn't another Lance. However, emotions weren't always rational and hers were scarred.

Was she selfish and wicked for wanting to take all she could of Simon, to replace the memories of a devastating failure of a marriage with the amazing beauty of Simon's lovemaking?

Simon stirred, his eyes flicked open and for several seconds they just stared at each other.

"What time is it?"

She went up on one elbow to look over his shoulder at the digital alarm clock. "A little after seven."

"We missed dinner."

Her stomach growled at the words, reminding her she'd missed her other meals today too. They'd made love right through lunch. "We could always go down and raid the kitchen."

"It's not that late. Jacob probably has something waiting for us."

The thought of facing the irascible old man after spending hours in Simon's bedroom daunted her. "Probably."

His hand cupped her chin. "What's the matter?"

"Nothing."

"Come on, baby. You've gone tense."

"Jacob probably thinks I'm a floozy."

"Floozy? Do they still use words like that in Southern California?" he asked with laughter in his voice.

"No, well, not that I've heard, but I bet Jacob does."

"You're not a floozy, Amanda."

"I know that. Women and men make love all the time without a major commitment."

His thumb brushed her lips. "But not you."

She felt way too vulnerable, but she couldn't lie. "Not me."

He kissed her so softly, so tenderly that she felt tears prick her eyes. "This isn't casual sex, Amanda. Not for me."

Her breath came out on a broken sigh. "Not for me either."

He didn't say anything else, which left her wondering what the afternoon had been, if not casual sex. No way did he love her, but he didn't sound like the past few hours had been an indulgence of physical pleasure and nothing else, either.

That would have to be enough. She put her hand over his on her face. "Shall we go get some dinner?"

He didn't say anything for a second, his gunmetal eyes probing her own, making her wish she could close them and hide whatever he might find.

Finally, his hand dropped from her. "Sure." He slid out of the other side of the bed. "Stay here while I run down and grab your suitcase."

"Okay."

She watched in hungry fascination as he covered his nakedness with a pair of *do bok* pants. He was only semierect, but he was still bigger than Lance had been with a full arousal.

Did the guy ever go totally soft?

He was funny about her seeing him completely

excited, though. She hadn't noticed at first, but he'd kept his body averted from her when they got out of the bath, wearing a towel until they'd gotten in the bed. And the last time they'd made love, he'd kept the sheet over the lower half of his body until just before joining their bodies.

He also hadn't asked her to put the condom on him. She'd been too shy to ask, but she wanted to touch him there.

Maybe she'd work up the courage later.

She was contemplating the prospect when Simon came back carrying not only her suitcase, but the rest of her things as well.

"Wouldn't it have been easier to just grab my suitcase?" She didn't need her laptop to get dressed.

He dropped the luggage at the end of the bed. "We'd just have to bring it up later. I thought I'd save myself a trip."

That sounded like she was moving into his bedroom. "Uh . . . Simon?"

He'd turned away to pull clothes out of the dresser. "What?"

"Am I sleeping here now?"

He spun around to face her. "Don't you want to?" He sounded defensive and his expression was wary.

"It's not that I don't want to, it's just that . . . Are you sure I won't be in the way? What about when you want to work?"

"You're not sleeping in my lab."

"But Jacob said you don't even like him to come up and clean when you're in a work mode."

He grabbed a pair of jeans and dark gray T-shirt from the drawer. "If you want your own space, just say so."

She thought about sleeping in Simon's arms, waking up with him and making love to him. "I'd rather sleep here."

Chapter 13

The next morning as she stared blindly at her computer screen, having just read an e-mail from Daniel, Amanda questioned the prudence of her decision to move into Simon's bedroom.

Who was she kidding? Prudence had nothing to do with it. For the first time she could remember, she had made a decision based wholly on emotion. She'd ignored the ramifications it might have for her career, the temporary nature of the liaison, and even how such a choice would impact how others like Jacob, Eric Brant, and her own coworkers saw her.

Why? Because she was in love, and she was discovering that emotion was more powerful than intellect, and more driving than reason. It had to be, or how could she have allowed herself to fall for Simon Brant?

But, until the merger went through, *if it went through*, he wasn't just a business associate, he was a key player for Extant Corp's competition, a *rival.* With his intransigence toward the merger, he also stood between her and success at her job. Their relationship, such as it was, was temporary. They were from totally different worlds and one day soon, she would have to go back to hers. He'd made that point and he was right.

Love should have no place in any equation that included him as a variable. Not when every indicator on both a business and personal level marked doom for anything lasting between them.

He wasn't looking for permanence with a woman. The only driving compulsions in his life were his inventions and computer designs.

The one woman he *had* ever considered marrying was the total opposite of Amanda. Elaine Brant was slim, gorgeous, and a social butterfly. She'd drawn Simon out of his quiet self-containment at dinner the other evening far more easily than Amanda ever could have done.

How could she have let herself love someone so programmed not to love her back?

If that incredible folly wasn't enough to convince her she'd lost her mind, she'd gone to bed with him. Okay. That part had been wonderful. More than wonderful. It had been life altering. She would never see herself the same way again now that she knew the sensual creature Simon's touch could evoke. Only what was going to happen to her when he decided he didn't want her in his bed anymore? Lance's rejection had hurt her; she feared that rejection from Simon could come close to destroying her.

If she had two brain cells to rub together, she would get off his island and never see him again. Because the longer she let herself be with him, the more it was going to hurt when it was over.

Had she so much as *considered* this yesterday when he'd come traipsing up the stairs with her things? No. *She'd moved in with him instead.*

It was incomprehensible to her. She was not an

impetuous person. She took her time making major
changes in her life. Look how long she had put up
with Lance. Yet, yesterday, she had been staying in
Simon's house and today, she was living with him.
She felt like she'd stepped onto one of the scare
rides at Disneyland with no hope of getting off.

The issues that had seemed unimportant yesterday loomed as shadowy giants in front of her today.

What would happen if Daniel found out she was
having an affair with Simon? Bile rose in her throat
at the thought that he would think she was following his smarmy advice.

When Daniel had given it, he had assumed she
was already sleeping with Simon. She had known
she wasn't. So, as ugly as the advice had been, it
had had no power to really touch her. Now she *was*
Simon's lover and, even though she'd done nothing wrong in regard to her business with him, she
felt like her professional integrity had been compromised.

She knew she wouldn't try to sway Simon's opinion with sex, but knowing that was what Daniel expected made her feel unclean anyway.

She hated feeling like that, but the only way to
change it seemed to be to stop being with Simon.
Her heart twisted painfully and she acknowledged
that she was already past the point of leaving Simon
without emotional damage.

She responded to an e-mail from one of her coworkers as the problem gnawed at her conscience.

What if she told Simon about Daniel's recom-
mendation and that she didn't want him to make
any decisions based on their intimacy? He might
scuttle the merger on the strength of his revulsion
toward Daniel alone. Simon had a lot more integrity than her boss. His reaction to the knowledge of what Daniel wanted her to do was bound

to be at least as bad as her own. No, she definitely should not tell Simon about that part, but she *could* still tell him that she didn't want to influence him with their personal relationship.

If he changed his mind about the merger, she wanted it to be because he was swayed by the facts she'd presented to him, not because of sex.

All she had to do was tell him.

Jumping up from the table Simon had installed in his bedroom for her use as a makeshift desk, she crossed the room to knock on the door to his laboratory. He didn't answer. She waited a few seconds and knocked again. Still nothing. She knew he was in there. She knocked one last time. She tried the handle. It turned.

Of course it did.

He didn't have to lock Jacob out. The housekeeper wouldn't dream of interrupting Simon during his work. Well, she couldn't wait for Simon to surface again to settle this issue. She couldn't work with it preying on her conscience like a hungry cayote.

She pushed the door open and peeked inside.

What an amazing room. Looking more like the lab for a large design team than one man's private sanctuary, it stretched at least ten feet beyond the size of the great room on the floor below.

Workbenches lined the three walls not covered in glass and two long tables bisected the center of the huge space. Several computer systems in various stages of build filled one entire workbench and impressive looking equipment with lots of buttons and displays resided on the worktable closest to her. The whir of several supercomputers struck her ears and an ozonelike smell permeated the room.

Her gaze flicked to a nearby corner filled with

equipment that looked like it had come straight off the Star Ship Enterprise. She wasn't very technical, but one of the big black devices looked like a laser to her, its red glow enhancing the room's space-age feel.

When she could tear her gaze away from the impressive array of equipment, she found Simon. He was at the other end of the room, sitting behind a U-shape desk made of the same flat-brushed metal material as his bedroom set. The rapid clicking of computer keys attested to his concentration on the laptop in front of him.

She walked toward him, stopping a couple of feet from the desk. "Simon."

He kept typing.

"Simon!"

His head jerked up, his eyes widening in shock at the sight of her.

It was a good thing she wasn't a corporate spy. She could have taken pictures of everything in the room before he noticed her. "I did knock."

He flicked a rather vague glance to the door. "I heard."

"So, why didn't you answer?" she asked with some exasperation. She'd stood out there knocking for something like five minutes.

He frowned, his gray gaze sliding back to the computer screen. "I'm right in the middle of something."

And she was an interruption he did not want. He didn't have to say it. Who else would have come knocking at his door? Knowing it had to be her, he'd opted not to answer.

Well, that was definitely telling her.

Why had she thought she needed to clarify this whole sex-business thing with him anyway? It was obvious Simon wasn't going to be swayed from his course of action by a few hours in bed with her. He couldn't even be bothered to answer the door when he was busy.

"I'm sorry I interrupted." She backed toward the door. "I'll leave. No more knocking, I promise."

She had her own work to do and would be better off concentrating on it than obsessing over something so unlikely as her being in the role of corporate Mata Hari with Simon as her victim. It was all Daniel's fault for making the revolting suggestion in the first place. Her boss had a lot to answer for.

She spun around and hurried from the room, closing the door softly behind her.

She slid into her chair and logged in to her remote access for work again. She needed to apprise Daniel of the situation with Simon, to tell her boss that Simon had listened to the entire proposal, but still hadn't changed his mind. She wanted to put it off because Daniel would respond in one of two ways. Neither of them did she look forward to.

One, he would give her another talk about doing whatever it took to gain Simon's cooperation and she just might scream at him this time. Two, he could as easily decide it was time to cut their losses and order her to return to Southern California.

She didn't want to leave. With the merger pretty much scuttled, she could take some vacation time and spend it with Simon without business to cloud things between them. That was supposing he would want her to stay, which was not a given.

If he didn't, she might just need the vacation time to pull herself together.

Now that she'd thought about it, she almost hoped Daniel did say she should forget the merger negotiations for now. With an irrational sense of anticipation, she flipped open her mobile phone and dialed her office. The phone on the other end had rung twice when she felt a hand on her shoulder.

She didn't have to look up to know it was Simon. Her body had developed a sixth sense for his presence.

She clicked the phone off before the receptionist had a chance to answer and forced herself to turn around and meet Simon's gaze. He didn't look angry.

She swallowed and smiled tentatively. "I'm sorry I barged in like that."

"What did you need?"

Now that she'd thought about it, the idea of telling Simon she wasn't trying to use sex as a manipulative tool seemed really silly. "Nothing important."

"You came into my lab."

She nodded. "I know. I'm sorry," she said again.

"I didn't mind you coming in."

She warmed slightly at that blunt declaration.

"But you were in the middle of something," she said, repeating his own words almost verbatim.

He grimaced. "I should have answered the door."

"Why?" She shrugged. "You don't answer the door for Jacob, do you?"

"You're not Jacob."

"No, I'm not." Not an old man, for sure. Not a housekeeper. Not exactly a lover . . . not exactly a business associate. What was she to Simon?

"I'm really glad about that." His grin was so sensual, it was a good thing she was already sitting down or her legs would have collapsed under her.

"Are you coming out for dinner tonight?" she asked, hoping he'd think that was what she'd gone haring in there to ask him.

"Actually, I was hoping we could have lunch together down on the dock and then maybe have a Tae Kwon Do session afterward."

Warmth filled her. "I'd like that a lot."

His thumb brushed her collarbone above the scooped neckline of her top. "I want to kiss you, but I'm afraid if I do that I'll carry you back to bed."

Delight that he found her desirable to that extent thrilled through her. "You've really got to watch these caveman tendencies you're developing."

He laughed, the sound deep, rich and very, very sexy. "I feel pretty primitive around you, sweetheart."

She loved it when he called her that. "It's mutual."

"So, why did you come into the lab?"

She hadn't fooled him. She didn't know why she'd thought she could. He was a genius inventor, trained to look minutely at all data. "I thought better of it. It wasn't anything important."

"Which one is it? You thought better of it, or it really wasn't all that important?"

"Both."

His thumb moved to the sensitive spot behind her ear and her concentration on the topic at hand was severely compromised.

"You've got me curious. It'll gnaw at me and I won't get anything done for the rest of the day."

She didn't believe that for a second. The man had more focus than the Hubble telescope. "Try to make me feel guilty, why don't you?" she teased, breathless from his small caresses.

"Is it working?"

She rolled her eyes. "No."

"I really want to know."

She sighed, facing the inevitable. Those amazing powers of concentration of his were focused on getting the information from her and he wasn't about to give up. The man could be so stubborn. Just look at how he'd kidnapped her yesterday. "You'll think it's stupid."

His fingertips trailed up her face. It felt good and it was all she could do not to reach up to trap his hand against her cheek and just hold it there.

He brushed her chin and then let his hand fall. "Nothing about you is stupid. Nothing."

"This is, believe me. But I'll tell you anyway." She owed it to him after pulling him away from his work. She inhaled, hoping she wouldn't sound as idiotic as she felt. "It's just that I got worried you might think, now that we're sleeping together, that I would try to convince you about the merger with a more personal form of persuasion."

"You're worried that I believe you're trying to manipulate me with mind-blowing sex?" He sounded only mildly curious.

She liked the mind-blowing part. "Yes." She smiled wryly to let him know how ridiculous she realized that supposition was.

"Are you?"

"What?"

"Are you trying to use your body to convince me about the merger?" He didn't look like he was teasing her, but again he didn't sound overly concerned by the prospect.

So much for Amanda Zachary as the newest corporate Mata Hari.

"How could you ask me something like that?" It hadn't occurred to her that he might actually have considered such a scenario. "I would never do something so despicable." Not to mention obviously impossible.

Unable to remain sitting with the confusion of emotions roiling through her, she shot up from her chair, knocking his hand away from her neck. "If that's what you think of me, maybe I should leave right now."

Stupid! That wasn't what she wanted. *Oh God, let him realize how wrong he is and ask me to stay.*

Daniel suggesting such a thing had made her angry. Simon believing she was capable of it hurt. But then, Daniel was just her boss. Simon was her lover. He should know her better. But her inner voice nagged: *The only thing he knows well is your body. You love him, but his feelings are a lot more basic. Why should he automatically trust in your integrity?*

"Amanda, you're the one that brought it up."

"I didn't think you'd believe something so vile about me," she said helplessly, pain radiating outward from the region of her heart.

"Then why did you come into my lab?"

The very reasonableness of the question fanned the flames of her anger. She was feeling vulnerable and she didn't like it. "Because I wanted to tell you I wasn't doing any such thing!"

"If it wasn't a possibility, why bring it up at all?"

"Because I'm not used to sleeping with business associates and I wanted to make sure you understood one had nothing to do with the other."

"I'm glad."

She glared. Bully for him. "Let's be real. It's not like it would ever have worked anyway."

He pulled her into his arms, seemingly oblivious to her stiffened body. "Are you sure about that, baby?"

"Of course I'm sure. You have too much integrity to make a business decision based on sex."

"Thank you." He bent down and kissed the side of her neck.

She shivered. "But it makes me really angry *you* think *I'm* some kind of slut who would use my body as a bartering tool."

His hold on her tightened. "No, I don't."

"But you said—"

His finger pressed against her lips. "I asked you an academic question. I did not mean to imply I believed the answer would be yes."

"Then why ask it?"

"Why come into my lab to tell it wasn't a possibility?"

"Because!" She took a deep breath, trying for a calm she was far from feeling. "Because I didn't want there to be any misunderstandings between us."

"Exactly."

Oh. Maybe she'd overreacted a little. "Are you sure you're not secretly wondering if I'm just going to bed with you to manipulate your attitude toward the merger?"

"Very sure."

She chewed on her bottom lip.

"Baby, in order for you to be the kind of woman who bargains with her body, you would have had to ask for something in exchange for what you gave me yesterday. You didn't."

"Maybe I was trying to soften you up."

"I don't get soft around you."

When his meaning sank in, she grinned despite a lingering ache inside. "I noticed that yesterday."

"I won't try to manipulate you with sex either."

"I never thought you would."

He squeezed her at the unsubtle dig. "Behave."

She nuzzled his chest. "It still feels funny."

A featherlight kiss landed on top of her head. "What does?"

"Making love with someone I'm doing business with. I'm afraid I'm going to lose my objectivity." She had the terrible feeling she already had.

"Are you going to give up the idea of the merger because I want you to?"

"No." Yet, if he told her she had to choose between the merger and him, she wasn't sure what she would do. Thankfully, she would not have to face that choice because Simon would never stoop to such measures. He was too confident of his ability to get his own way with straightforward means to resort to emotional blackmail as a weapon.

"Then there's nothing for you to worry about, is there?"

She shook her head. Nothing she was going to admit to.

"Do you have something urgent you were working on?" he asked in a voice that made her melt inside.

"No."

Then his mouth rocked over hers and she forgot all about the merger, Extant, and the phone call she would have to make later to her boss.

Simon had never found it a turn-on watching a woman eat before, but everything Amanda did excited him, especially now that his body knew what it felt like to make love to her. He cursed his own stupidity in waiting so long to touch her. All his worries seemed inconsequential now.

The thought that she might have left the island, and his life, without his ever having touched her passionate nature made him break out in a cold sweat.

He'd never had sex so good, but then he'd never had Amanda. She was the perfect lover. So responsive. So passionate. So giving.

So *temporary*. Once she realized he wasn't going to change his mind about the merger, he would lose her. Not because she was trying to use sex to convince him, but because her job was the most important thing in her life. She wouldn't thank him for messing things up for her.

He wondered if she would grow bored with his lifestyle before that even happened. Other women had, women he hadn't wanted as much as he wanted her. They'd made it clear that being with a man who became obsessed with his work to the point of forgetting they were there grew old real fast.

He'd done that this afternoon to Amanda. She hadn't said anything yet, but he was sure his failure to come out of his lab until dinner had upset her.

She wasn't acting like it, but women were good at hiding things like that. They didn't forget though, and then, one day, they walked away, saying he didn't respond to their needs. "I'm sorry I didn't come out for lunch like we planned."

Maybe he would get points for apologizing before it became a major issue.

She laid her fork on the edge of her plate and smiled so sweetly he wanted to wrap her up in his arms and never let go. *Right, Simon, women don't do forever with you.*

"You had to make up for lost time. So did I."

"But I missed our sparring session too."

"We can have one tonight if you like, but personally, I enjoyed the form of exercise we employed this morning too much to complain." She winked at him.

He was immediately ready for another bout of the kind of exercise she was talking about. "You're not mad at me?"

"No. Why should I be?" She looked genuinely puzzled. "We both chose to spend the time we should have been working, doing something far more personal and less productive. So, we had to forego the pleasure of a picnic lunch."

"But I forgot about you." Why had he said that? She didn't need to know. She'd come up with a plausible excuse and here he was rejecting the salvation it offered. Dumb, very dumb.

"I forgot about you too, to tell the truth. I had a lot of work to catch up on after taking all of yesterday off."

"You forgot me?" He found that disconcerting. He'd been yelled at, dumped, even slapped for his insensitivity by women, but he didn't think he'd ever been forgotten.

"Mmmm." She popped a bite of the blackened catfish Jacob had made for dinner into her mouth and chewed, making a humming sound of pleasure. "This is delicious."

"What if I had come out and wanted to go on our picnic?" he asked, unable to let the subject go.

She shrugged. "Then I would have remembered you."

"Would you have gone on the picnic with me?"

Her mouth twisted as she considered his question. "I'm not sure. Probably, but we would have had to keep it short."

"If you'd knocked on my lab door, I would have answered."

Her smile was radiant. "I'll remember that."

Jacob served chocolate-dipped strawberries and champagne after dinner. Simon enjoyed watching Amanda's sexy mouth bite into each succulent strawberry too much to eat his own dessert.

She stopped eating and looked at him. "Aren't you going to have dessert?"

"Later." Only, she was going to be the dessert. He wondered if Jacob had any of the chocolate sauce left.

"Oh." She pushed her dessert plate away from her. "Did you want to ask me anything about the merger?"

He shook his head. "Finish your strawberries."

The merger could wait. Forever, as far as he was concerned.

"I'm full."

He didn't believe her. "No, you aren't."

"Yes, I am."

Something about this scenario bothered him. "You were enjoying your dessert until I told you I wasn't eating mine."

She started to get up. "I'll just go get my briefcase. I thought of something this afternoon that you might be interested in regarding the two companies coming together."

He grabbed her wrist. "If I eat my dessert now, will you finish yours?" He was trying to understand what was going on, but he felt like he was missing an important element.

He hated feeling that way.

She sat back down, but she frowned at him. "Simon, this is ridiculous. You're making something out of nothing. I said I was full, can't we just leave it at that?"

"Jacob will be offended if you don't finish." Remembering the old man's reaction to having to serve them napoleons that had been sitting in the fridge the night before, Simon said, "He'll get cranky."

"Isn't he always?"

"Don't let him hear you say that." He reached across the table and pushed her dessert plate back in front of her.

"Look, it's not as if I need it. My hips won't thank me for the high-fat chocolate."

"You think you need to diet?" The idea shocked him. She was perfect.

"I could lose ten pounds, yes."

Like hell she could. "Taking your body below optimum weight can cause problems for your immune system."

"I'm not exactly anorexic."

He was beginning to wonder. "That's fortunate. Anorexia nervosa is a debilitating disease."

She rolled her eyes. "I was being sarcastic. I would think it was obvious that I don't have a problem with eating."

"How is it obvious?" he probed, feeling like he was getting closer to the missing element. Then, as often happened in his lab, several pieces of information clicked together in his head. "He told you that you were fat, didn't he?"

"He who?"

"Don't play dumb."

She looked away, with an air of fragility that had not been there seconds before. "I already told you Lance did not find me the epitome of perfect female form."

"Tell me about it, baby. Please."

She shook her head. "It's over."

"No, it's not."

She looked at him and the pain he saw in her face ripped at his gut.

He stood up and pulled her to her feet. "Come here."

Tugging her along, he made straight for his large, overstuffed sofa.

Chapter 14

Amanda let him pull her down onto the couch so they were facing each other. He wanted her to tell him about her marriage to Lance, but what woman wanted to admit to such a colossal failure? She let her gaze travel up his strong, broad chest to his face.

His expression was filled with a compassion she had never expected to receive. "Tell me what that bastard did to you."

"How can you be so sure he *did* anything?"

Simon's laugh was harsh. "I would have to be a blind idiot not to know that something had happened to you. You are the most beautiful woman I've ever known and you act like your body is grotesque."

"It's not that bad!"

"Maybe, but you sure as heck don't have a clue how lovely and sensual you are."

Maybe that was because she'd never been sensual with anyone but him. Part of her wanted to tell Simon about her past, but for him to understand her marriage, she had to tell him about her family. "My brother introduced me to Lance during my junior year in college. I didn't date. I was too shy. Too serious. Too sure I was as awkward and unattractive as my mother claimed. Besides, I didn't fit in with my Southern California peers."

He reached out and took both her hands, letting his thumbs rub soothingly over the backs of them, but remained silent.

She took a deep breath and let it out slowly. "Lance got along really well with my family. He was a lawyer with an impressive client list. My parents were both surprised he was interested in me. My brother told me how lucky I was."

"Did you love him?"

"I thought I did. I wanted so much for our relationship to work. I wanted to feel like I belonged to someone."

"But your family . . ."

Memories of her childhood still had the power to hurt. So, she usually suppressed them, but she wanted Simon to understand. "I was an 'oops' baby. My brother, Brice, is ten years older than me and the only child my parents wanted to have. My mother planned to have an abortion, but unfortunately for her, Grandfather's housekeeper had caught on to the fact she was pregnant. He threatened to cut her out of his will if she got rid of me."

Simon had gone rigid beside her. She could imagine. He'd lost his mother when he was a child, but from what he'd said, she had loved him. No one had loved Amanda in her entire life except for Jillian.

"I was three years old when Grandfather died. Alive, but not wanted. The only time my parents ever gave me even the least bit of approval was when I caught Lance's interest. I married him believing I would finally be accepted into my own family with the added bonus of having one of my own. I was on a euphoric cloud for the entire ten months of our engagement. Lance didn't even protest waiting until we were married to make love for the first time."

"You never slept with him?"

She shook her head. "I read a lot as a child. My sense of morality came from my books, not my family because they ignored me or criticized me. *Little Women*, *Anne of Green Gables*, *The Five Little Peppers*, and other classics—books that weren't exactly peopled by your typical Southern Californian."

She turned to stare out over the water, loving the peacefulness of the scene all over again. "My wedding night was a disaster. Lance wanted me to do things I'd never heard of. I was scared and embarrassed. Sex hurt. But that wasn't the worst of it. The most painful part of my wedding night was having Lance turn out the light so he could fantasize I had a different body."

"He told you that?"

She didn't look at Simon. "Yes. Over the two years of our marriage, he pestered me to have breast reduction surgery, watched every calorie I consumed, and nagged at me if I didn't work out at least an hour every day."

"Why did you stay with him?"

"Because I was used to not being loved, I guess. I'm not really sure. It hurt being married to him, but no more than it had hurt living at home. I kept trying to make my marriage work, but nothing I did could fix the problem."

"Your ex-husband is a bastard. That's not a problem you could fix."

She laughed hollowly. "He didn't want me and I was convinced that was my problem. I tried everything to seduce him, but it didn't work. Looking back, I don't know why I bothered. It wasn't as if I enjoyed being intimate with him. He was an extremely selfish, perverse lover." She shivered at her memories. "The last year we were married, we didn't have sex at all and, other than feeling like a total failure as a woman, I didn't care."

"You thought I didn't want you either."

Remembering the pain of Simon's rejection, she nodded.

"Why?"

"That day we had the sparring session, I thought you were going to kiss me. I leaned into you and you backed away. I was humiliated. It felt like Lance all over again. Only this time I really wanted to kiss, not just to prove that I could attract you as a woman, but because I *wanted* you."

"I wanted you too, but our relationship is complicated."

She turned her head and met the silvered gray of his gaze. "It's still complicated."

He didn't deny it. "But I can't keep my hands off you regardless."

She smiled a little. "Making love with you is so different."

"From the sounds of things, sex with your husband was less about intimacy than it was about control. He used his supposed lack of desire for you to make you do the things he wanted."

"I don't know what you mean."

"He controlled what you ate, how much you exercised. I'm damn glad he didn't talk you into that surgery. I find your breasts so sexy, just looking at them makes me want to come."

She threw herself in his arms and kissed him all over his face. "You make me feel good, Simon. Thank you."

He hugged her to him, settling her into his lap where she could feel the rigid proof of his words against her hip.

"Jacob found your pajamas in the guest room's bathroom garbage yesterday."

She tensed. "Did he?"

"I thought they must have landed there by accident, but Jacob didn't agree."

Jacob was too astute for his own good, she thought wrathfully.

Simon's hand rubbed against her back in a soothing motion. "Tell me why you threw away your pajamas."

She nestled against his chest. "I'd rather not. It was just a misunderstanding and it's over now."

"Does it have something to do with you thinking I didn't want you?" He sounded really disturbed by the prospect and she wished she could lie to him and say no, but she didn't want to lie to Simon. Ever.

"When Jacob told me you wanted to meet me in my room, I thought that was your unique way of setting up an assignation. You've got to admit your mind doesn't work like other people's," she said by way of an explanation for her folly.

"And when I came downstairs expecting you to tell me about the proposal, you were embarrassed."

"Humiliated. I'd got it wrong again."

"You didn't have it wrong. I had erotic dreams all night long about you in those sexy things. When I came down to breakfast and found out you were gone, I was ready to howl at the moon in frustration."

"The moon isn't out in the morning."

"Details."

"When I went into the bathroom, I stripped off the lingerie and tossed it away in a fit of angry despair. Lance had once told me how ridiculous I looked in sexy nightwear and I couldn't stand the thought you believed the same thing."

Suddenly she was being held away from him.

The compassionate, understanding Simon had been replaced by a furious man. He shook her shoulders. "How could you think that? I told you I wanted you! It was all I could do to keep myself from ripping those silky things off your even silkier body."

"How was I supposed to know that, with you rabbiting on about the proposal?"

"You moved in to my house for the express purpose of presenting that information to me, damn it." He sounded even angrier by that fact. "And the only reason you agreed to stay was so you could keep trying to convince me."

An incredible thought struck her all at once. It hurt Simon that she had stayed for business. "But you never let me know there could be anything between us but the merger."

"I told you I wanted you."

It was the second time he'd reminded her of that and this time she laughed. "Lance told me he loved me, but he showed me he didn't."

"Are you saying I showed you I didn't want you?" Simon's voice was dangerously controlled.

But she wasn't going to deny the truth. "Yes."

"Because I didn't put my desires for you above the business that is so all-important to you?" Each biting word came out with the power of a bullet.

And she knew, absolutely knew, in a blinding flash of clarity, that what he said was exactly right. She wanted Simon's feelings for her to come before everything else in his life and that was not going to happen. Not ever.

If she kept pushing, she could very well lose what they did have.

She did something she had vowed she'd never do again. She tried a bit of seduction. Rubbing the breasts he said he liked so much against him, she said, "I know you want me now."

It worked.

With a growl, she found herself lying full length on the sofa under Simon with his mouth devouring hers.

"You're sleeping with him?" Jillian's incredulous shriek blasted Amanda from the mobile phone's earpiece.

"You told me I should," she reminded her friend, who was taking the news of Amanda's affair with Simon in a completely unexpected way.

"I told you to go out with my friend, Dave, too, but you didn't do that!"

"I didn't want to go out with Dave." Or any of the other numerous men Jillian had tried to fix Amanda up with since the divorce.

"But you *wanted to go to bed* with Simon? I don't believe it. According to you, sex is God's joke on unsuspecting women."

"I was wrong about that." Remembered pleasure had Amanda's eyes flicking toward the closed lab door.

He'd said he would answer the door if she knocked. It was tempting, but she couldn't interrupt his work just because at the age of twenty-six she had finally discovered her female libido. Besides, she wasn't ready to risk the possibility of his rejection. She'd initiated that kiss on the sofa the other night, but Simon had already been aroused. She wasn't sure she'd ever have the confidence to approach him cold with seduction on her mind.

"Amanda?"

"Huh?" Indistinguishable words echoed in her mind telling her that Jillian had been talking the entire time she had been caught up in her thoughts of Simon.

"Do you really think this is a good idea?"

"That is a *really surprising* question coming from you." Jillian had been pushing her to start dating since before the divorce was final.

"I know." She could almost hear her friend doing that thing she did with her hair while she was thinking. "It's just that you're not into casual *amore*."

No, she wasn't. Casual love, sex, whatever you wanted to call it, wasn't something in her makeup. "It's not casual," she bit the bullet and admitted, "but it *is* love."

She'd called Jillian because she had to talk to someone about the overwhelming feelings Simon engendered in her, but saying the words out loud had been harder than she expected. It had also left her feeling stripped naked emotionally. She didn't even want to think how much worse it would be if she told *Simon* the truth about her feelings for him.

"*You're in love with him?*" Jillian was back to shrieking.

"Yes." No use prevaricating or trying to take the words back. They were true and Jillian would not be fooled by an attempt at retreat. "Do you really think I could have risked *making love* with him otherwise?"

"No. That's what has me worried." Her friend's voice dropped an octave with concern. "Sweetie, you pretend to be so tough, but you're not. You're one of the most fragile people I know and I'm scared to death this guy is going to hurt you."

"I'm a little nervous about it myself, but I don't seem to have a choice." She started doodling on a piece of paper. She needed Jill to see how potentially devastating, but equally inescapable this relationship with Simon had become for her. However, she didn't know if she had the words to make her friend understand.

"I never knew how powerful love could be. It's pretty much unstoppable." She could hear the lingering disbelief in her own voice. "Even though I know I'm going to end up hurting, I can't hold back from whatever Simon is willing to give me."

"His body."

"It's a great body, Jillian."

Her friend snorted laughter. "Amanda!"

"He cares about me, too. Maybe it's not love, but it's more than I ever got from Lance. Simon wants me to be happy while I'm with him." He did all sorts of little things to show her, like setting up this office area for her and gaining Jacob's agreement to let her watch Jillian's show every day on his television. "And he never criticizes me. He's sort of blind and tells me all the time how beautiful I am."

"Aw, honey."

"Jill, it's so amazing, but when I'm with him, I feel like I'm not just Amanda Zachary, junior executive and failure in the marriage stakes."

"You're not the failure," Jillian said fiercely.

"That's what Simon says too. He can't understand how Lance didn't want me. He said my ex must have been the most inept lover alive not to be able to please a responsive woman like me. *Can you imagine?*"

"I tried to tell you that not all men were like that jerk you married."

"Maybe not, but I don't think I would respond to other men the way I do to Simon. I want him, Jill, and I've never *wanted* another man, not like that."

Jillian, who had had an active love life since she was sixteen, would probably have a hard time understanding that. She wouldn't make fun of Amanda, though. She never had, no matter how far apart their perception of something was.

"So, tell me more about this guy. I've got that

he's hell on wheels in bed, but I want more info on what he's like out of it."

Jillian grilled Amanda about Simon for another twenty minutes, before letting her change the subject. Not that Amanda minded talking about the man she'd fallen in love with. She didn't, but the more she talked about him the more unlikely it seemed that a man like that would fall in love with her. However, when she flipped her cell phone closed forty minutes later, she was smiling.

Jill's initial reaction had surprised her, but the other woman had ended the call by saying, "Go for it."

The next morning, Amanda woke up to the feel of Simon's hand gently caressing her stomach. Her eyes fluttered open to his steel-gray gaze.

She smiled. "Hi."

He kissed her, tenderly, sweetly and oh so slowly. "Hi."

"You know what today is?" she asked.

His brows drew together then his expression cleared. "The five day anniversary since the first time we made love. What do you want to do to celebrate?"

She felt her heart constrict. He could be so romantic, even if he did tend to forget everyone else in the room when his mind started chewing on one of his projects.

"That too, but I was thinking that it's Saturday. I don't have to work today. How about you?"

She didn't think he kept regular hours, but maybe he could take a break today.

His forefinger drew a circle around her right nipple, causing the flesh to swell and stiffen immediately. "The only thing I want to work on today is us."

The breath stilled in her chest for a full five seconds and then it came whooshing out on a rush of air. Had he really said that? That he wanted to work on them . . . that there was a real *them* to work on, not just two people who were extremely compatible in bed?

Her thoughts short-circuited as he went about once again proving that compatibility.

Simon carried Amanda into the shower. She was right. When he was around her he had some major caveman tendencies, but she liked it. She might haughtily protest his habit of picking her up and carrying her around, but she always curled into him with a trusting sensuality that he found addictive.

Hell, everything about Amanda was addictive. From the way her breath hitched when he first probed the entrance to her body to the way she teased Jacob about having a crush on one of the female leads in Jillian's show. The warm sunshine that seemed such a natural part of her personality dispelled every lingering shadow in his soul but one. He could not dispel the knowledge that one day soon, she would be gone.

It made him determined to enjoy her to the fullest while he had her. His libido complied with an enthusiasm he hadn't known since his teens. Their recent lovemaking had been quick and fierce, the perfect beginning to a day spent entirely in her company.

He let her slide down his body, before reaching in to turn on the taps. She liked her shower hotter than he did, so he set the temperature on the two showerheads on the left higher than the overhead nozzle of the two on the right.

He felt a featherlight touch on his back and

turned around to face her. She had an odd expression on her face.

"What is it?"

"I was just touching you to see if you're real." Her eyes reflected an inexplicable wonder.

His knees about buckled and his recently satisfied male member surged with renewed arousal. "I'm real." Not only did he act like a caveman, he sounded like one, practically growling his response to her.

"Yes." Satisfaction laced her voice. Then she smiled and reached past him to test the water. "It's hot."

He nodded, still a little stunned by the awe he'd seen on her face for that brief moment.

They stepped into the oversize shower stall.

He'd had it built this way because he liked space around him. The five showerheads had been a luxury he'd decided to indulge in, which had turned out to be doubly decadent when he and Amanda washed beneath them. He had discovered some very interesting uses for the directed jets of water when making love with her, uses that made her blush and come apart with pleasure at the same time.

But today he wanted more than to make love with this beautiful woman full of stimulating contradictions. He wanted her to make love to him. It had taken him a while, but he'd finally realized that she almost never initiated their touching and that she was reticent about touching his body. He'd caught on right away that it wasn't because she didn't want to. She looked at him with a hunger that stirred his baser instincts, but she never acted on that hunger.

At first, he'd been glad. He'd been careful not to overwhelm her with his size, but she didn't show the slightest indication that she found his overt masculinity overwhelming. In fact, she went crazy when he touched her so deeply inside with his aroused flesh that he couldn't go any farther. She was tiny compared to him, but her passion made them the perfect fit.

Except, she didn't touch him and he was going hungry for the feel of her sweet little hands on his sex.

He handed the soap to her. "Wash me?"

Her head jerked up and she stared at him with those drown-in-me brown eyes. "All over?" she asked as if she needed his permission.

Oh, yeah. "Please."

Her eyes lit with anticipation. "I've been wanting to, but I wasn't sure . . ." her voice trailed off and she caressed him tentatively with the soap across his chest. "You'll tell me if I do it wrong, won't you?"

Damn that bastard she'd been married to.

Simon reached out and framed her face with his hands, making her look at him. "Any way you touch me is the right way. I'm dying for the feel of your hands on my skin. Amanda, don't you know you're the best lover I've ever had? Please, baby, don't let that bastard stop you from giving me what he was too stupid to want."

Her smile was misty, but brilliant. "Okay." She put the soap aside. "I want to feel you with my hands, both of them, alright?"

He supposed it would take time for those little hesitations to be completely dispelled. "It's more than all right. It's perfect."

He couldn't talk after that because her hands were doing things to him he'd dreamed of since the moment he met her. She started with his head, massaging his scalp, playing with the shoulder-length strands of his hair before moving on to touch his face with butterfly caresses. His eyelids slid shut as she brushed his cheekbones.

She outlined his lips with a fingertip. "I love your mouth, Simon."

He nipped at her finger. "My mouth loves your body, baby."

She laughed softly, sensually.

Then her hands were on his neck, lightly tracing his pulse. "Your heartbeat is a little fast, darling. Maybe you should have your blood pressure checked."

"It wouldn't do any good. It's always high when you're around."

A feathery kiss pressed against his pulse point. Her fingers trailed down his chest, zeroing in on the small brown disks of his male nipples. "They're just like mine. They like being touched too."

He couldn't make his mouth form a response. All he could do was groan with the teasing pleasure she was subjecting him to.

"Do they like other things, I wonder?"

She knew damn well they did. She'd sucked on him last night until he'd taken her in such frenzy that he'd been terrified he had hurt her until she screamed her release in his ear.

She suckled him, first one and then the other. She didn't linger and he didn't beg her to because he didn't want anything to delay her reaching the ultimate goal. A delicate bite on each nipple ended her torment of those erogenous zones.

Her mouth and hands moved downward, caressing a stomach that had gone rock hard with excitement. She outlined each one of his defined abdominal muscles. "You've got an amazing body." Her voice was husky and so sexy it was like a caress on his sensitized skin.

Then she went lower.

He stopped breathing, in a wealth of torment waiting for her to touch his most intimate male flesh, but in a move calculated to drive him insane, she bypassed his sex and went to the tensed muscles of his thighs. She caressed them with all ten fingertips, making him shudder and wonder if he was going to be able to stay standing.

His legs came close to collapsing when she caressed the back of his knees. "You're sensitive here."

"Yes," he managed to get out in a guttural voice.

"And here? Are you sensitive here too?" She brushed the inside of his thighs, letting the backs of her fingers make brief contact with his sacs.

He muttered a short, Anglo-Saxon term that he was usually careful not to use in a woman's presence.

She laughed. "Not yet, darling, but soon."

He liked it when she called him darling. It was intimate, as intimate as her touch.

"Amanda." His hips strained toward her, his erect flesh brushing against her face. "Please, baby, touch me there."

His hands were flattened against the warmed and wet tile of the shower stall, and every muscle in his body was tense with anticipation.

When she didn't say or do anything for several long seconds, he opened his eyes and looked down at her. She was staring at his sex with a sort of rapture. He felt a small amount of pre-ejaculate come out in testimony of how much that look turned him on.

She saw it and licked her lips, making him groan. She reached out with one delicate little fingertip and touched the bead of moisture at the tip of his penis. Then she brought it to her lips and tasted it.

He groaned. She was going to kill him with her innocently sensual curiosity.

She looked up at him, her eyes darkened almost to black with desire. "I like it."

"Oh, baby. . . ." How could he want to pound into her with every inch of his throbbing arousal, while at the same time wanting to hold her and kiss her with a tenderness he'd never felt for another woman?

Her fingers wrapped around him and he choked on his own breath. The tips did not quite touch.

"You're big, aren't you? I mean bigger than average." Her tone was that of a scientist gathering information and it made him smile despite the acuity of his need.

"I don't measure myself against other men," he said truthfully, if evasively.

"Well, you're a lot bigger than Lance was."

Something about the wording of that statement pricked at him until he had an insight that he could not quite believe. "Are you saying you don't have any other standard of comparison?"

She didn't look up at him, her attention was wholly engaged with his hardened rod. "I've never been intimate with any other man except you and Lance."

He wouldn't define what she'd had with her ex-husband as intimacy. "You're practically a virgin!"

Chapter 15

She did look up then, her expression wry. "I don't think you can be practically a virgin, that's sort of like being almost pregnant. You are or you aren't."

He didn't agree. Elaine three months pregnant was a whole different proposition than she had been in her final trimester with her first child. There were definitely levels to how pregnant a woman was. Just ask any man who had lived through a pregnancy with one. And there were levels to a woman's move from innocence to sexual experience as well.

"You're very innocent."

"But I'm learning all the time." Her smile should have warned him, but it didn't.

So when her hot, silky wet mouth closed around the head of his arousal, he went up in flames. He bucked toward her and she caressed his length with both her hands while swirling her tongue around his head.

"I'm going to come. You've got to stop."

She didn't let go. She didn't move her mouth. Instead, she sucked another inch inside the heated interior and moved on him with inexperienced, but highly erotic motions.

He felt like the top of his head was coming off,

but he wanted to be inside her when he climaxed. It was the sweetest sensation and one that had become an integral part of his complete satisfaction. He forced her head back and quickly lifting her under her armpits he lined their bodies up for his penetration. Her fingers dug into his shoulders as she spread her legs. Locking them around him, she settled onto his aching flesh in one slow downward thrust.

She was making love to him.

It felt better than he'd fantasized and he went over the brink almost immediately. She came with him, her body convulsing around his pulsing sex while her teeth locked onto his shoulder in pleasure-pain.

Panting from the cataclysmic explosion, he hugged her to him with arms like manacles. It was only as sanity returned in slow increments that the different quality in their lovemaking alerted him to a devastating reality. He had taken her without protection. Or rather, she'd taken him. Not that it mattered. His baby-making sperm were swimming inside her right now and that was the only reality he could grasp.

If she got pregnant, there was a chance he could convince her to stay with him. As quickly as the thought formed, he felt ashamed of it. She deserved something better than to be trapped into a long-term relationship.

Guilt followed the shame as close as one Siamese twin is to another. It was all his fault. She'd never had a lover outside of marriage, was as close to being a virgin as a once-married woman could get. He'd been the one to seduce her in the shower, to beg her to touch him . . . to lose control and enter her without putting on a condom first.

"Baby?"

"Mmm?"

"I didn't use anything."

She mumbled something against his chest.

"What?"

Suddenly, her head flipped back and she looked at him in shock. "Did you just say you didn't use anything?" Then she shook her head, her eyes wide and slightly wild. "Of course you didn't. We were in the shower." She looked down at their still-joined bodies. *"Oh, Simon, I'm so sorry."*

Even now, he didn't want to let her go and one hand settled under her behind. "You're not the one who forgot birth control."

She winced at his tone and he felt worse, but she made no attempt to distance herself from him physically.

"Actually, we both forgot. I didn't give it a thought, but it's all my fault that you did. I seduced you into such a frenzy, you weren't likely to remember anything mundane like that." She didn't sound as upset as she should.

If he didn't think it was beyond the realm of possibility, he would have said she sounded proud of herself even.

"Protection isn't exactly mundane."

"Well, it's not on par with making love either."

"Obviously," he said wryly. "Is pregnancy very likely?" He had to ask.

She blushed and if he hadn't been feeling so guilty, he would have laughed. She'd taken him into her mouth without a qualm, but blushed when asked about her menstrual cycle.

She bit her lip in a gesture that always made him feel both protective and horny. "Do you want the truth or a peace-providing lie?"

"The truth."

"If I remember high school health class correctly, we're on the outer edge of the zone."

He couldn't begin to explain the hope that took root inside him and just would not let go, nor could he explain the sudden surge of lust that had him hardening all over again.

Her eyes widened. "Simon?"

He felt heat in his own cheeks. How did you tell a modern woman who was involved in a uncommitted sexual relationship with you that the thought of getting her pregnant was a major turn-on? "I guess I'd better let you go."

Her dark brown eyes went liquid with desire. "Um . . . we've pretty much done the damage, haven't we?"

Was she saying she didn't want him to let her go? His arousal grew in response to the thought. "According to statistical averages, the added risk of pregnancy from a second unprotected encounter would be minimal."

She laughed, her breath hitching when he moved inside of her. "You sound just like a university lecturer."

"I feel like a man who is on the verge of something earth shaking."

"You say the sweetest things."

Amanda was the first woman who had ever seen him as even approaching romantic. "You say too much sometimes," he growled against her lips before taking them.

Two hours later, replete from a decadent brunch provided by Jacob, Amanda's hand rested in the warm clasp of Simon's as they walked along the shoreline. She'd been trying to work up enough sangfroid to mention that he didn't need to worry about contracting any nasty disease from her, but they'd both been avoiding the topic of their unprotected sex earlier and she didn't know how to open the subject up again.

She inhaled the clean salt air, enjoying the way it woke her senses. "You know, I can understand you wanting to live on an island. Everything is so fresh here, so clean and so quiet."

His hand squeezed hers. "I like it."

"I do too." Which was surprising considering where she was accustomed to living. "The water is cold though."

They were walking in their bare feet and her toes had gone numb from the frigid surf.

"If it weren't, the beaches would be a lot more crowded along with this island."

"I guess you're right." But it would still be nice to be able to feel her toes.

"My swimming pool is heated." His voice had dropped to that sexy tone that sent messages of delight to the secret places of her body.

"Is it?"

"You haven't been in it since you came."

"I didn't bring a suit." She'd packed for a business trip, one she'd expected to be much shorter than this one had become.

He smiled down at her, his usually cool gray eyes warm with the desire that was so much a part of their relationship now. "Swimming without is one of the privileges of owning your own pool."

"I've never been skinny dipping before." She'd never wanted to. She'd never had the confidence to want to put her body on display like that, but the idea of doing so with Simon was titillating rather than scary. Still . . . "What if Jacob came down to tell you that you had a phone message or something?"

"I'll tell him not to disturb us."

"Then he'll know what we're doing." As soon as the words left her mouth, she realized how ridiculous they sounded. It wasn't as if Jacob could actually miss the fact she'd moved into his boss's bed.

Simon didn't answer, but with an apologetic look, he lifted his watch and spoke into it. "Yes, Jacob?"

"Master Joey is on the phone."

"I'll be right up."

He looked down at Amanda. "It's my nephew. I promised to come and see him this week, but I forgot." He brushed her cheek. "Things got a little crazy."

She smiled, loving the way he made her feel when he touched her like that. "You'd better go see him today if you're going to keep your promise this week."

Simon nodded. "We'll have to put off our swim to another time. Come on, I'd better get up there before he talks Jacob into telling him another Secret Service story. Last time, Elaine was mad at me for a week."

"Why?" she gasped out, having to jog to keep up with Simon's long strides.

"Jacob's stories can get pretty gruesome."

She could imagine, the man loved to emote.

They reached the house a few seconds later and she left Simon to answer the phone while she went upstairs to check her e-mail. There was a message from Jill and she answered it. There was also an e-mail from her mother. She'd listed a condo in Amanda's building with her real estate agency and wanted to know if Amanda was interested in selling too.

Amanda deleted the message without replying. It was, after all, nothing but e-mail solicitation and she never replied to junk mail. She ignored the twinge of pain she experienced at the knowledge that that bit of salesmanship had been the first time her mother had bothered to contact her in over six months.

"Can you be ready to go in ten minutes?" Simon asked from just inside the bedroom doorway.

She turned off her computer and stood up. "Go where?"

"To see Joey, remember?"

"I didn't think you'd want to take me with you."

"Why the hell not?"

"It's a family thing. I'm not family." She wasn't treated like family by her own parents and brother, why on earth would Simon's relatives want her around?

"You're my girlfriend. That's close enough."

"Girlfriend?"

"Yes, girlfriend. Do you have a problem with that?" He looked wary.

She shook her head. "I just didn't realize you wanted anyone to know about us."

He ran his fingers back through the loose strands of his shoulder-length black hair, his expression frustrated. "When have I ever said that? I love sex with you, but you're not just a business associate I happen to be screwing. I thought you realized that."

"I do." Their relationship might not be permanent, but he'd never relegated it to merely sex either. She didn't know what to say to get that irritated expression off his gorgeous features. "I'll change my clothes."

She didn't have a lot of selection to choose from, but she assumed a visit with his nephew would be pretty casual. So, she pulled out her one pair of jeans and a white button-up blouse she usually wore with a suit. She cuffed the sleeves and left the top three buttons undone before slipping on a pair of white sandals.

She turned to face Simon. "I'm ready."

He had changed into a pair of black jeans and matching T-shirt. His hair was pulled back in a ponytail and he looked positively yummy.

He also looked very serious. "Amanda, are you embarrassed about my cousin knowing we're together?"

"No!" She crossed the room and put her hands on his forearms. "I didn't want to intrude. That's all."

"It could be pretty awkward with your boss if he realized you were sleeping with the enemy, I suppose."

Awkward wasn't the word she would use to describe the way Daniel would respond to such news. Glee might be a better candidate. "You're not the enemy," was all she said.

"No, I'm not." He stared down at her, an enigmatic expression in his gray eyes. "I wonder if you will remember that, if the merger doesn't go through."

He didn't give her a chance to reply, but pulled her out of the room. They jogged down the stairs and out through the great room onto the deck.

"Where are we going?"

He tugged her toward the stairway that connected the deck with the yard. "To my cousin's."

"But the car . . . ."

"We're taking the boat. Eric will pick us up from the pier."

"Oh." She followed Simon to the end of the deck where he lifted her onto the small yacht.

"Jacob's at the wheel, but I've got to cast off." He untied ropes that held the boat to the dock and then vaulted aboard when the last one had been loosened. He took a few minutes securing the rigging before coming back to her.

"It takes a little over an hour which isn't quite as fast as the ferry, but we don't have to worry about missing it coming home either."

"Jacob told me most of the island residents have their own boats."

"It's a matter of safety as well as necessity. You never know when ferry service is going to be interrupted."

She'd certainly found that out, not that she was complaining. "You don't have to worry about gossiping ferry officials either."

Simon's mouth quirked. "That's true."

True to his word, it only took an hour to reach the mainland and Eric was waiting for them at the pier.

He smiled when he saw Amanda. "Hi. How are the merger negotiations going?"

Her returning smile was rueful. "Your cousin is stubborn. He listened to the proposal and all the benefits I outlined to you, but I don't think it made any difference."

Simon's arm dropped casually around her shoulder. "But she's welcome to keep trying to change my mind."

Eric looked at Simon's hold on her and then at Amanda's face with a speculative gleam, but he said nothing. He opened the back passenger door on a silver Mercedes sedan. "Elaine and Joey are waiting at home."

"What about Jacob?" Amanda asked as Simon handed her into the backseat of the luxury car.

"He'll keep himself occupied."

"Won't he feel left out?"

Eric laughed from the front seat as he started the car. "Jacob is Simon's employee, not his best friend. You don't need to worry about him, Amanda."

She didn't agree entirely with that assessment and her look to Simon told him so.

"Jacob has an old friend he likes to visit when we come to the mainland. He doesn't feel neglected at all."

"Oh. Okay then." The irascible old man irritated her no end, but she liked him.

"I imagine being on the mainland feels good after so many days on the island," Eric said to her.

"I don't know. I think I could easily live there year round. Simon does it."

Eric's laugh filled this roomy interior of the car. "Yes, but Simon doesn't look at life the same way other people do. He prefers his solitude."

She did too, when that solitude included Simon, but she didn't say it. Her first comment could be construed as a broad hint to Simon that she wanted to stay already. She didn't want to make him uncomfortable or to sound like a clinging vine.

"How's Elaine?" Simon asked.

Eric's smile slipped. "Morning sick and emotional. I feel so helpless and it only gets worse. It's a darn good thing she only wants two children. I don't think I could go through this again."

Amanda's hand slipped to her stomach. She could be pregnant with Simon's baby. Would he feel the same way about pregnancy? Would he only want one child like her parents had or two like Eric and Elaine? Maybe he didn't want any.

The sobering thought pierced the sweet bubble surrounding her. If she was pregnant, she had every intention of staying that way. She didn't see abortion as an option for birth control, no matter what the rest of the country thought. She could never get rid of Simon's baby.

For a few sweet seconds she considered what it would be like to be married to Simon and pregnant with his child. As long as she was daydreaming she might as well put a toddler on her lap and serious dark haired little boy on the seat beside her. It was positively medieval, but she would love four children . . . with Simon as the father.

"Amanda?"

She snapped out of her reverie.

Simon's head was turned toward her from the front. "Eric asked how soon you would have to head back to California."

She couldn't help feeling the answer should have been of more interest to Simon than Eric, but it wasn't her lover who had brought it up.

"I . . . . There is no set time. Upper management really wants the merger. I'm doing my other work remotely, so it's not a problem for me to stay." Well, other than a lack of clothes. Maybe she would call Jillian and ask her to FedEx some things up from California.

Her business suits just didn't fit her current lifestyle with Simon.

"There must be some kind of deadline," Eric probed.

She turned her face away and looked out the car window. "I'm sure there is, but I don't know what it will be."

She didn't want to leave and talking about it depressed her, but Eric was right. Her boss was bound to have some cutoff point at which he'd call her back to California.

She began to doubt that belief as the next week progressed. Daniel had been extremely affable when she made her less than encouraging report on Monday regarding the merger.

She'd had the opportunity to discuss the merger

with Eric while Simon was busy playing with his nephew. Eric had reaffirmed his interest in the proposal. However, he'd made it clear that if Simon stayed opposed to it, he would withdraw his support rather than allow a family war to start over the issue.

Which was just as she'd suspected. Yet when she'd told Daniel, he had responded as if it were a minor consideration, not the major setback it was. He had told her to keep working on Simon, but she'd gotten the distinct impression something was going on she didn't know about.

However, she'd gleaned nothing from the remainder of their conversation and her carefully worded questions.

Tuesday, she had accompanied Simon to Brant Computers. He had wanted to meet with his design teams and had invited her along. He'd made it a point to introduce her to several Brant Computers employees. The difference in how he related to them and the way Extant's Executive Management Team related to the workforce was a revelation.

He'd left her in the company of an older woman who worked in the sustaining group during his meeting. After they left the company, Simon had asked her how she would feel if that woman were one of the ones forced out of a job by the merger.

She'd been forced to acknowledge: one, it was all too likely and two, she'd feel awful.

"She's worked for us since her husband died of pancreatic cancer fifteen years ago, leaving her a widow with two teenage children. I couldn't sleep at night if she had to start working at a fast food place because we let her go."

Simon's words still echoed in her mind and she had begun to see his adamant refusal to consider the merger in a different light. He wasn't a quirky genius who didn't understand the business world well enough to function efficiently in it. He was a deeply caring man who took the plight of his company very personally and, in his mind, his employees were the company.

Yet, he continued to discuss the finer points of her proposal with her. He made it a point to ask her at least one question a day, or bring up an argument that she was forced to parry. She didn't know if he did this as a sop to his conscience because of his promise to Elaine, or if he just wanted to remind Amanda why she was there.

Even if that wasn't his intention, it worked. She never forgot that she was a temporary aberration in Simon's life, not a permanent fixture. The issue of her possible pregnancy had not come up again and Simon had been scrupulous about protection since that time in the shower.

Part of her was terrified she would end up pregnant. What did she know about being a decent and loving parent? A single one at that. But there was this teeny-tiny person inside her that craved having someone who belonged to her, someone to whom she could belong.

She ignored those desires while trying to understand her boss's almost complete about-face. He was way too understanding about her lack of success with Simon and then today, she'd gotten an out-of-the-office response in reply to her e-mail asking him a question about something else.

It gave her a bad feeling.

She was afraid he had gone behind her back to talk to the other shareholders. What really preyed on her mind was the idea that she should warn Simon and Eric of the possibility. She owed Extant Corporation her loyalty as an employee and telling Simon and Eric anything would be tantamount to revealing confidential information. On the other hand, she was terrified her boss would start that family war both she and Eric were so intent on avoiding.

And if he was pursuing the other shareholders, he was violating his agreement to let her handle the merger negotiations at this point. She sighed as she stepped on a small dead branch that crackled under her feet. She felt torn apart by her divided loyalties and the impermanence of her association with Simon.

The watch on her wrist started to vibrate. Simon had given it to her on Monday. Both he and Jacob could buzz her within a mile radius via the small two-way radio that was part of the watch just like Simon's.

She lifted it and pressed a small button on the side. "Yes?"

"You got a visitor, missy."

Daniel was here! It had to be. Who else would come to see her? "I'm heading back now."

She'd been exploring the woods surrounding Simon's home. She loved the tall spindly trees that swayed like hula dancers when the wind gusted and the way their sparse branches let sunlight through, casting a dappled pattern onto the forest floor.

She approached the house from the front. The yellow Mustang convertible did not look like something her boss would rent. He drove a white BMW. It wasn't flashy, but it screamed status seeker, from the polished silver door handles to its shiny black wheels.

She jogged up to the house and went in through the front door. She could hear voices from the great room, but the words were indistinguishable. However, as she drew closer to the room, she could tell one of the voices was a woman. Definitely not Daniel. Maybe Elaine had come to visit.

She'd been really friendly the previous Saturday, especially after Simon had made it clear he and Amanda shared more than a business relationship. Amanda had thought it odd later that neither Eric, nor Elaine were concerned she was attempting to manipulate Simon with sex.

They obviously didn't see her as Mata Hari material either.

Jacob said something and the woman laughed. *Jillian.*

Amanda burst into the great room just as Jacob started laughing right along with Jillian. Dour-faced Jacob laughing?

"Jill! What are you doing here?"

Jillian spun around to face Amanda. "I came to surprise you." And with her characteristic grin she flew across the room to give Amanda a hug. "I checked in to the hotel and then came right over. You wouldn't believe this guy who works at the ferry. I asked for directions and he starts pumping me for information like he's the CIA or something."

Amanda laughed. "I'd believe you, trust me."

"He didn't even recognize me."

"Most people don't and that's how you like it, so don't whine."

Jillian dressed conservatively with her hair kept in an elegant up-do for her role on the soap opera, whereas in real life she tended to wear clothes that would look jarring on Madonna and let her hair riot around her head in a mass of auburn curls.

Jacob was back to looking dour. "I recognized her right away."

"You charmer, I think I'll keep you."

Red burnished Jacob's cheekbones and Amanda just about fainted. The man was definitely starstruck.

"Can I get you two some refreshments?" Jacob asked, at his polite best.

Amanda stifled a giggle at the amazing change in him. "Sure. I'll take Jill out to the deck. Do you know if Simon plans to surface soon?" It was just going on lunchtime and he'd come out to share it with her every day so far this week.

"As I have said in the past, Ms. Zachary, Mr. Brant is not a submarine."

"Be nice to me, or I won't let Jillian talk to you."

Jillian laughed and patted Jacob on the shoulder. "Don't worry. Her bark is much worse than her bite. She hasn't muzzled me in a year at least, but I do want to meet your boss. Will he be down for lunch?"

"I believe so. He has discovered an ongoing and sufficient motivator for leaving his lab in the middle of the day." He gave Amanda a significant look and it was her turn to blush.

Because while it was true that she and Simon shared lunch every day, it was also true that that wasn't the only thing they shared in the middle of the afternoon.

Jillian's brow rose. "Interesting. You two will have to be more circumspect now that I'm here, though. I'm very impressionable."

"You're impossible," Amanda replied. "Come on. Let's go out on the deck."

They were seated at the table, sipping freshly brewed ice tea with a twist of lemon when Jillian turned to Amanda, her face more serious than Amanda had ever seen it. "Tell me about this guy you're sleeping with. Are you pregnant yet?"

Chapter 16

Amanda's tea went down her windpipe and she started choking.

Jill jumped up and pounded her back. "I didn't mean to kill you with the question."

Amanda tried to wheeze out an answer, but she couldn't make her voice work.

Jill stood back. "Oh, hell. It's already happened hasn't it? I knew it! You're such a babe in the woods with men. What did he do, tell you not to worry, he'd pull out?"

Amanda's face felt sunburned and her throat hurt from coughing. "It wasn't like that. Sit down, please."

Jillian shook her head, her red hair waiving wildly. "I'm going to kill him."

"*Jill.*" Amanda reached out and grabbed her friend's flailing arm at the wrist. "Stop it. I'm not pregnant."

"Are you sure about that?"

At the sound of Simon's voice, Jillian spun around, ripping her arm from Amanda's grip. "You jerk! I suppose you don't think anything of—"

Amanda's hand on Jill's mouth cut her off. She'd jumped up from her seat the minute Jillian started in on Simon. "Calm that Irish temper down or I'm going to end up eating your words and being humiliated in the process."

Jillian's eyes narrowed, but she nodded. Amanda moved her hand and turned to see Simon's reaction to her friend's outburst. He wasn't looking at Jill.

His entire attention was on Amanda. "I thought your period wasn't due for another week."

If her face had felt sunburned before, it now felt like she'd sustained a third-degree burn. "It's not."

"Then how can you be sure you aren't pregnant? Did you take a test?"

The only thing needed to make this farce more embarrassing would be for Jacob to make an appearance. "No. How could I? I doubt your local store even carries them."

He smiled cynically. "Don't be so sure about that, but if you didn't take a test, you can't know. Yet, you told your friend you're not pregnant."

"All right!" She glared at both Jillian and Simon. "I should have said I don't think I'm pregnant, okay?"

Jillian opened her mouth to say something and Amanda forestalled her. "Before you go off again, it's not Simon's fault."

"Oh really?" Jillian was at her sarcastic best. "Are you saying you had sex with someone else?"

Even the thought of another man touching her like Simon had made her sick to her stomach. "No."

Simon looked at Jillian. "It is my fault. I'm the one who forgot protection."

"And I made you forget it." She was still a little awed by that fact. Not a rational reaction, she knew, but when a woman had spent her whole life being told she didn't measure up in the female stakes, it was definitely a *natural* one.

"You sound proud of yourself," Jill accused.

"I noticed that too," Simon agreed laconically.

Amanda felt attacked from two sides even though, logically she knew that in their own way both Simon and Jill wanted to protect her. "How do you want me to sound? Ashamed? I left my hair shirt in California along with any false front for emotions I don't feel."

"Are you saying you want to be pregnant?" Jill practically shrieked in astonishment.

"Lunch is served." The addition of Jacob's voice to the melee was more than Amanda could handle with equanimity.

She turned on the housekeeper cum security expert with blood in her eye. "Discretion is the mark of a proper butler."

"I was being discreet. I didn't mention that pregnant women need to keep up their strength, did I? Didn't comment on the fact that a woman pushing thirty and a man already there should be a little more savvy about birth control. Now that would have been indiscreet."

Simon choked on something that sounded suspiciously like a laugh and Amanda wanted to hit him.

Jillian was busy nodding her head vehemently. "You took the words right out of my mouth. They're both old enough to know better."

"Twenty-six is not pushing thirty," Amanda informed them all loftily. As topics for conversation went, her age outdid pregnancy by a wide margin.

She spun on her heel and went back into the house.

"Where are you going?" Simon demanded from behind her.

"Jacob said lunch was served and as he so delicately pointed out, if I am pregnant, I need to keep up my strength."

"Uh oh . . . ." Jill's singsong voice followed her.

"I know that tone. She's really miffed. Simon, you don't have a big screen television, do you?"

"No, he doesn't, but he does have a collection of *katanas* that would make admirable gardening implements." Amanda didn't bother turning around when she made the threat, but she knew the people still on the deck could hear her.

"What's a *katana*?" Jill asked.

"A Korean sword." Surprisingly, it was Jacob who answered. "The boss is partial to his collection. They're all one of a kind and some are over a hundred years old."

"And no way are you using them to dig in the garden, even if you are pregnant with my baby." Simon's voice whispered in her ear as he leaned around her to pull a chair out from the dining table for her to sit in.

"That is not something I want to discuss right now." She let herself be drawn into the chair and scooted up to the table.

Jacob and Jillian came into the room.

"You're eating with us, aren't you?" she asked Jacob, thinking an obviously starstruck fan would thwart Jillian's inevitable attempt to grill Amanda over the possible pregnancy.

His poorly disguised fascination with Hollywood would make an ideal topic for the lunch table.

One gray brow rose in question. "You want me to eat with you? Thought you'd be embarrassed talking about the baby in front of me."

"We are not going to discuss babies or the possibility of a pregnancy," she said repressively.

"We're not?" Jillian asked tauntingly.

"No," Amanda replied firmly as Simon took the chair kitty-corner to hers. "You can tell us all about the show. Are you going to end up married to your love interest?"

The look she gave Jillian told her friend to go with the flow or else.

Jillian went, but with a disgruntled look.

Simon wasn't surprised when Jillian came to find him in his gym. Amanda was working on an emergency e-mail she'd received from Extant Corporation and it was the first time Jillian had had all day to corner him alone.

"So which one of these is over a hundred years old?" she asked pointing to the wall on which his *katana* collection hung.

He indicated one near the center. "That one is actually three hundred years old."

"Wow. If something's more than ten years old in Hollywood, it's considered an antique." Her eyes were focused on the sword in question with definite awe.

He smiled and moved into his form.

She turned her head toward him, her expression set. "I'm worried about Amanda."

He liked her directness.

"Me too," he admitted as he pivoted on his foot for the next step of his form.

That seemed to surprise her and she idly fingered the handgrip on one of the swords. "She's not very experienced around men. I don't think she'd like me telling you that, but you should know."

"She told me I'm the only lover she's had besides that bastard she was married to."

Jillian laughed. "He's a bastard all right and you probably don't know the half of it, but I'm glad she told you she doesn't sleep around."

"She told me." And he'd liked hearing it. He went through his entire form in a series of rapid movements that left a light sheen of sweat on his skin.

When he stopped, Jillian was eyeing him speculatively. "Are you just playing with her?"

"What is this, a rendition on the 'what are your intentions' theme?" He grabbed a small towel and swiped at his face. "Isn't that something parents are supposed to ask?"

Jillian crossed her arms and glared at him. "Maybe it is, but Amanda's parents are dead losses where she's concerned. They were rotten to her growing up and completely wrote her off when she left Lance."

"They don't believe in divorce?" he asked, curious about every nuance of Amanda's life.

"They don't love their daughter." Jillian's voice was dripping with contempt. "They're more worried about appearances and business contacts than her happiness."

"You care about her." It wasn't a question. Jillian had flown up from Los Angeles to check on her friend. That showed genuine caring.

"I'm the only person in her life that does."

"No." He took a swig from his water bottle. "You're not."

"Then your intentions are honorable?"

"That's between Amanda and myself." And not something he could answer right now. It was too complicated. "I'm glad you care about her, but this is something you have to let her work out for herself."

"That's what I thought about Lance. I knew he was a smarmy toad, but I didn't say anything because she seemed so happy. By the time they'd been married a month, I bitterly regretted my silence."

Simon was beginning to understand Jillian's motivation for flying to her friend's rescue. "You felt responsible for her marrying someone that hurt her so much."

Her green eyes glistened with moisture. "Yes. She was so innocent and he wasn't."

"But she left him when he had an affair."

Jillian's laugh was harsh. "Lance had his first affair within months of their marriage and I think Amanda knew it, but she blamed herself for not being sexy enough. He was such a bastard. He rejected her every way a man can reject a woman and made her feel like it was her fault."

"They're divorced now." She had to have figured out at some point it wasn't her problem.

"Yes, thank God, but she's still vulnerable. She hasn't even dated since the divorce and then she falls into bed with you. Can you understand why I'm worried?"

He removed one of the *katanas* from the wall and began an ancient fighting routine. "She's decided to spread her wings, find out what she's been missing."

"Amanda's not like that."

He wished he shared Jillian's confidence. "Are you saying you think she's in love with me?"

Jillian averted her eyes and that said it all.

"I didn't think so. Look, I don't want to hurt her. Our relationship means a lot to me."

"I'm glad to hear that."

He finished the routine and started oiling the sword.

"What are you going to do if she turns up pregnant?"

"At the risk of repeating myself, that's between Amanda and me. You'll have to trust your friend to know what's best for herself."

"Like she did with Lance?" Bitter worry laced her voice.

He understood her pain, but he couldn't alleviate it. What he wanted and what Amanda wanted were probably two different things, but whatever happened, they had to work it out between themselves without anyone else's involvement.

Amanda waited with the car running for Jillian to come out of the bed-and-breakfast. She'd called her on the cell to say she was here a minute ago.

Jillian had shocked her the night before when she had refused Simon's offer to stay at his house. She'd said her clothes and everything were already unpacked in her room. Then she had asked Amanda to come over to Port Mulqueen to spend the day with her today.

Amanda couldn't say no, not even knowing it was losing a whole day of the limited time she had left with Simon. A Saturday. Jillian had flown up from Los Angeles because she was worried about Amanda. Because she cared. Amanda refused to dismiss that as unimportant.

Besides, a day spent with just the girls held some appeal. For some reason she didn't understand, Simon had suggested inviting Elaine to join them. When Jillian had learned that Elaine was his cousin's wife, she'd gone along with the idea wholeheartedly. Amanda had no problem understanding what motivated her friend. She wanted to pump Elaine about Simon.

The passenger door opened and then Jillian slid in. "Sorry I didn't come down right away. I had to finish making some plans."

"What plans? I thought we were just going to drive into Seattle and go shopping."

Jillian shook her head. "Change of itinerary."

"What change?"

"I'm not telling. It's a surprise."

"Does Elaine know?"

"Nope."

Amanda frowned and started the car. "She's pregnant, remember. One of your forays into extreme sports would not be the way to spend the day."

"Don't worry, we're not doing anything risky to pregnant women." Jill eyed Amanda's stomach significantly.

"Stop that. It's highly unlikely I'm pregnant."

Jillian sobered. "What happened?"

"I seduced Simon in the shower. We both forgot."

"You seduced him?" The disbelief in Jillian's voice said it all.

Her friend knew how hard it was for Amanda to initiate sex. "He asked me to."

"Smart man," Jillian said under her breath.

Amanda didn't reply.

"So, is it likely?"

She repeated what she'd told Simon that day in the shower to Jillian.

"Are you going to buy a pregnancy test kit while we're out and about today?"

"I'm due to start in a week."

"Do you really want to stew over it for another six or seven days?"

Amanda sighed. "No, but how accurate can a test be? It has only been a week."

"There are some that claim ninety-eight percent accuracy after two days."

"How do you know?"

"Television. Some of us watch more than pretaped programs that skip all the commercials."

"I'll think about it."

Jillian didn't push it and Amanda was grateful.

They pulled up in front of Elaine's house a few minutes later. The door opened immediately and Elaine came out. Jillian jumped out of the car and moved to the backseat so Elaine could sit up front.

Elaine smiled her thanks as she slid into her seat. "I'm not too big for the backseat yet, but I get carsick if I try to ride in the back."

"Bummer," Jillian said.

"At least I'm not morning sick all day long like I was with Joey. That was a real bummer."

"It should be against the law to be morning sick past eleven A.M.," Jill said facetiously.

They all laughed.

"So, where are we going?" Amanda asked Jillian.

"Get on I-5 going south."

"Very mysterious." She turned to Elaine. "Maybe you'd better navigate. I was on I-5 coming from the airport, but I'm not sure if I remember how to get there."

It took half an hour to reach the freeway from Port Mulqueen. Once they were headed south, Amanda again asked Jillian where they were going. Jillian referred to a piece of paper she pulled from her oversize holdall and gave Amanda an exit number to take.

Elaine smiled. "This is fun."

"I'm reserving judgment," Amanda said.

Jillian snorted. "You're going to love it."

"I'm surprised you got her away from Simon. She's barely left the island since their first meeting."

Amanda felt her cheeks heat. "I was supposed to be convincing Simon about the merger."

"Oh, I could tell that the merger was uppermost on both your minds last Saturday."

Remembering Simon's openly affectionate manner, she understood Elaine's teasing. "By then we'd become personally involved."

"Is that what you call it?" Jillian asked, tongue-in-cheek.

"What would you call it, smarty pants?" Amanda demanded.

"Incredible sex if it managed to get you off the wagon of abstinence."

"Is it incredible with Simon?" Elaine asked, sounding very disbelieving.

"Don't you know?" Amanda returned.

"No. We dated for a while, but it never got that serious."

It had been serious enough for Simon to consider marriage, but he and Elaine hadn't slept together. For some reason that made Amanda feel better. "I've never experienced anything like it."

"That's the way it is with the man you love."

"Watch it you two, I think I'm too young for this conversation," Jillian piped up from the backseat.

"That will be the day," Amanda chided back.

Laughter filled the car and the tension that had held her all week long as she wondered what was going on between her and Simon, and what her boss was up to, dissipated.

Amanda pulled the car into the small strip mall's parking lot. The gray buildings housed a women's only fitness facility, a bank, something called Shinga'ar and a couple of restaurants. Maybe Jill wanted to go to the women's only workout place, but Amanda hadn't brought anything to work out in and she hadn't seen a gym bag when Elaine got into the car.

"Park there in front of Shinga'ar."

Amanda obeyed Jill's command and saw that the store was actually a salon.

Jillian unclipped her seat belt and opened the back door. "Let's go ladies, our *shinga'ar* awaits."

Elaine turned to Amanda. "What's a *shinga'ar*?"

"Beats me. Knowing Jillian, it's more than just the name of the salon."

"You're so right, Amanda. Now stop dawdling. Our appointment is for ten."

Considering the fact that it was five minutes to, Amanda did as Jillian suggested.

They walked into the salon and were greeted by a lovely Indian woman, dressed in a green sari outfit with a matching jewel on her forehead. A melodious tinkling accompanied her every movement.

"Good morning, you are Miss St. Clair?"

"Yes," Jillian replied, "but call me Jillian."

"And these are Miss Zachary and Mrs. Brant?"

"Please, call me Elaine."

Amanda said something similar and the woman smiled. "I am Geetha. Are you ready for your *shinga'ar*?"

"I don't know," Amanda said, "What is it?"

"The shinga'ar is the whole person makeover. The hair. The clothes. The jewelry. The makeup."

"You do all that?" Elaine was looking around the shop as if trying to understand how that could be so.

"Not usually, no, but your friend made special arrangements." She indicated the back room with a fluid movement of her elegant arm and her multiple bracelets clinked together softly. "I have brought in a special selection of clothes and jewelry."

"Trust you to come up with something totally unique, but I don't want my hair cut off." Simon's blatant enjoyment of her hair gave her far too much pleasure.

"Do not worry." Geetha beckoned with her perfectly manicured hand. "Come. I will show you some pictures."

Amanda followed her to the other side of the reception desk. On it was a large flat panel monitor. Geetha clicked a button and an image materialized. It was a beautiful woman, her makeup exotic, her dress alluring. That picture was followed by another and then another. Each woman looked too perfect to be real. They all had jewels on their foreheads, some wore bracelets like Geetha's, others wore sexy dangling earrings, one woman had henna tattoos on her hands, but they all had one thing in common. They were gorgeous.

She didn't think for a minute that Geetha could perform such a miraculous transformation on her, but the thought of going back to Simon tonight dressed and made up so appealingly filled her with anticipation.

"I knew you'd like the idea," Jillian said, "Your eyes are shining with a positively wicked light."

Amanda laughed and Elaine said, "This is just the sort of thing a pregnant woman needs to indulge in. How did you ever find this place?"

"I've got a friend in LA who has a sister who lives up here. She came in for Shinga'ar's Grand Opening and then told her sister all about it. Kali told me about it when she found out I was coming up here for the weekend."

"Shall we get started?" Geetha asked.

Starting meant being led to a room at the back of the salon and undergoing an allover body massage and herbal wrap. Afterward, Geetha gave them all white cotton robes to don and thongs for their feet. She then fed them a light lunch from one of the restaurants nearby.

This was followed by manicures, pedicures and makeovers. The makeovers included having their eyebrows threaded. It was like getting them waxed, but didn't hurt as much and Geetha was meticulous in shaping Amanda's eyebrows into slim, feminine curves that made her brown eyes stand out.

True to her word, Geetha did not cut Amanda's

hair, but she did take it out of its customary French twist and put it up in juice-can size rollers all over Amanda's head. When she took them out, Amanda's hair fell in big curls that Geetha brushed into soft waves which she pulled back from Amanda's face with a jeweled clip.

When Amanda turned to look in the mirror, an exotic stranger stared back at her.

"Do you want henna tattoos before we select your clothes?" Geetha asked.

Elaine refused, not sure if the henna would be good for the baby. Jillian asked how long they would last and had to decline with obvious regret when Geetha said at least a week. That left the other two women looking at Amanda expectantly.

"I don't want my hands tattooed, I'm sorry." She smiled at Geetha, not wanting to offend the woman.

"What about something on your shoulder blade?" Elaine asked.

"Be daring, have her put something sexy in your cleavage." Jillian smiled devilishly.

"What about something around your belly button?" Geetha asked when Amanda remained silent.

The only person who would see it would be Simon. "Like what?"

Geetha indicated a page of swirling designs.

Amanda selected one that looked almost like lacework.

Both Jillian and Elaine insisted on watching her have it done.

When Geetha was finished, she let Amanda see in the mirror.

"All it needs is a jewel and I'll look like a belly dancer."

Geetha's soft smile shone and she left the room. She came back a moment later carrying something glittery in her hand.

She handed it to Amanda. "It has adhesive on it. If you do not submerge it, it could last for a week. If you go in the Jacuzzi or pool, it may come off sooner."

Decadent thrills were curling through Amanda and she didn't even hesitate. She took the red, ruby-looking gem and put it in her belly button. "It feels funny."

With the henna tattoo and jewel, her tummy didn't look like it belonged to her.

"You need to learn to belly dance. It's too bad we don't have time today." Jillian winked.

"I think that's going to drive Simon wild," Elaine said.

Amanda blushed under the subtle makeup Geetha had applied, all the while hoping Elaine was right.

"Now the clothes and jewelry."

They followed Geetha into another room. Colorful silks filled a portable wardrobe. Amanda was surprised to see that the silks were not all saris. Some were dresses cut in simple but flattering lines. Jillian chose a flamboyant lime green-and- gold sari with a gold undershirt.

Elaine opted for a sari as well, saying the style hid the small pooch announcing her pregnancy. However, hers was a more conservative pattern in a soft yellow and tan.

Amanda was torn. Part of her wanted one of the exotic saris, but another part of her didn't want to go the whole length of the transformation to a woman of another culture. Geetha suggested she try on a dress in blood red. Depending on how the light hit it, it shimmered black as well. It looked demure until she got it on. The high neck was offset by a butterfly cutout right over the plunge of her cleavage.

There was almost no back at all, exposing her skin from below her shoulder blades right down to her tailbone. No way could she wear a bra with this dress. Turning to look at the side profile and the way the skirt clung to her until mid-thigh where it swirled out, she thought she'd have to forego her panties as well. They were leaving a line.

"You've got to take that one," Jillian cried.

Amanda stared at the now extremely sexy, exotic woman in the mirror. "I feel practically naked." And once she got rid of her bra and panties, she would be.

"It looks beautiful on you." Elaine's voice rang with sincere admiration.

Geetha clinched it by handing her a pair of shoes that were no more than a bow and delicate heels. And they matched the two-tone deep red-black of the dress.

Amanda slid them on. "How did you know to have my size?"

Jillian looked guilty. "I knew the dress I wanted you to wear. I sort of had this planned."

"But Elaine . . ." She could understand Jillian making plans for her and Amanda from LA, but Elaine too? That made no sense.

"Saris are one size fits all." And the simple sandals they wore with them were in neutral leather tones, easily going with any sari selected.

Amanda turned back to the mirror. She had never looked like this in her life and she liked it. "Wow."

"Now, the jewelry."

Both Elaine and Jillian affixed jewels that matched their dresses to their foreheads.

Amanda refused one. "It wouldn't really go, and besides I've already got a jewel on."

She did, however, allow Geetha to slide about a dozen black glass bracelets on her left wrist that tinkled when she moved her arm. Elaine wanted an anklet and Jillian opted for bracelets on both arms.

When they were ready to leave, Amanda was shocked to see that it was after five.

"We'd better get back or I'll miss the last ferry back to the island tonight."

"Don't worry about it," Jillian said, "I called Simon this morning and we're all having dinner on his yacht at the Port Mulqueen pier."

"That sounds perfect." Elaine smiled. "A woman shouldn't get dressed up, just to go home and have dinner in front of the television set."

Amanda sincerely doubted that Elaine and Eric made a habit of eating in front of the TV, but she smiled. She understood the sentiment.

She even shared it, along with a certain amount of trepidation at how Simon was going to react to her makeover.

Chapter 17

———————

The closer they got to the pier, the more nervous Amanda became.

How would Simon react to her new image? She hadn't tried anything sexy on him since the night she'd worn the cami and tap pants only to discover he'd wanted her proposal and not her. Simon seemed to prefer her naked. That had been hard enough to get used to, but the prospect of appearing before him in her almost not-there dress was making her shake in her spike-heeled sandals.

She could remember times she'd gone to great lengths to look nice for Lance when he hadn't commented at all. Worse had been the times he'd found something to criticize. Simon wasn't like that. She knew he wasn't, but she couldn't seem to quiet the dancing gorillas that had taken up residence in her stomach.

She pulled her rental car into the lot attached to the pier. Jillian and Elaine got out, taking time to adjust their saris. They looked gorgeous and mysteriously foreign. Amanda climbed out of the car and locked it.

She was afraid to look toward Simon's moorage in case he was there waiting. She wasn't ready to see him yet, to acknowledge his reaction to her

new look. She approached the end of the pier
where Simon docked with her eyes focused on the
ground in front of her as if her life depended on
watching each step. In the sexy sandals, it just
might. Or at least her dignity.

Like a small child, she was operating on the
principle that if she couldn't see him, he couldn't
see her.

Elaine and Jillian discussed the merits of shopping in Seattle versus LA. Thankfully, they seemed
content with her own silence.

Her skin tingled and she knew he was there,
watching her approach. She almost stopped walking, but she managed to keep her feet moving forward. Each step she took increased the tension
inside her until she couldn't help looking up.

She had to see his reaction.

Just as she had known it would be, Simon's
yacht was in its moorage and he stood on the deck
waiting for them. Their eyes met across the distance separating them. His were devouring her
with ravaging force.

Elaine called out a greeting to him, but he didn't
respond. His eyes did not so much as flicker in their
intent regard.

Jillian said something and Elaine laughed. The
words didn't register for Amanda, so she had no idea
what the two women found so amusing. Her attention was locked on the man standing so still on the
deck. His gunmetal gaze moved over every inch of
her body with tactile force. Goose bumps broke
out on flesh that felt as if it had been caressed.

Her mouth went dry and she tried to swallow.

She reached the yacht. She was peripherally
aware of Elaine and Jillian walking up a gangplank
that had not been used on the previous trip she'd
taken on Simon's yacht. A male voice indicated that

either Eric or Jacob had come out to greet them. Amanda could not force her attention away from Simon long enough to look and ascertain which.

She stopped at the end of the gangplank. Simon started moving toward her and she waited for him, feeling paralyzed by the look in his eyes.

When he reached her his hands came out to cup her face. "You're beautiful."

Two words that meant so much.

His head lowered and he kissed her softly, almost reverently. "I wish now that I hadn't agreed to have dinner with the others."

Her hands rose of their own volition to rest against his chest. She could feel the heat of him through the thin black silk of his dress shirt. He was wearing a pair of black slacks as well and he had pulled his hair back into a ponytail. "You look pretty nice yourself. I don't think I've ever seen you in anything but jeans."

"Right now, I want to see you out of that dress."

She tilted her head to one side, flirting in a way she'd never done. "Don't you like it?"

He laughed. "It's sexy as hell, but it does too good a job of teasing me with what is underneath."

"Not a whole lot."

His eyes closed and he tilted his head back. "I'm not going to last through dinner." Then he looked at her again, his face a study in male frustration. "What constitutes not a whole lot? I have to know so I can torment myself for the next few hours with what I can't have."

"You know the stay-ups I like to wear?"

His gaze slid down her body to her black silk clad legs and he nodded. "Uh huh."

"That's it."

His head snapped back. *"Just you and a pair of thigh-highs?"*

"Yep." She watched in fascination as sweat broke out on his upper lip.

"Baby, I'm not going to make it." He did sound like a man who was dying.

She inched closer so his scent and heat surrounded her. "Sure you will."

He swallowed convulsively and ran a fingertip around the cutout between her breasts. "This is nice."

She trembled. "I like butterflies."

"So do I, but I've never seen a more beautiful one." His finger rested directly on her exposed cleavage. "I want to taste you here more than I want to take my next breath."

Her breath hitched, pressing the flesh of her breasts against his fingertip. "I don't think you should do that in front of the others."

His finger ran down the line where her breasts were pressed together by the cut of the dress. "They've gone inside."

"They have?" How had he noticed? It was all she could do to remember they had even been there.

"Yes."

"Someone else might see." She was trying so hard to stay sane. He wasn't making it easy.

He looked down at the rigid peaks obvious beneath the thin material of her bodice. "I want to put my mouth over them and suck on them through your dress."

She shivered, her knees weakened, and she felt herself going damp between her legs. "Stop it. I'm not going to be able to sit down pretty soon."

"I can't walk already."

She looked down and felt her insides melt at the blatant evidence that her sexy new look definitely affected Simon.

"Oh, Simon."

"Don't say my name like that."

Her head snapped up and she looked at him, half-hurt by the harsh tone in his voice. "Why not?"

"Because it makes me want to strip you naked and take you on the gangplank."

"Not a good idea, cousin. You can get arrested in Port Mulqueen for stuff like that. I think it's called indecent exposure."

She peeked around Simon and there stood Eric, looking incredibly amused. She felt her face flush and looked at Simon to find a matching burnished color slashing across his cheekbones.

"Jacob's waiting to serve the appetizers until you come inside. Elaine is hungry. Pregnant women get cranky when they're hungry. She and Jacob are close to coming to blows."

"We'd better go save Elaine," Amanda said with a small smile at Simon.

Eric chuckled. "I think Jacob is in greater danger, besides our guest is waiting to say hello to Amanda."

Tension filled Simon's body at Eric's words and the look he gave his cousin could have stripped paint. Something was definitely wrong. Had he and Eric argued about the merger while the women had been gone? She could easily see Simon taking advantage of Elaine's absence to launch a full-scale battle with Eric regarding Extant's proposal. Simon was protective of Elaine's feelings. He'd made that clear during their first meeting in Eric's office and again when Elaine and Eric had come to the island for dinner.

She longed to know if that was because Simon's natural protective instincts extended to her as a woman in his family or if he still cared for the woman he had once considered marrying.

Her musings stopped as Simon placed a heavily proprietary arm around her waist and began walking her up the gangplank.

Eric noted it and grinned at Simon and then winked at her.

What in the world was going on?

Simon barely controlled the urge to take off his shirt and put it around Amanda's body before letting her walk into the lounge. He'd spent the last hour in the company of her ex-husband. The guy was too smooth to be real, but his California golden image was undeniable. A lot of women would find his looks irresistible.

Amanda had married the man.

She must have been taken in by the looks and rehearsed charm at one time. According to Jillian, she'd even stayed married to the guy after the first affair. Had she loved him that much?

He'd hurt her, but women didn't always stop loving men that hurt them, even if they worked up the emotional stamina for a divorce. And here she was looking sexier than she probably ever had. Lance Rogers was bound to be hit right in the libido with what he'd given up.

Simon was watching for it as they walked into the lounge.

Lance noticed Amanda before she noticed him and his eyes widened at the sight, an arrogant smile playing around his lips. "Hello, Amanda."

Her entire body went stiff beside Simon and she stopped dead two feet into the room. "Lance?"

Simon couldn't read anything from her voice except shock. Not welcome, not revulsion, just shock.

Lance's smile grew. "Yes, it's me. Surprised, sweetheart?"

Simon felt his own body tense at the endearment. Damn it, no man had the right to call her sweetheart but him.

"What are you doing here?" she asked in a flat tone.

"I've been in town for the last couple of days talking over the merger with Eric." He was all golden boy charm. "You look fantastic, Amanda. Very exotic. It's a new image for you."

"You don't even work for Extant Corporation." To Simon's pleasure, she didn't respond to the compliments on her appearance.

Lance's smile was more predatory than disarming. "Not strictly, no. But they have my law firm on retainer. Your boss approached me to help negotiate the deal. Friendly mergers are one of my specialties. Eric and I have had some good discussions over the past week."

"Why wasn't I told?" Amanda asked in that same flat tone that was beginning to bother Simon.

He didn't know what it concealed.

"Is that really something you want to discuss in front of our hosts? If you insist on hearing the details right now, perhaps Simon will lend us a stateroom to talk."

The pretty boy was taking Amanda to a stateroom over Simon's dead body. His hold on her tightened.

Her head came up and her eyes met his for a brief moment, not long enough for any meaningful communication but sufficient time for him to see that she was operating in a state of contained shock.

"The details can wait." She turned toward his cousin. "You didn't mention that Lance had come to discuss the merger with you."

Eric looked discomfited by Amanda's monotone as well, or maybe it was the accusation implied by her question. "He told me you knew he was here."

"I didn't."

Lance didn't look bothered by the denial. "Let's not play games, Amanda. You knew Daniel would be sending someone." He looked significantly at Simon's hold on Amanda. "It's obvious you've lost the objectivity necessary to act as negotiator."

Amanda tensed further and pulled away, going further into the room and putting distance between her and Simon. He wanted to snatch her back, but the way she held herself so stiffly made him wary of pushing her.

"My relationship with Simon has absolutely nothing to do with the merger." At least she was admitting they had a relationship.

For a minute there, he thought she might be gearing up to deny it.

"You're right about one thing, this isn't the time or the place to discuss Extant business." She took a deep breath and let it out. "We *will* talk later, but I can't help wondering why I wasn't called back to California if, as you've implied, Daniel believes my professional integrity has been compromised."

"You know why, but if you really want me to spell it out to you, I'll gladly do so later." Lance's condescending tone grated on Simon's nerves.

He wondered how the pretty boy would look wet from a dunking in the Sound.

"Fine, you do that." She looked toward the doorway. "I assume that now Simon and I have arrived, Jacob is going to start serving the food?"

Whether it was because he'd been standing outside the room, listening, or because of his amazing timing, Jacob came in at that moment with a tray of *hors d'oeuvres*. Showing intelligence, if a bit belated, he offered the tray to Elaine first.

When the tray came to Amanda, she declined anything.

"I don't know how you can wait until dinner. It's been hours since lunch, aren't you hungry?" Elaine popped a miniature puff pastry in her mouth. "I'm starving."

Lance smiled winningly at Elaine. "With a figure like yours, you can indulge, but Amanda can't afford to partake of every course of dinner."

Fury rolled through Simon like a tidal wave and his vision of Lance was surrounded by a red haze.

"Keep your opinions of Amanda's figure to yourself," Jillian added with a voice that could have shred steel.

Lance put his hands up in a gesture of surrender. "Hey, I didn't mean to offend. I was just trying to explain why Amanda hadn't taken any of the appetizers."

"I'm capable of explaining my own actions when necessary." The words were said firmly, but the look in her beautiful brown eyes was too damn vulnerable for Simon's liking.

Lance shrugged. "Sure."

Simon picked up a canapé and walked over to Amanda. He stopped in front of her and she looked up, her eyes asking a question.

"I think your body is perfect, sweetheart. Now try this, it's one of Jacob's personal concoctions."

Her mouth opened slightly, but not enough for him to slide the small goody between her luscious lips. She stared at him and suddenly he felt like he was waging a battle between the present and the past that still tormented her. He would win because losing was not an option. Lance had had his time with Amanda and he'd screwed it up. Simon wasn't making the same mistakes. He wasn't even tempted to.

"Open up, baby. Trust me."

Her lips parted further and he slid the morsel into her mouth. He brushed her lips with his fingertip before he withdrew his hand and signaled for Jacob to bring the tray of appetizers to him. This time he chose a mini-quiche. He put it to her lips and felt like a conquering king when she accepted it without protest.

Jacob turned away and put the tray of *hors d'oeuvres* on one of the small tables. "Dinner will be on the table in fifteen minutes." He left with all the dignity of a Victorian butler.

Simon winked at Amanda; her eyes warmed, though she didn't smile. "He's playing a role again," she whispered.

Simon nodded. "He's a frustrated thespian. He never got to go undercover on his Secret Service detail and he has latent frustrated desires."

"You'd better watch out or he's going to follow Jillian back to Hollywood. Then where would you be?"

"No chance. He hates smog."

"There is that."

Good. Amanda was sounding more normal.

"So tell me about this *shinga'ar* thing," Eric said from his position beside Elaine on one of the small sofas.

Elaine and Jill launched into an animated description of how they had spent the day. Simon half-listened while getting a glass of wine for Amanda.

He handed it to her. "Do you want anything else?"

She shook her head. "I'll wait for dinner."

"You're not fat."

"Sometimes I see myself through other people's eyes. I don't mean to."

Looking at her incredibly sexy and downright feminine persona, he smiled. "Then see yourself through my eyes. You're perfect."

She got drawn into the conversation by Jill before she could answer.

Jacob called them into dinner a few minutes later. Lance had not said anything else offensive to Amanda, but he'd let his gaze zone in way too often on the curves he'd disparaged earlier. Amanda seemed oblivious as with each passing minute she slipped more firmly back into the cool, buttoned-down façade she had put on when she first came to Washington State.

She looked sexier than any woman Simon had ever known, but was acting as asexual as an amoeba.

He was tempted to kiss her senseless just to break through the defensive wall growing around her, but the fragility under her surface kept him from doing it. He wished he knew what was causing that fragility. Was she still susceptible to her ex-husband or was it because her company had sent him to Port Mulqueen without telling her?

She wasn't giving anything away.

Why the hell had Eric invited Lance to join them for dinner in the first place? Making up numbers. Like Jillian would have cared if she were the odd one out. That woman had enough confidence to accompany a friend on her honeymoon and still have a good time. To give his cousin the benefit of the doubt, the first Eric had heard of Lance being Amanda's ex was when Simon had brought it up just before the women got back.

Lance sure as hell hadn't said anything. The man was obviously economical with the truth and if he was an example of Extant Corporation's management style, Simon was doubly determined to prevent any merger from taking place.

Amanda stood with Simon to see his other guests off the boat. Barely leashed tension communicated itself to her and her nerves wound another notch tighter. Was he thinking she had been aware of Daniel's plan to send Lance to meet with Eric? Was he angry with her?

He hadn't acted angry when he had been cajoling her to eat the canapé. Stress had a bad effect on her appetite, especially stress related to Lance, but Simon had been determined not to give her that coping mechanism. She was glad, but she couldn't tell what he was thinking now.

There had been times over dinner when the look in Simon's eyes had been positively violent.

He didn't like Lance. Simon was too self-contained to be obvious about something like that, but certain gestures and the measured tone he used when talking to Lance had made it clear to her.

"I didn't know he was in Washington."

Simon didn't look at her. "He said you did."

"He lied. He's good at that."

Simon's shrug said it didn't matter and cold seeped into her, making her shiver.

"It was nice of Jacob to drive Jill back to her bed-and-breakfast." No one had suggested Jillian ride with the Brants and Lance. Probably because they all wanted to avoid bloodshed.

"He's starstruck."

"I thought so too." She smiled fully for the first time since seeing Lance that night. "I told you. You're going to have to watch him with Jill. She may not get him to Southern California, but she's got connections up here as well."

"He plays more roles as my employee than he could ever land in a real production."

"No doubt." She sighed and turned away from the disappearing taillights.

Simon wasn't looking at them, his eyes were on her.

"Lance is smooth."

She grimaced. "He works at it."

"He could be a model."

Too true. "He was on a Calvin Klein billboard when he was an undergraduate."

"Do you still love him?"

The question blindsided her. Hadn't Simon heard her when she told him how Lance had treated her? "No!"

"You sound adamant."

"I am." She couldn't believe he was thinking along those lines. "Simon, Lance is not a lovable person. I was more enamored with the idea of getting my family's approval than I was with him before we got married and by the time we got divorced, I despised him."

"You said he didn't want you."

"He didn't." Why was he bringing this up now? Didn't he realize that even though she was over her ex-husband, the memories of her marriage still had the power to wound. Failure hurt. Failing at the most basic definition of who you were—like being a woman—was devastatingly painful.

"His eyes were glued to your chest all night. Like hell he doesn't want you."

"What?" She felt disoriented. Simon sounded jealous, yet she couldn't believe he thought there was a need to be so.

"He wanted to get you alone in a stateroom."

"To talk business," she said with some exasperation.

"With the way he was looking at you, I don't think business would have been the first thing on the agenda."

She'd been worried that Simon might think she had been working behind his back on the merger, and here he was, suffering from a bout of male possessiveness. Lance had not been possessive. It felt . . . She had to think about it. Different, and sort of nice.

"You think Lance would make a pass at me?" It was so laughable that she smiled. "No way." Less amusing was her next thought. *You think I would succumb?*

"I didn't say that."

"But you're jealous." Her mind boggled. Simon, the most gorgeous and masculine man she'd ever known, not to mention a lover most women would die for, was jealous.

"Yes," he bit out.

She laid her hand on his arm. "There's no need. The only man I want is you." How could he not see that? She vibrated like a tuning fork when he came into the room and wilted like a dead flower when they had to be separated.

Was he blind?

"You were married to him." It was almost an accusation.

"It was a lousy marriage."

"Jillian said you didn't divorce him after the first affair."

Jillian had a big mouth and she had a tendency to draw her own conclusions. They weren't always right.

"I didn't know about the affairs, not for sure anyway." She willed him to believe her. She'd stayed married for too long to a complete jerk, but she had not been a total doormat. "Until I walked in on him."

"That's when you realized he was having an affair?"

"Yes. I suppose I should have suspected before, the way he found it so easy to reject me physically. Maybe I was willfully blind, but I didn't know."

"What happened?"

"I went to his office on a Saturday to see if he was there. It was an off chance. He usually golfed on Saturdays, but he wasn't answering his cell phone. I needed something. I can't even remember now what it was, but I remember what I saw." It still made her sick. It had been so sordid.

"He was with another woman."

She remembered Jill had said almost the same thing. "Yes, but they weren't alone."

"He had two women with him?" Simon asked with disgust.

Would that have hurt less? Maybe. If she hadn't known either of the women. "Worse."

"How?"

"I discovered my husband was bisexual."

"He was with a woman *and* a man?"

"Yes. He hadn't touched me sexually in a year and there he was with two of them. They were panting, grunting, sweaty . . . there was this smell, like they'd been going at it a long time. They didn't even notice me, they were so lost to reality in their lust. I left. When I told Lance I wanted a divorce, I didn't tell him what I'd seen, just that I knew he was having an affair."

She shuddered with remembered distress. "He didn't even bother to deny it. He told me it was my fault that he had to seek sexual release elsewhere. That I wasn't enough woman for him. He was furious with me for insisting on the divorce. Do you know he had the gall to suggest I get counseling?"

Simon's expression went from savage to so tender, her heart cried. "Aw, baby." He pulled her into his chest. "I'm sorry. What a bastard. If I'd known all of this before, I wouldn't have let him on my yacht."

She knew he was telling the truth. Simon wasn't Eric. He didn't allow himself to be bound by socially correct behavior.

He squeezed her tighter and incredibly, her body reacted to the pressure of his. "You're lucky you didn't end up with some disease."

"I know." She rubbed her cheek against his black silk shirt. "The Monday after I found him in his office, I went to the doctor and demanded they run every test imaginable. It was humiliating, but I couldn't live with the uncertainty." The memory wasn't as wounding in Simon's arms as it had always been before. "Who knows what level of protection he exercised in his perverse sexual games?"

"Considering his selfish arrogance, that's a damn good question." Simon's body heat surrounded her like a security blanket. "I want to hurt him." The level of fury in Simon's voice shook her.

"Don't. Please don't let it matter. It's over, and now I'm really thankful he found me such a sexual turnoff."

Simon stood there rubbing her back for several minutes in silence. Thoughts of her marriage with Lance were relegated to her brain's garbage incinerator as the heat that Simon's gentle touching evoked burned them up.

The cold breeze coming off the water could not diminish the lava-like desire flowing through her.

She moved subtly against him and he sucked in air.

"You turn me on without trying," he said in a voice guaranteed to melt her insides to liquid honey.

Chapter 18

She didn't doubt him.

The evidence was pressing against her stomach.

"I'm glad." So very glad.

"I can't believe your family was mad at you for divorcing the bastard," Simon burst out.

She didn't want to think about it anymore, but an image of the man Lance had been with rose before her like a specter. "My parents love my brother. They don't even tolerate me."

"So?"

"The man that made up the final third of that lewd *ménage à trois* with Lance that day was my brother." She'd never told anyone, not even Jillian.

When she had stopped going to family events, her parents hadn't cared. She'd never been forced to explain why she couldn't stand to be in the same room as her brother. They were all too busy vilifying her for divorcing such an upwardly mobile man with all those great connections for their real estate business. She now realized her brother had pushed her at Lance to cover his own bisexuality. A trait that didn't go over well in the business community, even in Southern California.

Simon said something that made her ears burn. She tilted her head back to smile at him, the pain of her brother's betrayal submerged in the pleasure she found in Simon's company. "My thoughts exactly."

He swept her up into his arms without any warning, looking pretty fierce.

"Are we playing another fantasy? Are you the marauding privateer now?"

"Privateers were not considered marauders. Pirates marauded."

She clung to his neck. "Are you playing pirate, or just caveman . . . again?"

He stopped and looked down at her, his gaze silver with emotion. "Do pirates get to capture princesses?"

A lump formed in her throat. He said the most amazing things. She smiled brilliantly at him, despite the wetness she couldn't quite conceal in her eyes. "It depends."

"On what?" He'd started moving again and was carrying her along the short corridor that opened onto the staterooms.

"On what pirates do with princesses."

"Ravish them."

"In that case, I would say it's a certainty. Pirates are the very best at capturing princesses."

"Then I'm a pirate, because you, Amanda, are definitely my princess."

She wouldn't let herself believe he meant what she wanted him to mean, that she ruled his heart. But even so, the words touched her deeply. "You're a very sexy pirate. I like the fact you have both eyes and no hook."

He laughed as he leaned down to open a door. "You'll be really grateful for both hands by the time the night is over."

"Will I?" she teased, knowing he was right, but it wouldn't take all night. She was thankful right now as anticipation of what he would do with those hands rolled over her in a hot wave.

He carried her into the stateroom. It was bigger than she expected, with a custom-built bed occupying most of the space. He dropped her onto the bed in a flurry of red silk. She landed with her skirt exposing the top of one of her stay-up stockings.

"I think you'd better take the dress off, captive." The words were diffident. The tone was not.

She gave him a saucy look. "Why's that?"

"Because if you don't, it's going to end up ripped."

She had never been wanted to the point of having her clothes ripped off. The concept that Simon could want her that much excited her.

She stretched back against the bed, raising her arms above her head in a way that made every curve move under the sensuous silk of the dress. "Really?"

Simon's expression turned feral. "I'm not kidding, baby."

It was a beautiful dress, but not as beautiful as the look of desire in Simon's eyes. "Show me."

His eyes widened, then narrowed, and he came over her in a predatory rush that made her gasp. One of his hands slid into the butterfly cutout of her dress, straining the fabric to its limit. He cupped her ripeness. She couldn't help scooting back a couple of inches that gained her exactly nothing.

"Nervous, baby?" he asked mockingly, his hand squeezing her in erotic repetitions.

"Excited," she corrected. Conquering warrior, pirate, it didn't matter . . . Simon would never hurt her.

Something came over him at her response and his other hand went to join the first. When he found the opening too small for both hands, he yanked at it and the sound of rending silk filled the silence of the stateroom.

Her breasts were exposed, framed by the frayed edges of the torn red fabric.

Simon leaned back to look at her. "They're fantastic, sweetheart. So beautiful, they're a Heavenly work of art."

She shuddered and heat pooled between her legs as her heart swelled with emotion. "Are you going to touch me?"

Had he ripped open her bodice just to look?

His smile was all masculine sex appeal. "Oh, yeah."

Then he started doing just that, using his mouth and his hands to tease her flesh into a state of aching need.

"Oh, Simon . . . . Please. Yes. Don't stop."

His sensual laughter acted like a further stimulant to her senses. "I couldn't stop, baby. Not even if I wanted to and I don't. I'm going to touch you all night long."

But he did stop, long enough to tear his own shirt off, sending jet black buttons flying, and then he was kicking off his pants, exposing an erection of rather daunting magnitude. It was a good thing she hadn't gotten a good look at him before they made love the first time. She would have run screaming, sure they wouldn't fit, but they did and he touched her so deeply sometimes, it felt spiritual.

He came down on top of her, pressing the hot skin of his muscular chest against her soft flesh and she cried out at the indescribable feel of it. He teased her with his body, rubbing himself between her legs, the silk abrading both of them. If it felt as sensual to him as it did to her, he was going to climax before he got inside her. She felt on the verge of orgasm herself.

"You are so sexy, Amanda. So beautiful." He whispered more compliments, interspersing them with things he wanted to do to her as he kissed her face and neck and breasts.

She writhed under him, desperate for a connection he seemed intent on denying.

She wanted her dress off. Now.

Loving the freedom to touch him, she ran her nails down his back, the pirate fantasy forgotten. She didn't feel like a captive. She felt like a woman being tormented by her man.

"Simon, I want to be naked," she wailed.

The hiss of rending silk was followed by the feel of his hardness against her wet and swollen labia. He stroked his flesh against hers without penetration for several seconds.

"I want you, Simon! Now. Please. . . ."

He reared up and backward; when he returned to her, he was holding a condom. "Put it on me."

She sat up, breathing hard, and pulled off the remnants of her dress. She discarded it, a violent ache to pleasure him holding her in its grip. She lifted the weight of each breast in her hands, then leaning forward, she rubbed her hardened nipples against his even harder erection.

He groaned.

Arrows of sensations shot straight from her stiff peaks to the very core of her.

A wantonness she'd never known pulsed with the rapid beat of her heart; she pressed her breasts around him and he shouted out.

"What are you trying to do to me?"

"Make you feel as good as you make me feel."

He choked on whatever he tried to say next as she slid the soft tunnel of her breasts up and down his length. She'd never done anything like this, but Simon made her feel wild. As her generous curves pressed against the base of his manhood, she bent her head forward and delicately licked the top.

Bucking toward her mouth, he made an inarticulate sound of need. "More, baby. I need more of you."

She understood and with one final kiss to the tip of his erection, she released his rigid flesh from its resilient prison. Excited by performing this task for the first time, she tore open the condom package. She took as much time as she dared sliding the latex down his length, wanting to prolong the touch of her fingers on him.

"I love touching you," she whispered from a throat raw with passion.

"I love your touch, but it's got to be now."

With that, he exploded into movement, lifting her up and back and pressing himself between her legs, all in one desperate motion. A single rocking of his hips saw him sheathed in her heated wetness and she moaned at the pleasure of being one with him. She felt connected to him on every level at that moment.

"I love you, Simon. I love you!"

He responded in a frenzied series of thrusts that sent her into a vortex of pleasure so deep, she didn't think she'd ever come out of it. She convulsed around him, the rippling sensations going on and on and on as he continued to pound into her with driving force. Then his body bowed and he yelled her name as he came.

Afterward, she fell asleep with him still inside her.

Amanda didn't stir, even when he gently pulled himself from her body. She sprawled on top of the comforter with her arms thrown wide and her legs parted in the position of their loving. One dark brown curl lay nestled around her still-turgid nipple. The rest of her hair was a wild tangle around her head and she looked like a pagan queen well satisfied by her lover.

She'd been satisfied all right.

How many times had she convulsed in orgasm? He'd been too busy slamming into her with uncontrolled need to keep count, but it had seemed to last forever. And she had screamed her throat raw. He bet she didn't even realize it, but toward the end she'd done no more than croak his name.

She probably didn't realize she'd said she loved him either. Sex talk . . . only Amanda didn't indulge in that. Not yet anyway. That was something they could play with another time, later. If they had a later.

From the sound of things, her boss wasn't happy with her handling of the merger. What a jerk to have sent someone up to help with the negotiation and not even tell her. Especially her ex-husband. Her boss had to have the sensitivity of a rhinoceros. Or he was so displeased with Amanda's inability to get Simon to agree to the merger, these actions were like a corporate slap on her wrist. Would she be called back to California?

Could he convince her to stay?

She'd said she loved him.

In the throws of a mind-blowing climax, he reminded himself. But she had said the words.

What did words mean? If she meant them . . . then, everything.

He made quick work of taking care of the condom and then went back to the stateroom. Not surprisingly, Amanda hadn't moved. He lifted her limp body so he could pull the covers over her, then slid into bed beside her, curling his big body around her smaller one.

Content, he slept.

Amanda laid her fork down. "When are you sailing back to the island?"

"Don't you mean we?" Simon leaned back in his chair, his empty breakfast plate pushed out of the way and measured her with a look.

She wished she did. "I have to bring my car." Too bad. She had never made the crossing on the yacht in daylight. The view would be spectacular.

"Why don't you leave it here? You don't need it on the island. If you want to come into Port Mulqueen and I can't take you, Jacob can drive you to the ferry."

For a woman who had been fiercely independent for the past few years, the idea was much too tantalizing. "I don't know."

"You afraid of my driving, missy?" Jacob asked from his position by the galley sink.

"Of course not."

"Then leave your car here," Simon instructed.

"All right." She could always pick it up later, but the opportunity to go with Simon today was irresistible. "So, what time are we leaving?"

"Did you want to invite Jill to sail with us?" he asked instead of answering.

"I would, but she told me that she's meeting some friends from acting school in Seattle today."

"Then I guess we can leave any time."

"I need to meet with Lance before we go."

"No."

She stared at Simon, shocked at his vehement denial. Despite his tendency to want his own way, she hadn't expected him to try to interfere with her like this. Not about business.

"I need to find out what's going on with Extant."

"Call him." Simon picked up his coffee cup and took a long sip, his steady regard a little unnerving.

"I'd rather talk face-to-face." Lance lied too easily and too well. She needed all the extra help she could get and seeing his face when he answered her questions would be a step above tonal qualities over the phone lines.

"I don't want you alone with him."

"Don't be ridiculous. I've had to meet with Lance on several occasions since the divorce. Besides, that really isn't a decision for you to make."

His expression said otherwise. "I'm not trying to make the decision for you."

Right. "Like you weren't trying to make the decision for me when you kidnapped me on the island and blackmailed me into staying?"

"I lured you into staying. I didn't blackmail you."

"Semantics."

"I know he treated you like the untouchable woman while you were married and I can't pretend I'm not glad for that after what you told me last night, but he wants you now. Men recognize lust for their women in other men."

"Am I your woman?"

"Haven't we had this discussion already?"

Was he referring to their talk regarding her status as his girlfriend? She guessed he was. Only one didn't seem quite as serious as the other and she desperately wanted to know how serious about her he was.

She hadn't been so lost to passion the night before, that she hadn't noticed his silence in the face of her avowal of love. No answering declaration. No mention of it whatsoever, in fact.

"Even if he is lusting, and to be honest I think

your perception is biased, I don't want him. So there's no problem."

"Problem is the boss doesn't want you alone with the guy," Jacob inserted.

She turned to frown at him. "I've got enough to deal with here. I don't need your interference."

"Gettin' sassy, ain't ya? See what a makeover will do for a woman?"

She let out an exaggerated sigh. "I'm not made over anymore."

"You're wearing your hair down and your face looks different. You're made over all right."

"Let me clue you into something, Jacob. I could have my hair in a bun and a bag over my head and I would still object to both your and Simon's interference in my plans."

"I want to spend the day with you and I don't want your ex-husband or your job to take any part of that away from me. Is that so much to ask? It's Sunday, Amanda. Most people take Sundays off. You don't see me headed home to my lab do you?"

No, she didn't. "Would you be if I wasn't here?"

He shrugged. "Probably. I'm working on something pretty important right now."

But spending the day with her was more important. "All right. I'll deal with it tomorrow."

Simon's smile was full of male satisfaction, but she couldn't work up any resentment because his eyes reflected a relief that touched her. He cared. He might not love her, but he cared in a way no one but Jillian ever had.

Sailing back to the island during the day turned out to be everything that Amanda imagined it would be. She loved standing at the rail, Simon behind her, surrounding her with his arms and the warmth of his body as the cold breeze off the ocean made her skin sting with awareness. The views were spectacular. They even saw whales in the distance and Jacob slowed the yacht to a crawl so Amanda could watch them play in the water.

She forced herself to forget her worries and to concentrate on being with Simon.

And true to his word, when they got home, Simon didn't disappear into his lab. He didn't disappear at all. His focus was entirely on her and she couldn't help wondering what it would be like to spend the rest of her life with this man. Late in the afternoon, he talked her into a sparring session, insisting she needed more work on her form. He touched her a lot more than was strictly necessary, but now that she did not have to hide her reaction to the brush of his body against hers, the Tae Kwon Do sessions were sheer pleasure.

He made love to her gently and slowly that night, keeping her on the brink of completion until she shouted his name and her love. He didn't return the words, but he was so gentle with her as he prepared them both for sleep that warm tears leaked out of her eyes.

He kissed them away and pulled her into his body to hold her through the night like he'd done every time they slept together since the first bout of passion they had shared.

"You said Jacob would take me to the ferry if I wanted to go into Port Mulqueen." Simon wasn't being gentle now. He was being stubborn and she wasn't having any of it. "I'll walk to the ferry terminal if I have to."

Stormy gray eyes narrowed. "It's six miles."

"Do you doubt I could do it?" In her current

mood, she could jog the distance in her sensible pumps.

He leaned back against the kitchen counter and crossed his arms. "We agreed you wouldn't be alone with him."

"We agreed I would deal with it today and that's what I'm doing."

"What's the problem with calling him?"

"It's a meeting that needs to happen face-to-face." She had questions she wanted answers to, answers that would come more than just from the words Lance might say.

Simon didn't say anything, his expression set in grim lines.

She sighed. "Look, if it helps, we're meeting in a restaurant. We're not going to be alone."

"But you insist on meeting him?"

She couldn't read anything from Simon's voice. "Yes."

He straightened. "Then I guess I'll get Jacob to drive you."

He turned to go, but she reached out and touched his arm. "Simon, this has nothing to do with us."

He spun to face her with the grace and speed he showed in the gym. "That's what I'm afraid of." He grabbed her and kissed her hard, then set her away from him before leaving to get Jacob.

She stood there in bewildered surprise for several minutes until Jacob's impatient summons started her moving toward the front door.

She had a forty-five-minute ferry ride in which to think about Simon's reaction. He was really worried about Lance and she couldn't imagine why. She wouldn't let Lance touch her with a barge pole.

He was a poisonous spider under those California golden looks and she had no desire to ever again spend time in his sticky web.

Her mind was still engaged with thoughts of Simon and what his overprotectiveness could mean in terms of emotional commitment when she walked into the restaurant to meet Lance. He was sitting in a booth by the window overlooking the pier.

Sliding into the seat opposite him, she offered a polite nod, but no smile. "Hello, Lance."

"Amanda. Back to the business persona, I see." He looked her over like a buyer for a used car, his expression saying there were plenty of flaws even if he hadn't found them yet. "The night before last was certainly a departure from your normal style." His gaze fixed directly on her chest in a way that it had rarely done when they were married. "That red dress had sex written all over it."

The implication was nauseating. "I'm not here to discuss my taste in clothes and I have absolutely no interest in your opinion of how I dress."

"Are you sure about that?"

She pushed her napkin and cutlery aside, and signaled to the waitress for a cup of coffee. "Very sure. The only thing about you that interests me is an explanation of what you're doing on my project and why I wasn't told you were in Port Mulqueen."

He grimaced, the perfect looks of his face marred by lines of distaste. "You're such an abrasive person, Amanda. Talking business does not preclude observing the social niceties."

"There is nothing nice about you Lance. It may have taken me a few years to figure it out, but all my blinders are off in regard to your character." She would not let him sidetrack her with his critical attitude. "Now answer my question."

She didn't care if he thought she was a female version of Attila the Hun; she wanted details.

He took a long draw on his ice tea, purposefully drawing out his answer.

When she merely sat there, silent and staring, he gave in. "You weren't getting the job done." He stopped and did that measuring thing with his eyes again. "It's easy to see why now, even if a bit difficult to believe. I never would have thought you were the type to put her personal life ahead of the job."

"Are you trying to imply that I'm somehow responsible for Simon's adamant desire to keep Brant Computers privately held?"

"Please." Lance's tone patronized her. "Your career is hinging on this deal. You want it to go through all right, but the problem lies in the fact you're obviously more concerned about getting boinked than getting the job done."

The crude accusation annoyed her, but she didn't buy it. Nothing short of a miracle was going to convince Simon Brant that Brant Computers was better off merged with its competitor, Extant Corporation. She'd tried and her failure had not been due to lack of business acumen or effort.

She relaxed against the booth. "We aren't all controlled by our libido and it's no use you trying to judge me by your standards. They don't mesh with mine."

His eyes narrowed and she knew he'd gotten the implied insult.

"If I wasn't getting the job done to Extant's satisfaction, why wasn't I told?" It really bothered her that her boss would go around her like this.

"You were left to deal with Simon, which seemed to be your preferred method of pursuing the merger." Lance's voice dripped innuendo. "Daniel thought someone else would be more effective at shoring up support from Eric Brant for the merger."

"That doesn't explain why I wasn't told."

"You didn't need to know."

"How can you say that? It's my project."

"But it's Extant's merger. You're a cog in the wheel, Amanda, not the driveline."

The waitress laid a platter of appetizers in front of them.

Amanda ignored the food, but Lance took a sautéed mushroom and popped it in his mouth. "I don't know why you're complaining. You weren't taken off the project and you weren't required to pursue a line of inquiry other than the one you chose to do."

"I was the initial negotiator with Eric Brant and his opinion was not the one holding up forward momentum on the merger."

"The management team felt that a more aggressive approach needed to be made to him."

"So they sent you?"

"I often work in a similar vein for my clients. You know that."

Lance did have experience in negotiations, but he still wasn't an employee of Extant. He was usually brought in when his clients were looking for more than a smooth negotiator. Why had upper management decided to bring in legal muscle at this juncture?

"How does Daniel think you'll succeed where I've failed?" There was a plan and she wanted to know what it was.

Lance waited to answer, taking time to eat another appetizer before talking again. "I'm working on showing Eric Brant what a visionary move the merger will be and convincing him to go ahead without Simon's endorsement."

She'd been afraid of that, knowing in her gut that a man who thought she should use sex as a manipulative tool wouldn't balk at starting a family war. She had hoped Daniel would be held back by Simon's threat to go elsewhere with his designs if the merger went through.

Apparently, her hope had been in vain. "So, what are you using to convince Eric of the 'vision'? Smoke and mirrors?"

"Not at all. Your initial proposal and subsequent number-crunching were sufficient basis to begin my talks with Eric. Your analysis wasn't bad, by the way, but the presentation was too generic. I improved on it, of course."

"Daniel gave you my reports without talking to me about it?"

Her proposal had not been in the company's public domain. Those numbers and supposedly boring analysis belonged to her. Corporate common courtesy dictated that Daniel asked before using them for his own work, much less giving them to someone outside the company.

Lance gave her a pitying look. "You didn't expect him to ignore their potential just because you were too busy shacking up with the competition to use them, did you?"

She ignored the comment about shacking up. For all intents and purposes, that was what she'd been doing and she could hardly take offense at the truth. However, she did not accept that her relationship with Simon had prevented her from doing her job. "I already presented that material to both Eric and Simon Brant. The potential wasn't being wasted."

"I presented it again with a few conclusions of my own." He smiled smugly. "I think we've got Eric Brant solidly in favor of the merger."

"He's always been in favor of the merger," she replied with exasperation. Didn't anyone at the head office understand that the problem was Simon, not Eric? "It's *Simon* who won't be budged."

"That's not a problem."

Clearly her boss was convinced of that or Lance wouldn't be in Port Mulqueen. "Did Daniel mention to you that if Brant Computers goes public, Simon will sell his new designs to the highest bidder?"

Lance shrugged. "He's bluffing and if you weren't so blinded by his *personal attributes*, you would realize that."

"If you make one more crude, snide or suggestive comment in regard to my relationship with Simon Brant, I'm going to make taking apart a big screen television and letting it crash to the floor seem like an act of mercy." She bared her teeth in an imitation of a smile. "As for Simon, you don't know him. He doesn't play corporate head games. It's not a bluff. He feels really strongly about keeping the company family held."

Lance shrugged again, his expression chilling in its calculation. "If Simon Brant attempts to sell his designs to the highest bidder, he'll be in for one hell of a legal battle."

"He didn't sign an intellectual property rights agreement for Brant Computers. He gives them his designs because it's his company, not because he's legally required to do so."

"There are such things as implied contracts, Amanda. Didn't you learn anything in your business law course?"

Implied contracts? She ignored the dig, feeling sick to her stomach. "What you are proposing isn't ethical."

Lance laughed and it was not a nice sound. "Grow up, Amanda."

"I am an adult. A moral adult, which is something I realize you have no familiarity with."

"Sticks and stones, sweetheart."

"Simon is not an asset on Brant Computer's spreadsheet." The nausea in her stomach increased. "You can't force him to design for the merged companies."

"We'll see."

Amanda stood up, not bothering to hide her disgust. "Yes, we will. Eric won't support a bogus lawsuit and Simon is no patsy. In fact, he's a hundred times the man you could even think of being."

Lance rolled his eyes. "Anything else, Amanda?"

"Yes." She smiled, a real smile born of joy from the experiences that led to the thought she was about to express. "You're a lousy sex partner as well as morally corrupt. I now know what it means to be satisfied by my lover and I have to wonder how much you paid the women you had affairs with, because it sure as hell wasn't your prowess in the bedroom that convinced them to have sex with you."

It would have been a very effective exit line if it wasn't followed by an unexpected dash to the women's restroom where she lost her breakfast.

Chapter 19

She used her cell phone to call Daniel from the ferry.

He wasn't answering on his mobile and, according to his voice mail that morning when she'd tried to reach him before going to see Lance, he was still out of town.

She closed the flip phone wishing desperately that Jillian hadn't flown back to LA the night before.

Amanda needed someone to talk to.

Her work was blowing up around her ears and she very much feared that wasn't the only thing that would be exploding in the next nine months. If that bout of nausea in the restroom meant what she thought it did, her waistline was going to do a fair amount of exploding as well.

Panic curled through her, fighting with anger for supremacy. She was furious with her boss for going behind her back and sending Lance to negotiate with Eric. It showed such a complete lack of respect for her professionally that she had to wonder why he'd sent her on the mission alone in the first place. And betrayal twisted her insides as she thought of the ammunition he'd armed Lance with—her work.

Beyond that, she was sickened by their proposed plans to use legal means to force Simon to design for the merged company. She didn't know if it would work, but it would drive a huge wedge between him and his cousin. If the merger went through, their relationship would be strained enough.

It wasn't right.

She wanted to warn Simon and tell him about her suspicion that Daniel was working on the other shareholders in an attempt to override Simon at a shareholders' meeting with their votes added to Eric's. Amidst all that was her worry that Extant Corporation knew details about Simon's current projects that they shouldn't know. She had no idea how they'd gotten the information, but Daniel had certainly implied they had it.

But she still worked for Extant and she could not convince herself that she had the right to say anything as long as she was an employee of the company.

The fact that she wanted to say anything at all was a huge deviation from the way she would have responded before meeting Simon Brant and falling in love with him. A few weeks ago, her entire future had been bound up with her job. That wasn't true anymore. Even if Simon didn't want her as a permanent fixture in his life, she was afraid that, in one way or another, she was going to be.

She laid her hand over her stomach, the queasy feeling not gone completely. Whether that was due to the rocking motion of the ferry or something inside her own body would be determined when she reached Simon's house and used the early pregnancy test kit she'd bought after leaving the restaurant.

* * *

"Amanda . . ."

At the sound of Simon calling her name, she came out of the bathroom, feeling curiously light-headed.

All she saw was Simon's back. He'd turned around and headed back out of the room already.

"I'm right here."

He pivoted back to face her, his expression strangely blank. "So you are. Where's your watch?"

She'd forgotten to put the combination watch-com-munication unit on that morning. "I don't know, beside the bed probably."

He turned to look and her gaze followed his. Sure enough, there it was on the nightstand.

"Simon, I—"

"Eric just called," he interrupted, swinging back to face her. "Our second cousins are demanding a special meeting of the shareholders to discuss the proposed merger with Extant Corporation."

It was her worst fears realized. Dizziness came over her and she swayed. "I see."

"Do you?"

She nodded, still too loopy from what she had learned in the bathroom to measure her responses. "I expected something like this."

"Are you saying you knew your boss was talking to the other shareholders for Brant Computers?"

Her brow wrinkled at the flat tone in Simon's voice.

"Yes." She'd known. She hadn't wanted it to be true, but she'd suspected and it turned out her suspicions were right.

"So, what was this all about?" He swept his hand toward the bed. "Your way of keeping me occupied while your boss got my cousins hot for the merger?"

"What?" His words didn't make any sense.

"You promised me you weren't using sex to manipulate me into agreeing to the merger, but I should have asked a different question, shouldn't I?"

Suddenly his meaning became clear, and so did the reason why Daniel hadn't told her he was sending Lance to Port Mulqueen. She had unwittingly done exactly what Simon had accused her of. Daniel had used her like a paid prostitute. Knowing she wasn't guilty in her own heart was little consolation with Simon looking at her with such a wealth of disgust in his gunmetal eyes. Daniel had used her, but the possibility that Simon believed she'd done it on purpose, gutted her.

She went hot, then cold with the most excruciating pain. "You think I made love to you to—" She clapped her hand over her mouth and ran back into the bathroom.

She barely made it to the sink before being sick. She hadn't eaten anything since coming back to the island, so she dry-heaved and it hurt. But then everything hurt right now. She couldn't get a deep breath and hot tears burned a path down her cheeks as she bent over the sink.

Two strong arms came around her. One held a washcloth which he wet under the tap and then used to wipe her face.

"Shh, baby. It's okay. Relax."

She closed her eyes and let him comfort her because she felt physically too weak to fight him and her emotions were decimated.

Her stomach finally settled and he swept her into his arms, carrying her back into the bedroom.

He laid her gently on the bed. His hand brushed her cheek, but she kept her eyes shut. She didn't want to look at him right now, didn't want to see eyes she was used to seeing burn with passion, or light up with humor, or with what she'd convinced herself was caring, now burn with resentment. It hurt.

"Amanda . . ."

She turned away from him and curled up on her side. "Lance thinks that if they get the merger through, the combined companies can force you to give them first option on your designs with some kind of legal injunction based on implied contracts."

She spoke quietly, but she knew he could hear her.

His hand settled on her shoulder. "Baby—"

"And I think Daniel knows whatever it is you're working on right now."

Now Simon knew it all. If Eric had waited to call just one hour, she would have told Simon everything and he would never have accused her of something so despicable. She would never have had to know what a low opinion he had of her morals, or that whatever he felt for her, it wasn't love.

You didn't think things like that about people you loved. She didn't have a lot of experience with the emotion, but she knew deep in her heart that she would not have even considered a similar scenario with Simon in the deceiving role. She'd never entertained doubts about him using sex to manipulate her either, not like he'd wondered about her in the beginning.

But then, she loved him.

"That doesn't matter." Simon's voice was gravelly above her.

She shook his hand off her shoulder. "It's all that matters."

Damn it. Why was she so weak right now? She just wanted to get up and leave, but she didn't think her legs would hold her. And where would she go? Not back to Port Mulqueen. Her job there was over. Her job was over, period.

She could go home.

She was unemployed, but she still had her condo. After faxing in her resignation without giving notice, she doubted she'd get any kind of reference. It might be a while before she found another job. If things got really tight, she could list it with her mother's real estate agency and make at least one person happy.

He rolled her onto her back by exerting steady pressure on her shoulder. His gray gaze was mesmerizing. "Are you pregnant with my baby, Amanda?"

"Yes."

"I'm glad."

Was he? She guessed he could be. You didn't have to love the mother of your child to want it, did you? Simon would be a wonderful father, but that wasn't something she could deal with thinking about right now. She'd never considered being a single parent, giving birth to a child by a man who didn't love her.

"What are you going to do about the merger?"

"Eric's on his way over now. We're going to talk."

"I hope you can work it out between you."

Simon looked down at the woman he had made love to so exquisitely the night before. She had burned like living flame in his arms and told him she loved him. Her Hershey dark chocolate eyes were lifeless now, as if that incredible fire had gone out and all that remained was dead ashes.

She was talking about the merger as if it was the only thing that mattered.

As if being pregnant with his child didn't matter.

As if he didn't matter.

She wanted him and Eric to work things out, but

there was no room for compromise. He couldn't agree to the merger, especially after what she'd just told him about her boss's plans. He didn't want corrupt management working with his company.

He wished he could give her what she wanted. Make it all right and make her happy, but he couldn't.

He touched her again, relieved when she didn't reject him. "I'm sorry."

"Me too."

He wanted to ask where they went from there, but she looked so fragile and he wasn't sure he could take the answer when it came. Maybe she didn't think they went anywhere. Maybe *they* were a done deal as far as she was concerned.

She'd admitted to knowing her boss was working behind the scenes to make the merger go ahead, but accusing her of using sex to keep him occupied in the meantime had been stupid. He was the one who had kidnapped her and convinced her to stay. She had too many hang-ups about her own ability to attract a man to have planned to use it in some nefarious manner.

He was an idiot.

And his idiocy had been born of jealousy, along with a feeling of betrayal which he should not have experienced. He knew her job came first. Right from the beginning, he'd known that. But he'd wanted more and so, had made her pay for it when he didn't get it.

Remembering the sound of her heaving over the sink, the pasty white complexion of her face and the tears, he felt like the world's biggest heel.

"You have nothing to apologize for, but I do. I shouldn't have accused you of using what we have. I know it wasn't like that."

Her eyes begged him to mean it, for once her

emotions as clear to him as a perfectly polished optical lens.

He pulled her into his arms, holding her so tight she squeaked.

He loosened his hold just a little. "Please, Amanda. Forgive me. I didn't mean it."

She cuddled into him and he felt like he'd cracked the secret to fiber-optic computer processing.

"Are you sure?" Her voice was muffled by his chest.

"Positive. I was the one who kidnapped you, remember?"

"I remember, but I thought you had forgotten." That was all she said, but he sensed there was more going on in her mind.

He also sensed that right now she had no intention of opening up to him.

They stayed that way for a long time, her allowing him to hold her. Finally, she squirmed in his arms and he let her move back a little so he could see her face.

"Do you think you can convince Eric to vote against the merger?"

"I don't know." Remembering her words earlier, he asked, "Why did you tell me about Daniel and Lance's plans?"

"Because what they want to do is wrong. I tried to talk Daniel out of starting a family war, but he wouldn't listen."

"He doesn't care about anything but the bottom line."

Far from being offended by that indictment against her boss, she nodded her head sadly. "You're right. He even wanted me to try to convince you to change your mind using sex as my weapon."

"Is that where you got the idea I might be worried about it?"

"Yes." Her voice was small, almost like a child's.

"He's a bastard, honey."

"But a smart one. He and Lance are going to do their best to overrule you at the shareholder meeting."

"They won't be there. The only people allowed in the room are shareholders and their legal representative."

"Then be prepared for Lance suddenly taking on one of your cousins as a client."

She was right. He smiled grimly. "I'll be ready for him." He laid his hand across her belly. "Are you happy about the baby?"

"I don't know. It's all such a shock." She put her hand on top of his. "I'd rather not talk about any of that until this thing with the merger has been decided."

He almost asked her if she was going to withhold the baby from him if he succeeded in scuttling the merger, but stopped himself in time. He did not need another "dumb man" moment for her to file away in her memory banks and use as reference material when they did get around to talking about the baby and the future.

"Okay. Eric's going to be here soon. I'd better get downstairs."

She nodded, her expression hiding her emotions and her thoughts. "I think I'll go for a walk."

In other words, she was giving him time alone with his cousin.

Simon leaned down and kissed her, putting feelings he could not yet put into words into the pressure of his lips. Her response was everything it had always been and he shuddered inwardly with relief.

"I really am sorry for being such an idiot," he said when he pulled away.

"Thank you, Simon. That means a lot to me."
He left her with a soft smile curving her lips.

Eric lounged back on the sofa, looking a hell of a lot more relaxed than Simon felt. "So you're saying Amanda told you that her boss plans to sue you for your designs if the merger goes through and you make good on your threat to put them up for the highest bidder?"

"It's not a threat, Eric."

"Yeah. I know that, you know that. But, according to Amanda, Extant management thinks you're bluffing."

"Right. The legal recourse is a contingency plan." Eric nodded. "It's not a very good plan."

"They're counting on you being as numb to ethics as they are."

"Bastards."

That was pretty much what Simon thought too.

"That Lance Rogers is a smooth operator, but under the surface he's slime."

"Glad to hear you figured that out."

"I didn't like the way he treated Amanda at dinner the other night, and you know how I feel about being lied to. He was so sure I wouldn't care that he'd told me she knew he was in Port Mulqueen when she didn't, that he didn't even bother to apologize for it."

Simon told Eric the bare bones about Amanda's marriage to Lance. He didn't expose her private pain and humiliation, but he wanted his cousin to know what kind of man Lance was. "And he's the guy Extant Corporation chose to replace Amanda as negotiator for the deal."

Arctic lights glinted in Eric's blue gaze. "A big part of my approval of this deal was wrapped up in

Amanda. She's a straight player. That spoke well for Extant."

"You said *was*. You're no longer one-hundred percent behind the deal?"

"Are you kidding? They went behind our backs and approached the other shareholders, they sent a second negotiator who is pure slime, but their plans to try to force you to sell your designs to the merged company is the clincher for me. If this is the way Extant Corporation's management operates, there's no way I'm merging my company with theirs."

Simon smiled. Extant's attempt to force his hand had backfired magnificently. "Amanda also thinks they've got some inside knowledge into what I'm working on."

Eric looked shocked. "How could they have that?"

"I'm not sure, but my guess is they've had someone monitoring my supply purchases. Some of the equipment and components I'm using right now have very limited application."

"But you don't make your purchases through the company. Even if they had an inside man, and I'm not convinced they do, your activities couldn't be tracked through Brant Computers."

"But if they learned the names of my suppliers, hacked into my credit card records or even monitored deliveries via the ferry, they could get some idea."

"What are you working on right now that has Extant Corp so interested in acquiring you and Brant Computers?"

"I'm close to proof of concept on a fiber-optic processor."

Eric whistled. "The first company out with that baby is going to take over lead position in the industry."

"Yes."

"No wonder you've been so against the merger."

"I'm against it because I think it's wrong."

Eric sighed. "You've made me do a lot of thinking the past month and last week when Rogers was making such an effort to sell me on the merger, I realized how many of his arguments completely dismissed employee welfare."

"Amanda didn't. She believed that merging the companies would be best for the employees in the long run."

"Does she still believe it?"

Simon looked out the window where he could see Amanda's small figure in the distance. "I don't know, but whatever she believes, she told me what they were planning to do."

"She's in love with you."

Warmth coursed through Simon. "Yeah, I think she is."

"How do you feel about her?"

"I want her to stay. She belongs to me."

"Does she realize that?"

"I don't know. She may decide to dump me when I cost her her job success."

Eric shook his head. "Are you blind? She told you what you needed to know to convince me to side with you on the merger."

"She couldn't know it would have that affect on you."

"Sure she did. Simon, Amanda and I have been talking the proposed merger for weeks. She knew me pretty well by the time she flew up from California. She knew that I would go ballistic at the idea of them trying to trump up that implied contract crap."

"You think she knew she was scuttling the last chance at the merger going through?"

Eric looked at him like he was brain-dead, which was not an expression Simon was used to receiving. "Yes."

For the first time in days, real hope took root in Simon that he and Amanda had a future. "So what do you think my chances are of convincing her to stay in Washington permanently?"

"If the question is accompanied by a marriage proposal, I'd say pretty darn good. Amanda is a traditional little thing despite the fact that she looked like sex personified the other night."

Remembering her in the dress he'd ripped from her luscious body had a predictable effect on Simon. "I think you're right."

She was not a woman who would look at single motherhood with equanimity, but his stupid accusation had made her back off from discussing the baby until after the merger issue was settled. He'd thought maybe that was because she wasn't sure how she felt about a man who would damage her career, but now he realized she didn't want him thinking their relationship had anything to do with the merger.

She really loved him and he'd screwed up. Badly.

He had to do something to make it right, something to show her how important she was to him and how much he trusted her.

"Eric, there's something I need to do."

When he had finished outlining his plan to Eric and explaining the reason it was necessary, his cousin's expression was grim. "I think you're right. Women in love are vulnerable. Thinking you don't trust her is sure to be tearing her apart."

Simon hated believing that, but he knew Eric was right. "You're not worried I might be making a mistake?" Simon was sure of her, but Eric wasn't the one in love.

"No. I trust you and you trust her. That's all I need to know."

"Okay. Let's work out the details."

Eric sat up and pulled out his PDA. "I'll take notes and then get the legal documents drawn up this afternoon."

Amanda curled into the warmth of Simon's body. The last couple of days had been strange. She hadn't told him she had resigned from her job, but instead of treating her like the enemy, he'd been gentle with her. He made no mention of the merger or the baby, but he treated her like spun glass, making love to her so tenderly she felt loved even though he never said the words.

Jill was convinced he did love her, or so she had said repeatedly during their daily phone chats. Amanda wasn't so sure. Simon would never dismiss the mother of his child. He had too much integrity. If nothing else, he would make sure they remained friends.

He hadn't felt like a mere friend last night though. He'd felt like a man who could never get enough of her. He'd woken her several times to make love throughout the night, doing little for her sleep but a great deal for her sense of value to him as a woman.

"What are you thinking about, sweetheart?" Simon's hand brushed over her stomach and came to rest just over her womb.

"You," she said honestly.

"Good thoughts?"

She wiggled her bottom against him. "Yes."

His hand moved to her hips to still her movement. "Stop that. We've got to get up. The shareholder meeting is at eleven and the crossing takes an hour."

"I remember." She rubbed her cheek against the arm under her head. "I think I'll just stay here this time. There's no reason for me to go."

"I want you with me."

Did he mean he wanted her support before and after the meeting? If so, he was showing her a certain level of trust, believing she would be there for him. Her heart desperately needed that small boost after his accusations the other day. He'd apologized, but later she'd wondered if he'd only done so because he felt guilty about upsetting her when she was pregnant with his baby.

"All right, I'll come. I can stay on the yacht while you're in the meeting."

"I've made arrangements for you to be there."

"I thought only family could be there."

"Family or shareholders."

"Well, since all the shareholders are family, that's pretty much the same thing, isn't it?"

"In a way."

"So, how did you arrange for me to be there?"

"I worked it out with Eric. Don't worry about it. It's all set and I'm not claiming you as my legal representative, if that's what's worrying you."

"No. You don't lie. You wouldn't do that."

"But Lance Rogers would."

"I'm sure he has."

"You're right. He's the named legal counsel for Alana St. John, one of my second cousins."

Darn Lance anyway. He was such a slimy toad. "I'm sorry, Simon."

"Don't be, baby." He hugged her. "It's going to be fine."

"You mean Eric is going to stand with you?"

He kissed the sensitive hollow behind her ear. "Did you expect anything else after telling me Extant's plans for the merged companies?"

She hadn't, but since Simon had been so silent on the merger, she had wondered if Eric had decided to back the merger regardless of the deviousness of its management. "Not really."

"That's what Eric said. He said you'd gotten to know him pretty well."

"I did. In the things that are important, you two are a lot alike."

"That's what I was counting on when I first started arguing with him about the merger. I figured given enough time, he'd come around to my point of view. It turns out your boss's belief that my cousin is as unethical as he is made my further argument unnecessary."

It was probably time to tell Simon the truth about that. "He's not my boss anymore."

She found herself flipped on her back with Simon looming above her, his eyes stormy with anger. "Are you telling me they fired you over this business?"

She shook her head against the pillow and smiled up at him. He cared. He might not know it yet, or trust her as much as she trusted him, but this was not mere relief that she was out of the enemy camp she was seeing here. "I resigned."

"Oh, baby."

The kiss was voracious and led to other things, forcing them to take the fastest shower on record and for her to board the yacht for crossing to the mainland with wet hair.

Chapter 20

Amanda walked into the boardroom behind Simon and Eric. As she had expected, Lance sat at one end of the table with some people she didn't recognize. Simon's second cousins, she surmised, the only other shareholders. No doubt Daniel was waiting somewhere close by for Lance to call with the outcome of the meeting.

Lance met her gaze with his own, his eyes reflecting both derision and a certain level of smugness.

She did not acknowledge him in any way and took her seat to Simon's right. He squeezed her shoulder before sitting down himself and turning to confer briefly with Eric.

As both President of Brant Computers and Chairman of the Board, Eric called the meeting to order. "In the interests of saving time, would someone like to put forth a motion in regard to the current business on the agenda?"

The only piece of business on the agenda that Amanda was aware of was the proposed merger.

Lance raised his pen in indication he wished to be recognized by the chair.

"Yes, Mr. Rogers?"

"It is my client's understanding that Brant Computers' bylaws stipulate no one outside the family and their legal representatives are allowed to attend shareholder meetings."

Eric inclined his head. "In point of fact the bylaws stipulate that no one outside the shareholders or their legal representatives may attend such meetings."

"If Ms. Zachary is attempting to pass herself off as legal representation for Simon Brant, I must point out she is neither a lawyer nor an attorney. She has no legal right to practice law in the state of Washington."

"The same could be said of you, Mr. Rogers. You've passed the California bar, not that for our state, I believe." Eric didn't fidget or indicate nervousness in any way. "However, neither point is relevant as our bylaws do not indicate whether or not the legal representation for shareholders needs to be practicing in the law profession."

"I would like to go on record expressing my client's dissatisfaction with this proceeding."

"So noted. However, unless your client wishes to take legal issue with the ambiguity of our bylaws, I propose we move forward."

Lance turned and conferred with a dark-haired woman, presumably Alana St. John.

He turned back to face Eric. "My client is willing to allow the proceedings to go forward."

"How fortunate." The sarcasm in Eric's tone was barely perceptible.

Ms. St. John made a motion to merge Brant Computers with Extant Corporation.

In that moment, Amanda experienced an overwhelming sense of relief that Simon had convinced Eric to stand with him. He'd been right all along. Brant Computers was a family run company and the employees mattered, ethics mattered, and doing what was right mattered to the management.

Extant was interested in the bottom line only

and Daniel's most recent behavior had put the difference between the two companies in stark relief.

Another second cousin seconded the motion and Eric called for discussion.

"I move that discussion be waived and that we proceed directly to a vote." Simon's voice was even and firm, with no emotional inflection whatsoever.

Lance's eyes narrowed in surprise and his gaze swung to Eric then back to Simon. "You don't want to argue against the merger?" he asked.

Simon's gray eyes were steady and unreadable. "No."

Lance's gaze swung to Amanda. She stared back. He was going to lose and in her mind it couldn't have happened to a more deserving candidate. She couldn't feel much one way or the other for the second cousins he had duped into playing as his patsies. None of them had contacted either Simon or Eric before going ahead and calling for the special shareholder meeting.

Brant Computers was an income producer for them, but they weren't close to the company or the men who ran it.

Lance said, "I would like a moment to reiterate both the short and long-term benefits to Brant Computers that a merger with Extant Corporation would bring."

Eric indicated Lance should proceed.

Which he did. After he had been talking for a while, the secretary recording the meeting said that five minutes had been reached.

"Your time is up, Mr. Rogers."

Lance stopped talking, but looked annoyed.

"Is there any rebuttal?"

No one indicated they wished to speak.

"In that case, we will move directly to the vote."

Once again, Lance's pen was in the air.

"Yes, Mr. Rogers?"

"According to parliamentary procedure, if there is no one else wishing to take the floor, I should be allowed to continue."

"If you had read the company bylaws more thoroughly, Mr. Rogers, you would have noted that our meetings are run with an adaptation of Robert's Rules. This is one of Brant Computers' adaptations."

Eric referred to a section of the bylaws which Lance immediately looked up.

He read it, then lifted his head. "The adaptation is as you say."

Eric didn't bother to reply.

He called for a vote. Each of the second cousins voted in favor.

Eric turned to Amanda. "Which way do you vote?"

"What?" For some reason she flushed with heat. "I'm not a shareholder."

"As of the day before yesterday you are. Simon Brant signed over thirty-seven percent of his stock in Brant Computers to you which constitutes eleven percent of the total company shares."

Even in the deep state of shock that Eric's words had thrown her into, she could do the math. Simon had given her the deciding vote. She turned to him. He was looking at her, a warmth and trust in his eyes she could not mistake.

Tears clogged the back of her throat.

He trusted her with the future of Brant Computers in her hands, with his future as well, and he had signed over those shares before she had told him about resigning from Extant.

"I vote nay." Her voice shook with emotion, but she couldn't help it.

"I also vote nay." Simon didn't look away from her as he said it and she could not look away from him.

"I vote nay as well." Eric's words were accompanied by a gasp from the other end of the table.

It was quickly followed by an eruption of gabbled voices. Evidently Lance had told the second cousins that Eric would be voting in favor of the merger. They weren't happy.

Eric called the room to order again. "There is one more piece of business."

Looking highly irritated, Ms. St. John asked, "What is it?"

"Simon and I are prepared to buy your stock and the stock of the other shareholders at fifteen percent above market value, but only if you all agree to sell."

"What if only one of us wants to sell?" asked a man who looked enough like the dark-haired woman to indicate he was her brother.

"We will pay market value and no more."

"But you still want to buy the shares?"

"Yes. However, the additional fifteen percent is only on offer until we leave this room. Once the meeting is adjourned, the offer will be withdrawn."

Amanda was still shaken from Eric's revelation that she was a shareholder. This move of his and Simon's went right over her head, as did the second eruption of voices from the other end of the table.

"If you sell, you'll regret it. Simon Brant is working on the next generation of computer technology. If Brant Computers is the first to market with the concept, your shares will increase in value astronomically," Lance was urging.

"The operative word here is if. I won't confirm or deny the content of Simon's current experiments. His work is and has always been confidential." Eric's blue eyes were colder than Amanda had ever seen them. "Which leads to the obvious question of how you came by the belief that Simon is working on next generation technology."

Lance actually sneered. "Don't be dense. Extant Corporation would be foolish not to keep an eye on its competitors."

"Even more foolish to be slapped with an injunction and lawsuit for hacking into confidential information files." Simon spoke, having turned away from her to face Lance. "You can bet I'll know exactly who gained illegal entry into my supply records and how it was done, within the next week."

Lance's expression left no one in the room in any doubt that information had been obtained in just that way. "Go for it," he said however, in a false show of bravado.

Or maybe not so false. It wasn't his neck on the line.

In the end, some of the second cousins refused to sell their stock. The others were angry that they wouldn't get the extra fifteen percent, but they did negotiate for an eight percent increase over market value with the stipulation that if Brant Computers was first to market with a fiber-optic processor, they would receive an additional seven percent.

"Are you sure you two won't come for dinner? Elaine and I would love to have you over."

Simon shook his head, his hand on Amanda's shoulder. There was this irrational fear that if he didn't hold onto her, she would disappear. Until he got things settled between them, that fear was not going to go away.

"Another time. Right now, I just want to head back to the island." He turned to Amanda. "Is that all right, sweetheart?"

Her expression was sending him messages that made his knees go weak. "Yes."

Eric laughed. "You two are better entertainment

than a live performance at Cheney Stadium." He squeezed Amanda's arm. "Be kind to him, honey. I never thought I'd see the day when Simon was more interested in a woman than his experiments."

She smiled, moving into Simon's side and sliding her arm around his waist. "I'll be as nice as he'll let me be."

Eric winked at Simon. "It looks like you've got it sewn up, buddy. I'll let you get to it."

He turned and walked back to his car in the pier parking lot.

Simon looked down at Amanda. She'd dressed in her buttoned-up business attire, but something was different. Maybe it was the twinkle of mischief in her eyes, or the fact that he knew the bra and panties she was wearing under the conservative gray suit was scandalous in design.

"Do I?"

She tilted her head in that adorable way she had. "Do you what?"

"Have you all sewn up?"

"Hmmm . . ." She thought about it and even though he knew she was teasing him, tension started to seep into his body.

"I guess it depends on what you mean by sewn up," she finally said.

"Come on." He took her hand. "I'll explain it on board." He wasn't asking the most important question of his life on the gangplank to his yacht.

She let him lead her aboard.

He stopped once they were on deck. "Do you want to stay outside for a while?" The sun was shining and she had a marked preference for the outdoors.

She nodded, but pulled her hand from his. "Let me go in and change my clothes. Then we can relax together on the forward deck, okay?"

"Sounds good." He let her go, knowing that if

he went with her, the minute her clothes were off he would forget his noble intention to talk and do something far more physically active. While making love with Amanda was the most pleasurable thing he'd ever known, settling their future was more important at the moment.

He headed to the forward deck, removing his jacket and tie along the way. He undid the first few buttons on his white silk dress shirt and cuffed the sleeves, before sitting on one of the deck loungers.

Amanda was only gone a few minutes, enough time for Jacob to have been and gone, leaving a tray of chilled water and finger size sandwiches *to tempt the little mother's appetite.* It wasn't exactly wine and roses, but Simon didn't want the superficial trappings of romance. He wanted the real deal and Amanda in any setting was it.

She'd taken off her shoes and thigh-highs and changed into a pair of mouth-watering, hip-hugging denim shorts. Her formfitting white singlet showed a tantalizing strip of skin and the top of her temporary tattoo above the waistband of her shorts as well as the shadows of two dark points that indicated she'd left her bra off.

She was beautiful.

She was pulling pins from her hair as she walked toward him, the magnificent mass of chestnut silk floating down in a cloud around her face just as she stopped in front of him. "Hi."

He had to make an effort to breathe. "Nice outfit."

"Jill brought it up with the other clothes she picked up at my apartment. I wasn't going to wear it, but around you . . ." She shrugged, but her expression told him the rest. She trusted him not to criticize her like her ex-husband had done.

"It looks great." Better than great. "But it's going to pay hell with my desire to talk."

"I like knowing that," she admitted as she sat on the edge of the lounger beside his.

"Like you were proud of yourself when you seduced me past the point of remembering to use protection?" He'd caught on to her.

She laughed. "Yes." The smile faded. "It was so new. I can't tell you how incredible it feels to be wholly a woman and not think there's a major part of my femaleness missing."

"And you don't mind being pregnant?"

She bit her lip. "I wish it had happened in marriage. I guess I'm old-fashioned, but I think a baby should have the benefit of two loving parents."

"Ours will. Do you doubt it?" Did she think he would dismiss his responsibility to her and the baby, leaving her to fend for herself?

She shook her head. "Oh no. I don't doubt you. You're going to be a fantastic father." She laid her hand over the tummy he loved touching. "I love the baby already. I'm going to be the best mother I can and make him or her feel so wanted."

Not like her parents had done with her. She didn't have to say it, he knew she would do it differently. Amanda had so much love in her small body, she radiated with it.

She smiled softly at him. "I'm really glad I'm carrying your baby."

"But you wish it had happened after we were married?"

She went completely still. "Are we getting married?"

A four letter word went zinging through his brain. He was screwing this up. He was supposed to ask her, not assume.

Operating under a compulsion stronger than any that had ever sent him disappearing into his lab, he stood up, taking her with him. He had to get this right. His whole future was at stake here.

There was one thing he had always gotten right with her and he took shameless advantage of it. Molding his mouth over her slightly parted lips, he gave her the emotion he found so difficult to vocalize.

And he found something in return. Warmth. Generosity. Love. He could taste her love. It had always been there for him, he realized now, waiting to flood his parched heart like the warmest, wettest rain.

He pulled back just far enough so he could look into the liquid depths of her Hershey-brown eyes. "I love you, Amanda." It had been so easy to say. Why had he waited so long?

Those eyes drenched. "I didn't think you did." She took a shuddering breath as two rivulets of tears trickled down her face. "I told you I loved you. Over and over again, but you didn't say anything. Nobody but Jillian has ever loved me. I didn't think you could."

He wanted to dispel her fear and remembered pain. All he had was words. "Baby, how could I not love you? When I'm with you, I am whole. The shadows disappear; the frozen places in my soul melt. I've never known anything like it. Relationships before were always wrong. I didn't understand why, but now I do. Love isn't physical, though I think that's a part of it. It's spiritual and it doesn't happen just because you want it to. It's the most precious gift life has to offer."

She swiped at her eyes. "I know, believe me."

But she didn't believe he really did. Because he was the man she loved, she didn't see how inadequately he fit with the rest of the world.

"I was in college when I was fifteen."

She looked quizzical. "I remember."

"I discovered sex and older women. One woman

in particular. I'd had a few girlfriends, but this woman was special. She made my head come off, or so I thought until I met you. Now I know what she gave me were minor explosions. With you, it's nuclear."

Amanda liked his description of how she affected him because it was mutual. "What happened with the woman?"

Simon's gray gaze went unfocused as he looked back into the past. His jaw tightened. "One night I went to pick her up in the dorm. I wasn't old enough to drive even, but I was having sex with this twenty-year-old woman. I'd go to her dorm room and she'd drive if we went out. Usually we stayed there."

"Anyway, that night the door was open and one of her friends was in there with her. They were joking around, talking about me and what a stud I was. At first I felt great, but then she said I was just a kid though I knew how to use my cock, and that it was big enough to really pleasure a woman. She speculated on how big I would be when I was a full-grown man and then offered me to her friend when she was done with me."

The pain in Simon's voice added to the fury growing in Amanda. "That perverted, pedophile bitch!"

"She was hardly a pedophile. I was full-grown physically and I lived in the adult world, Amanda."

"She hurt you and she knew what she was doing. She knew you were vulnerable and too young for her." Rage filled her on behalf of that younger Simon, who had believed that sex was love and that he'd find acceptance with a woman who was using him for her own physical gratification. "What did you do then?"

"I ran. I met Jacob that night. He was still in the Secret Service at the time, but on vacation where I went to college. He stopped me from doing something really stupid and helped me to refocus my energy on doing something with the amazing intellect God had given me."

"Is that when you stopped living like the rest of the world?"

"I never lived like other people, Amanda. I don't think like other men. I forget things, get lost in my experiments, work out in my gym in the middle of the night and collect ancient fighting swords because they fascinate me. I'm not normal, baby. I'll never fit."

She wrapped her arms around him and hugged him tight. "You may not be normal, but you're perfect for me. I love you so much, Simon. So, so much."

"I wasn't sure you did. I don't have a lot of experience with romance and less with love. It took me a while to figure out what I felt for you, even longer to determine you loved me."

That didn't make any sense. She'd told him. "I said it. Repeatedly."

"During lovemaking." His chin rested on top of her head. "Never any other time. I thought it was just sex talk."

She felt the heat in her cheeks from a blush as she remembered what she was usually doing when she shouted out her love for Simon. "It wasn't. I really love you."

"I figured that out." She could hear the satisfaction in his voice.

"But you accused me of using sex to keep you occupied while Daniel drummed up shareholder support for the merger," she reminded him.

"Elaine calls them 'dumb man' moments. She says Eric has them occasionally, but she loves him anyway."

The last sounded like a question and she smiled

against his shirt front. "I didn't stop loving you, but it hurt."

"I'll never do it again."

She believed him. "I know." There would be other "dumb man" moments, just as she would mess up, but Simon trusted her and he would never make an accusation based on a lack of that again.

He leaned back and cupped her face, his gaze intent on seeing into her soul—or so it felt. "Are you sure?"

She lifted her hands to cover his. "I'm sure. You gave me the deciding vote, Simon." Choking up with emotion again, she had to take several deep breaths before going on. "You trusted me with your future before you knew I'd quit my job. I'll never forget that."

"And will you always remember I love you?"

She tilted her pelvis forward, rubbing against the bulge that had been there since she walked outside. "How long are we talking here?"

He kissed her. Hard. When he lifted his head, they were both short of breath.

"A lifetime. Living without you is not an option I can accept." He sounded like he meant it.

She wondered what he would do if she said she had different plans. She didn't. There was nothing more she wanted out of life than to live the rest of it with Simon, but still. . . . He was a smart, creative guy. His method of convincing her would almost be worth holding off her answer. Almost.

"When I divorced Lance, I never wanted to get married again." She'd never wanted to be that vulnerable to hurt again.

His body tensed. "I'm nothing like him."

"I know that." She brushed his chest, her hand tucking into the opening and laying against his heart. "You're so much more than any man I've ever known. You're such a gorgeous guy, I thought you had security to keep the groupies at bay." He smiled, like he thought she was joking. She wasn't.

"You have an integrity I could trust my life to. You care so much for others that it humbles me." Even being a near-total recluse, his concern for the employees of Brant Computers had eclipsed Eric's. "You're strong physically, emotionally, and mentally. You're the perfect father for my children."

Leaning forward, she kissed the exposed patch of skin in his shirt's opening. "I never want to leave you. If you need the words: I'll marry you, Simon, and spend the rest of my life glad that I did."

He shuddered, almost with relief. "I never want you to leave. I want to tie you to me with marriage, with love, with our baby. You belong to me. I belong to you. It's perfect."

She felt like crying again, she was so happy.

"Don't cry, baby." Then he kissed her, a beautiful seal to their commitment.

After several minutes of pure pleasure, he withdrew his mouth from hers. "Big or small?"

Deliberately misunderstanding him, she reached down and caressed him intimately. "It feels pretty big to me."

He growled and grabbed her wrist. "I meant the wedding."

"I don't care as long as it's soon and Jillian can be there." She'd had the big wedding and it had all been for show. They could get married in the pastor's office with Jillian and Eric as witnesses and she would feel more married, more secure, than she ever had with Lance.

They got married on the yacht two weeks later. Jillian was indeed there, as were Eric, Elaine and Joey. Jacob catered the reception for the small group before scuttling everyone off the yacht. He then piloted Amanda and Simon to a deserted stretch of ocean. Amanda was finishing some final touches on the stateroom when she heard a powerboat come alongside and then leave again a few minutes later.

She looked around the room, a sense of anticipation curling through her insides. She'd imagined this scene once before, but this time she *knew* Simon wanted her. Not the presentation of a business proposal. Nothing but her this time.

Simon tapped on the stateroom door and pushed it slowly open. Amanda had disappeared the minute they left the dock, telling him not to come down until they were at anchor. Well, they'd dropped anchor and Jacob was gone. Had she heard the boat that came to pick him up?

He wondered if she would realize its significance, but then his brain short-circuited like a wet power supply without a ground strap. The stateroom was filled with soft light, sheer scarves covering the small lamps and diffusing their glow into a golden haze. Some kind of Eastern music was playing in the background and Amanda stood in the middle of the bed looking like a pasha's favorite concubine from the harem.

Her outfit seemed to be made up of several sheer veils and scarves and not much else. When he walked in, she started swaying, clicking small gold castanets in beat with the music. The lines of her body swayed sinuously against the silk giving him a glimpse of a rosy peaked curve here and creamy white thigh there.

Blood and heat surged into his sex and he started tearing off his tuxedo. She kept dancing, her body's gyrations making sweat break out all over his body.

"Is this another fantasy?"

She shook her head, her dark hair sliding across her unfettered breasts sensually. "No. This is for real. I love you and I want to give myself to you completely. I want to be every fantasy for you. I want you to be every fantasy for me, but not live in fantasy. I want to dress up for you and dance for you and seduce you the way you seduce me."

Naked, he crossed to the bed. "Your love is the most seductive force in the world, baby, but you keep right on dancing. I'm so turned on, I ache with it."

Her arms moved gracefully around her, drawing attention to different parts of her beautiful body, while she silently enticed him. Suddenly he understood the gift she was giving him. It was the same one he'd given her in the boardroom of Brant Computers. Complete trust. She trusted him to want her, to love her, to affirm her, although she'd learned so well not to trust.

He couldn't help it. He swung her off the bed and into his arms. "I love you, Amanda. Everything about you."

She looped her arms around his neck. "I love you, Simon. Don't ever let go of me."

"Never. Don't ever let go of me."

Her arms tightened convulsively. "Never."

And then she kissed him, long and slow and sweet. "You're my husband."

"You're my wife." The words were sweeter to him than any decadent dessert.

"We may not fit in with the rest of the world, but we belong together."

Wetness burned in his eyes, but he blinked it away. "We fit."

"Perfectly."

And they proved it, once again joining body, soul and spirit.

Please turn the page for an exciting
preview of Lucy Monroe's
COME UP AND SEE ME SOMETIME.

Also available right now from Zebra!

Alex had been totally silent since tucking Isabel into the passenger seat of his car.

She had tried valiantly to focus her attention out the window. She wanted to ignore him. To pretend that the whole evening had never happened, but she kept stealing glances at him out of the corner of her eye.

It just wasn't fair. She'd been attracted to him from the moment he'd entered her office, and it hurt to find out that the only thing about her that interested him was her client list, or rather the name of one client in particular.

He pulled into a parking spot in front of her condo and killed the engine.

"I could have lied." His voice startled her, coming as it did after so many minutes of silence.

She opened her car door. "What would be the point? You must have already figured out that you weren't going to get what you wanted from me."

She stepped out of the car, proud of her exit line.

Alex followed her to the door, standing motionless as she searched for her key. "What exactly is that, Isabel?"

Her head snapped up and she stared at him.

The question, asked in far too soft a voice, sent a sensual thrill skittering down her spine that had absolutely no business being there after what she'd learned about him.

The man was definitely acting dangerous again.

"We've been all through this. You want my client's name."

He reached behind her and she went motionless, unable to function with his nearness.

He started pulling out her hairpins. "Are you sure that's all I want from you?"

She wanted to yell at him not to do this to her but refused to give him the satisfaction. "Of course. It's not as if you're attracted to me or anything."

The way he was looking at her belied that comment, and the feel of her hair falling from its French twist set off alarms inside her. "Even if you were," she said in a breathy voice, "you must realize that after the way you attempted to use me, I couldn't trust you."

He shook his head and moved closer. "I didn't lie about my reasons for taking you out when you asked about them. Why would I lie about being attracted to you now?"

She found herself crowded against her front door and had to fight the urge to pull him the final few inches until their bodies touched. Her skin felt hot and tight, while a heavy sensation pooled in her belly.

"Maybe you are somewhat attracted to me, but we both know that isn't why you asked me to dinner." She'd tried to sound firm and cool this time, but once again managed only to reveal her physical reaction to him through a voice way too soft and inviting.

He put his hands against the door, one on either side of her head, enfolding her in his presence, overwhelming her with his male scent and the heat emanating from his big body so close to her own. "Is that so important?"

She swallowed. "Yes."

His eyes devoured her while he brushed one finger down her cheek. "I don't agree."

Warm, firm lips drowned her protest as he moved his hands from the door to cradle her head.

His mouth slanted over hers in a sensual assault. She told herself that she should not respond to his kiss, but his mouth was so hungry. His passion fed her own.

Her body started to melt as he sucked her lower lip into his mouth and nibbled on it.

Had she ever kissed before? Really kissed? If this conflagration of her senses was a kiss, then nothing she'd shared with her former dates counted as such because this was unique. This was passion. It felt too good to even think about stopping. She heard a moan and realized that it was hers.

Her defenses were completely helpless in the face of such sensual mastery and her reaction to his kiss.

Her moan acted like a catalyst for him and his hard-muscled body squashed her into the door, the evidence of his arousal pressing against her as they made contact from chest to tangled legs. The rough passion-filled movement—at odds with the tender way he cradled her head and the now gently nipping kisses he was giving her lips—affected her body in an unexpected way.

She felt warm everywhere, particularly in her most feminine place. Not only was she hot there, but she felt empty and swollen at the same time. She tipped her pelvis toward him, seeking some sort of connection that would assuage the ache growing in her innermost being.

He made a harsh sound and his mouth moved over hers, demanding that she open her lips to his invasion. Unable and unwilling to deny him, she let her lips part. He swept inside with his tongue and she tasted tiramisu and masculine ardor. The combination was both erotic and overwhelming.

Her new favorite dessert. Even chocolate didn't taste this good.

Running her hands over the raw silk of his shirt, she gloried in the textured fabric and the hard muscles underneath. She wanted to touch him everywhere, to have him touch her.

She had the first half of his shirt buttons undone and one spaghetti strap was perilously low on her arm when he tore his mouth away from hers. "Key."

Key? Her mind was lost in an unprecedented sexual frenzy. Nothing made sense except the feel of his body against hers.

Since he wouldn't kiss her, she kissed him—along his jaw, down his neck. She had made it to his chest when he shoved himself away from her.

"Baby, you are killing me."

The chilly evening air buffeted her with the loss of the heat generated by Alex's body. She shivered with unsatisfied desire and cold, trying to understand why he'd pulled away.

"Your key. Isabel, give me the key to your door."

She was so disoriented that she did just that.

Alex rammed the key into the lock and shoved open the door. He turned and lifted her in his arms and carried her into the hallway, pushing the door shut with his foot.

"Lock it," he ordered.

She did.

"Where's your bedroom?"

The flat question finally broke through the passion dulling her brain's activity.

She vehemently shook her head, fear slicing through her. And not fear that this man would take more than she willingly offered but rather fear that she would offer too much. If she'd ever had this volatile a reaction to a man before, she would not be such an inexperienced twenty-eight-year-old woman.

She was sure of it.

That inexperienced status was not going to end tonight, however. She had allowed herself to get carried away on the porch, but she wasn't about to make love with a man who had tried to use her.

"No, Alex. You can't take me to bed."

Lucy also has a wonderful story appearing in
STAR QUALITY, an anthology from Brava
currently on sale.

*Meet three people with a little something special whose
love lives are about to turn wild, crazy, sensual, and
oh-so-hot. Blame it on the moon? Sure. But who's
complaining, anyway . . .*

STAR QUALITY

New York Times bestselling author
Lori Foster
<u>Once in a Blue Moon</u>

It's all because of that stupid blue moon. That's
what Stan Tucker thinks as he walks through
Delicious, Ohio, suddenly privy to everyone's
innermost thoughts, a gift courtesy of a rare blue
moon. What most people have on their minds is
boring—grocery lists, work woes, appointments.
But not Jenna Rowan's super-private thoughts.
The pretty, shy bookstore owner is having decid-
edly hot thoughts about Stan . . . naked, sweaty,
not-for-primetime thoughts. Stan's lusted after
Jenna for ages, but he never thought the proper
lady was interested. Now that he knows, he
intends to do something about it, and this time,
he won't be the only one howling at the moon . . .

Lucy Monroe
<u>Moon Magnetism</u>

Ivy Kendall dreads the full moon. For
generations, women in her family have been ex-

tremely magnetic on that day—which was fine fifty years ago but not in the age of hard drives and cell phones. That's why the hotel manager has resisted the technological improvements her boss wants her to implement. Now, the sexy, dynamic Blake Hawthorne is coming to insist on the upgrades in person. Shoot, he'll probably fire her. Being around Blake makes her body go as haywire as a full moon, maybe even more. And as long as she's going to be out of a job soon, there's no reason not to use a little of that magnetism to her advantage, luring him into an elevator where the only electricity that will work is the kind they generate themselves . . .

Dianne Castell
<u>Moonstruck</u>

For years, Julia Simon has had the worst luck, married to a man who cheated on her left, right, and center. Now, the pretty divorcee is ready for her luck to change, and it is . . . big time. Ever since she unknowingly performed a Blue Moon ritual, Julia's wishes seem to be coming true. So why not wish for wild, unbridled passionate sex with hunky P.I. Marc Adams? Well, because when it happens, it's so amazingly good, that's why. Now, with the blue moon due to end in three days' time, Julia can only wonder if it's just a spell or the start of a whole new life . . .

Be careful of wishful thinking. It just might get you everything . . .

Say Yes! To Sizzling Romance by
Lori Foster

__Too Much Temptation

0-7582-0431-0 $6.99US/$9.99CAN

Grace Jenkins feels too awkward and insecure to free the passionate woman inside her. But that hasn't stopped her from dreaming about Noah Harper. Gorgeous, strong and sexy, his rough edge beneath the polish promises no mercy in the bedroom. When Grace learns Noah's engagement has ended in scandal, she shyly offers him her support and her friendship. But Noah's looking for something extra . . .

__Never Too Much

0-7582-0087-0 $6.99US/$9.99CAN

A confirmed bachelor, Ben Badwin has had his share of women, and he likes them as wild and uninhibited as his desires. Nothing at all like the brash, wholesomely cute woman who just strutted into his diner. But something about Sierra Murphy's independent attitude makes Ben's fantasies run wild. He'd love to dazzle her with his sensual skills . . . to make her want him as badly as he suddenly wants her . . .

__Say No to Joe?

0-8217-7512-X $6.99US/$9.99CAN

Joe Winston can have any woman—except the one he really wants. Secretly, Luna Clark may lust after Joe, but she's made it clear that she's too smart to fall for him. He can just keep holding his breath, thank you very much. But now, Luna's inherited two kids who need more than she alone can give in a small town that seems hell-bent on driving them away. She needs someone to help out . . . someone who can't be intimidated . . . someone just like Joe.

__When Bruce Met Cyn

0-8217-7513-8 $6.99US/$9.99CAN

Compassionate and kind, Bruce Kelly understands that everyone makes mistakes, even if he's never actually done anything but color inside the lines. Nobody's perfect, but Bruce is about to meet a woman who's perfect for him. He's determined to show her that he can be trusted. And if that means proving it by being the absolute gentleman at all times, then so be it. No matter how many cold showers it takes . . .

Available Wherever Books Are Sold!

Visit our website at **www.kensingtonbooks.com**.

**Discover the Thrill of
Romance with**

Lisa Plumley

__Making Over Mike
0-8217-7110-8 $5.99US/$7.99CAN

Amanda Connor is a life coach—not a magician! Granted, as a
publicity stunt for her new business, the savvy entrepreneur has
promised to transform some poor slob into a perfectly balanced
example of modern manhood. But Mike Cavaco gives "raw material"
new meaning.

__Falling for April
0-8217-7111-6 $5.99US/$7.99CAN

Her hometown gourmet catering company may be in a slump, but
April Finnegan isn't about to begin again. Determined to save her
business, she sets out to win some local sponsors, unaware she's not
the only one with that idea. Turns out wealthy department store mogul
Ryan Forrester is one step—and thousands of dollars—ahead of her.

__Reconsidering Riley
0-8217-7340-2 $5.99US/$7.99CAN

Jayne Murphy's best-selling relationship manual *Heartbreak 101* was
inspired by her all-too-personal experience with gorgeous, capable . . .
outdoorsy . . . Riley Davis, who stole her heart—and promptly skipped
town with it. Now, Jayne's organized a workshop for dumpees. But it
becomes hell on her heart when the leader for her group's week-long
nature jaunt turns out to be none other than a certain . . .

Available Wherever Books Are Sold!

Visit our website at **www.kensingtonbooks.com**.